OAK LAWN PUBLIC LIBRARY
3 1186 00806 7464

S0-BEF-675

SPOONFUL

CHRIS MENDIUS

Anything Goes Publishing
Oak Park, IL 60302

ISBN: 978-0-578-09541-7

Cover design by Joseph Taylor:
www.JoeTaylorArt.com

Printed in the United States of America

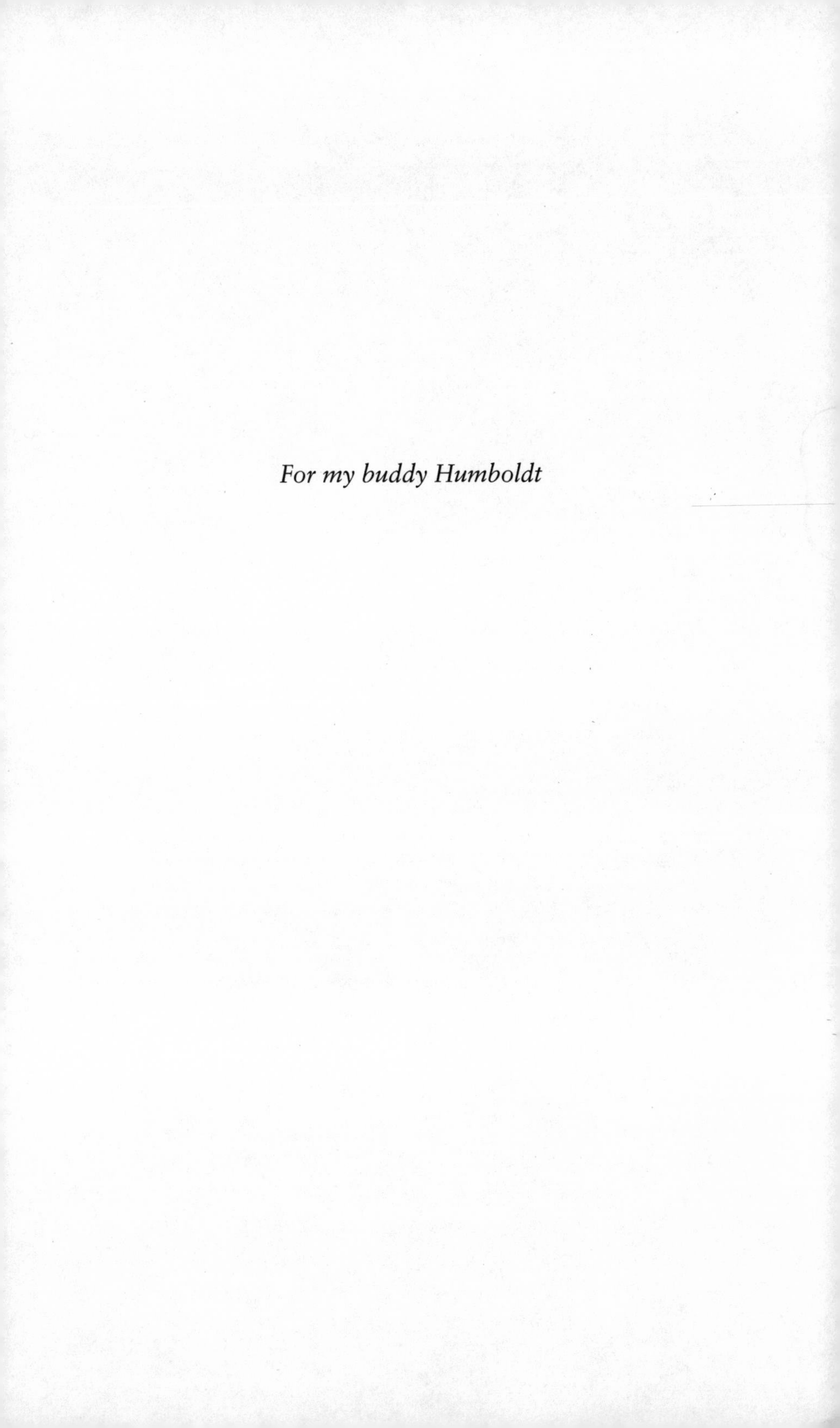

For my buddy Humboldt

Men lie about that spoonful
Some cry about that spoonful
Some die about that spoonful
Everybody fight about a spoonful

Willie Dixon (1915-1992)

CHAPTER ONE

Nobody ever says, "When I grow up, I want to be a junkie."

Then again, nobody ever says, "When I grow up, I want to be an accounting clerk, or an insurance adjuster or some middle manager with a potbelly and a bad case of acid reflux." It just happens. Life races by and you wonder where it all went wrong. You're parked in front of a computer all day, getting fat and slowly losing your mind as you tap on the keyboard. A debit here. A credit there. Maybe you're beating up some poor slob who just lost his house in a flood or bracing yourself for the next round of layoffs, hoping and praying your little corner of the corporate bureaucracy doesn't get eliminated. Or maybe you have a habit and you're ransacking some luxury condo, desperately searching for something small, valuable and easily pawned. So what? Lots of people live shitty lives they didn't plan. Why get worked up about it? Or so I sometimes told myself back then. Other times, I just said, "Fuck it."

That's what I said when Sal asked me to help him rob this woman he dropped off at Midway Airport earlier that day. She was some up-and-coming marketing executive at General Mills who had just moved into the area. Her latest promotion meant a weeklong trip to the company headquarters in Minneapolis for the next level of corporate indoctrination. According to him, she was cute too, "like Chloe Sevigny, only older and stacked."

"Who's that?" I asked.

Sal was a film buff, always tossing out the names of actors and actresses in movies nobody ever saw. Since I had watched hundreds of videos with him and had the freakish tendency to never forget a face, I usually knew who he meant.

"The chick that got dead-horsed at the end of *Kids*," said Sal.

"No shit?" I knew exactly who he was talking about. She was cute. I felt bad for her character. She passed out in the last scene of the movie and got raped by some little scumbag that was carrying AIDS. "Why didn't you ask her out?"

"Believe me, I wanted to, but then I figured that would be kind of…" Sal paused, searching. "Short-sighted."

Short-sighted, indeed. That sounded funny coming from a guy who seldom thought beyond the next fix. Even so, he did have a plan. Sal drove a cab part-time. Whenever he had a fare going to the airport, he would chat them up in a friendly yet detached way that put even the most uptight assholes at ease. He'd go on and on, regaling them with recommendations from his cousin Vinny who knew all about the city they were visiting. The stories always involved some great place to go or something really good to eat.

"My cousin Vinny lives in Cincinnati," he'd say. "I never been there, but he says no matter what, you gotta make sure you try some Skyline chili. They even got vegetarian."

He also knew about a lot of great deals.

"My cousin Vinny goes to Vegas every year. Loses his ass most of the time but he eats well. He says there's a place right off the Strip. I forget the name. Supposedly they got the best twenty-four-ounce rib eye in town for under ten bucks."

He wouldn't even stop when he found out where they were going and for how long. Why should he? Sal liked to talk and people liked to talk to him. Especially hipsters and women. This was back in the late nineties when heroin chic had already been shamed off the pages of fashion magazines but was still alive and well on the streets of the hip urban neighborhoods where we ran. That worked out great for Sal. Pale and sinewy with tattoos curled around his forearms, he was a real blood-and-guts dopefiend with the willowy good looks of a rock star. People always said he was a dead ringer for Kurt Cobain, whose face was still all over the place. I could see the resemblance, except Sal had the jet black hair of his Sicilian ancestors. Before he got the idea to troll for a mark, Sal often parlayed his grungy appeal into a phone number or an offer to meet somewhere for a drink. One time he even fucked some woman in a McDonald's parking lot on the way to O'Hare.

No such luck for our girl from General Mills.

Sal wanted to break into her place, steal whatever he could and then send his real cousin Tony over there. A hardworking family man with a small home-security business, Tony would hopefully make a sale. If he did, Sal would get a kickback which he would split with me, provided of course I was there when he got it.

"Pretty smart, huh?" Sal smiled.

"What if she's already got a security system?"

Sal got quiet, considering the possibility.

"I'm surprised you didn't think of that," I said.

"You're handy," Sal said finally. "You could cut the wires."

"I don't think so, Sal. I don't have any tools and besides, those systems are usually wired so you can't do that."

He looked at me skeptically.

"It's not like in the movies," I added for good measure.

"Well," Sal frowned. "Fuck it. Let's just go over there and see what happens. You never know."

Despite the twist with his cousin, I thought the scheme sounded pretty lame. Sal had already knocked over a couple places on his own but mostly came away without much to show for his trouble. One time he stole a computer screen and forgot the tower.

"That's the part that matters," I told him.

"What do I know about computers?"

Another time, he got a Harman/Kardon amplifier, only to have it stolen from his cab when he stopped for cigarettes. Bottom line, Sal needed help. And though breaking into people's houses was definitely not my thing, we were short without many prospects. Aside from fixing the occasional leaky pipe in the courtyard building where Sal and I shared a rundown garden unit, my own bread and butter involved mostly credit card fraud, retail theft and small-time dope deals. But things had gotten trickier, thanks to better security and the upscale demographic shift of our Wicker Park neighborhood. Developers were buying up properties in the area and all these yuppie types were moving in. That meant a stronger police presence on the streets. Granted, these were Chicago cops who weren't the most industrious but they still slowed things down.

"So where are we going?" I asked.

"North of Division," said Sal. "We'll park a block over and sneak down the alley behind Smoke Daddy."

"That's cool."

Sal fired up a Marlboro and I joined him. With the excitement of our impending caper, I had completely forgotten to service the nicotine addiction yapping at my heels like a pesky lap dog. I had another priority, one I could feel stirring in my legs and back. We hadn't fixed for hours and the sickness was already creeping into my limbs. My stomach was in bad shape too, though I couldn't tell if that was the smack calling or my nerves. Either way, I felt intensely uncomfortable, wishing for nothing more than to be on the other side of our risky business and hoping to hell I wouldn't find myself locked up at Cook County.

A couple long drags and we were there. I made sure to park my '81 Mustang GT—a real beater Sal had aptly dubbed "The Disgustang"—under the one streetlight that didn't work. The block was lined with mostly small frame homes, but there were a few of the generic brick and block three-flats that had recently gone up all over the North Side. They towered above the houses nearby, their oppressive height crushing the rest of the street while at the same time trumpeting its so-called revitalization.

"I wonder who lives in there," said Sal, tilting his head at the nearest building. A sign in front read: "Two bedroom units from the low 300's. Only 1 unit left!"

"They probably got some nice stuff," I said, thinking how much I hated those places.

"That's the spirit," said Sal. "You want to move into the hood, you gotta pay the price. Remember what that dude said?"

"Yeah, yeah, yeah," I grumbled. He was referring to some old-timer we used to see around our neighborhood.

"What's the difference between a pioneer and a settler?" Sal asked, ignoring my attitude.

"The pioneer has an arrow in his back."

"Fuckin' A," he said. "And that makes us the Indians!"

"Please." I never bought that.

"What? Why not?"

"Why not? Because we're not exactly indigenous people being run off our land."

"Yeah, well. I watch the History Channel too, and I say we are."

"Fine." It wasn't worth arguing about. "So you say we are."

"Besides," he went on. "For all these people moving in here, this is just a pit stop on the way to Schaumburg or Naperville."

"And so what if it is? What do you care?"

"They're gonna drain the life out of this whole area and make a killing," Sal said bitterly. "And I don't know about you, but I'm not gonna let that happen without getting mine." He let his statement sink in before he spoke up again. "You ready?"

I wasn't anywhere near ready but I could feel his impatience building in the dark, smoky interior of the car.

"Fuck it," I said. "Let's go."

We climbed out and headed around the corner into the alley. The night air was still thick with humidity. It had been a scorching day and the darkness brought little relief.

"Take these," said Sal, handing me a pair of rubber gloves.

"Wow." I was blown away. Sal wasn't one to take precautions of any kind. "Is this really necessary?"

"You never know," he said. "It can't hurt, especially since they got both our prints on file."

He had a point but I still had to fuck with him a little.

"I'm impressed," I said. "You sure you're not just angling to give me a rectal exam?"

"Very funny," Sal said absently. He was examining each building that we passed. Unlike the street where we parked, the block this woman lived on had only a couple rundown single-family homes and one big conversion. The rest were those awful three-flats.

"I can't tell these places apart," I said.

"Me neither."

"But you know the address, right?"

"Not really."

"What do you mean 'not really'?" I tried to sound incredulous, but it was no use since Sal knew I knew he was always pulling fly-by-night shit like that. "How the fuck are we gonna find it?"

"It's right there," he announced.

"How do you know?" I wanted to be sure.

"She told me she drives an Acura," he said, his hand shaking as he pointed to a sporty white sedan parked next to a mini SUV on a concrete pad. It was a good thing he asked about the car.

"It looks like somebody's home," I said, noting the SUV.

"That must be the guy on the first floor," said Sal.

We walked past the car to a gated cast-iron fence separating the parking area from a tiny patch of grass behind the three-story building. A wood porch with steps connecting each level was attached to the back of the structure. The top two units were completely dark. Some lights in the front of the first-floor unit were on, though the room that led out back was also dark.

"He's probably chilling in the front room," said Sal.

"Let's hope he's passed out drunk."

"Let's hope."

I would've felt much better if the whole place was empty but I knew there was no backing out at the point. Hoping to get lucky, we checked the gate. It was locked so we scanned the area for something to toss over the pointed finials at the top.

"Over there," I said, heading toward a dumpster parked behind the place two doors down. A roll of torn-out carpeting, filthy and matted, hung over the edge. Sal flicked out the pearl-handled switchblade he carried on him at all times and hacked off a piece about the size of a throw rug. We ran back to the gate, draped the carpet over the top and quickly climbed over.

So far, so good.

"She lives on the second floor," Sal whispered. "The unit on the top floor hasn't sold yet."

"Maybe I'll make an offer."

"Put your gloves on." Sal gave me a nudge.

We snapped on the tight plastic gloves and skulked up the porch stairs while a noisy air-conditioning unit hummed away on the opposite side of the lot. Walking past the rear of the first-floor condo, I was relieved to hear muffled voices and what sounded like some sporting event emanating from inside.

"Cubs are playing," I remembered.

"Go Cubs go," said Sal.

We crept up another flight of stairs to the landing outside the second-floor condo and peeked through the back window. The place was completely dark inside, which was good. However, the door only had one of those small semicircular windows in the top of it. I had hoped to break the glass and reach the dead bolt inside but the window was too far away from the lock.

"Any ideas?" I asked.

"Just kick it in."

"What?" I thought he was crazy.

"Just do it!" Sal barked. He lowered his voice again. "If you don't want to, get out of the way."

"Are you kidding?"

"I've done it before," said Sal. "It ain't pretty, but I know I can do it. Just stand back."

"Hold on, hold on," I said. If anybody was gonna kick in that door, it would be me. I was no bruiser but I had Sal by at least thirty pounds.

"Just put your foot right here," Sal said as he laid his hand on the door just below the lock. "As hard as you can. I'm telling you, the jamb will splinter just like that."

"And what if there's an alarm?"

"We'll hear it," said Sal. "And we'll run like hell."

I nodded grudgingly. We certainly weren't on our way to the criminal hall of fame but the plan made sense. And much as I didn't relish the thought of kicking in that door, I wanted to get off the porch before some nosy neighbor saw us. So without further delay, I took a deep breath, clenched my fists and planted my size ten right smack dab in the spot where Sal told me and, sure as shit, the door flew open with a deafening crash. A tense moment of silence passed before we figured it was safe to keep going.

"C'mon!" said Sal, hustling me inside.

We closed the door behind us and Sal tiptoed through to the front door while I listened at the back. The light from the alley shone through the window, illuminating all the maple, granite and stainless steel around me. I was in the kitchen.

"You hear anyone?" I asked in the loudest whisper I could muster. Sal didn't answer and that was fine with me. No news is good news in a situation like that. Another minute and I figured we were okay on my end, so I decided to see what Sal was up to. I walked down a short hallway through the dining area into the front room where I found him crouched down with his ear to the floor. A cheer erupted at the gathering below us.

"Cubs are winning," he said.

"Wow." I glanced around, taking in the space. "Three hundred grand and you can still hear the neighbors."

"How about that?" said Sal, getting up.

We had a look around, making sure not to turn on any lights. Between the moon, the streetlights and my Zippo, we could see everything we needed. The place was airy and probably quite sunny during the day with all the windows. Our girl had plenty of room for all her furniture, modern, well-matched and very grown-up. It wasn't anything like the places where we hung out, but I could imagine being the guy that comes over there. You could sit down on the leather sofa or the armchair, have a glass of wine or a mixed drink, take in a baseball game or a video on her twenty-seven-inch TV and get laid afterwards. Not a bad way to live.

"How about the stereo?" I asked, noticing the shelf system she had set up next to the TV.

Sal walked over to get a closer look. "It's a Denon," he said. "Impressive but a little big. Let's see what else she's got. Try to be neat. I feel bad enough for our girl as it is."

"You don't have to tell me," I said.

We made our way back to the two bedrooms. Sal took the one used as an office, while I searched her sleeping quarters. Walking into the bedroom of this strange woman, my heart began to race like I was some horny teenager about to get lucky. The space was so neat and feminine with the faint scent of lingering perfume. The bed was big, at least queen-size, piled high with pillows and a soft down comforter pulled over crisp sheets so white they seemed to glow in the dark. She had a bookcase headboard with a clock radio and one of those sound machines from The Sharper Image. Some fashion magazines were neatly stacked nearby along with a couple of paperbacks. A painted wicker chair sat in the corner, the perfect place to sit down and try on any of the twenty or so pairs of shoes she had in the rack inside the closet. A dresser with a matching framed mirror was ideally located on the wall opposite the bed. I pictured it, watching myself with her, Chloe Sevigny, only older and stacked.

I shivered and felt a cramp in my stomach and I remembered why I was there. I flicked on my lighter to see what was on the surface of the dresser, three framed photos off to one side. In the first, an older couple lounged on a sunny veranda, martini glasses in hand. In the next, a guy straight out of the frat house grinned like a buffoon with our girl, judging by Sal's uncanny description, hanging all over him. In the last photo, she stood arm-in-arm with another young woman who was also pretty hot.

"Find anything?" Sal called from the other room.

What the fuck? Focus. I should have taken the office. Snooping around her room was starting to creep me out.

"I don't know," I said, scanning the dresser again. Off to the other side, I found a bottle of perfume and...booyah!

A jewelry box.

I reached out, but before I could open it, Sal appeared next to me with a laptop computer under his arm.

"Fuck!" I said.

"Check it out," he smiled. "I thought for sure she'd have this with her on the trip."

"The company probably gives..." I never got to finish.

Sal suddenly shushed me, thrusting his hand over my mouth as we both heard the voices in the front room.

CHAPTER TWO

"I am so fucked up, Steve," a woman slurred. "I don't know what got into me tonight."

"We're just having fun," some guy replied. "Nothing wrong with that, right?" He didn't sound nearly as drunk.

"You sure Kim won't mind?" said the woman.

"Of course not."

Hearing them talk, I mentally cursed out Sal for getting us into the wrong unit. What a fuckhead. I reached for the doorknob and Sal tried to stop me, but I brushed him aside and cracked the door to take a look. I'll be damned if Sal wasn't right after all. I caught a glimpse of the guy's face and immediately recognized the tool from the picture on the dresser. So who the hell was she?

"I'm gonna have a beer," said the guy. "You want one?"

"I think I've had enough."

"You sure?" he asked. "You don't have to drive."

"It's a good thing too," she giggled. "I can barely walk anywhere tonight."

"You really have to get a place in the city," said the guy.

"Don't remind me," she mumbled. "Kim has it made over here."

"Who the fuck is that?" Sal whispered in my ear.

"The guy is her boyfriend," I whispered back.

"And who is she?"

At first glance I thought she was the other woman in the photo but on my second look I realized that wasn't the case. This chick had darker hair and wasn't nearly as pretty. Whoever she was, I found Sal's curiosity annoying, given our predicament.

"Well?" Sal nudged me.

"I don't know, Sal. Why don't you go out there and ask her?"

We were totally fucked. My heart was beating so loudly, I thought for sure they would hear it. I took a deep breath and let it out as quietly as I could before stealing another peek. The two of them were now making out on the couch.

"Jesus, can you believe this?" whispered Sal.

I might have thought he was still outraged at the infidelity we had stumbled upon, if not for the frantic gulps of air I could hear him taking so close to me.

"We gotta get the fuck out of here," Sal whispered, unmistakably desperate. We retreated back into the room, as if some distance from the scene outside might somehow save us. Then we heard footsteps coming closer and closer. Sal moved back toward the door, taking a position directly behind it. I heard a muffled click and noticed he had drawn his switchblade.

My God.

I rushed over and placed my hand on the knife, shaking my head. He resisted at first, his eyes glowing with fear. I stood firm and he relented, folding up the blade and sliding it back into his pocket. I took another quick look and saw the girl duck into the bathroom just outside the room where we were hiding. She closed the door behind her and we heard the guy walk back to the kitchen.

"Now's our chance," whispered Sal.

"Definitely." I hesitated, searching my mind for a plan until it came to me. "Let me go first," I told Sal. "Stay close behind. If the guy comes out, I'll take care of him. Just get your ass out the front door and get to the car."

"You sure? I could give you a hand."

Sal was tough in the sense that he could take a beating but he wasn't the best in a fight. He would probably just get in the way.

"I'll be fine," I nodded and reached for the doorknob but Sal grabbed me first. I turned and saw him hold up his hand, counting off one... two...three.

I opened the door.

Wouldn't you know it? That very moment, the girl came out of the bathroom and almost bumped into us. We were all dumbstruck at first. Then she let loose with a hysterical shriek, and we got our cue to make a break for the door. I knew the guy would be coming so I stopped short, only to leave Sal fumbling with the lock.

"What the fuck!" I shouted.

"I can't get it open!"

Like the hapless victim in countless slasher movies, we were screwed, thanks to some door that inexplicably wouldn't open.

Then I heard the footsteps.

"Hit the lights!" I yelled. Sal got the door open and the room went dark just as the guy caught me from behind, his arms wrapped around my waist like he was making an open-field tackle. I smashed into the hardwood floor with him on my back. The impact knocked the wind out of me. As I frantically struggled for a breath, he dug his chin into my shoulder blade, an old wrestling move I recalled from high school gym class. The guy felt like a wrestler too. He wasn't big but he was strong, with hard, veiny arms.

"Call the police!" he shouted.

The girl stopped shrieking long enough to run into the kitchen and I knew I was fucked. Hearing Sal bound down the stairs outside the apartment, I wished like hell I had told him to stick around. I needed help. The guy reached under my arm and up toward my neck. He was going for the full nelson.

No fucking way.

I could not lose this fight. He got one arm up and around my neck and started to push the other one through when I got my breath back. I tried to wriggle free but he was too strong. I felt him close behind me, literally breathing down my neck. I snapped my head back and got lucky, catching him on the chin. The unmistakable pop of bones colliding through flesh rang out like music to my ears. He let out a whimper and his grip slackened, giving me the chance to shrug him off of me and crawl away. As I climbed to my feet, I turned and saw him lying there on the floor in a stream of light coming in from the landing outside.

This motherfucker.

I wanted to kick him in the head for good measure but he looked pretty fucked up already, half knocked out with a mouth full of blood. Besides, I heard the girl on the phone in the kitchen and I knew I had to get the fuck out of there. I dashed out the front door and practically leaped down the stairs, only to almost collide with the guy who lived below as he came out of his condo with a couple of friends. They must have heard the commotion.

"What the hell is going on?" he asked.

He stepped toward me with his friends backing him up. They were young guys, white. They wore fitted baseball caps and looked like they drank too much beer. They also looked ready for a fight. There was no way I would let guys like this jam me up.

"Step off, motherfucker!" I reached under the front of my shirt for the gun I pretended to have shoved in my jeans. It was a cheap trick that Sal taught me one day when we were copping on the street in some shitty West Side neighborhood. A couple toughs came up to rob us and we bluffed our way out.

These guys fell for it too. Either that or they were the ones bluffing. Maybe they weren't ready for a fight after all. They took one look at me—unshaven and drenched with sweat, pumped from the fight upstairs—and froze in place. It's a good thing too. If they hadn't backed off when they did, my plan was to take the first guy down so fast and so hard, the others would've wanted no part of me. Thankfully it didn't come to that. They immediately shrank back from my charade and I bolted out the front of the building.

I figured they were at least watching me, so I ran across the street and hopped a couple fences to get to the alley on the other side of the block. I headed north and doubled back across the street to the other block where Sal was waiting in the driver's seat, nervously puffing on a cigarette.

"Jesus Christ, what took you so long?" he asked as I tossed him the keys and collapsed in the passenger seat.

"You don't want to know." I lit up my own cigarette.

Sal studied me for a moment. I was panting and disheveled with blood smeared on my cheek from the small gash in my scalp.

"That guy must have been tough," he said.

"Crazy is more like it," I said, wiping off my face. "Motherfucker came at me full on. Can you believe that shit? I could have been some…I don't know, straight thug, with a knife or a gun." Thinking about it got me mad as hell. "Shit, I could've stomped the motherfucker to death! And the guy downstairs too!"

"What about him?"

"He came out as I was running down the stairs, him and his douchebag crew. You should have seen these guys with their beer guts and their goatees."

"You're kidding!" Sal was appalled. "What did you do?"

"What else?" I said. "I pretended I was packing."

"These fucking people, man." said Sal, truly disgusted. "They got no fucking clue. They move in and they think they own the place."

"Tell me about it."

"What happened with the chick?"

"She was on the phone when I ran out of there."

"I knew I should have stuck around."

"Can we please get rolling here?" I swallowed hard, tasting the bile bubbling around in my stomach. "The fucking police are gonna be all over the place in a couple minutes."

"You don't have to tell me twice," said Sal. He started the car, dropped it into gear and juked and jagged up a few side streets before turning north on Damen, where we had to pull over for a pair of rollers speeding down to the scene.

"There they go," he said as we both watched the flashing red and blue lights slowly disappear from the rearview mirror.

"What the fuck are we gonna do now?" I couldn't care less about the police. We had other more pressing concerns.

"What do you mean?"

"You know goddamn well what I mean."

"What else?" Sal cracked a smile and reached under his seat. "We're gonna head over to Stella's and make her a deal on this fine piece of electronic equipment."

He pulled out the laptop computer he had shown me earlier and I could all but hear an army of robed singers, belting out the "Hallelujah Chorus" in my head. I thought for sure he had left it in the condo. I should have known better.

"Holy shit!" I said. "I can't believe you got it."

"Of course I got it."

Words cannot describe the relief that washed over my entire being. I would've hugged the crazy bastard if we weren't driving.

"You're like Mr. Pink," I said finally.

Mr. Pink was Sal's favorite character from his favorite movie of all time, *Reservoir Dogs*. Mr. Pink's quick mind, foul mouth and relentless professionalism were all attributes Sal strove for in his own pursuits. For a little while, Sal even stopped tipping, thanks to Mr. Pink's objection to the fact that some jobs are deemed tip-worthy while others aren't. I was more of a Mr. White kind of guy myself, slow and steady, brutal when I had to be, yet considerate to people around me. I was the one who got Sal to start tipping again after seeing him stiff one too many a poor waitress working the shithole diners where we often ate. Yet I could still appreciate Mr. Pink's appeal. Even though the robbery turned into a bloodbath, he still got out with all the diamonds.

"Am I the only fucking professional around here?" said Sal, rattling off Mr. Pink's signature line.

"I guess so." I didn't mind giving Sal his props that night.

"Fuckin' A," he said. "We still gotta move. This thing ain't gonna be worth dry shit tonight if Stella's closed up."

"Hit it," I said.

Sal shoved the laptop back under the seat and stepped on the gas. We weren't holding and even if we were, another beater speeding down the street isn't likely to attract much attention from Chicago's finest. We were on our way to Uptown Pawn. At that hour, the store was already closed. The owner, a hard-boiled Polish woman named Stella, lived in an apartment upstairs, along with her dim-witted nephew Nicolas who helped her out at the store. She never liked anyone dropping by after hours but she seemed to have a soft spot for Sal and me. If we got there before she sat down in front of the TV with her nightcap of orange sherbet and vodka, she'd probably be willing to make a deal. If not, we were shit out of luck.

"So what do you think of Joe Frat and that skank?" asked Sal as we headed east before racing up Ashland Avenue. "Cheating on our girl, in her own condo, no less!"

"I'm scandalized," I said. "What do you care?"

"I think it's bullshit. I just don't get it. You got a nice girl, with a nice place...how you gonna risk all that just for some cheap piece of ass?"

"I think that was one of her friends too," I said.

"How shitty is that?"

"People do it all the time," I said. "Maybe our girl's a cunt."

"No way," he said. "She was nice, sweet even."

"Then why the fuck did you want to rob her?"

"One thing has nothing to do with the other."

"Whatever." I didn't know why we were even talking about this but I went on anyway. "Somehow, some way, our girl is not all that. Maybe she works all the time and won't shut up about her job. Maybe she doesn't like to party. Maybe she doesn't like to give head."

"That's fucked up," said Sal.

"You never know," I said. "You never know what somebody's really like until you're in a relationship. That guy was an asshole and she can clearly do better, but he had his reasons, whether they make sense to you or not."

"I just think it's a shame."

"I don't know what to tell you, Sal."

I got quiet and Sal did too. The temporary victory with the laptop that had allowed for our frivolous discussion gave way to silent tension about our prospects. Even if we caught a break with Stella, we still had a long way to go.

A few more blocks and we pulled over to the curb directly in front of the darkened brick storefront. Stella had already turned off the lights and retired upstairs. Behind the retractable security grill, I could barely make out a few items in the window: an electric guitar, a television and a compound miter saw. The unlit neon sign read: Top $$$ for goods!

"Fuck! What time is Leno on?"

"I have no fucking idea."

Sal wheeled the car around to the alley in back and parked right next to the battered door to Stella's garage. He grabbed the laptop and we hopped the chain-link fence around her lot. We only made it a few steps along the concrete walk when her barking German shepherd appeared out of nowhere.

“Easy, Max,” said Sal, holding out his hand. The dog quieted down and came over to sniff us both. We stroked him a few times and made our way over to the set of old wooden steps that led up to the apartment above the store.

“Lights are still on,” I said hopefully.

We climbed up to a landing crowded with overgrown geranium pots outside the door. A noisy air conditioner jutted out from the back window, the curtains inside tightly drawn.

Sal flashed a tentative look at me. “Shall I?”

“Be my guest,” I said.

He was about to rap on the door when it swung open and Nicolas appeared. Hulking and slovenly, he smelled of alcohol and had a revolver in his hand. He stuck it in Sal’s face and scowled.

“What do you want?”

CHAPTER THREE

"What the fuck, Nicolas?" Sal jumped back and hit me, almost knocking us both down the stairs.

"We just want to talk to Stella," I said.

"Who is it?" Stella called out from behind Nicolas in her thick Eastern bloc accent.

"Michael and Sal," said Nicolas, lowering the gun. He looked us up and down with naked contempt. I never understood how such a big dumb goon could be so judgmental.

"Tell them I am closed," said Stella.

"She's closed," said Nicolas.

"Tell them to come back tomorrow," said Stella.

"Come back tomorrow," said Nicolas.

"It is eleven o'clock at night," said Stella.

"It's eleven..."

"Jesus Christ, Stella," said Sal. "Would you just come out here and talk to us?"

"Watch it, you!" Nicolas took a step towards him.

"It is all right, Nico." Stella appeared in the doorway in her long terry cloth robe. Her flowing brown hair, prominently streaked with gray, had been brushed out over one shoulder. She took a sip from the glass in her hand and stroked his arm, and I caught a glimpse of her faded beauty.

"I will handle this," she said.

He gave us one last hard look before turning back inside.

"Boys," Stella admonished us. "You know better than to come here this late. I am tired. Nico too."

"We're sorry, Stella," I said. "We just..." My voice trailed off under the scrutiny of her gaze.

"We came across something really special," Sal jumped in. "And we didn't want to let the unfortunately late hour deprive you of an excellent opportunity."

"Thank you so much," said Stella. She knew Sal was full of shit. "You still should not have come. You boys need to learn some patience. You need to learn the rules."

Patience. The rules. I almost laughed out loud.

Sal looked down, straining to appear contrite. "We're really..."

Stella raised her hand, cutting him off. "Do not tell me you are sorry. Just do not do this again."

"We won't," I said.

"Promise," said Sal.

"Very well," Stella sighed and stepped aside. She led us into her kitchen, a cramped, modest space that hadn't been updated since the sixties. A bottle of Belvedere vodka, probably the most luxurious item in the entire apartment, sat on the marred laminate countertop. She took a moment to refresh her drink. "You were saying."

"Yes, of course," Sal continued his pitch. "I was saying that this is your chance to update your merchandise, to ah...you know, freshen things up, get in on the new economy."

"New economy?" I asked, forgetting my place in the conversation.

"That's right," said Sal, ignoring my thoughtless interruption. "It's all about computers these days." He lifted up the laptop he was holding under his arm.

"What is that?" asked Stella, slipping on the bifocals she had strung around her neck.

"It's a computer," I said. "Top of the line."

"Really?" asked Stella. "Where do you type?"

"It folds up," said Sal. He started to fiddle around with the laptop before moving over to her small wood dinette. "Michael?" he asked, his voice ringing with frustration.

I went over there to help. "It's right here," I said, noticing the slide lock on the front of the unit. I flipped up the screen and Stella came over to take a look.

"It is very small," she said.

"That's the point," said Sal. "It's portable, so you can take it wherever you want."

"What about the cord?"

"It runs on a battery," I said.

"What happens when the battery runs out?"

"I'm sure Nico can pick up a cord at Radio Shack," said Sal.

"I am not sure, boys."

Stella took another sip from her drink and pursed her lips like she always did when she was about to beat us up. So far, so good. I really didn't give a fuck what she gave us, as long as it was more than a hundred dollars.

"I will give you three hundred," she said finally.

My heart leaped into my throat. Fuck, yeah! I was about to sound my approval when Sal opened his big mouth.

"Gimme a break, Stella," he said. "This thing is worth ten times that and you know it."

"I know no such thing," Stella said. "And even if it is worth what you say, nobody that comes into my store will pay that much."

"Five hundred," said Sal.

Stella stared at him without saying a word.

"Oh, come on, Stella," said Sal. "You expect us…"

"How about four?" I cut him off.

They both glared at me but Stella started talking first.

"You two come to my house in the middle of the night."

"It's hardly the middle of the night," said Sal.

"It is late! My store is closed!" Stella snapped. "But I let you in anyway. I hear you out and I make you a fair offer. And what do you do in return? Insult me!"

Nicolas reappeared behind her, a menacing scowl etched into his coarse features. Seeing him, Sal raised his hands in submission.

"We're just talking here."

Nicolas stood there, silent and disapproving. Despite the urgent business at hand, a big part of me wanted to go over there and kick him in the balls as hard as I could.

"Three hundred fifty," said Stella. "Not a penny more."

"We'll take it," I said, nudging Sal. Stella was through fucking around and so was I.

•

"We could've done better," said Sal.

"Bullshit," I said, taking a drag on my cigarette.

I felt achy and sore and I wanted to concentrate on the road, but I had to set Sal straight. "We're lucky we got anything. We're lucky Nicolas didn't throw our asses out the back door."

"Fuck that," said Sal. "You could take him."

"Not the way I feel right now."

"Maybe not," he shrugged.

He had to be hurting too, though he never let on. Sal was always tougher than me in that way. He quit grousing about the deal at Stella's and we spent the rest of our trip to the West Side with the only noise in the car coming from the air whipping through the open windows. We were headed to our house connection on Erie Street. Rundown two-flats and three-flats built from dirty, brown bricks lined the block. Groups of people, most of them young black men, hung out on the front porches and stoops.

This was the usual scene if the weather was decent. They drank forty-ounce bottles of beer from brown paper bags and smoked menthol cigarettes and ditch weed. Every now and then some hoochie mama would come by strutting her stuff and they would whistle at her. One might make a play and get lucky, strolling off for some action. Mostly they laughed and talked shit. When they saw guys like Sal and me come around, they didn't think twice. We were nothing special, just a couple junkies. I recognized most of the neighbors. Sometimes I got a reserved nod, like they recognized me too. Given some of the nasty spots to score, street corners where they'd rather stomp your guts out than sell you a dime bag, this was a nice place to go.

I parked behind another beater and we got out and crossed the street to the only building with a front door at ground level. Sal hit the buzzer and we heard a window open overhead.

"Hold on, baby," Janet called down to us from the front bay in the first-floor walk-up, her long cinnamon weave spilling over the sill. She closed the window and disappeared. Moments later, her brother Aaron came to the door.

"Yo, yo, yo," he said.

Short, dark and ripped, with a carved jaw and pale blue eyes, Aaron had a deep baritone voice that belied his height. He stepped aside and we hustled up a half flight of stairs to the apartment he shared with Janet and the rest of the family. Sal gave a quick knock and we heard Aaron's other sister answer from behind the door. Her name was Theresa but everyone called her T. She made it her business to lock up whenever anyone stepped out, even for a minute.

"Who's that?"

"Sal and Michael," said Sal.

"What you want?"

"We're collecting donations for the United Negro College Fund," said Sal. "Would like to contribute?"

"Nigga, did you just say 'negro'?" asked Aaron.

"What's wrong with that?" Sal asked with feigned cluelessness.

Aaron ignored him and turned toward the door.

"Open up, T!"

Dead bolts popped, latches clicked and the door creaked open. As usual, T was puffing on a Kool, her tracksuit hanging off her rail-thin frame and a red scarf pulled tightly around her head.

"Very funny," she said.

Sal smiled. "A mind is a terrible thing to waste."

"Y'all should know." T narrowed her eyes at him and turned to me, gesturing at my torn, sweaty clothes. "Damn, boy! What happened to you? Working overtime again?"

Older and saltier than Aaron and Janet, T had that old-school ghetto edge that made it mandatory to fuck with guys like us.

"Don't even start," I said as we brushed past her.

We went into the dining room, a dim crowded space with spare furniture, cardboard boxes and some old milk crates lining the walls. Janet came in wearing a hooded Tommy Hilfiger sweatshirt zipped up just enough to contain her massive breasts. She gave Sal a kiss on the cheek and looked at me.

"How y'all doing?"

"Anything going on?" I asked.

That was the question. I was so wound up to know, the words seemed to float through the air.

"Not yet," said Janet. "We still waiting on the package."

Goddamn-motherfucking-cocksucking-shit!

Four words you never want to hear: waiting on the package. I rubbed my temples, took a deep breath and tried to chill.

"But it's on the way, right?" asked Sal.

"Don't worry, baby," Janet caressed his back. "It's coming."

"When?" I asked, exhaling slowly.

"He's around the way," said Janet. "I just beeped him."

"Maybe we should hit that spot on Cicero," I said.

"They waiting over there, too," said Aaron.

He would know. The connection came through his affiliation with the Vice Lords, the street gang that controlled most of the drug traffic on the West Side of Chicago. Though he was tight with the leadership, Aaron was never a full-fledged member.

"They some thug-ass niggas," he always said.

The Vice Lords had a reputation for being ruthless and violent, but the gang bangers we saw on the street always showed a lot of respect for Aaron. It made me wonder about him the way you might wonder about someone you know who has fought in a war. Maybe he wasn't some thug but Aaron never could've made it as long as he had without seriously proving himself at some point.

"Fuck," I almost groaned.

"Y'all want something to drink?" asked T.

"No thanks." My stomach was in knots.

"I'll have some Tampico," said Sal.

"I'll take some too, Mama," a voice boomed.

I jumped and T let loose with a jarring cackle.

"Damn, you edgy!" she said.

Her son Mookie strolled out from one of the back bedrooms. A colossal slab of muscle and bone with an intense gaze, he was T's pride and joy and the star fullback for the Whitney Young Magnet High School football team. Heading into his senior year, he had already been actively recruited by Division One stalwarts Ohio State, Miami and USC. The kid was going places.

"You ready?" Mookie casually shoved Sal.

"You best knock that shit off, homey," said Sal.

"What you gonna do?"

"I'm gonna take it to the hole, that's what." Sal pretended to front but Mookie just dismissed him.

"Yeah, whatever."

T came out from the kitchen with a couple of glasses of orange drink so bright they seemed to glow. Sal took his and gulped some down, exhaling with annoying satisfaction.

"Nectar of the gods," he said.

"We on, or what?" said Mookie.

"Bring it, bitch," said Sal.

Mookie headed back to his bedroom with Sal right behind him. On the days we had to wait, Sal played Nintendo basketball with Mookie while I hung out with the rest of the family in the living room. Mookie's father was long gone, but T had a man named Maurice she had been with for almost ten years, or so we heard. He was older than T, though I couldn't say how much. Lean, with forearms like Popeye, Maurice was an old-school junkie and a real survivor who knew how to work the system. Between an ongoing disability scam with Cook County and his small time hustles on the side, he managed pretty well.

"Michael, my man. How you feelin'?" Maurice asked as I came in and collapsed next to him.

We were on one of two couches awkwardly situated around a makeshift sleeping area. Some talking head on CNN was running his mouth from the old console TV across from us.

"I'm hanging tough," I said with a deep breath.

Maurice knew where I was coming from. "That's how we do."

"Listen to y'all," T's cousin Clifford spoke up from the other couch. "You *could* just put that junk down."

An ornery retired city worker with a sagging midsection and a mouth full of rotting teeth, he and his morbidly obese diabetic wife Beverly had fallen on hard times. They had been shacked up in the living room ever since Sal and I started coming around there. We had never seen either one of them leave the apartment and we had never seen Beverly get off the couch.

Clifford went on, badgering Maurice. “But you whipped, like your man Clinton. Only it ain’t pussy that got you.”

“Clifford!” Beverly smacked him on the arm.

Maurice fired back and the two of them got into it. A couple old-time products of entrenched urban blight, Maurice and Clifford had that vague political awareness I chalked up to almost anyone who lived through the sixties. They both read the *Chicago Sun-Times* every day and usually agreed about things, but the Lewinsky scandal had been percolating in the press for months and Clifford was really down on Clinton. Maurice blamed the Republicans for being on a witch hunt. They were just a bunch of crackers, and anyone who couldn’t see that was just plain blind.

When I wasn’t biting my lip, waiting for the connection, I got a kick out of hearing those guys talk. That night, I was in a strange mood, vacillating between giddy anticipation and soul-crushing anxiety. Having gotten through the burglary, messy as it was, and the subsequent deal with Stella and that ape Nicolas, I had a lot to be thankful for. Much could have gone wrong that didn’t. Yet I couldn’t shake the chill of my disease and the gnawing doubt that went with it. The smack was still out there, somewhere. Janet said it was just around the way but that didn’t mean shit. The guy could still get busted or capped. Something could happen.

“Oh, stop it, y’all,” Beverly told Clifford and Maurice. A simple woman who laughed a lot, she always tried to keep things friendly. “Michael don’t want to hear that nonsense. Ain’t that right?”

Before I could reply she kept going.

“I don’t know why y’all keep hollering at each other when you know damn well it don’t make no difference. The man’s gonna do what the man’s gonna do! Now gimme that clicker,” said Beverly.

Huffing and puffing, she shifted her frame and thrust one flabby arm toward a table littered with snack food wrappers, empty pop cans and an overflowing ashtray. She came up a few inches short so I grabbed the remote control and handed it to her.

“Here you go, Bev,” I said.

“Thank you, honey,” she smiled.

“What you gonna do now?” asked Clifford.

"I'm gonna see who's on Arsenio."

"Damn, woman," said Clifford. "It's just a rerun anyway. Besides, we watching this."

"Don't sound like it to me."

She changed the channel and things went from bad to worse when Milli Vanilli appeared on the screen.

CHAPTER FOUR

"So what's this I hear?" asked T.

She and Aaron came into the living room where I was slow roasting in my own private hell. I didn't know which was worse, the pit in my stomach or the two clowns spinning around on TV.

"Girl you know it's true

Ooh, ooh, ooh I love you..."

"This crazy motherfucker beat down some white boy after robbing his place," T said to Maurice. "Ain't that some shit?"

"Damn," Maurice chuckled. "Is that how you do? Next thing, you gonna be snatching purses. Old ladies better watch out."

"From now on, we gonna have to pat these motherfuckers down," said Aaron. "We might be next."

"It wasn't like that," I protested but it was no use.

Sal and his big mouth. They continued to rib me and all I could do was take it. A part of me didn't care anyway. They knew what we were about. Besides, with every minute that passed, I became more and more distracted by...well, the minutes that passed.

Where the fuck was the connection?

The buzzer rang and I caught my breath.

Janet bounded past me to the window. "It's him."

I heard the chorus in my head once more.

Haaa...llelujah!

Aaron went down to get the door and came back with a husky, middle-aged guy in a white T-shirt, baggy jeans and Sox cap. They headed straight for the kitchen. Less than a minute later, Aaron walked him out, handing off a paper bag to Janet. She took it back to the room she shared with Maurice and T. I had seen her do this a few times before so I knew the drill. She took a bigger piece, usually a half ounce or so, and divided it up into dime bags that weighed around a tenth of a gram. Since the weight was too small to be accurately measured with any scale they had laying around, Janet made the cut using what looked like a miniature baking pan with tiny indentations she packed full of product. The doses were then transferred to tin foil or wax packs, each marked with the black heart Aaron used to identify his particular brand.

"How many you taking?" asked Aaron.

"Two dozen," I said, hoping for a break.

"Gimme two twenty," said Aaron.

"You got it." Bonus bags! I loved that. "A couple twenties of blow too," I said, referring to the bigger packages of coke they had that cost twice as much. Sal and I weren't much into blow anymore but sometimes we still needed a little boost.

"Make it two sixty," he said.

I counted out the bills and handed them over.

"C'mon back," Aaron motioned toward the bedroom.

"Don't mind if I do," I said, deliberately avoiding Clifford's disapproving stare. It was on now. I pushed myself up from the couch, running the finances through my mind while I still had the time to think clearly. Sal and I rarely blew so much at once but we had made an exceptional score that night and agreed to stock up. Besides, we still had almost a hundred left for incidentals, maybe a meal or two and a few drinks when all was said and done.

"Where you goin', punk?" Mookie called after Sal who had just come out to the hallway.

"I'm forfeiting."

"Whatever," said Mookie. He sounded annoyed, like he always was when Sal would quit playing to get high.

"What's the word?" I asked Aaron.

"Supposed to be tight." He looked serious. "For real."

"No shit?" Sal's eyes lit up. "I'm gonna slam one right now."

"No way, not here," said Aaron. "You know how T get."

T never liked us fixing in her place. "This ain't no shooting gallery," she often said.

As far as we knew, T never did smack or blow. She let Aaron and Janet run both through the apartment but hard drugs weren't her thing. T smoked weed and she sold it too, in ten-dollar packages we called "T-bags." They were decent quality with the buds stuffed into tiny manila envelopes that came in handy when you were out and about. Along with Clifford, T was the only one with a bug up her ass about people slamming dope over there.

I couldn't blame her. For T, it was all about doing right by Mookie. He was a good kid with a real shot at making something of himself and she didn't want anything fucking it up. She had a tough enough time between Maurice and Janet, who both got high regularly, but she could always draw the line at our white asses.

"I think we should get going," I said. We had what we needed and I didn't want any trouble.

"Gimme a minute," said Sal.

He wasn't leaving without fixing first.

Maurice came up behind me, his voice lowered.

"Ain't no thang," he said, "Just be quick about it."

I nodded, immediately understanding the deal. We'd be okay as long as we hooked him up. A couple of bags were a small price to pay for the instant gratification Maurice's offer afforded us.

"This on you," Aaron told Maurice. He looked hard at Sal and me. "Y'all motherfuckers go easy now."

"Fuckin' A." said Sal, rubbing his hands together.

Janet came out and handed me a Ziploc bag with our packs in it. I reached inside for two and slipped them to Maurice.

"Bev got some hypes in the medicine cabinet," he said in a low voice. "I'll be out sitting with T."

"I can fix you, baby," Janet smiled at Sal before turning toward me. "If you up, I'll fix you too."

Now that was an offer I couldn't refuse.

Janet fetched a couple of the disposable hypodermic needles Beverly used for her insulin injections and went into her room. Sal quickly followed and I was right behind him. We took a seat on the floor near Janet's bed against the far wall. An improvised partition made from dark sheets and a clothesline separated her sleeping area from T's. Janet reached under her bed for the orange Nike shoebox where she kept her works, sat down between us and got busy.

Sitting so close, watching those huge breasts sway with each movement of her body, my mind began to wander. I was in good hands. The sexy black nurse was going to take my pain away. I could see why Sal liked to party with her and it occurred to me he was probably fucking her too. I could imagine them getting it on. They got high, they felt good, one thing led to another. It was only natural. It could've just as easily been me, although I wasn't as smooth as Sal and Janet had never fixed me before. I almost got distracted by the possibilities when I caught a whiff of the smack in the cooker and all I could think about was getting off.

"I'll do you first, Michael." Janet loaded up the syringe and handed me the worn leather belt she used to tie off. I hardly needed it with my arms, hard and veiny as they were. I wrapped it around my bicep anyway and clenched my fist a couple times. Janet zeroed in on the sweet spot—just inside my elbow—and stared up at me with those angelic brown eyes. "You ready?"

"Fuck yeah." I couldn't stand it anymore.

She pushed the needle in and we both gazed at the cylinder. I felt my heart pump and a tiny red cloud streamed into the clear liquid inside it. The whole night had led up to this moment.

Janet depressed the plunger and I was off.

The dope crashed into my system like a wave hitting me on a secluded beach. But instead of falling on sand or rocks it felt like I was landing in a giant down pillow. Suddenly I didn't have a care in the world beyond fawning appreciation for the sublime warmth consuming every inch of my body. The rush sucked me down into a deep nod before releasing me long enough to flash on my harrowing night. Rough as things had gone, it didn't seem that bad anymore. That's how it works with heroin. Once you feel that rush, it doesn't matter what the fuck you had to do to score. It was worth it.

"He good," I heard Janet say in the distance.

I dropped out again and before I knew it, I was lifting my chin off my chest while Sal rambled on in his best cockney accent, his voice heavy and coarse with labored ecstasy.

"Oh bliss! Bliss and heaven. Oh, it was gorgeousness and gorgeousity made flesh. It was like a bird of rarest-spun heaven metal or like silvery wine flowing in a spaceship, gravity all nonsense now. As I slooshied, I knew such lovely pictures!"

He was quoting his second favorite movie character of all time, Alex DeLarge from *A Clockwork Orange*.

"You off the hook, baby," said Janet as she gathered up her works. "How you doing, Michael?"

"Fuck," I nodded languidly.

"That's good," said Janet.

"Y'all motherfuckers better not be slamming in there!"

T was right outside the door but she sounded far, far away. At least Maurice had held her off long enough to get the job done.

"I think it's time y'all be going." Janet stashed everything back under her bed and slowly stood up, extending her arm to Sal. She helped him to his feet and turned to me.

"Fuck," I said once more.

"Feeling a bit shagged and fagged and fashed, huh?" Sal leaned down to pull me up but I waved him off.

"I got it, I got it," I said. "All gorgeousness and bliss and gravity and shit."

"I don't know what the hell y'all talking about," said Janet.

"Me neither." I smiled and reached for the sky, twisting to scratch my back which itched from the dope.

Janet opened the door and we walked out of the room.

"You wanna go again?" asked Mookie. He was coming down the hall with another glass of Tampico.

"No, man," said Sal. "I better give you a break today."

"Punk," he said, disappearing back into his room.

By now, I wasn't in any hurry to get home. I could've easily hung out and watched them play Nintendo or gone out to the living room to listen to another round between Maurice and Clifford.

"We could hang out for a bit," I shrugged.

"Not today," said Sal. "I think T's a little hot."

"She'll get over it," said Janet. "But I gotta get the rest of the package ready for the hoppers."

"They waitin', girl," said Aaron. He came toward us, nodding as we passed him. "Y'all be careful driving."

We headed back out through the dining room where T sat at the table, flipping through a copy of Ebony magazine. Arsenio was gone. Beverly, Clifford and Maurice were now glued to some old western.

"See you guys," said Sal.

"You boys be good," said Beverly.

T raised her eyebrows and looked up at us skeptically.

"Later, T," I said, trying to sound casual and coherent.

"Uh-huh." She took a drag off her cigarette, watching us.

We tried to make a quick exit but the multitude of locks on the fortified wood door jammed us up. Sal fumbled pathetically, locking and unlocking, turning the handle both ways, all to no avail. It was like a slow-motion replay of his earlier attempt to get out the front door of our girl's condo.

"Hold on," said T. "Y'all gonna fuck up my security system."

She got up and quickly undid the locks, pulling the door open and sending us on our way.

•

Though we were feeling no pain, Sal and I couldn't help but notice the mood on the street had gotten much more tense. A salt-and-pepper team of narcs had some hoppers up against the wall across the street. It didn't look like anything serious but people on the block were definitely irritated by this familiar sight.

"Where were y'all last night when my basement got broke into?" asked a woman in a light green hospital uniform as she walked past, lugging some groceries she had picked up at the corner store.

"Say that!" said some toothless old-timer on a nearby stoop. He shook his head and sipped a forty wrapped in a paper bag.

The narcs ignored them and went on about their business. Nobody seemed to be holding. That was good. For all we knew, one of these guys was on his way over to Aaron's for the package. Better they get rousted on the way in than on the way out.

"Fucking pigs," Sal muttered.

We had to walk right past them to get to my car. I knew Sal had our score crotched and I just wanted to get out of there without any incident. The narcs, a grizzled white guy with a handlebar mustache and a buff black guy with a shaved head and a goatee, didn't look familiar, but that didn't matter. They didn't have to know us to know what we were about. Cops, especially narcs, notice everything. They sure as hell weren't likely to miss a couple of hopped up white guys skulking down some ghetto sidewalk. Our only hope was for the hoppers to keep them occupied until we got out of there.

"Where the fuck you goin'?" asked the black narc as he stepped away from the line of kids to block our path.

"I'm just trying to get to my car," I said.

"I'll bet you are." He looked me up and down as he popped the gum in his mouth. "Coming back from your auntie's, huh?"

"We've got some friends down here," said Sal. "Why? Is that against the law?"

The narc snapped his neck in Sal's direction and narrowed his eyes. "What the fuck did you say?"

At that point, the white narc cut the hoppers loose.

"I see any of you knuckleheads out here again tonight," he called after them, "and I'm hauling you in for curfew."

The kids were out of there in no time, leaving the white narc free to break our balls with his partner. We were fucked. And much as I was inclined to blame Sal and his lip, I knew better. We were in trouble the moment either one of those guys laid eyes on us.

"Check out these two," the black narc said with marked disdain. "Up against the wall," he motioned to Sal and me.

"This is fucking bullshit," I said.

"Ain't that some racial profilin' right there," the old-timer laughed and took a swig.

"Sir, no comments please," said the white narc.

"Don't pay me no mind, officer," said the old-timer.

The people on the street didn't seem to harbor any ill will toward us, but they sure got a kick out of the whole scene. They milled around at a distance, watching as Sal and I each assumed the position, hands against the wall, legs spread. Too bad for them the show didn't last. As soon as the white narc started to pat me down, we heard gunshots in the distance. Seconds later, their radios crackled with an urgent message.

"Shots fired on the fifty-two hundred block of West Superior!"

"Motherfuck!" said the black narc.

"Let's roll!" said his partner. He shoved me away from him and pointed at us both. "You two, get the fuck outta here!"

With that, they hopped into their gray Caprice sedan and sped off in the direction of the gunfire.

•

"Fuck, man," said Sal, "I thought we'd never make it back."

"Tell me about it."

We were standing on the dank little patch of concrete outside our garden apartment in south Wicker Park. Still really high, I had some difficulty getting my key in the lock. I finally got the door open and we stepped inside. Sal groped around for the light but before he could flip it on, somebody sprang from the darkness and tackled me for the second time that night.

CHAPTER FIVE

"Fuck, Dante!" I yelled as I got slammed into the couch.

If it had been his place I broke into earlier, I would've been shit out of luck. Dante was Sal's cousin and my best friend next to Sal. I had known them both since grade school. We all grew up together in Elmwood Park, or "EP" as we called it, a working class town just west of Chicago with a large Italian-American population.

The quintessential Italian stallion, Dante was a former all-state middle linebacker and captain of our high school football team, the Elmwood Park Tigers. More than ten years had passed since his glory days on the gridiron, but Dante still had the aggressive tendencies that made him such a devastating force when he was out there. He was also in excellent shape, big, strong and fast. Getting hit by Dante was like running into an oak tree.

Knowing we hid a key on the trim over our front door, he often took the liberty of letting himself inside whenever he got too shitfaced to drive back out to EP. He still lived out there in his mom's basement. After years of drinking, fighting and dead-end jobs, Dante had never managed to pull together enough money to get a place of his own, if he even wanted one.

"Got ya!" He gave me one final punch in the chest before settling back into our ratty upholstered armchair.

"Good thing Dante wasn't dating our girl," said Sal.

"I was just thinking that," I agreed.

"Who's your girl?" A familiar voice called from the kitchen.

"Yeah," said another. "We thought we were your girls."

Lila and Sherry came out to join us, each holding a cigarette in one hand and a bottle of Miller High Life in the other. Two hot girls who knew how to have fun, they were always welcome at our place, especially Lila. They came around pretty often. Dante and Lila had a serious thing going and Sherry was way into Sal. The two of them fucked when we hung out but he always kept her at arm's length. Sal got laid all the time and saw no reason to settle down, although Sherry was a total sweetheart and he did really like her.

"So what's all this about your girl?" she asked Sal playfully.

"Never mind," he said. "So what are you guys doing here?"

"What the fuck does it look like?" said Dante. He gulped down the rest of his beer and let out a loud, crisp belch. "Partying!"

"We expected to see you guys over at Spoonful," said Lila. She tried to scoot past Dante but he pulled her down on his lap, copping a quick feel in the process. "Would you stop?" she laughed.

The way Lila handled Dante reminded me of an overworked zookeeper struggling with some large, frisky animal. Dante gave her a quick squeeze and released her. She planted a kiss on the top of his head and got up to get another beer. Dante and I watched her go–she had a great ass—before he leveled his gaze at me.

"So where were you guys anyway?"

"Nowhere," I said.

Dante started to say something but decided not to bother. He knew our deal and he didn't like it. Dante drank. Once in a while he took a puff on a joint. On extremely rare occasions, when he was totally drunk—maybe at a bachelor party or New Year's Eve gathering with some old football buddies—he might sample some blow if it was shoved in his face. That was it. He never touched smack and hated the fact that his two best friends were a couple of stone-cold junkies.

"Drugs are for losers," he always said. "That's why you have to go into the hood to buy 'em."

"Does that mean everyone in the hood is a loser?" Sal asked as if it were a real question and not a thinly veiled jab.

"Only the white guys," said Dante. He usually let Sal get the better of him but not always.

"How about some music?" asked Sal.

"Sounds great," said Sherry as she bent over to pick through a pile of CD's left on the couch. She also had a great ass. Sal was a lucky guy, not that it seemed to matter much to him.

"What do you want to hear?" he asked.

"Surprise us," said Lila.

"Very well," he nodded, retreating into his thoughts until his eyes lit up. "I got it."

Sal made his way over to our version of an entertainment center, nothing more than a nicked up coffee table with a nineteen-inch color TV, an old VCR and a patchwork of cast-off stereo components piled on top. As he rummaged through the CDs piled underneath, I remembered the sweet mini-component system our girl had in her perfect little place. I looked around, surveying our own shabby digs, cramped and cluttered, all peeling paint and tattered furniture. For a moment, I wished that we at least had a better stereo. Then I felt that lovely surge of warmth, deep in my bones, and I realized our sound system and even our shitty apartment were just fine.

"It's on now," said Sal. He turned and gave me a poke in the ribs, causing me to raise my head. "No nodding, you."

I was still flying pretty high and couldn't help but drop out here and there. I hated to nod out like some bust-out junkie with my chin on my chest, but I didn't have much choice when the rush pulled me under. I tried to tune in when a slightly distorted familiar bass intro tumbled out of the speakers.

"All right!" said Sherry. She set her beer down and shimmied over to Sal as the rest of the music kicked in.

"Never too soon to be through
Being cool too much too soon
Too much for me, too much for you
You're gonna lose in time..."

Sal took Sherry by the hand and spun her around, pushing up against her from behind as she pumped her body rhythmically to the beat. It wasn't long before his hands were almost completely buried under her shirt. That's when I noticed Lila in Dante's lap. The two of them were making out like they were the only people in the room. With everyone else paired off, I was grateful to head into the bedroom in back and close the door behind me. It had been a long night. I thought about fixing again, one last shot of heaven to blast me into dreamland, but I was bone tired and comfortable enough to lie down in the clearing of dirty clothes on the rug. If Sal or Dante wanted the bed, they could have it. It didn't matter what anyone did around me. I knew I would sleep like the dead.

•

Hours later, my eyes snapped open. I could hear the sounds of early morning in the city, the rhythmic clap of shoes against concrete on the sidewalk above. I sat up and rubbed the sleep from my eyes. When I reached into my shirt pocket for my cigarettes, there was only one left. Sal must have pillaged the rest. I lit up and glanced around the room where sunlight crept in through cracks in the bent aluminum shades. Sal and Sherry were sacked out on the lumpy mattress, the wrinkled sheet awkwardly twisted around their naked bodies. Even with Sal's pasty arms wrapped around her, Sherry looked fine, sort of like a poor man's Elle McPherson.

I was puffing on my cigarette, checking her out, when the sound of light footsteps outside the room interrupted me. I crawled over to the door and cracked it open just wide enough to see Lila, in her pink wife beater and black lace panties, step into the bathroom. She caught my gaze and smiled, mouthing the words "good morning."

My heart began to race and my stomach fluttered a bit. I turned my attention back to the bed and the nightstand next to it where Sal and I kept the stash. It wasn't far enough for me to get up so I crawled over there and pulled open the drawer. After a quick count, I immediately realized why Sal was still crashed out. No big deal. Now it was my turn. With company in the house, I needed a little extra something so I decided to treat myself to some blow. I opened up one of the twenties and dumped half into my wake-up fix, then cooked and slammed it before I took the last drag on my cigarette.

Good morning, indeed!

I took a heavy breath, feeling a nod one second and a bell ringer the next. Once I climbed to my feet, I walked out to the living room to check on Dante. He was sprawled on the couch, still out cold. I doubled back to the bathroom. The door was hanging slightly ajar. I started to push it open when the rush hit me again.

Bliss and heaven, as Sal would say.

Another deep breath and I was ready. I pushed the door open and found Lila sitting on the closed toilet seat with her panties on the floor by her feet, smoking a cigarette.

She stood up, tall and leggy with her nipples all but poking through the tight cotton fabric stretched across her firm round breasts. I pulled her towards me and she whispered in my ear.

"What took you so long?"

•

Tender and loving though nasty when it counted, Lila might have been Dante's girlfriend but she was my girl. It had been that way ever since shortly after we met, almost two years before. That's when Lila and her co-worker at the time, a hot Asian chick named Nikki with fake tits and a foul mouth, showed up to Dante's bachelor party. They were the cream of the crop at Anything Goes, a premium service that provided entertainment for parties and other "mild to WILD" occasions. They were supposed have the best Two-Girl Bi-Show around, so I hired them to do a first-class send-off for our man Dante. He was set to marry Donatella Melchiorre, a nice Italian girl from EP and the daughter of one of his father's business partners. The plan was for the two of them to get married, move into a brand new house built by one of Mr. Melchiorre's associates and Dante would get some cushy position working for somebody's father. The whole thing might as well have been an arranged marriage but Dante was up for it. That is, he was up for it until the night he laid eyes on Lila.

She and Nikki swooped into the party and by the time they were oiled-up and on all fours, taking turns licking each other's nether regions, Dante was in love and I was intrigued. There was something irresistible about the way Lila handled herself, not to mention a room full of drunken meatheads who all thought they knew what she was about just because they saw her work a double-headed dildo. Nikki was hard with plenty of attitude, enough to keep the animals at bay but not without a struggle. Lila was friendly and sweet. She kept it fun, and though she was totally naked and outnumbered ten to one, she had the proceedings under complete control. Her looks certainly helped. A strawberry blonde with golden-brown eyes and slightly exaggerated features—sort of like a cross between Judy Garland and Cher—her physical beauty was stunning. I wanted Lila the moment I saw her, but she really had me when I got to know her better.

Lila was smart. And she was into stuff. She didn't have Sal's encyclopedic knowledge of film but she had seen many of the same movies. She was also a voracious reader with a freakishly eclectic collection of books written by everyone from Dr. Seuss to Hunter S. Thompson. She wasn't a drunk or a junkie but she could appreciate the lifestyle. First and foremost, Lila was a painter. Inspired by classic rock and the sixties, she was working on a series called "Icons." They featured blown-up photographic images of dead rock stars, each juxtaposed over a painted background of blended reds, golds and browns. The stripping and the lesbian act were a way to pay the rent and squirrel away some money for the future, maybe to open a gallery or start some other creative business.

"You want to go get some breakfast?" Lila asked as she slipped her panties back on. We were still in the bathroom, having just fucked in front of the mirror over the sink.

"What about Dante?" I said.

"Trust me, he'll be out for at least a couple more hours. We'll bring something back for him." Lila turned to check herself in the mirror. She pulled her hair into a ponytail, straightened her shirt and gave me a quick kiss, speaking softly into my ear.

"Brush your teeth before we go."

•

"So how late were you guys up?" I asked.

"Late," said Lila. She gingerly blew on her coffee before taking a sip. We were each perched on a wobbly stool in front of the curvy chrome-trimmed counter at Leo's Lunchroom, a homey little hole-in-the-wall not far from us. The place was bustling but not quite packed. It was still early and many of the hipsters and other urban types that frequented Leo's gritty confines were used to sleeping late. I waved my cup at the guy behind the counter. A scruffy twenty-something with wire-rimmed glasses and a soul patch, he didn't exactly specialize in prompt service.

"Regular," I said.

He nodded and sloshed some coffee in my cup.

"So what are you doing today?" asked Lila.

"Chilling, hopefully. You?"

"Sherry and I have a party at Excalibur tonight." She took another sip of coffee and kept her eyes on me. I knew she was checking out my reaction to this news.

"Anybody I know?" I joked lamely. I lit up a cigarette and took a long drag, searching for anything to distract myself from my mental image of Lila working a party. Like a frayed tag rubbing against the back of my neck, an annoying little psychic ache began to work on me. I concentrated on the rush and got a little relief. I hated to feel even a hint of jealousy but I couldn't help it, so I always needed to hide that side of me from Lila. She didn't need to be burdened any more than she already was. Things were weird enough with her and Dante and me. She didn't need any shit about her job on top of all that. Besides, who the fuck was I to make any demands?

Our arrangement suited me pretty well, though I wrestled with some guilt about Dante. Still, there was no denying the big hungry part of me that wanted her all to myself. The unfortunate reality was Dante fell for her first. In the middle of his bachelor party, he called poor Donatella and broke off the engagement, effectively terminating his father's most profitable business relationship. In doing so, he pretty much torched his future, all for Lila. She was so touched by his reckless affection she decided to take up with him. There was a lot to love about Dante and she did love him. She just needed more. I sometimes rationalized that my thing with Lila allowed her to stay with him, but deep down I knew that was probably bullshit. The truth was, Lila was something special. There was no way I was letting go of the little part of her I got.

"Michael?" Lila snapped her fingers before my eyes. "Hello?"

I started and looked at her.

"Where do you go?" she asked. "When you're off like that?"

"Nowhere really."

"Someday I want to join you."

"I don't think so."

"You don't think so, huh?" Lila shook her head. "With or without you, I'll do what I want."

I was at a loss. Lila had never come at me like that before. I made it perfectly clear I got high from the moment we met. Lying was pain in the balls. I refused to go to the trouble with anyone I chose to know. It was bad enough needing a story for people foisted on me by circumstance, like my landlord or my mom. I was glad Lila was so cool, but the idea of turning her on made me uneasy.

"You need to be careful," I said warily.

She looked at me, silent and tense.

"Anything to eat?" asked soul patch.

"We need a minute," I told him.

"I need an order," he warned.

"Some more coffee," I said. "And a ham and cheese, to go."

"No sandwiches until after eleven," said soul patch.

"Fuck." I scratched my head and felt my last rush.

"How about scrambled egg and cheese with whole wheat bread?" said Lila as I dropped back into the scene. "Only put the eggs and cheese on the bread. And three of them, please."

"To go?" asked soul patch.

"Definitely," she said. "The coffee too."

•

"So what happened to you last night?" asked Dante. He wolfed down the last bite of his sandwich and took a swig of beer.

"How the fuck can you drink that?" Sal cringed.

"Hair of the dog, motherfucker," said Dante. "You should talk." He turned his attention back to me. "So?"

"So what?" I was getting irritated. The blow from my wake-up had me a little tweaked and I wanted to get right, but everyone was already up and taking turns in the bathroom. The wait was killing me and I was tempted to just sit down on the couch, but I never felt comfortable fixing out in the open when Dante was around.

"Why'd you pussy out?" he asked. "The night was young."

"The night was anything but young," I said.

"Oh yeah?" Dante looked puzzled. "And why's that?"

Sherry emerged from the bathroom, finally.

"Thanks for the coffee," she said with a sunny glance at the cup on the table in front of Dante.

"And the sandwiches," he said.

"Don't mention it."

I got up and started to head for the bathroom when I flashed on the robbery the night before. I was glad nobody knew about it. Dante had some idea about the shady shit Sal and I pulled but he never wanted any details and we were happy not to give them. The girls never knew anything. That's how Sal and I both wanted it.

"We gotta run," said Lila, jingling her keys. She got up to leave though Sherry stayed seated, sipping her coffee.

"Where's Sal?" she asked.

"See you girls later," he yelled from the bedroom.

"Okay," said Sherry. She stood up and grabbed her purse, looking a little put off.

"Not so fast, honey," Dante called to Lila. He got up to give her a deep kiss as he grabbed her ass. "You working later?"

"I'll see you around midnight," said Lila. She stroked his arm and directed her gaze at me. "Are you coming out tonight?"

"I'll make sure he does," said Dante. He grabbed a hold of me and I knew there was no getting away, so I tried to end it early. When he got me in a headlock, I punched him in the kidneys.

"Fuck, Michael." He grimaced and let go.

"When are you guys going to grow up?" Lila asked as she grabbed Sherry and hustled her out, slamming the door behind them.

"What the hell is her problem?" Dante asked me.

"I have no idea," I said, but I thought I knew. She had seemed a little sour ever since we got back from Leo's, where I had been so down on the prospect of her getting high.

"No?" He gave me an ominous look and lowered his voice. "You sure about that?"

"What are you talking about?"

My throat was suddenly so dry I could barely get the words out. Dante squinted like he always did when he was mulling something over. A moment passed and he pulled me close as if to tell me a secret. I tensed up, thinking for sure he would smell Lila on me.

"I gotta ask you something," he said.

CHAPTER SIX

"Is Lila getting high?" asked Dante.

"What?" I tried to appear concerned in spite of the immense relief washing over me. I doubt I could've pulled off an effective denial if he had asked if I was fucking Lila. Not that Dante was so far off. Given my earlier conversation with her, I knew Lila wasn't getting high but I also knew she wanted to try it.

"I know I couldn't stop her if I wanted to," said Dante. "I'm not stupid. But if that's what's up, I wanna know. Something's going on. She's acting different."

"Don't worry," I said. "She's not using."

"You sure?"

"Believe me, I would know. Sal would know."

"Know what?" said Sal. He came out of the bedroom, eyes glazed, rubbing the bull's-eye tattoo inside his left elbow.

"Nothing," said Dante.

Sal shrugged and went into the kitchen.

"I'm telling you." I wanted to convince Dante.

"Fine," he nodded at me. "Good. I know I'm kind of a ball-breaker about the dope and I know I don't have a lot of control over her, but I still want the truth."

"Don't worry," I said, trying to ignore the guilty conscience screaming in my head. "Okay?"

"Yeah, okay. Thanks, Michael." He took a swig of his beer. "Oh, there's something else I wanted to talk to you about."

"What's that?"

"I ran into this kid last week outside Wrigley Field. Maybe you remember his older brother, kind of a tough guy. I played against him in the eighty-eight semi's, Jeff Brady. He was a guard at New Trier. I kicked his ass." Dante smiled and faded into the past. "I fuckin' walked all over him for the first half."

"I remember," I said, recalling the game. Most people we saw around were bored by Dante's stories, but not me. I watched him play and it was unforgettable. He was like a high school version of Samurai Mike Singletary, only white. With his size, speed and ferocious attitude, Dante was the kind of player that struck fear in the hearts of quarterbacks and anyone else unfortunate enough to have the ball when he was on the field.

"I got three sacks," Dante said. "I don't know what the coach told him at halftime but he came out of that locker room a completely different player for the rest of the game."

"You still got in a few good shots though," I said.

"Yeah but he burned me, straight up," Dante's face fell as he recalled the play. "Got me on a counter as I tried to switch direction. Laid my ass out. They got over twenty yards."

"Fuck it, Dante." I tried to purge my mind of the jarring image of him laid out on a football field. I was at that game but I must've gone to smoke a bowl or drink a beer because I would've never forgotten Dante getting his ass kicked. "That's one play."

"I know," he said. "It's fucked up. I made so many good plays, I can't remember them all. But the few times I got burned, I can never forget." Dante pondered this for a moment before moving on. "Anyway, like I was saying, I ran into this guy's kid brother. His name's Mark. He's up at Northwestern."

"How'd he even know who you were?" I said.

"I hung out with Brady a few times after running into him on Rush Street one night," said Dante. "I even went to a couple parties up in Winnetka. Or was it Wilmette? I forget. "

"Oh, yeah." I vaguely remembered that period when Dante was sometimes AWOL. Sal and I were doing a lot of blow back then. "What's the guy doing now?"

"He's some kind of lawyer," said Dante. "Lives in Washington. Anyway, I know it's not my thing but for some reason the kid asked me if I knew where to score some coke."

"No shit?" After our harrowing mission the night before, I was in the mood for a slam dunk. "You got a number?"

Dante patted himself down and finally handed over a wadded piece of paper he dug out of his jeans.

"So," Sal walked out of the kitchen sipping a glass of orange juice. "Who's up for a flick?"

•

Dante called in sick and got an earful from his boss over at the loading dock where he drove a forklift part-time.

"Fuck him," said Dante, tossing the phone on the couch.

"Who does that guy think he is?" said Sal.

There was a brief burst of commiseration about shitty jobs and asshole bosses and how life sucks.

"And then you die," Sal flipped out a cigarette and lit up. "But not yet. And right now we are going to Paris."

He popped in a videotape and introduced Dante to a taste of French cinema. *La Femme Nikita* was on the bill. Dante loved the movie so much he wanted to watch it again, and Sal was happy to oblige. The super called and I spent the afternoon resetting the toilet in some old lady's apartment upstairs. It had leaked for so long that the wood floor underneath was completely rotten. The job was a pain in the balls, but considering the break we got on our rent—two hundred plus utilities—I didn't mind getting a call every now and then. By the time I got back, Sal and Dante had left France and were almost done with *The Empire Strikes Back*. I slammed another bag and joined them for *Return of the Jedi*. Dante ordered a pepperoni pizza and afterward, we headed out to our favorite haunt.

•

A dark little gem off the beaten path, Spoonful was known for spicy chili, live music and a refreshing lack of yuppies and poseurs. We knew that could change at any time but so far people like us still had the run of the place. Spoonful was divided into two sections, the front and the back, with a narrow little corridor connecting them. The front was where they served the chili. The back was where the bands played. I had made some calls earlier and arranged for the kid Dante told me about to meet us in the back.

"Double Crown and a High Life," I told Dana.

"You're not gonna fall out on me," she said. A butch chick with a pair of killer sleeves, Dana kept the drinks flowing with the perfect blend of familiarity and attitude.

"This is it for me," I said. "I'm going easy tonight."

"Then keep an eye on him," she gestured to Dante, who was leaning against the wall draining a longneck.

"He'll be cool," I said.

"Uh-huh." Dana sounded skeptical. She handed me my drink and I slipped her a ten, leaving the change. I took a gulp, savoring the taste of the whiskey and that warm, fuzzy feeling of the alcohol seeping into my system. I finished it off and grabbed my beer.

"Who's playing tonight?" I asked Dana.

"The Blacks," she said.

"The Blacks? I don't think I've seen them before."

"You would remember," she said. "They really lay it down."

I sipped my beer and noticed Dante waving me over.

"What's up?" I said.

"The kid's here," said Dante. He pointed to a pair of guys in their early twenties, college types with that affected slacker look. The shorter of the two had some whiskers on his chin. The other was clean-shaven and wore one of those tattered baseball caps that probably came straight off the rack from Abercrombie & Fitch.

"Which one is he?" I asked.

"The tall one," said Dante.

"Nice hat," said Sal.

The short guy went to the bar while the other one waved to Dante before coming over to join us.

"Dante, dude, what's up?" he asked, extending his hand.

"Hey, uh…" Dante stumbled on the guy's name.

"Mark," said the guy.

"Mark," Dante repeated. "This is Michael and Sal."

We all shook hands and made the requisite bullshit small talk. Mark told us how he had trouble finding a place to park.

"You could always take the el," said Sal, half fucking with him.

"That's true," Mark nodded politely and an awkward silence set in until the shorter guy came over with a couple of beers.

"What's goin' on?" he said. "I'm Steve." The guy extended his hand and new introductions were made. Then we got right to it.

"So how can I help you guys?" I asked.

"We're looking for a couple OZs," said Mark.

Sal had a funny exclamation he had used ever since we were kids. He said he got from his uncle Paulie, a low-level wise guy from New Jersey. If someone abruptly said or did something nasty or crazy or generally out of pocket—like a couple arguing and he calls her a cunt or she mocks him for having a little dick—Sal would say, "Oh!" Sometimes all it took was some pooh-butt frat boy asking for two ounces of blow like he's ordering a beer.

"Oh!" exclaimed Sal.

I shook my head and took a moment to think it over. Anything over an ounce was pretty serious, certainly more than you would expect from a couple of part-timers like those two.

"How do I know you guys aren't cops?" I asked. I knew it was highly unlikely they were anything but what they seemed to be, but you can never be too careful.

"C'mon, dude," said Mark. "Didn't Dante tell you?"

"Yeah, yeah, yeah. He played ball with your brother. I heard. Thing is, that was over ten years ago." I looked Mark right in the eye. "And you were just a kid back then."

"Still is," snorted Sal.

"How about this?" said Steve as he pulled his shirt down in back to reveal a small tattoo on his shoulder blade. Three capital Xs.

"Triple X," said Sal. "Nothing wrong with that."

"Triple Chi," Steve corrected him. "It's our fraternity. Jesus Christ, I'm a senior in college! I'm not a cop!"

"So what?" Sal was getting a kick out of winding this guy up. "Cops can't be in fraternities?"

"What about the Fraternal Order of Police?" asked Dante.

Even though I knew he knew better, Sal said that was an excellent question. Mark tried to explain the difference between his fraternity and the Fraternal Order of Police but Sal and Dante started talking over him.

Steve tried to jump in, too. I listened to them go back and forth and I could tell we were okay. These guys weren't cool but they weren't cops either.

"No problem," I raised my voice, ending the exchange.

"How much?" asked Steve.

"Twenty-two," I said.

"Fuck," said Mark. "That's a little steep."

"And I want half up front," I added.

"What?" Steve's eyes bugged out like I had just asked to fuck his sister. "You gotta be joking!"

"Take it or leave it."

I didn't give a rat's ass what these two had to say about it. If they had other options, they wouldn't have been talking to me.

"Dude," said Mark, "be reasonable."

"You be reasonable," I said. "I'm going into the hood to get this shit. All I gotta do is get rousted with the cash and I'm fucked. It's risky enough just getting out of the car. Why should it be all my money on the line?"

"How do we know you're not gonna rip us off?" asked Steve.

"You know where I hang," I said. "If you don't believe me, ask Dana behind the bar. We come in here all the time."

"I don't know, dude." Mark shook his head, thinking.

"Besides, why would I beat you guys out of eleven hundred bucks when I can make a lot more on the up and up?" They still weren't convinced so I spelled it out for them. "You guys look like a couple good prospects. I'm sure you got lots of people lined up in the frat house and the dorms, ready to party or pull an all-nighter. They got money coming in every month from Mom and Dad..."

"Fine," Steve cut me off. "When can we do this?"

"Once I get the cash, a couple days, tops."

"Will you take a check?" asked Mark.

Sal choked on his beer, laughing out loud. All I could think about was how fucked-up it was that guys like this would probably be running the country someday.

•

Two hours later, the band was about to start. Mark and Steve were still hanging around, getting plowed with Dante as he regaled them with football war stories. Sal and I were chilling, talking to some of the other people who came for the show. Just as Dana had told us, a few of them said that The Blacks were the shit. And though nobody could exactly describe the music, they all pretty much said that the band was one of a kind.

"Fuckin' A," said Sal as the house lights dimmed.

The stage was nothing more than an elevated cove in the far end of the room. The space was pretty cramped once the band's equipment was all packed in there. They had everything you could imagine, including a banjo, a trumpet and a huge upright bass with a pair of naked ladies painted on the front, flanking the strings. No wonder nobody could describe their sound. The band soon came out and opened up with a rocking tune layered with gritty riffs straight out of the honky-tonk. Everyone in the house started moving. Sal drifted back toward the bar as I got sucked into the show.

"Red is passing through my head
Might be wise a while
I will murder that dear little girl
Who never smiles..."

Between the music, beer and smack, I was so chilled I slipped into a sort of trancelike state. I was staring at the stage when I felt the soft touch of a hand on my arm.

"Nice ink," a female voice purred in my ear.

I had a tattoo on my forearm, a lizard with a long tail that wrapped around my elbow and extended all the way up to my bicep. I got comments on it all the time.

"Thanks," I said, trying to sound smooth. I got my game on and turned to meet whoever it was, hoping she would be of interest.

"You dog!" said Lila. She was standing right next to me, trying to contain her laughter.

"What?" I wanted to act cool but she had already seen the surprise in my face. "I knew it was you," I lied.

"Uh-huh." Lila raised her eyebrows at me with exaggerated outrage and I knew she was just busting my chops.

"Where's Dante?" I asked, always on the lookout.

"Still getting wasted with his new friends."

"They're not so bad."

"I'm sure their mothers think they're just fine."

I was about to respond when a noisy disturbance at the end of the bar distracted me. I turned just a second too late to catch what happened but I could see Dante, facing off with some guy standing next to him. They were both spattered with blood.

CHAPTER SEVEN

"What the fuck, Dante!" yelled Dana.

I had just hustled over to see what was going on. Steve was off to the side, swaying from a few too many. Mark was doubled over on the grimy floor. One of the regulars, a wiry guy named Lee, stood nearby with a crumpled cocktail napkin pressed against his bloody nose. Dante faced him, fists clenched.

"Dante slugged Lee," Sal explained.

"What? Why?"

"Ask him," said Sal.

I turned to Dante. He looked like he was ready to stand down. At least he had unclenched one of his fists, even if it was to grab his beer. I heard the band start up again behind me.

"Jesus, Dante," I said. "You just had to throw a punch, huh?"

"It's cool, Michael," said Dante, his voice a little slurred.

"It's not cool!" I berated him. "This is our place. We know Lee! He doesn't deserve that shit."

"That was fucked up, man," said Lee. He was no pushover but he knew better than to raise a hand to Dante. A broken nose would just be the start. Still, he was pissed off and not afraid to say so.

"You shouldn't have tagged him," said Dante.

Lee just shook his head in disgust and wiped something off his shirt with his bloody napkin. I leaned in for a closer look at Mark and the pinkish brown puddle on the floor around him. As soon as I got a whiff, I put two and two together. Mark must have puked on Lee, who responded by punching him in the gut. Dante bloodied Lee's nose in return. I took a step back, trying not to gag.

"Classic, huh?" said Sal, struggling not to laugh.

"It's not funny," said Lila. She walked over and took Dante by the arm. "Let's go."

"Aw, honey," said Dante. He pulled his arm away from her. "I'm just gonna finish this last one."

"The hell you are!" said Dana. She snatched the bottle from his hand and tossed it in the garbage behind the bar.

"Fuck you!" yelled Dante. "Fuckin' dyke!"

"Get him outta here!" Dana turned to Lila, furious. "I mean it, Lila! Don't make me call the cops!"

•

"That was seriously fucked up last night," said Sal. He rubbed his nose and settled into the couch, a tall glass of orange juice on the coffee table in front of him.

"Tell me about it." My voice trailed off as I felt the rush. The first fix of the day was always the best. "And I was really starting to dig the band too."

"I can't believe Dante punched Lee in the nose."

"I can't believe that kid puked on him. Rough night for Lee." I lit a cigarette. "And I can't believe Dante called Dana a dyke."

"She is a dyke," he said.

"Is she?" I wasn't sure. "I thought she just looked like one. But it doesn't matter. Either way, it was a fucked up thing to say."

"That it was." Sal scratched his chest, thinking. "I hope she doesn't hold this little incident against all of us. We didn't have anything to do with that bullshit."

"She'll get over it." I sat up in my chair. "I just hope those fucking idiots aren't all talk."

"Yeah, those guys were something else." said Sal. "Talk about a couple amateurs. Who pukes in a bar?"

"He said he had some sorta twenty-four hour bug."

"Oh, I'm sure," Sal snorted.

"At least I'm getting half the money up front."

"What about the rest?" he asked. "I'm driving later. I could try to line up another job or two."

"Thanks, but no thanks," I said. The mere thought of kicking in somebody else's door was enough to make me shudder.

"I should get a hundred or so in fares anyway."

"Don't sweat it," I said. "Maybe you could make some calls. I'll have an extra half ounce or so to unload after I step on the package I get together for these guys."

"Fuckin' A," he said. "I'm on it."

Sal ran through a few names while my mind drifted off. I had a grinding list of errands that included a ride up to Mark's frat house on the Northwestern campus in Evanston, a stop at the bank in EP and a trip to Stella's. And before any of that, I had to run out to the West Side to make sure Aaron was cool with the order. It would have been a hell of a lot easier if I could've just given him a call.

•

"You know, a guy named Alexander Graham Bell came up with this really handy invention," I said. "Maybe you've heard of it..."

"Nigga, fuck that," Aaron said, cutting me off. "I'll talk on the phone when I'm in the pen."

"I didn't realize you were going to the pen," I said.

"Ain't nobody goin' to the pen," said T. "You know why?"

"Because we don't talk on the phone," said Aaron.

"I get it, I get it," I said.

They were smart not to talk business over the wires but it was still a pain in the ass to have to make the trip out just to ask a question. We walked in and sat down at the dining room table. Clifford and Beverly were glued to an especially rowdy episode of *The Jerry Springer Show*. Maurice flipped through the Sun-Times, unfazed. He got up and walked past us into the kitchen.

"Michael, my man," he said. "Where Sal at?"

"He's chilling."

"Nothing wrong with that," Maurice nodded.

"Not when he got you to do the runnin'," T said, needling me.

She was always trying to wind me up. She knew Sal slacked a lot but he was my partner. What could I do? When you're ripping and running, you need someone you can count on. Sal was that someone. Sure, he didn't always pull his weight. Sometimes I carried him, just because I could. The deals were my thing. They were relatively easy money but they required resources and organization and discipline. You had to be able to get the money together. You had to sell the drugs before doing them all. You couldn't beat a guy like Aaron down on the price and you couldn't insult your customers, even if they were a couple of clueless frat boys. As it was, I barely had what it took to pull these deals off without any "help" from Sal.

"This is something different," I said. "It's not for us."

"Yeah?" Aaron sounded curious. "What we talking about?"

"Blow," I said. "A couple ounces."

"Damn!" said T. "What? Y'all rob a bank?"

"Can you do it?" I looked at Aaron.

"I can do anything," said Aaron. "When I see the money."

"How much?" I asked.

Aaron furrowed his brow for a moment, thinking.

"His math ain't so good," said T. She seemed pretty happy to hear my request and it made me wonder what her end on all this was.

"Sixteen," Aaron said finally. "And just so we clear," he snarled at T, "my math is tight."

"I'm just playin'," she said with a smile.

"Cool," I absently told Aaron as I crunched some numbers in my head. Based on the smaller deals I had done before—no more than a half ounce at a time—I'd expected to pay around eighteen. I was already up two hundred. "When can we do it?"

"Holler at me tomorrow," said Aaron.

•

"I'm really sorry about last night, dude," said Mark.

I had no doubt about that. I couldn't tell if he was sick or just hung over but he looked terrible, his eyes red and his face oddly pale. He wore a "Hooters" T-shirt with stained sweats.

"You want a beer?" he asked.

"Uh, no thanks," I said.

I couldn't think of anything I wanted less. It was barely two in the afternoon, not to mention the combined smell of oxidized alcohol, body odor and cherry Glade was almost enough to make me puke myself. I was in Mark's room at the Triple Chi house, a real den of iniquity. With a fully stocked bar and a real wood counter, a Graphics bong in plain sight, plenty of seating and a monster A/V system complete with a library of hardcore titles like *Barnyard Betty* and *Fist-O-Rama*, the space had all the essentials for serious partying. It was hard to believe somebody actually lived in this room, let alone went to classes. I didn't even see any books.

"I gotta run," I said.

"Sure," said Mark. "Let me just get that for you."

He shuffled behind the bar and crouched down, disappearing for a moment before popping back up with a knot of twenties. He handed them over and I did a quick count.

"Looks good," I said.

Just then, the door opened and Steve came in.

"Hey, dude," he said to me. "How about this guy last night, huh?"

"That was something, all right," I nodded.

It was embarrassing talking with these two guys about what happened. I wasn't sure why they kept bringing it up. Maybe public vomiting was more acceptable in a frat house. College life. I just wanted to get the fuck out of there. I had business to do.

"So when can you do it?" Steve asked.

"I'll be back tomorrow sometime."

"You sure?" said Steve. "We can come to you."

"Positive," I said. "I'll call you beforehand."

•

"Take as long as you need," said the woman.

Young and attractive, she had a nurturing air about her, like an Asian masseuse or a stewardess in first class on an overseas flight. Something about the small private rooms there in the basement of the Midwest Bank and Trust in Elmwood Park always made me feel like I was really being attended to well. Maybe it was the way the bank employee took me down there, like she was leading me into some inner sanctum. Maybe it was the complimentary coffee with real half-and-half in the dedicated kitchenette. Maybe it was her hushed tone and the way she said, "Take as long as you need."

I sat down at the square table in the center of the room. The space was so quiet I could hear the hum of the fluorescent lights overhead. I glanced around, looking for a camera. I had never seen one before but I always felt compelled to check. I turned my attention back to the table where a three by ten by twenty-inch painted steel box sat before me with all my earthly wealth inside. I flipped back the cover and took a look, my heart fluttering from the entirely irrational fear that it might just be empty.

Nope. It was there.

I pulled out my dad's Rolex Presidential watch. An eighteen-carat solid gold masterpiece with a diamond-encrusted bezel, it was on his wrist the day he dropped dead from a massive heart attack on the sixteenth hole at Medinah Country Club. At fifty-one years of age, he managed to outlive a million-dollar life insurance policy by less than two years. Though he was golfing with one of his many rich clients at the time, my mom would be left almost completely broke after all his assets were liquidated to pay off his mountain of debt. She was lucky to hold on to the house. With my sister only a year from graduating with her finance degree from the University of Illinois, my mom thought it only proper for me to get the watch since I wouldn't be going to college after all.

Sad as it was, I'm not crying about things. That's what happened. I was lucky to get the watch and it was a miracle I still had it. I also had an envelope with the insurance policy for it and a small stack of United States Savings Bonds purchased on the day I was born, December 7, 1970. That was it. Somehow, some way, I had managed to go all this time without selling off my pitiful inheritance. I examined the watch, noting its heavy weight in my hands. I waved it back and forth and the second hand came to life, sweeping around the dial with the perfectly smooth stroke that characterized the Rolex movement. Swiss craftsmanship at its finest. There was no way I could wear a watch like this but I always liked knowing it was mine. Hopefully it would be back in its steel box before long.

•

"You must think I am stupid," said Stella. She was peering at the tiny gears visible through the back of the watch, her bifocals perched on the end of her nose. Nicolas hovered nearby.

"It's no fake," I said. "That watch is worth at least five thousand dollars."

"More like ten," said Stella.

"Jesus. You're kidding."

"I do not kid," said Stella, her Slavic accent dripping off each syllable. She handed me the watch and folded her arms. "But I have no use for a watch like this."

"Excuse me?"

"It has surely been stolen," said Stella.

I glanced around the dimly lit room where we were standing. The space was crowded with stolen merchandise: TVs, VCRs, power tools, guitars, a drum kit. Maybe someone was coming back for the drums or the tools but I doubted it. I saw the laptop Sal and I dropped off a couple nights before. A tag hung over the screen with the price $1,200 scrawled across it in red marker.

"What about all this stuff?" I said.

"I don't know what you mean," said Stella.

"You know exactly what I mean!" I said, raising my voice from exasperation. Nicolas tensed up and got in my face, so furious at this affront to Stella he couldn't seem to find any words.

"You," he finally sputtered, pointing his meaty finger right at my nose. He would've gone on but Stella raised her hand.

"Enough, Nico." Stella was gentle but firm. She cast a wary look at the security camera hanging above the entrance.

"The camera, Nico. Turn it off."

"What?" He seemed confused. "Why?"

"Do as I say." Stella snapped her fingers.

Nicolas quickly disappeared through the door behind the counter and Stella stood there, not saying a word. He returned a minute later. When she still didn't say anything, I spoke up.

"I just want a loan, Stella," I said. "I'm coming back."

"Sure you are," said Stella.

"I mean it," I said. "This was my dad's watch."

"Your father?" She sounded thoughtful, like the idea that a father of mine could own a watch like this was somehow plausible and somewhat interesting.

"Yes, my dad." I said, thankful that I had come prepared. I whipped out the insurance policy and pointed to his name on the document.

"See? Michael Lira."

Stella looked at the wrinkled paper, then at the watch and then at me. I had no idea what was running through her mind. She had always approached me like I was someone with more promise than I showed, like I wasn't beyond hope, despite all evidence to the contrary. I might have thought this was just her way, the tough but fair pawnbroker eking out a living while maintaining her unbowed humanity, but I knew better. I had seen Stella treat too many of her so-called customers like the lowlife scumbags they were. Even Sal got his share of attitude from her. Whatever her reasons, Stella sometimes tried to get through to me, like I was somehow better than all this.

"Are you sure about this, Michael?" she asked.

"I'm positive," I said.

"Once it is gone." She held up her hands.

"I know how it works." I was getting fed up with her concern and just wanted my money. "Why the fuck do you care anyway?"

"Watch your mouth!" barked Nicolas.

"Nico." Stella calmly shook her head at him and fixed a cold gaze on me. "How much do you need?"

•

By the time I got back home, the sun had set and my body ached all over. I unlocked the door and stepped inside, only to catch Sherry walking out of the bedroom with nothing but a sheen of sweat covering her naked body.

"Oops! Sorry, Michael."

She quickly ducked into the bathroom as I called after her.

"Don't apologize. I should be thanking you."

"You're sweet," I heard her say as she turned the shower on. A minute later, Sal emerged from the room in a pair of plaid boxers.

"Michael, man," he said. "Long day?"

CHAPTER EIGHT

"This fucking heat is killing me," said Sal.

He took a long drag off the smoldering cigarette pinched between his fingers and flicked his ash out the open window.

"Tell me about it," I said.

Without thinking, I shifted my body only to curse myself for upsetting the damp mold of denim, flesh and worn fabric upholstery underneath me.

"You need to get some AC up in this bitch," said Aaron. He spoke up from the cramped backseat, his deep voice cutting through the stagnant mix of smoke and heat inside the car. Sweat glistened from his dark brown skin like a protective coating.

"I'll get right on that," I said as I lit up my own cigarette.

We were parked on a desolate stretch of Harrison Street not that far from T's place just off the Eisenhower Expressway. A steady stream of traffic whirred by overhead. The August sun beat down on the shit-brown exterior of the vehicle, slowly roasting all three of us.

"What's taking these guys?" I wondered out loud, glancing in the rearview mirror at Aaron.

"They'll be here," he said.

I was sweaty and irritable but I wasn't worried. That's just the way it works when you score. You go wherever you have to and you wait as long as it takes. Sometimes it jumps off quickly. Sometime it doesn't. Nobody likes it but everybody knows the deal.

"What the fuck are we doing out here by the scary projects anyway?" asked Sal. "Couldn't we hook up over at your place?"

"Y'all wanna get jacked up coming out the house?" asked Aaron.

"Ain't no police over here."

"I can see that. No garbage men either," said Sal, peering out his window. "Jesus, check out those two!"

A courtyard building covering half the block sat across a tiny patch of grass overgrown with weeds and strewn with trash. A washed-out monolith of crumbling bricks and broken glass, it had long been abandoned, first by the residents, then by the city. Now it served as a sort of junkie clearinghouse. Ratty dopefiends of every stripe wandered in and out of several doorways like zombies.

"Which two?" I asked.

"Over there." Sal tilted his head over his shoulder. A man and woman, both painfully thin, huddled in front of a boarded-up entrance to the first bank of tenements off the street. The man held a flame to one end of a charred glass pipe while sucking on the other end. The woman pawed at him greedily, unable to wait her turn.

"Fuckin' rock stars," said Aaron.

"Like two fat kids with one candy bar," said Sal.

I found the scene too depressing to comment on though it did make me grateful not to be a crackhead.

"Here they come," said Aaron.

We all turned our attention to a royal blue Caprice sedan with chrome rims and tinted windows coming toward us. The car pulled over to the curb on the opposite side of the street a little ways in front of us. The driver's window came down and a young black guy wearing a Cardinals baseball hat and a hard look nodded casually.

"Ahight," said Aaron.

"Go get 'em," said Sal as he opened the door and moved his seat forward so Aaron could slip out.

"Sit tight," he called back, striding toward the other car.

"You think those guys are strapped?" asked Sal.

"I'm sure. I bet Aaron is too."

"We should have a gun," he said.

"It's crazy for us to come down here with a gun."

"Are you kidding? It's crazy to come down here *without* a gun." Sal glanced around. "Look at this place. If I didn't know better, I'd think we were on the set of *Dawn of the Dead*."

"Wasn't that in a shopping mall?"

"You know what I mean."

We watched Aaron in the back of the other car. I'm sure they had the AC going in there. I took a deep breath and slicked my hair back with the sweat on my brow. Fuck the heat and the trash and the rock stars. I needed to keep my eye on the ball.

"Jesus, how long does it take to hand over some blow?" said Sal.

"They're probably counting the money," I said, taking a couple quick drags before flicking my cigarette out the window.

"Can I get a ride?" A female voice invaded the car.

We turned to see a woman standing outside Sal's door. She was long and lean, in biker shorts and a hot pink tube top, with a chocolate-brown complexion and a long brunette weave.

"Excuse me?" I asked. At first glance she seemed out of place here, but then I noticed her full lips were chapped and brittle and her sunken eyes had an unmistakably desperate look.

"Just around the block," she said.

I still didn't get it.

"I'll suck your dick for a hit," she said.

"Oh!" exclaimed Sal.

"Thanks, but ah," I paused, not quite sure how respond. I had never received such a direct proposition. I wasn't interested but I didn't want to be rude.

"C'mon," she pleaded. "It won't take but a minute." She looked at Sal. "How about you? I'll suck your dick for all the change in that ashtray." She gestured to the pile of quarters, dimes and nickels—at least five dollars' worth—that had accumulated there.

"That belongs to him," Sal said nonchalantly.

"Get your motherfuckin' fiend ass outta here!" Aaron's voice boomed. He marched up from behind and grabbed her by the elbow. His grip was so tight, the thick veins wrapped around his forearm bulged when he took hold of her.

"Ouch!" she cried, spinning around to face him. "Keep your motherfuckin' hands off..." Her voice trailed off the moment she was confronted with Aaron's furious gaze.

"You heard me!" He opened his hand and gave her a sharp crack on the ass that sent her scurrying away from the car.

•

"You ever notice how good blow smells like money?" said Sal.

Back at our place with the air conditioner we had rigged up in the front window blowing cool, musty air into the apartment, I was relieved to be out of the heat with the deal behind us. Sal was on the couch and I was in my chair. An old carnival mirror with a hooded executioner holding Ozzy Osbournes's severed head sat on the coffee table between us. One of the few relics of my youth I hadn't lost or thrown out, it almost wasn't big enough for the contents of the two sealed packs I set down on the scratched surface. Each pack held a white rock about half the size of a golf ball with a yellowish tint and a visibly flaky texture. Sal tore one open and took a whiff.

"See what I mean?" he said, handing me the pack.

I smelled it myself. "Definitely."

"I wonder why that is," said Sal.

"I think it's a psychological thing," I said. "Good blow smells a certain way. You make money selling it. You spend money buying it. After a while, you associate the smell with the money."

"I once heard that most cash has a tiny bit of cocaine residue on it," said Sal. "Especially in Miami."

"Who knows?" I said as I went to work. I had to crush up the two rocks and mix in the Inositol, a member of the vitamin B-complex family that comes in the form of a tasteless white powder. I could add one part to four and have my cake and eat it too.

"You think those guys will have something to say about the lack of rocks?" asked Sal. Anyone who's ever scored knows blow that's all powder has usually been cut with something.

"They can say whatever they want as long as they pay me."

I wasn't concerned about complaints from these guys. I just wanted to get this thing done and over with.

"You gonna take a ride with me today?"

"I'd love to," said Sal as he sat back and stretched. "But after the Star Wars trilogy the other day, I've been anxious to reconnect with my more sophisticated cinematic tastes."

"What's on the bill?" I asked.

"*The Killer*," said Sal. "Followed by *Hard Boiled*."

"Sophisticated, huh?"

"These are the subtitled versions."

"Well, don't strain your eyes," I said dryly.

It would be nice if he came along for company but I wasn't about to make something of it. Sal had already done his part, making some calls to unload the extra half ounce. Lila's boss Candice was taking a quarter and another one was going to Paul, a hard-charging stockbroker with a serious taste for blow. He had dated my sister Fran a few years before in what was the most unlikely pairing I could imagine. I was relieved for her sake when Fran decided to cut him loose. But I always got a kick out of Paul and we stayed in touch, mainly because he liked to party so much. He also had cash to burn and was happy to do it. Paul and Candice were easy money stops and Sal had lined them up. I really couldn't expect much more.

•

"You made it," said Mark as he stepped aside.

His eyes were glazed and the room smelled of fresh bong hits. I went inside amid hoots and howls coming from a couple fresh-faced guys slouched across the couch. They were gawking at a grainy video of some chick getting fucked by a pig.

"Just think," said one of them. "That's somebody's daughter!"

"Or their sister," said the other. "Come to think of it, you have a sister, don't you?"

"Fuck you, asslick! Besides, that pig's better looking than that chick you were with last weekend."

I turned to Mark. "You think we could clear this mother out?"

"No problem," said Mark. I chalked up his nervous, overly apologetic vibe to the weed. "I'll get Steve too."

"You do that."

I went over to peruse the CDs while Mark hustled his little frat buddies out of the room. A minute later, Steve came through the door and we got right down to it.

"So where's all the rocks, dude?" he frowned, rubbing the whiskers on his chin as he stared at the blow.

"What can I tell you?" I lied. "It's from the bottom of a key."

"So what? This is the shake?" Steve asked, as if he was looking at a bag of ditch weed.

"It's different with coke," said Mark.

"Whatever." Steve didn't really know what he was talking about but he was suspicious and he was on to something. I had cut the blow, but it was still worth every penny he was paying.

"Hey, man," I said as coolly as I could. "If you don't want it, I'll just take these off your hands right now." I reached for the packs but Mark stopped me.

"There's no need for all that." He looked at Steve. "Right?"

Steve stood there silent, arms folded.

"Fuck this," I said, pouring it on. I grabbed the packs and Steve finally broke.

"Easy, dude," he said. "We'll take it. Just try to get some more rocks next time, would you?"

"I'll get what I get," I said. Fuck him.

I took my money and walked out, almost positive I'd be hearing from them again. Even stepped on, the blow I got from Aaron was way better than anything these guys could score. And if they didn't get that, fuck 'em. They would just be problems.

I got back into my car thinking about my next stop. Candice was Lila and Sherry's boss over at Anything Goes. Sal thought to call her and I was glad he did. She wanted a quarter and she didn't mind paying for it. Best of all, I wouldn't hear shit about shake.

•

"Hey, sweetheart," mouthed Candice as I entered.

She waved me into the stuffy waiting area of an old storefront office probably once used for a neighborhood chiropractor or tax accountant. A petite, middle-aged woman with blonde highlights and a cheerful demeanor, she sipped a bottle of Evian while talking enthusiastically on the headset phone.

"Not when you consider what you're getting. Ask anyone who's ever hired us. They'll tell you Anything Goes shows are worth every penny. In addition to keeping the bachelor completely engaged—no pun intended—that price also includes hot sixty-nine and strap-on action as well as vaginal and anal penetration with a wide assortment of dildos, vibrators and even fruits and vegetables. Pretty much anything you can think of except fisting."

She waited while the guy on the phone asked a question.

"That would be a hundred dollars more and I would need to know in advance, since not all our girls can do it."

Another question.

"We accept cash only, but there's no contract or deposit required. You simply tell us where and when you want us and we'll be there." Candice listened some more and ended the conversation.

"Absolutely. And thank you so much for calling."

By that time, she had made her way back behind the old steel desk in the far end of the office. She hit a button on one of two cell phones in front of the computer monitor, removed her headset and looked up at me with a roll of bills in her hand.

"Boy, am I glad to see you," she said.

•

"So when are we getting you into the market?" asked Paul. He emerged from his kitchen with a sly grin that really brought out the dimples in his cheeks.

"You're joking, right?" I turned to look out at the clear dusk sky hanging over Lake Michigan. Though I had been up there twice before, the view from the 69th floor of Lake Point Tower still overwhelmed me. Paul handed me a highball glass filled with ice cubes, Grey Goose and a splash of tonic.

I took a sip and winced. "Wow."

He pulled a remote control from the hip pocket of his slacks and aimed it at a sculpted console built into the wall across from us. A jazz melody instantly filled the room.

"You like Thelonious Monk?" he asked.

"In a background sort of way," I said.

"I know what you mean."

Paul took a sip of his own drink and planted himself on the leather sofa in front of a solid glass coffee table surrounded by austere upholstered chairs. A massive canvas spattered and streaked with bright colors hung on the wall behind him.

"So what do you say?" Paul asked as he reached under the couch for a plate with a razor blade on it. He dumped out the contents of the bag I sold him, picked up the blade and dug into the pile.

"About what?" I finally turned away from the view.

"The market," said Paul. Using a series of quick, fluid motions, he spun out a pair of long, curved rails.

"I don't know anything about it," I said. "Except maybe that it's too risky."

"Too risky?" Paul guffawed as he pulled a clip full of bills from his pocket, peeled one off and rolled it up.

"For a sucker like me anyway," I clarified. Not that I really considered myself to be a sucker, but stocks weren't my game. Besides, the market was a big reason my dad died broke and I always suspected the stress might even have contributed to his heart attack.

Paul quickly snorted up the two lines, dipped his fingers into his drink and dabbed his nostrils before taking a sip.

"No different than anything else where money is involved," he said. "You just have to know the right people. Speaking of which, I can't tell you how glad I was to hear from Sal."

"Oh yeah?" I figured as much.

"My guy just got busted," he said. "But that wasn't the only reason. How's Fran doing?"

I hadn't spoken to my older sister in months, not since the blowout we had after I lit up a cigarette around her six year old, my nephew. Paul was asking the wrong guy.

"She's..." I shrugged. "You know. She's Fran."

"Yeah, I know," Paul nodded thoughtfully. "Anyway, like I was saying...you don't have to be an expert on stocks to make money in this market." He flipped out a cigarette and motioned to a carved stone piece sitting on one of several shelves displaying small sculptures from Asia and Africa. "Grab that ashtray, would you?"

"I thought that was a work of art," I said.

"It's also an ashtray."

I set it down and lit up as well.

"It's like the other day," Paul went on, cutting some more lines. "I hired this kid, right out of college. He comes in to the office. It's his first day and all. I show him his desk, introduce him to everyone and get him started, then head into my office to make some calls. A couple hours later, I come by to check on the kid and he's dug in by his desk poring over all these graphs and shit."

"What's wrong with that?" I had no idea.

"Nothing, if you wanna take it in the ass from guys like me," Paul let loose with a jarring cackle. "I told him that, too. I said, 'Look kid, we don't build rocket ships here, we ride 'em!'"

"That's pretty good," I nodded. Paul was nuts.

"I'm telling you, there's nothing to it," he said.

•

After promising to follow a hot tip on the NASDAQ, I finally extricated myself from Paul's place and headed out west. With almost two grand in my pocket, I was tempted to stock up until Christmas, or as close as I could get. Then I remembered my dad's watch sitting there in Stella's safe. I just couldn't blow all my money on dope, not without getting it back first. When I got to T's place, she told me Janet was out with "my boy." I didn't know what she meant until Aaron informed me I was already on the hook for ten bags. Fucking Sal. Aaron hooked me up with twenty more and I was on my way.

I went back to home to relax and zone out, but when I got there I was immediately assaulted by the passionate moans emanating from the bedroom. Living in such tight quarters with a guy like Sal, I could usually tune out that kind of thing, but I was too jazzed from running and gunning all day. So I fixed up and went over to Lila's. I figured she would be there alone, since Candice told me there weren't any parties that night and Dante had a new job as a security guard in some factory on the South Side. I would've called first but I didn't want to take the chance she might tell me not to come.

CHAPTER NINE

"Michael." Lila stood frozen in the doorway, clearly surprised to see me standing there.

"Aren't you gonna ask me in?"

"I didn't realize you needed to be asked." She smiled and I knew I hadn't made a mistake.

"I'm like a vampire."

She looked at me blankly.

"That means I can't come in unless you invite me," I said as I stepped over the threshold.

"I see." Lila closed the door behind me.

"You gotta watch *Buffy*," I said. Sal and I loved that show.

Lila walked past me without a word and I remembered she didn't even own a TV.

"So what are you up to?" I asked.

"Painting."

Lila lived south of Sal and me in East Village. Still pretty rough, the neighborhood was just starting to show signs of change. Longtime residents were moving out and developers were moving in. They were tearing down houses and putting up three flats and converting all the best apartments into condos. Lila had heard rumors from some of the other tenants—all of them artists, hipsters or eccentrics of some sort—that their building, the old Stackman Brothers Toy Factory, was going condo any day. They would throw a couple cans of paint on the walls, put in some Euro cabinets and stainless appliances and make a fortune.

"Where do we go then?" asked Lila.

We all wondered the same thing. Lila had a great place, the perfect blend of chaos and comfort. A lofted space with exposed ductwork and a cinder-block exterior wall, her apartment had no interior walls but still felt oddly cozy. The kitchen was nothing more than a corner with an icebox from the fifties, a single-bowl sink, a hotplate and a six-foot section of painted steel cabinets with a stainless counter. A colorful Native American wool blanket lay strewn across a double mattress on the floor. Her books were stuffed into a shelf unit nearby, along with some photography magazines. Next to that, she had a small boombox on the floor with CDs and cassettes stacked around it. The Clash was playing.

The windows on the south wall were all wide open. Two had box fans wedged between the sash and the sill. One blew air into the apartment and the other sucked air out, creating a slight breeze everywhere you walked. Other than a small dinette, a pair of beanbag chairs and an antique wardrobe, the place was empty except for all the massive oil-streaked canvases. Many were simply luxurious concoctions of color and stroke and texture, sort of like Impressionistic visions of the surfaces of other planets or post-apocalyptic seas and skies. Her Icons series hung on the west wall. Jim Morrison, Jimi Hendrix and Janis Joplin all kept watch over everyone who entered, their famous faces swimming in layered swirls of paint. We stopped behind her easel.

"What are you working on?" I asked.

"Another icon."

"Let me guess," I said. "John Lennon?"

"Close." Lila led me around the front where I instantly recognized the bleary-eyed countenance. "Brian Jones."

"Cool," I said, taking in the work. The colors were brighter than usual, mostly royal blues and reds.

"Think of a Union Jack, melting," said Lila.

"Definitely." I felt a surge of appreciation for Lila and her paintings. "Hey, you want to go to the movies?"

"You're joking, right?" said Lila. "Look at me."

Raggedy as she was in her paint-smeared wife beater and low-slung jeans, I couldn't see any reason not to go out. I was sure she had been cooped up working all day and needed to relax.

"I'm serious." I glanced at my watch. Nine-fifteen. "We can still catch most of the last shows."

"What do you want to see?"

"I don't know. Why don't we just run over to the Logan and see what they got?"

"Why didn't call you first?" Lila scrutinized me closely. This was out of the ordinary for us and she knew I knew it.

"What's that?" I pretended not to hear her.

"You always call before coming."

"Not always," I said.

Lila raised her eyebrows, waiting for a real answer.

"I guess I thought you'd tell me not come."

"But you wanted to anyway."

"Yes," I said.

"What about what I want?" she said.

"Hey, look." I felt a surge of anxiety. I didn't know where Lila was going with all this but I was pretty sure it was nowhere I wanted to be. "I'm here asking you if you want to go to the movies."

"Well, I'll tell you exactly what I want." Lila narrowed her eyes at me and waited a beat. My stomach clenched as I steeled myself to hear what was coming. "I want a bucket of popcorn with extra butter and some Milk Duds," she said.

I let out a deep breath and felt my stomach loosen up.

"One of these days, Lila." I shook my fist at her.

"You gonna send me to the moon?"

•

"Have you seen *Saving Private Ryan*?" asked Lila. We were standing on the curb, looking up at the marquee.

"Twice," I said. "I'd see it again, just for the first twenty minutes. Storming the beach at Normandy. It's really something."

"I've heard," said Lila. "I'm just not up for war tonight."

"I've never even heard of *The Negotiator*," I said.

"Kevin Spacey and Samuel L. Jackson are in it," said Lila.

"That's right," I remembered. "It's some cop drama, the usual Hollywood summer shit."

"What about *Out of Sight*?" said Lila. "I read the book by Elmore Leonard. It's a sleazy tale. You'd like it."

"I can't stand George Clooney," I said.

"C'mon," said Lila. "What about *From Dusk Till Dawn*?"

"I'll give him that."

"Besides, I know you must like Jennifer Lopez."

"Who's that?" I had no idea.

"She was the scheming wife in *U Turn*."

"Oh yeah." I remembered her, a hot Latina with a nice round ass. "She was pretty good in that."

"Let's do it," said Lila, taking my arm.

We bought our tickets and went inside. I wasn't hungry but the popcorn and candy were part of the deal.

"Jesus, look at the line." I hated lines.

"What's the hurry?" Lila asked.

She took my hand and pulled me in the direction of the concession stand where we got behind a noisy group of three young couples. White suburban transplants all the way, they looked like they stepped off the pages of an Eddie Bauer catalog. I would've bet money they each had their own customized unit in one or another of the faceless condos taking over the North Side. They were talking and laughing and joking, no doubt lubed up from a few drinks before the show. They seemed oblivious to us until one of the guys caught a glimpse of Lila and turned white as a sheet. As soon as they got their snacks and walked away, I nudged her.

"Did you know that guy?"

"Sherry and I did his bachelor party two months ago," said Lila, glancing in his direction.

"You're kidding!" The words slipped out with a vehement edge that I instantly regretted.

"No, I'm not." Lila sounded annoyed. "Why would I be kidding about that?"

"I don't know," I said. "I didn't mean…forget it, really." I felt like I was walking through a minefield.

"I sure hope so," said Lila. "Because the last thing I need from you is some jealous bullshit."

"I hear you, Lila," I said. "I'm not going there, trust me."

"Okay, Michael," Lila said. "I believe you, but it's difficult when I hear that tone in your voice."

"I'm sorry," I said, trying hard to figure out what to say that would defuse the situation. "I just got caught off guard."

"Off guard?" I had clearly chosen the wrong words. "What does that mean? Do you need some kind of special warning any time we might run into someone that's seen me naked? Or should I just make sure to keep it to myself next time?"

As cool as I thought I was, a big part of me wished she would just keep it to herself though I didn't want to admit it. The whole sorry mess was my fault anyway. What the hell was I thinking? How else would Lila know a guy like that?

"Can we just move on?" I said. "I'm sorry, really."

Lila pursed her lips. "It's okay," she said. "It's just...there's nothing wrong with what I do. I refuse to feel ashamed about it."

"You're right. You shouldn't. It won't happen again."

I felt like such an asshole. The last thing I wanted to do was hurt her feelings. And who was I to pass judgment on what she did to pay her bills? I pulled her close, squeezing her tight. To my relief, she relaxed in my arms.

"Any day now," griped some goateed slacker behind us.

I would've told him to shut the fuck up but I didn't want to ruin the mood I had worked so hard to restore. We were at the front of the line and the kid behind the counter was all ears.

"Medium popcorn with extra butter and a box of Milk Duds for the lady," I said. "And I'll take a large Coke."

"Make that two, please," added Lila.

•

The movie was better than I expected. I liked the way the story unfolded, with flashbacks and seemingly unrelated characters and plotlines that all intertwined. The guy Don Cheadle played reminded of a skinnier, more brutal version of Aaron, and to my surprise, I liked George Clooney. But my mind kept wandering back to the image of that guy feeling Lila up at his bachelor party. I tried to put the scene out of my mind but I just kept coming back to it.

Fucking yuppie douchebag.

If not for stripping and other forms of prostitution, a guy like that wouldn't have a snowball's chance in hell of laying his hands on a woman like Lila. As it was, her choice of vocation was somewhat of a mystery to me. Though she came from a fucked-up family, Lila had resources. Her father was a Beverly Hills lawyer with a thriving divorce practice and a third wife. Her mother was a bipolar alcoholic and a former actress living off the fortune Lila's grandfather made as a B-rate movie producer. Lila had a decent relationship with both her parents, at least compared to most people I knew.

She also had an education, not to mention some real work experience. After graduating from UCLA with a bachelor's degree in fine arts, Lila moved to New York City to work in some big name art gallery. The job had prestige but didn't pay very well so she made ends meet working as a freelance artist's model. When the gallery went belly up and Lila got tired of sitting around naked, she abandoned the commercial side of the art scene and started painting on her own. She ended up moving to Chicago with a boyfriend, another painter who sounded like a real asshole from what I heard. The relationship ended badly and he went back to New York after less than a year. That's when Lila met Nikki, the chick who got her into stripping.

"I'm still naked but at least now I get to move around," Lila once said. "And the pay is a lot better."

•

When the movie let out, Lila and I each went to the bathroom. By that time, the bloody conclusion of the film had worked its magic, and I had completely forgotten about the douchebag Lila recognized before the show. I wasn't until he stepped up to the urinal next to me that it all flooded back into my mind. I tried to be cool, staring at the white ceramic tiles before me. But as I zipped up, I thought for sure I saw him smirk. One of his friends was in there too, along with a few others forming a line. I didn't give a fuck.

"You got a fucking problem?" I asked him.

The guy swallowed hard and quickly zipped up his pants. His friend stepped toward me.

"Back the fuck off, motherfucker!" I growled.

The guy wanted nothing to do with me. Neither of them did, or anyone else waiting under the glaring fluorescent lights in that cramped bathroom. I could feel their eyeballs on me.

"What the fuck are you looking at?" I pushed past them out the door where Lila was waiting for me in the lobby.

"That was fast," I said, hoping to hell she hadn't noticed the scene I just made.

"I was the first one," said Lila. "Good thing, huh?" She tilted her head in the direction of the ladies room where the line ran all the way out the door.

"Yeah," I said. "Good thing."

"You want to get some ice cream?"

•

Fifteen minutes later, Lila and I were nestled in one of the cozy, semicircular booths at Margie's Candies. She perused the menu while I examined the old-time mini jukebox mounted over our table.

"Do these things work?" I wondered out loud.

"They do aesthetically," said Lila. She set the menu down and looked around. "I love this place."

A trip to Margie's was like a trip through time. A Chicago landmark since the 1920s, the place was a virtual museum of knickknacks, newspaper clippings and assorted mementos dating back for decades. They even had an autographed picture of The Beatles from when they stopped there after playing Comiskey Park back in 1965.

"What are you getting?" I asked.

"I can't decide between a root-beer float and a hot-fudge sundae," she said. "How about you?"

"Decisions, decisions," I said. "I'm getting the same thing I always get, a chocolate malt with extra malt."

"Extra malt," Lila mused. "That's unusual."

"It's the only way to make sure they really put the malt in there," I said. "Otherwise it's just a shake."

"The horror!" Lila mocked me.

•

"I can't believe I ate the whole thing," said Lila as she walked into her apartment, rubbing her stomach.

"Popcorn, Milk Duds and a hot-fudge sundae," I said. "I don't know where you put it all."

I reached out to grab her by the waist but she slipped away. Maybe tonight was not the night. I never quite knew with Lila. With Dante and other considerations, it was ultimately her call. And it looked like that call wasn't going my way. Fuck it, I told myself. I could always go home and get high.

"I really had fun tonight, Michael," said Lila. The faint sadness in her voice set me on edge.

"Me too," I said tentatively.

"I wish it could always be like this."

"I do too," I confessed. That's as far as I would go. While I occasionally imagined having Lila all to myself, the reality was I shared her with Dante. "Look, I really need to..."

"What?" Lila cut me off. "Let me guess. You need to go, right? I'll bet you can't stay another minute."

"Lila, please." I tried to deny it but she had me. Ever since I realized I wasn't getting laid that night, the fix stashed in my coat had been looming larger and larger in my head.

"Don't even bother, Michael. I know what you're about." Lila grabbed my arm and turned it over, exposing the track marks hidden in my tattoo. "Must be nice not to need anyone."

What could I possibly say to that?

"I'm going back to California," she said abruptly. "I'm through with Chicago. And Dante. And you." Lila looked at me, the gold in her eyes glistening with tears.

"For God's sake, Lila." I felt a hot flash of desperation. "It doesn't have to be all that."

"All that?" Lila sounded bitter. "I'm sorry if you think I'm making too much of my happiness."

"I didn't realize you were unhappy," I said.

"I didn't either." She seemed as surprised by her own words as I was. "I don't know what's going on with me. But I want something more. I need something more."

"And you think you're gonna find it in California?"

"I doubt it," she said. "But at least I'll find something new."

I felt a pit in my stomach. I always knew Lila would eventually break up with Dante. When she did, I wouldn't be able to see her for a while.

My hope was after things cooled off, we could resume some covert affair. When I was really reaching, I told myself that someday Dante would get over her, and uncomfortable though it might be at first, we could see each other openly. It never occurred to me she would just pick up and leave. And now that it was on the table, I was starting to freak out. I took a deep, frantic breath and stepped back. Lila noticed my distress.

"Michael? Are you okay?"

"I have to go." I suddenly felt the sickness all over me.

"No, you don't." Lila came over and gently took my hands. "`You can stay right here." She pulled me close and peered into my eyes and I almost cried. "But you have to let me join you."

CHAPTER TEN

Heroin, Lila and me were a threesome made in heaven. Far from some personal apocalypse, the night I got Lila high brought us closer than ever before. She stayed in Chicago and we spent many more evenings like that one, though we often didn't make it out of her apartment. We would put some music on, have sex and take turns getting off afterward. I taught her how to fix and she was a natural, quick and clean. I could just sit back and Lila would take care of me. When it was her turn, I couldn't wait to see the ecstasy wash over her face. And as much as Lila took to the feeling, I was relieved to see she seemed fine going without it. I didn't want to see her get saddled with a habit and I sure as hell didn't want Dante to find out. I was glad things at his new job were going well.

"I can't complain," he said. "I kinda like working at night. It's quiet. Nobody bothers you. There's even a little tavern across the street that's open when my shift ends."

Nothing like a beer at seven o'clock in the morning.

When Sal didn't have his own thing going, he sometimes badgered me about where I was always off to. I told him I was hooking up with my old girlfriend Tina. The two of them never got along.

"She's kind of stuck-up," he said. "You can do a lot better."

"What can I tell you?" I lied. "She's easy."

That's all Sal needed to hear. He would've been disgusted to learn about Lila and me, so I made sure he didn't find out. It wasn't too hard. I had a lot going on besides my trysts with Lila. Mark and Steve, who we had taken to calling Frat Row, turned out to be an incredible connection. After that first deal, I hooked them up five more times in the next three weeks. By the time I got my watch back from Stella a month later, I had almost ten grand in cash to add to the Rolex in my safe deposit box. Some of that came from Paul and a few guys he knew down at the Chicago Board of Trade. We called them the CBOT Crew. These guys were something else. They were all big, like basketball players, only thicker.

"They gotta be that size to make the trades," said Sal. "All that yelling and screaming down in the pit? Think about it."

They also had a twisted, predatory edge about them. Loud and profane to a fault, they were always declaring how this or that person needed to be fucked in the ass or mouth. Those guys would've done just fine in prison. They were big, nasty brutes, raking in the cash and spending it on strippers and blow. Guys like that even made Lila think twice before taking her clothes off.

"They're a gang bang waiting to happen," she said.

Nice. They were certainly unpleasant, so much so that even I didn't want to deal with them. Besides, I had enough on my plate with the constant shuttling between the West Side, the Triple Chi house and Paul's cocaine-fantasy condo on Lake Shore Drive. So I sent them up to Northwestern to score through Mark and Steve.

"Good thinking. Let Frat Row deal with those animals," said Sal.

And they did. Another month passed and I went back to the bank, this time with twenty grand. I was getting it done, though all the running was starting to take its toll. I started spiking some of my fixes with a little blow just to keep my wits about me.

"Watch that shit," Sal warned.

Easy for him to say. I was the one busting my ass. It would've been much less hassle to just sit back and wait for a knock on the door, but I never liked people coming to my place to score. If they only stayed for a minute, it looked suspicious to the neighbors. If they wanted to stick around and party and you didn't like them, it was awkward. I wasn't worried much about getting robbed, but that was always a possibility. People get hooked. They get desperate. They know you have drugs in the house. The next thing you know, your door gets kicked in and you have a gun in your face. Driving around with drugs carried some risk but as long as I didn't give the police a reason to pull me over, I felt like I had more control over the situation. I just needed something for Sal to do. The last thing I wanted was to get dragged into any more capers.

"Listen, man," I told Sal. "No more break-ins as long we got this other thing going, okay?"

"Are you asking me or telling me?"

"I just don't want to get busted over some stupid shit."

"Then you can stay home," said Sal.

"I'm definitely staying home," I said. "You should too."

"This is *your* thing, Michael," Sal snapped. "I know we share the stash and all and I appreciate that, but I like to earn. And don't give me any shit about driving either. Fuck that."

"Fair enough. I could use some help."

I had been reluctant to let Sal handle the blow but I really did need a hand. So I had him take care of Candice and a few other people we knew, and I set him up right. I even kicked back a few grand to Dante for hooking me up with Frat Row in the first place.

"You don't have to do that," he said.

"Think of it as residual commission."

"What the fuck is that?"

We went back and forth, but he eventually took the money while I kept rolling. I was so busy, I started farming out some of my maintenance duties at the building. No more leaking toilets or rotten floors for me. I even got my car fixed, did the brakes and replaced the CV joints along with the exhaust.

"All you need is a paint job now," said Sal.

Aaron and T and the rest of the family could not have been more pleased. I know Aaron didn't make as much off me as he did from retail sales through his hoppers but it was easy money, free and clear of all that corner bullshit. I could see the results around the apartment. They bought Mookie a stereo system that really brought his Nintendo game to life and they also got a new TV, a thirty-two-inch monster with built-in surround sound. Beverly was so thrilled, she actually got up off the couch to hug me.

"Ain't that somethin', Michael?" she gushed, squeezing me so tight I almost lost my breath.

"You the man, Michael," said Maurice.

T was always in a good mood. She started getting her hair and her nails done. And I heard talk about them getting a bigger place, maybe even a house. Aaron was even looking into real estate just as an investment. I was blown away when I heard that.

"Why not?" he said. "They buildin' right next to Cabrini. Ain't but a matter of time before they get to the West Side."

That got me thinking hard. Maybe all this "revitalization" wasn't so bad after all. Houses and small apartment buildings were changing hands everywhere you looked. Speculators were fixing up the houses or tearing them down to build larger, more expensive ones in their place. Developers were rehabbing apartments all over the city to sell as condos. I asked around and learned that some properties in my neighborhood were just getting flipped, straight up, without shit being done to them. People were making money hand over fist.

Why not, indeed.

I considered it for a while, only to get caught up in my usual routine. What did I know about real estate anyway? Other than the nondescript bungalow where I grew up in EP, the only places I ever lived were a string of shitty apartments. Legitimate finance was a mystery to me. I had never taken out a loan of any kind. I didn't have a credit card. I didn't even have a bank account. I had a safe deposit box with some cash and a few bonds and a really nice watch. That was all I had in the world and I didn't have the guts to put it on the line. Besides, I was already doing fine.

Why go and fuck it up?

CHAPTER ELEVEN

"So what are you gonna be?" asked Sal.

"I don't know," I said. "Probably a zombie."

"You can never go wrong with a zombie," he approved. "Hey, you should be an OD!"

"What? That's fucked up."

"No, it's not. If you're a zombie then you had to die somehow. And it'll be easy to pull together. You break off a hype, tape it to your arm, put some blue makeup on your face and be done with it."

"So why don't you do that?" I said.

"Because I'm Mr. Pink," he said. "Remember?"

How could I forget? We had been invited to the annual Halloween party at Triple Chi. Mark said it was their biggest party of the year and all kinds of people came by. Against my better judgment, I brought it up to Sal and we all decided to go. Sherry and Dante were down as soon as I mentioned it. Lila, having gone to college and been to her share of frat parties, took some convincing. I'm not sure why I bothered. I guess the party sounded fun at first. All of us in costume. Cooler weather. But as the date drew closer, I began to feel uneasy. I made sure to let Mark and Steve know I wouldn't be bringing anything with me so they needed to stock up beforehand. One less thing to worry about, but I still couldn't shake the feeling that something really fucked up might go down.

•

On Halloween night, Lila walked in as Elvira, Mistress of the Dark, in a black low-cut gown slit up to her thighs, a long black wig, and fishnet stockings. Sherry was a sexed-up version of the White Witch from The Lion, the Witch and the Wardrobe.

"It was Lila's idea," Sherry said with a shrug. "I've never even heard of that story."

"I thought it would be cool if we did sort of a black and white witch thing," said Lila.

"You two look great," I said.

"Don't they?" Dante agreed. He was decked out as the Viking superhero Thor, complete with a big plastic battle hammer.

"Michael..." Lila looked me up and down, grimacing when she saw the hype dangling from my arm. "What are you supposed to be?"

"An OD," said Sal as he came out of the bedroom in a plain black suit and tie with a crisp white shirt. The suit had come from the Salvation Army. It was baggy and threadbare and perfect for his costume. His hair was slicked back behind his ears and he was sporting a goatee he grew just for the occasion. He had a toy pistol tucked in the front of his slacks.

"I don't get it," said Dante.

"Michael nodded right out of this world," Sal lowered his voice, speaking in the ominous tone of a horror show narrator. "Only to be reanimated as one of the living dead!"

"Like a zombie?" said Sherry.

"Nothing gets by the White Witch!" Sal grinned fiendishly and grabbed her by the waist.

"I think it's a little ghoulish," said Lila.

"We're going to a frat party," I said. "Anything goes."

"Don't remind me," said Lila as she lit up a cigarette.

"Hey," I said. "We can pull the plug on this thing anytime."

"But we're all dressed up," said Sherry.

"There's a party over at Spoonful," said Lila.

"Fuck that," said Sal. "Half the place won't even be in costume."

"C'mon, you guys," said Sherry. "We go there all the time. This will be something different. It'll be fun."

•

"Ladies, ladies, come on in," said Mark when he got an eyeful of Lila and Sherry.

He looked pretty ridiculous with an oversize Chicago Bulls uniform hanging from his bony frame. The giant pair of Nike high-tops on his feet only made it worse. I was just happy not to see any barnyard porn going on the TV.

"Who the fuck are you supposed to be?" asked Sal.

"A big, goofy white guy," said Dante.

"Will Perdue," Mark said defensively as he turned to point out the name on his jersey.

"Exactly!" Sal had a laugh and Dante too. Even Mark joined in.

"At least you're not an OD," said Lila.

"What do you mean?" said Mark. Lila pointed in my direction and he almost jumped back. "Whoa!"

"What's the matter?" I said. "Scared of zombies?"

I had to admit, I did look creepy. After talking to Maurice, who had personally witnessed several fatal overdoses, I decided to go lighter on the blue. I used it to accent my lips and the tips of my fingers, while giving the rest of my visible skin the grayish pallor of a corpse. I wore a torn flannel with my left sleeve rolled up. A syringe protruded from the inside of my elbow, with fake blood streaming down my forearm.

"You look nasty, dude," said Steve. He came into the room sporting a handlebar mustache, fake chest hair and the cheesy leatherman getup from the Village People.

"Look who's talking," I said.

"Like my outfit?" Steve asked with an affected lisp.

"Nice look. What do your frat brothers think of your choice of costume?" Sal goaded him.

"Who cares?" said Steve. "I get more ass than a toilet seat."

"I'm sure the guy in the Village People did too," Sal snorted. "Hell, he probably got a lot of ass on a toilet seat."

"Enough already," said Dante. He was shutting it down before Steve had a chance to escalate the crude conversation. "We're in mixed company here."

"You're right," said Steve, turning towards the girls. "My bad. Sorry. Would you lovely ladies like a drink? Maybe a little something to get this party started?"

Lila and Sherry looked at each other and nodded agreeably.

"What have you got?" asked Sherry.

Steve cracked open a fresh bottle of Stoli for them and we all did a little blow, except for Dante who went to work on some Crown Royal. I did a couple shots with him but that was it. Sal and I had fixed up before coming over so I was good to go. Mark put some music on and the volume got higher and higher with each round of lines. Every so often, somebody would start pounding on the door. Soon one of us would become vaguely aware of the noise and we'd yell to Mark or Steve and one of those guys would check and see who was there.

Mark's girlfriend Lisa dropped in made up like a slutty Snow White. She had a friend in a cheerleader uniform with her. It didn't take long to see that they weren't into the scene at all. It might have been the blow that pissed them off, but I'm sure the smoking hot black and white witches on the couch didn't go over well either. After a short spat between Lisa and Mark, the girls left the room in a huff. A pimp came by next, all done up in a faux leopard-skin suit. He had a whore on each arm, blondes straight from the sorority house, taking full advantage of the opportunity to dress and act the part.

"I should have gone to college," Sal lamented.

This led Dante to go into his own sorry tale about how he had a full ride to Michigan State until some shithead kicked in his knee during a brawl the summer after graduation.

"Whatever happened to that guy?" asked Steve.

"Who the fuck cares?" said Dante vehemently. "All I know is if I ran into him on the street, I'd stomp his fuckin' guts out."

His outburst left an awkward silence that lasted until someone started furiously pounding on the door.

"What the fuck!" said Mark. "Who is it?"

"Head droog in charge," a voice called back.

Steve hustled over and tore open the door only to find Alex DeLarge from A Clockwork Orange standing outside, cane in hand.

"Welly, welly, welly, welly, welly, welly, well," said Sal. "To what do we owe the extreme pleasure of this surprising visit?"

"Viddy well, little brother. Viddy well," said Alex.

He and Sal went back and forth, trading lines from the movie. Alex had a drink and a bump and left the room. Others came and went after him. The Crow, Beetlejuice and, of course, Satan put in an appearance. Most of them just hung out for a minute, waiting patiently by the door for Mark or Steve to set them up.

"Business is good," I said.

"Can't complain," said Steve.

I was relieved the night appeared to be a success. Everyone got along really well, drinking and snorting and talking.

Then the CBOT Crew showed up.

Brad was barrel-chested and broad with a crushing grip. He always struck me as the unofficial leader of the crew. Jack was from the UK. Lean and pasty, he spoke with a faded cockney accent and had a psychotic gleam in his eyes, like he was up for anything. Greg was just a big guy with a blank stare who tagged along most of the time. He was the tamest of the three, which wasn't saying much. They piled into the room like they had rented it for the night. Not big on cordiality, they didn't bother with introductions.

"Michael, you crazy motherfucker, what's up?" said Brad. "I almost didn't recognize you with all that shit on your face."

"Where's your costume?" I asked.

"Fuck that," said Brad.

"We're going as date rapists," said Greg.

"Charming," I heard Lila mutter.

"You can't go as yourself, you cunt," said Jack.

"Suck my cock, you limey prick," said Greg. He laughed and punched Jack in the arm. Jack came back with a blow to Greg's thigh and the two of them grabbed each other like pro wrestlers. They began to push and shove, knocking over a few drinks in the process. Sal and the girls stepped back to make room while I kept an eye on Dante. So far, he was just watching the fracas but I doubted that would last. Mark and Steve made a lame attempt to break things up but they were clearly in over their heads. Finally, Brad stepped in.

"Chill out, you stupid fucks," he growled.

Greg and Jack tugged on each other a little longer before both pulled away, panting heavily.

"Cunt," said Jack.

"Bitch," said Greg.

"I'm glad we got that straight." Brad shook his head and turned to Mark. "We need a couple eightballs over here. And I'll take a Stoli rocks." He flipped a banded wad of cash in Mark's direction. Mark bobbled it at first but finally made the catch.

"Two?" he asked, fidgeting with the money.

"A couple means two," Brad sneered. "We also need a plate or a mirror while you're at it."

"You got a framed picture of your mum?" asked Jack.

"Very funny," Mark said with resignation.

Watching him, I felt a moment of guilt for unleashing these goons on Frat Row like I did, but it quickly passed. The CBOT Crew spread out on the two couches in front of the TV, leering at Lila and Sherry who were forced to scoot to one side and share a cushion. Mark walked over to them with their order and a white plate.

"How about a movie?" Greg asked with a lecherous grin.

Mark shot a nervous glance in my direction. He saw the potential situation we had on our hands. Dante had just shut down some crude banter and now the CBOT Crew wanted to put on some porn.

"Why don't we all head downstairs for a bit?" I said. "Join the rest of the party."

"That's a good idea," said Sal, finally tuning in. He gently pulled Dante towards the door. Lila rolled her eyes but Sherry was down. She bumped hips with Lila.

"C'mon, girl," she said. "Get into the groove!"

•

"Holy shit," said Sal.

We were heading down the main staircase into the foyer where two long tables were set up as makeshift bars. Vampires and goblins and French maids and superheroes and all sorts of other characters from movies and books were lined up six deep. A DJ spun records at a deafening volume in the adjoining living room, a vast open space packed with more costumed revelers drinking and dancing.

"Wow," said Lila.

"Now this is a party!" said Sherry.

All coked up and finally somewhere to go. Sherry grabbed Lila by the hand and dragged her out to the dance floor.

"Jesus, how long were we up there?" I asked Sal.

"More than three hours," he said.

"Fuck." I hated crowds. "Maybe we should just go."

"Not yet," said Sal. "Give Sherry a chance to dance it off."

"Let's get some drinks," said Dante.

We fought our way up to one of the bars and quickly got served, thanks to a good word from Alex DeLarge.

"Take care of these droogs!" he yelled, fingering his nose at the Joker who was manning the tap. We got our plastic cups of beer and found a clearing not far from where Lila and Sherry were dancing. The only way to communicate was by shouting, so we all just stood there watching the people around us. Every so often, Sal would yell some observation in my ear.

"Check out Cinderella at twelve o'clock!"

"How about Young Frankenstein?"

Dante was quiet. Too quiet. He had been drinking steadily since we got there with no blow or anything else to prop him up. I got the feeling that if he opened his mouth, he might be a slurring mess. One could never tell with Dante. Sometimes he held his liquor like an Irish cop. Other times, not so much.

Before long, we saw the CBOT Crew descend the stairs. They bullied their way to the front of the line to get some drinks and took a spot on the floor next to us.

"What's up?" I said.

Brad just nodded back at me with glazed eyes, his jaw twitching periodically. Greg and Jack didn't look much better.

"You ready to go?" I asked Sal.

"I guess," he said, tipping his cup to finish his beer. "But Lila and Sherry look like they're still having fun."

We turned to check them out. Sal was right. They were dancing with each other and the people around them. Maybe it was the costumes, maybe it was the way they moved, but there wasn't anyone else out there that could hold a candle to either one of them.

I heard a voice in my ear. "You gotta love fishnet stockings!"

"Excuse me?" I turned to see Greg standing between me and Dante with a nasty smirk across his mug.

"Fishnet stockings, you gotta love 'em!" He said it loud enough for me and everyone else around us to hear. "Like on the witch out there," he gestured to Lila. "I'd love to get those legs wrapped around my neck tonight. Think you could hook me up?"

And just like that, Dante came to life.

"I'll hook you up, motherfucker!" he said.

Greg turned just in time for Dante's fist to land square on his mouth. A sickening crack rang out and I felt warm blood spatter across my cheek as something hard glanced off my forehead. Greg flew back into the wall and Dante jumped on him, grabbing his shirt with one hand and pummeling his face with the other. He got in a few good shots, knocking out at least one more tooth before Brad or Jack even knew what was going on. When they came to life and made their move, Sal and I did what we could to jam them up. Sal sucker punched Jack in the back of the head. He was momentarily stunned but quickly recovered. I jumped on Brad's back, hanging from his neck with one arm while using the other to land blow after blow on the side of his face. The music stopped and people were backing away from us. I lost track of what was happening around me and the next thing I knew, Dante pulled me off Brad and quickly dropped him with a flurry of punches. Brad hit the floor and Sal kicked him in the head a couple times, prompting horrified gasps from the crowd. Dante stumbled away from the scene and we followed him to the front door where the Northwestern University Police picked us up.

"I'll call you for bail, honey," Dante yelled to Lila as they shoved him in the car.

•

An hour later, Dante, Sal and I were cuffed to a wood bench under a blinding fluorescent light in the holding area outside the booking room of the Evanston Police Department. Once the campus cops learned we weren't students, they wasted no time turning us over to them. According to the officer behind the glass, the whole CBOT Crew was in the hospital. Dante sat stoically in his Viking costume, examining the cuts on his fists. Sal was starting to freak out.

"We are so fucked," he groaned.

He would be sick before long. By morning, I would be too. Sal was right. We were truly fucked. Besides the immediate crisis, the gravy train had screeched to a sudden halt tonight. Between Frat Row and the

CBOT Crew, I had a really good thing going there for a while. A genuine enterprise. Like Maurice said, I was the man. I wondered if I could somehow salvage the connections and if it was even worth the trouble. Things like that always fall apart. Nothing is forever.

"Dante Casciani?"

We looked up at the officer who emerged from the booking room. A husky black woman with a mellow disposition, she was a refreshing change from the aggressive hard-ons who had hauled us in.

"Right here." Dante raised his bloody hand.

"You aren't gonna give me any trouble now," said the officer as she uncuffed him.

"No, ma'am," said Dante.

No, ma'am. No, sir. We hated cops but we knew enough not to let it show. Unless you're already fucked, like we were with those narcs on the West Side, it's best to check your attitude.

"When can we make our call?" Sal asked.

"After booking," said the officer.

Sal bit his lip. He looked like he was about to cry.

"Don't sweat," Dante reassured him. "Lila will get you out too."

Lila. God bless her. With a pile of money in the bank and a solid connection to the real world of accounts and credit and whatever else you needed to be a citizen, she was our only hope. I was grateful to have her, though I hated being so helpless. The more I sat there and thought about everything, the more I wanted a change. I was sick and tired of being a slave to smack and all the bullshit that went with it. Fuck Frat Row. Fuck the CBOT Crew. I took a deep breath.

"How are you holding up?" asked Sal.

I tried to speak but the words got caught in my throat.

Sal searched my expression for a response. "Michael?"

I finally blurted it out. "I'm gonna kick."

CHAPTER TWELVE

"What? You gotta be fucking kidding!" Sal was completely beside himself. I knew he would be.

"Watch that now," said the officer.

"Good for you," Dante said to me.

"Let's go, son," said the officer. She started to lead Dante away but he stopped after a few steps.

"You can do it, Michael," he called over his shoulder. "Hang tough, buddy."

"I thought you said you weren't going to be any trouble," said the officer. "You're gonna have to finish this later."

Dante nodded and did as he was told. The door closed behind them and Sal spoke up again.

"Jesus, Michael," he said. "What the fuck are you thinking?"

"Look at us." I jingled the cuffs. "We're in jail."

"What does that have to do with getting high?"

"You're joking, right?"

"Not at all. Break it down for me."

"It doesn't matter," I insisted. "I've made up my mind."

"Just like that, huh?" Sal was pissed. "And I get no say? When did all this jump off anyway?"

"What the fuck, Sal? You gonna shoot dope your whole life?"

The words came out louder than I intended and we noticed the officer behind the glass poke his head up.

"Don't get too excited now," Sal said to the guy. "We've already been searched." He continued in a hushed but no less furious tone. "Why the fuck not?"

"Gee, I don't know," I paused, as if I had to think it over. "Maybe because it's bad for you?"

"So is greasy food," Sal argued. "Are you going on a diet too? Why don't you quit smoking while you're at it?"

"Maybe I will."

"You might as well put a bullet in your head."

"Don't be such a drama queen."

"Look who's talking. 'I've made up my mind.' Jesus!"

"I'm sick and tired of the bullshit, Sal." I was also sick and tired of arguing with him.

"You don't know the meaning of the word sick," grumbled Sal.

"I guess I'll find out."

Sal and I had kicked almost two years before, mainly just to see if we could. It was awful, like having a debilitating combination of food poisoning and the flu, with periodic muscle cramps so strong you can't help but clutch yourself in pain. We would've said 'fuck it' but both of us were too sick to score. Once we made it through all that, we decided to stay off dope. A month passed with no discernible improvement in our lives and we promptly resumed getting high.

"Just so you know," Maurice told us back then, "you gonna catch more and more hell each time you put it down."

I wasn't especially concerned. We kicked and it sucked but I always figured we could do it again if we had to.

"Sal Bono?" The officer who took Dante was back.

"Yes, ma'am." Sal held up his cuffed hand, making it easier for her to unlock him. He looked at me, resigned.

"So what's the plan?"

I was hoping Sal would join me but after his withering objections, I wasn't sure anymore.

"What do you mean?" I said.

"You know damn well," he said. "How are we gonna do it?"

What a relief. I knew I'd never last a week without him.

"Let's go, son," said the officer. Sal looked at me.

"Well?" he asked.

"We'll stay here," I said.

"Say what?" said the officer.

•

I got booked for drunk and disorderly conduct and aggravated battery. Sal did, too, along with an extra charge for possession of drug paraphernalia. We both declined our phone calls.

"I'd like to just take some time and think about the error of my ways," Sal said to the officer in charge.

The guy didn't think that was funny but he was too busy dealing with the stream of idiots coming in that night to make something of it. We were locked up in a small pen with the other Halloween casualties who continued to join us into the early morning hours.

They didn't get around to booking us until noon the next day. Then they shipped us off south to another holding cell, this time in Cook County Jail. Given our condition, they gave us each a six-by-ten-foot concrete and cinder-block cell with a stainless steel cot and glaring overhead lights. By that night, it must have sounded like the Tower of London circa 1600. I remember watching a documentary on the torture chamber they had in there. Other than the array of macabre devices like the rack and the iron maiden, what I remembered best were the dramatized screams of agony. Grown men, crying like babies from the unspeakable suffering being inflicted upon them.

Sal and I were no better.

As hard as it was to kick the first time around, this was exponentially worse. Maurice once told us about a guy who blew half his ear off trying to shoot himself because he couldn't stand the pain of withdrawal. At the time, I thought that sounded crazy but now I understood. If I could have slit my wrists or flung myself out a window, I would've done so without a second thought. Those first two days were the worst forty-eight hours of my life. It was everything that getting high is not. I said before that once you feel that rush, whatever you had to do to score was worth it.

Kicking was the exact opposite.

When I wasn't puking or retching, I was a quaking, sweating mess with every muscle in my body tight as a clenched fist. I felt like I could drop dead any minute. Unsettling as it must've been to have me around, I was downright manageable compared to Sal. He was like some wild beast raging against the pain. He had to be restrained by the entire night shift before getting a heavy dose of sedatives and a trip to Cook County Hospital, not that they could do much for him. The guards were just so freaked out by his condition they wanted him off their hands. After he was gone, they took me to the infirmary where I got a warm blanket and an unlimited supply of Pepto-Bismol.

•

"How was it?" asked Lila.

"You don't wanna know."

I fired up a cigarette and took a long drag, my first in three days. We were zipping down Western Avenue in Lila's peppy little Honda Civic. She had rolled down all the windows because I reeked so badly from kicking in jail. The cool air whipping through the car rushed over my face, gradually bringing me back to life.

"Where's Dante?" I asked.

"Sleeping at my place," she said. "He said he was sorry he couldn't come. He worked last night."

"What about Sal?"

"They're going to release him tomorrow," said Lila. She seemed strangely preoccupied, taking a long drag on her own cigarette.

I nodded and searched her expression.

"What's wrong?" I asked.

"Nothing."

"You seem like there's something on your mind."

"I'm happy you're getting your life together, Michael." Lila gave me a sideways glance. "Any other big changes on the horizon?"

"I haven't really given it much thought yet," I said. "Nothing that concerns you, Lila."

"Are you sure?"

"Hell, yeah." I felt so wrung out and raw, I needed her more than ever. "What do you think?"

"I don't know what to think."

"I should be asking you about big changes," I said. "A couple months ago, I was ready to follow you out to California."

Having never admitted that to myself, it was an odd thing to tell Lila.

"Really?" Lila looked surprised. "You would have done that?"

"I didn't want to you to go."

"It didn't even occur to me that you would leave Chicago," she said. "Leave Dante? And Sal?"

"I didn't want to," I said. "But I would have."

"Well, I'm glad I stayed."

"Me too."

We drove in silence a minute before she spoke again.

"Aren't you going to miss it?" she asked.

"Miss what?"

"You know." Lila lowered her voice. "Heroin."

Just hearing the word uttered out loud gave me chills.

"I'm sure," I said, thinking. "I don't miss it right now but I know I will at some point. Probably sooner rather than later."

"Like a codependent relationship," said Lila.

"I don't know if it's all that." I wasn't even sure what that meant. "You know...I can still fix you if you want."

"No, thank you..." Lila's voice trailed off and I got the idea she had not yet grasped the implications of my newfound abstinence. "I'll be fine," she said finally.

"Okay." I wasn't convinced. "You just make sure and let me know. Don't do anything on your own."

"I won't."

"Promise me."

"I promise."

"Good." I sat back in my seat, satisfied that she meant it.

"Oh, I've got something I want to show you," she said.

"What's that?"

"No, I need to take you to it."

I was in no shape to go anywhere but she sounded so excited, I didn't want to bring her down.

"Sure," I said, trying to muster some enthusiasm. "But let's stop at my place first. I need a shower and a change of clothes before I rejoin the world."

"Of course," said Lila.

I grabbed the rearview mirror and examined my reflection. Between the smudged traces of makeup from my costume and the dark circles under my eyes, I looked like more like a zombie than ever.

"Jesus," I said.

"Don't worry," Lila smiled. "We'll get you cleaned up good. I'll even wash your back."

•

After a long hot shower, Lila and I got dressed and she put on some Nirvana while I rummaged through the stash. Sal and I had eleven bags left. Coming across them, I felt my heart race.

No fucking way, I told myself.

Recalling the misery of the last few days, I meant it too. I thought about offering a bag to Lila but watching her get high seemed like more than I could handle at the moment. Digging a little deeper in the drawer, I found what I was looking for, the last T-bag in the apartment, as far as I knew. Lila and I polished it off, smoking a few bowls as we lounged on the couch.

"Man." I was stoned.

"Feel better?" asked Lila.

"That sure hit the spot."

"What did?"

"All of it."

"You're a long way from jail now," Lila winked at me and lit up a cigarette. She took a drag and threw her head back, blowing a thin stream of smoke toward the ceiling.

"Ready to take a ride with me?"

"Sure," I nodded languidly and pushed myself to my feet.

•

It didn't occur to me to ask where we were going until I was back in the passenger seat of Lila's car.

"Spoonful," she said.

"It's kind of early, don't you think?"

The sun had just gone down and I wasn't ready for the night to begin. I wasn't ready to start drinking either.

"I have a party tonight," said Lila.

"On a Wednesday?"

"Why not?"

"No reason." I knew to shut my mouth. The last thing I wanted to do was to get into it with Lila about her job.

"It's not a bachelor party," she said. "Probably just some Japanese businessmen living it up."

The thought of some Japanese businessman pawing Lila in a matter of hours made my skin crawl but I didn't let it show. I was searching for something to say when Lila found a parking spot right in front. A neon sign with retro flare glowed incandescent blue overhead. A long curved spoon with a jazzy rendition of the word "Spoonful," beginning with a giant S, streamed over the top of it.

"They got a new sign," said Lila.

"It sure is bright," I said with grim recognition. I liked the old sign much better. A wood placard with the name scrawled in red paint, it was anonymous and gritty and looked like something hanging on the creaky door to some backwoods smokehouse. All I saw now was a flashy invitation to wreck the party.

"I like it," said Lila.

She reached for the door but I beat her to it. "Allow me."

"Why, thank you," said Lila as she walked by and gave me a quick bump with her hip. I followed her inside.

A well-worn blues bar from back in the day before blues bars where anything special, Spoonful was owned by a reclusive old head named Danny. In the five or so years we had been going there, I only caught a glimpse of him a handful of times. A mutated cross between Lyle Lovett and Andy Warhol, Danny had the pickled look of a junkie. This once led to some speculation about the name of his place.

"Spoonful?" said Sal. "Come on! What else could it be?"

"It's from the Willie Dixon song," I said.

"You're both wrong," said Dante. "It's 'cause of the chili."

Maybe. Their chili was the best I ever had. The super-secret recipe was rumored to have come from John Lee Hooker's second wife Maude. The only food they served besides olives, it came in a plastic bowl with a plastic spoon. You could get it with or without beans. Without beans, it would scorch the digestive tracts of most normal people. The beans cooled it down some. If you still couldn't take it, oyster crackers were provided upon request.

"Hey, guys," Dana nodded as we came in. She was pouring a couple beers while some Creedence played in the background.

"I heard you were in the clink," she said to me.

"I was framed," I said.

"Right," Dana nodded skeptically. "What are you drinking?"

"Diet Coke," said Lila.

Dana looked at me, "Michael?"

"Hmmmm," I paused, my stomach still churning a little bit. "I'll just take a ginger ale."

"Holy shit," said Dana. "Don't tell me you went and got religion up in there."

"Don't worry," said Lila. "He's only mildly reformed."

"Well, that's a relief," said Dana. She served up our drinks and I started to take a seat at the bar.

"Hold on," said Lila. She turned to Dana, tilting her head toward the back. "How about the lights?"

"I'll hit 'em now," said Dana.

"This way," said Lila. She took my hand and led me away from the bar. "Close your eyes."

"What?" I hated surprises.

"Just do it."

"Fine," I said. Given all that Lila had done for me today, the least I could do was play along.

"Careful." She gently guided me through the corridor that led to the back where the bands played. "Okay, you can open them now."

I opened my eyes only to see several of Lila's paintings hanging on the brick wall opposite the bar.

"Hey!" I said, taking them in. "Brian Jones turned out great."

"Thanks," she said with endearing pride.

I walked over to get a closer look.

"I don't understand. Did Danny buy all these?"

"No, but I did give him Einstein. It was his favorite."

"No shit. Did he come over to your place?"

"Dana showed him my portfolio," said Lila.

"And how did you get her to do that?"

"I just asked."

"I see," I looked at Lila with an overt trace of mischief. I had teased her many times before about Dana having a thing for her.

"It was no big deal," she said, ignoring my insinuation. "I got the idea when they put up the new sign."

"Well," I turned back to the paintings. "They certainly add a touch of class to this place."

"They're not here permanently," said Lila. "Danny just agreed to let me hang them for a little while, you know, to get some exposure. He really loved my work."

"That's cool, Lila." I pulled her close. "I'm happy for you, really. I hope some big shot comes in here and makes the discovery of a lifetime." I hugged her tight for a moment before letting her go. "What are they going for anyway?"

"I have no idea," said Lila. "If anyone asks, they can make an offer. I'm just glad to get them out there."

•

Lila and I sat at the bar and finished our drinks before she ran me back to my place. She had a couple hours before the party and I tried to convince her to come inside.

"Not tonight," she said with a firm but gentle look that told me not to push too hard.

"That's cool." I leaned over the gear stick to give her a kiss and we ended up making out a little before she pulled away from me.

"I really have to go," she said.

I reluctantly climbed out of the car.

"I'm going to the bank tomorrow," I said, referring to the money I owed her for bail.

"There's no rush."

"That's right." I gave her another quick kiss. "I keep forgetting you're about to become rich and famous."

I closed the door and she sped off. Watching her go, I shuddered from an aftershock of the withdrawal I had just gone through. I felt much shakier now that I was alone. After taking a deep breath and waiting until the feeling passed, I headed down to my apartment. I managed to get the door unlocked and stumbled inside, only to be caught completely off guard by a booming voice.

"Let's go, motherfucker!" said Dante.

CHAPTER THIRTEEN

"Jesus Christ!"

My heart was thumping against my chest so hard I could feel it through my shirt. Here was Dante in my place where I just fucked Lila less than an hour before. Minutes ago, my tongue had been in her mouth. There had been some close calls with Dante before but this was by far the closest. I was sure he knew. I studied him hard.

"What are you staring at?" Dante squinted at me for a second before he twisted open a bottle of beer and flicked the cap, shooting it through the air into our kitchen trashcan.

"Two points!" he called out.

I knew then I was safe.

"What the fuck?" I took a deep breath and sat down in the armchair. "Aren't you supposed to be working tonight?"

"Not till eleven-thirty," he said, swigging his beer.

"Shouldn't you be sleeping?"

"What's your problem, Michael?"

"No problem," I said. "I feel like shit. I've been in jail the last three days. I've been kicking, for Christ's sake."

"Imagine how Sal feels."

"Sal's had it better than me. At least he's in the hospital."

"That's right," he said. "And we're going to see him."

"Isn't he technically still under arrest?"

"Nope. Lila posted his bail the same time she did yours."

"So then he's coming home tomorrow at the latest."

"I don't give a fuck. We can still go see him."

"He's probably zonked on sedatives."

"Then we won't bother him."

"I just don't see the point," I said without much hope of changing his mind. Dante was insanely stubborn when he got an idea into his head about what needed to be done.

"You don't have to see the point," he said. "We're gonna visit him because that's what friends do. You should know that. When I got my knee kicked in you guys came to visit me, right?"

Every day for almost a week.

"I've never forgotten that," Dante went on, his voice momentarily quavering. "You guys really came through. After I woke up from the operation all I could think about was how my life was fucked. I ruined everything. And then you guys showed up and I saw that I still had my friends. I can't tell you how much that meant to me."

Hearing Dante's appeal, I was suddenly racked with guilt about Lila. And coming off the smack like I was, it hurt like never before. For the first time in a while, I felt like a real scumbag. I felt so bad, I tried to tell myself I would stop seeing her, that it was all part of some new better way of living I began when I decided to kick. Then I stopped lying to myself and I felt even worse. The least I could do was take a ride with him.

"Let's go," I said.

•

After a quick trip to the corner store for some Saltine crackers and a bottled water, we climbed into Dante's battered Iroc and raced back up Western Avenue. He had some Boston jamming so loud my ears felt like they were bleeding.

"Is that too loud?" he shouted over the music.

I shook my head. I was glad not to have to talk.

"So what time did you get out anyway?" he asked, finally dialing it down low enough for my hearing to come back.

"Lila picked me up around four, I guess," I said, adding a couple hours to account for the time we hung out at my apartment.

"Yeah?" He looked at me. "And?"

He seemed like he was waiting for some specific response and I got nervous again.

"And...what?"

"Did you guys go by Spoonful?"

"Yeah, we did," I said. Relief poured over me like the hot shower I took only hours before. "The paintings look great."

"Don't they?" A hearty smile lit up Dante's face. "Lila's gonna show us all someday."

"I bet she will," I said as Dante cranked up the music again.

•

By the time we got up to Sal's floor in the massive, crumbling shithole that was Cook County Hospital, visiting hours were almost over and nobody was at the desk. When one of the nurses finally showed up, she tried to turn us away. Somehow I convinced her we would behave like ideal guests for a very short visit.

"You better," she warned us. "He needs rest."

I don't know what the big fuss was about. When we got to the room, he already had two visitors with him.

"Yo, yo, yo," said Aaron. He sat in a chair by the door, paging through the Tribune's Metro section.

"Hey, Michael," said Janet. She was in another chair at the foot of Sal's hospital bed, rubbing his feet.

"Fuck," Sal said. "Now I know I must be dreaming."

"I don't know why you say that," said Dante.

I did. It was surreal as hell seeing Aaron and Janet up there in the same room as Dante. I knew they got out and around. Janet had recently been to our apartment. But I sure as hell didn't expect to see either one of them in Sal's shabby hospital room and Sal didn't expect to see me yet, not after what I just went through.

"How the hell did you get this guy out?" He motioned to me.

"It wasn't so hard," said Dante. "He wanted to come."

"Sure he did," Sal said, recognizing that was probably a crock of shit. He was fully aware of Dante's powers of persuasion.

As the host of this unlikely gathering, Sal made the introductions. Aaron and Dante shook hands, each no doubt trying to get a read on the other. When Sal introduced Janet, Dante greeted her in a polite and thoroughly awkward manner.

"How do you do?" he said, extending his hand.

Janet gave him a puzzled look and Sal almost laughed out loud.

Aaron seemed to take their reactions as his cue.

"We outta here," he said.

"Where you goin'?" said Sal. "It's early. You haven't even seen them change my bedpan yet."

"You one crazy motherfucker." Aaron shook his head. He never seemed too amused by Sal's sense of humor. "It's time to go, girl." He grabbed Janet's arm and gave Sal a meaningful look. "Think on that," he said before turning and nodding to Dante and me as he marched out of the room.

"Bye, y'all," said Janet as she hustled after him.

I took Janet's seat, sliding the chair away from the bed.

"You aren't gonna rub my feet?" asked Sal.

"I'll pass," I said, wondering what Aaron told Sal to think on.

"Who's the fuckin' yo?" Dante said finally.

"Oh!" exclaimed Sal.

"Just some guy we know," I said.

"He's from the hood," said Sal. "Which I guess, technically, means he's a loser. Right, Dante?"

"Knock it off, Sal," said Dante. "I was talking about white guys going *into* the hood. So how do you know him?"

"Jesus, Dante, how do you think we know him?" I asked.

"That's what I figured," said Dante.

"I also kick it every now and then with Janet," said Sal.

"Uh-huh," said Dante. He looked at Sal. "And you didn't just happen to partake in anything, did you?"

"Nope," said Sal. "But I could have."

He turned to me, lifting the arm with the IV in it. "Janet offered me a direct deposit."

I was impressed he passed on that offer.

"How did they even know you were here?" I asked.

"You know Aaron," said Sal. "Always got his ear to the street."

"C'mon." I wasn't buying it.

"I beeped Janet," said Sal.

"How?" I looked around but didn't see a phone.

"One of the nurses has a mobile phone," said Sal.

"What for?" I asked him.

"I don't know. Maybe she wants to be reached at all times. Maybe she's horny, waiting on that booty call."

"Not the nurse," I said. "Janet. Why'd you beep her?"

"I was lonely up here," said Sal. "And bored."

"I told ya!" Dante looked at me, vindicated.

"And I wanted a couple T-bags," said Sal.

"And Aaron just came along for the ride?"

"Janet never learned to drive."

"You mean to tell me Aaron left his hoppers on the corner, all by themselves, just to shuttle his little sister down here to see your scroungy ass and drop off a little weed?"

"Well," he said, "He *was* wondering what was up, what with us going all MIA and shit."

"And what did you tell him?"

"I told him we're clean now," said Sal. "You know, and ah...you probably wouldn't be rolling through there anytime soon."

I figured as much. "And what did he say?"

"He said he understood...though he wasn't sure what one thing had to do with the other."

"Aaron said that?"

"Not in so many words."

I just stared at him.

"Look, man," Sal went on. "It's your thing. It's your call."

"It doesn't have to be my thing." I meant it too. Sal was free to make a go of it if he wanted to. I wouldn't stop him but I wouldn't help him either.

"So how's the food in here?" Dante asked, changing the subject.

"I wouldn't fucking know," said Sal. "I haven't eaten since Saturday. And I'm in no hurry. Lunch smelled so bad I wouldn't even let 'em bring the tray in the room."

"Some hospital food is pretty good," said Dante.

"Maybe," Sal said. "But not in this dump, I'm sure."

"So what are you gonna do with a couple T-bags in here anyway?" I asked, looking around again. Sal had lucked into a private room but you still couldn't smoke in there. "You can't just light up."

"I probably can with the nurse with the phone." Sal folded his arms behind his head and laid his head on his pillow. "My girl Nita has taken quite a shine to me."

What a piece of work.

"Always got something going," Dante said with admiration.

"Hey, man," said Sal. "I just use what I got to get what I want."

"So what time they letting you out?" I asked.

"See, that's the thing." Sal's expression became guarded. "I gotta stick around for a couple more days."

•

"What the hell is Hep C again?" asked Dante.

"Hepatitis C," I said. "It's a virus."

We were back in his car, heading south back home. No sooner had Sal given us the bad news when a buxom Latina nurse came by to announce the end of visiting hours.

"Nita and I need some privacy up in here," Sal said with a grin.

"We don't want to cramp your style," said Dante, playing along.

I was too shell-shocked from Sal's newfound health issue to even fake my part of the conversation.

"Michael?" asked Sal.

"Yeah?"

"I'll call you guys when they let me out," he said.

"And we'll be here to pick you up," said Dante as he gave me a gentle but firm nudge. "Let's go."

The whole way down to the car, my mind raced through the implications of what I just learned. Sal and I, even close as we were, tried not to share needles, but there were a few times we had no choice. As far as I knew, we hadn't shared "partners," either, not since we each took a turn with Rosemary Amato junior year of high school. I came close with Sherry one time. It was late and we were shitfaced. Lila had gone home with Dante and Sal was down for the count. Sherry and I messed around and started to get undressed. Then she made an offhanded comment about how she was a little sore down there from the night before with Sal and I got turned off thinking about his big dick. I never got another chance with Sherry, but that still didn't mean I was in the clear. I probably had Hep C anyway, which meant Lila could have it and Dante too.

"What does it do?" asked Dante.

"It fucks up your liver."

"And what does your liver do?"

"A lot of important shit!" Sometimes Dante's general ignorance really got to me. "Remember your Uncle Joe?"

He died of cirrhosis our freshman year. Joe was Dante's dad's younger brother. He was a wild guy who did two tours in Vietnam. We all looked up to him when we were kids. He used to do card tricks and take us for rides on his Harley, a vintage model with an American flag gas tank like the one in *Easy Rider*. A beefy guy with a hearty laugh, he left an emaciated corpse that we almost didn't recognize at his funeral.

"Why you gotta go and bring that up?"

"I'm sorry," I muttered.

"Goddamn it, Michael," said Dante. "Sal's gonna be just fine."

He dropped me off without a word. By that time I was so far into my head, I didn't care. I wanted more than anything to see Lila. I tried to put her out of my mind, but the image of some sleazy little Japanese businessman with his hands all over her made me want to put my fist through a wall. I didn't understand how Dante could stand it. When I walked inside, I could all but hear the smack calling my name. With our remaining bags still stashed in the nightstand, I knew I would never make it through the night.

•

"Michael, my man." Maurice slapped me on the back. "Thank you."

He meant it too. I could see that in the way he strolled back to the bathroom, clenching the bags I had just given him.

"You sure enough made his night," T said, watching him go.

"You should have flushed it right down the toilet," said Clifford. He and Beverly were parked in front of the TV with a bowl of Doritos between them. "Saved you a trip out here."

"Ain't no cause for that," T frowned.

I agreed. I had never flushed a bag of dope and I sure as hell wasn't about to start. That was just plain wrong.

"I'm just saying," said Clifford. "I ain't had so much as a drop to drink since 1992. You know how I did it?"

"We all done heard a thousand times," said Beverly. "You poured your last beer down the toilet and that was it."

"That's right," said Clifford. "From that day on, I told myself, 'I might as well just go on and drink from the toilet as have me another beer.'"

Yeah, yeah, yeah. And I might as well shoot poison into my veins. I had heard it all before.

"Good for you, Michael," said Beverly. "You're gonna be a lot better off without that dope."

Aaron rolled his eyes. "So that's it, huh? You stop slamming and now you through with them college boys too? Just like that? They up there steady rolling and you just gonna walk away from that? Don't make no sense."

"I don't know," I said. I really didn't want to get into it with him. "Did you hear what happened?"

"Sal told me," said Aaron.

"Your boy sounds rough," said T as she lit up a cigarette.

"He is," I said. "Dante's a fucking bull on two legs."

"Maybe you leave him home next time," said Aaron.

"I don't think there's gonna be a next time."

"Sure," said T. "I heard that one before."

"We'll see," I said. He was probably right but I didn't care. "I'm just sick of the bullshit. Running around here and there, dealing with all these assholes."

"So what you gonna do?" he asked.

"I don't know," I said. "Get a job?"

"Shiiittt," said T.

"Ain't nothing wrong with that," said Clifford.

"Talk about bullshit," said Aaron. "What kind of job you gonna get? You gonna be one of these motherfuckers slingin' coffee? What's that green place goin' up all over?"

"Starbucks," said Janet as she walked into the kitchen. "How you doin', Michael?"

"Not so good," I said.

"That's right," said Aaron. "You gonna put on a little apron, get you a visor and shit."

"I know they hirin' over at Church's," said T.

"You guys are real comedians," I said.

"We just playin' with you." She pushed herself back from the table and got up. "You want something to drink?"

"No, thanks," I said. "I gotta get going."

"You want something else?" asked T.

"Gimme five," I said, referring to some T-bags. I handed her a couple of wrinkled twenties and a ten.

"Comin' right up."

•

After smoking a fatty with T, I headed out to my car, where I saw that same salt-and-pepper team of narcs slowly roll past. They eyeballed me long and hard but didn't stop. Even though I was holding the T-bags, a big part of me wanted to flip them the bird.

Fuck you, motherfuckers! I'm clean now.

Cold comfort. I drove home, making a quick stop at the corner store for a six-pack of High Life. My plan was to spend the rest of the evening smoking and drinking and vegging out in front of *Scarface* or *King of New York* or some other flick I had seen a thousand times before. When I got inside, I dropped the beer in the fridge and walked back out to the TV. As I passed by the phone, the blinking red light on the answering machine caught my eye.

Who the fuck could that be?

I cracked open my beer and took a few sips. I sure as hell didn't want to talk to anybody and I didn't give a shit who wanted to talk to me either. I stood there totally stoned, letting my mind wander over the possibilities. Maybe it was Frat Row, already trying to smooth things over.

"We need to see you, dude," Mark would say.

Maybe it was Paul or Candice or some chick looking for Sal. Then again, maybe it was Lila. Her party was done and she wanted me to come over after all. Suddenly filled with hope, I hit the button, only to recoil at the sound of a familiar voice.

"Michael? Are you there? It's your mother. Please call me."

We hadn't spoken in months. It was nothing personal. We just didn't have much to talk about, at least not much that interested me. My mom wasn't bad, as far as moms go. She did her best with kind of a shitty lot, but she was a total nag, like a lot of parents without much going on in their own lives. Identifying herself as my mother was her way of taking a shot at me for not calling or visiting in so long. With the holidays coming up, I knew I'd see her soon enough. There was no reason to pick up the phone.

CHAPTER FOURTEEN

"When is Thanksgiving anyway?" asked Sal.

"Three weeks from Thursday," I said. "And Theo's birthday is the day after, or the day after that, I forget."

"Some uncle you are."

"Whatever."

Sal and I were smoking a bowl and chilling on the couch at our place, each nursing a can of pop. Dante and Lila had just brought him home from the hospital. Since his viral load was relatively low, they decided against any immediate treatment. Instead, he got a visit from some NA chick doing volunteer outreach work at the hospital. A former heroin addict and prostitute, she went over the dos and don'ts of living with Hep C. According to Sal, they really hit it off.

"She almost made the cut," he said.

"Get outta here." I had to press him.

"If I went to a meeting or two, I could hit that no problem." Sal continued, thinking. "Of course I'd need a Magnum. If you ask me, that's the worst thing about this shit."

"What else is there?" I asked.

"I'm supposed to inform my sexual partners," said Sal.

"That should be fun. Can you even remember them all?"

"Fuck, no. Some of them, I never even knew their names in the first place."

The worst thing for me was the fear I had exposed Lila and Dante, but I sure as fuck couldn't tell Sal about that. It was still good to have him back, though I had planned for a little more time to myself to maybe find a job or get something going. There was some new construction in our neighborhood and I thought I could get work at one of the sites. I could always carry lumber or haul debris. The best jobs, pulling wire or laying pipe, usually went to union guys, but more and more I had noticed some of that work going to crews of Mexicans and Polacks. They were doing everything from concrete to roofing, so not all the builders were locked into the unions. I just needed something that paid a decent hourly wage. That was my plan, anyway. So far, all I had done was watch movies and plow through T-bags, the last being the one I just finished off with Sal.

"So when's the last time you talked to her?" he asked.

"Who?"

"Your mom, Michael. Remember? We were talking about her?"

I was so stoned, not to mention preoccupied by the Hep C and other shit, it was hard to remember much of anything.

"You should know. You were there." I said. "Fourth of July.

"Of course," he recalled. Sal, Dante and I had gone over to my mom's house for an impromptu cookout. It didn't end well.

"You gonna come out for Theo's birthday or what?" I asked.

"Do I have a choice?"

"Stay home if you want."

"I don't think so." Sal took a long hit, blowing out a thick cloud of smoke. "Somebody's gotta keep you in line."

"Good luck."

Sal and I finished that bowl and many more over the course of a film noir marathon that included *The Killing, Asphalt Jungle* and Sal's favorite, *The Set-Up*.

"I love the happy ending," he said.

"I'm not sure I'd call that happy.".

The movie was about a washed-up boxer who doesn't know when to quit. In the end, he has no choice after getting both hands broken by some goon for refusing to throw a fight.

"He doesn't end up dead or in jail," said Sal. "Not to mention, he gets the girl."

"That's all it takes, huh?"

"What more do you want?"

"I don't know." I tried to think of something.

"We should be so lucky," said Sal as he lit up a cigarette.

"Maybe." He was right but I didn't want to admit it.

"You hungry?" asked Sal.

•

"Two High Lifes and two bowls, one with beans and crackers." I handed Dana a twenty dollar bill.

"Beans and crackers?" she balked, knowing our usual order. "Who's the pussy tonight?"

"Even I gotta step on it every now and then," said Sal.

"Don't we all," Dana laughed.

"The place is dead tonight," I said. Thursdays were usually pretty big nights at Spoonful.

"Give it another hour," she said.

I looked at my watch. Nine o'clock. Sitting in front of the tube all day, I thought for sure it was later.

"Who's playing tonight?" asked Sal.

"Junior Kimbrough," said Dana. She slid two beers and two bowls of chili across the bar along with my change.

"Never heard of him," I said.

"He's an old-timer," she said. "Straight out of the Delta."

"Cool," said Sal as he dug into his chili. "I could go for some gritty Mississippi blues."

"Sounds good to me," I said. "Hey, did you see Lila's paintings?"

"You bet," said Sal. "That's totally cool. I just hope they don't end up on the walls of some douchebag's condo."

"Fuck it," I said, digging in to my chili. "As long as she gets paid, who cares?"

"I still think it would be shame."

"I didn't realize you were so sentimental."

"I didn't either," he said. "Must be the smack, or the lack of it rather. By the way, what are you gonna do now?"

"I figured I'd get a little head on and watch the band."

"Not *now* now," said Sal. "I mean in general, now that we kicked. What are you gonna do?"

"I don't know." I sipped my beer. "I was hoping to work construction. God knows there's enough going on all around us."

“Dream on,” said Sal. “Those jobs all go through the Hall.”

“Maybe,” I said. “But I’ve still seen plenty of scabs out there humping wood and bricks and everything else.”

“Fuck that,” said Sal.

“What are you gonna do?”

“Drive,” he said. “Somebody’s gotta find us some capers.”

“Don’t even think about it, Sal. I told you before. You’re on your own with all that.”

“We’ll see,” said Sal. “At the very least, I might find me a nice sugar mama, you know, lighten the load some.”

“You do that,” I said.

Just thinking about another break-in with Sal made me uneasy. I was glad he didn’t push it. We finished our chili and drank a few beers, taking periodic breaks to roast up in the alley out back.

Before long, the place filled up, and a salty old guy who looked like Fred Sanford shuffled out and took the stage. He picked up a guitar and started laying down a hypnotic blues rhythm and soon the rest of the band joined him. Sherry showed up with her friend Jasmine, a hot black chick who had just started working at Anything Goes. Sal was totally checking her out, initiating short bursts of conversation whenever he could. Everything he said was loaded with innuendo and she was into it, though she seemed to be holding back. I kept waiting for some reaction from Sherry but she didn’t seem to mind. I was also waiting for Lila. I finally asked about her, as casually as I could given how much I wanted to see her. Sherry told me Lila said she wasn’t up for going out.

“She’s probably painting,” I told myself out loud.

“Of course!” said Sherry. “I didn’t even think of that.” She turned to Jasmine and pointed out Lila’s paintings on the wall.

“Who’s the groovy brother?” asked Jasmine.

“That’s Jimi Hendrix,” said Sal, rolling his eyes at me. How could anyone not recognize Jimi Hendrix?

At the end of the night, we all went back to our place and smoked a joint and drank a few more beers. My mood had significantly deteriorated by then and it showed. Sal was working his ass off to get something going with Sherry and Jasmine. I didn’t want to jam him up so I made up an excuse to go out.

"I'm gonna pick up some more beer," I said.

"Good idea," Sal winked at me.

I took a walk, hoping he would either close the deal or shut it down by the time I got back. The night was cool and clear with the unmistakable smell of fallen leaves in the air. People were coming home, walking in small, chatty groups or quiet couples. Some stumbled out of cabs. They mostly looked happy or drunk or both.

Someone on the first floor of a brick three-flat on the next block was having what sounded like a jamming party. You could hear people inside singing along with "Black Dog." It sounded like so much fun, I wondered what they were like. I hoped they were cool, but Zeppelin was so popular you could never tell. They were probably just your typical fuckwads who only knew Zeppelin IV.

I walked up to Division where there was a lot more action. I saw a couple of familiar faces but managed to keep going without getting caught in any conversation. I went east one block and headed back home where I listened at the door. When I didn't hear anything, I figured it was safe to go inside. Sal was passed out on the couch alone. He must have been more fucked up than I thought. It was a good thing too. If he had been awake, I would've suggested we run out to the West Side and he would've gone for it in a New York minute. As it was, I just pulled his shoes off, tossed a coat over him and wandered back to the bedroom to crash.

•

The next day, I got up early while Sal was still out cold. Anxious to get going before I got trapped in a haze of weed, videotapes and munchies, I hopped in the shower and ran out for some Dunkin' Donuts coffee before hitting the bricks. I only had to walk a block or two to get to several building sites already bustling with activity. I approached the first place I saw, a brick two-flat they were converting into a single-family home. A truck was parked out front, stacked high with four-by-ten sheets of drywall. A big, solid-looking guy with a square jaw and bright blue eyes marched through the open frame of the front door.

"Who's in charge?" I asked as he brushed past me without a word. "Hey, buddy." I followed after him.

He turned and shook his head. "No, no."

I was lucky to get that much out of him. Most of those Polish construction workers didn't know a word of English. I walked from one unit to the other, getting little more than a blank look when I asked for the boss. If they were Mexicans I could have at least said "el jefe" and possibly gotten somewhere. The next two sites weren't much better. When I did finally happen upon someone who could talk to me, the guy practically laughed in my face.

"I got all the help I need, guy," he said. "You should have been here when we were gutting the place."

•

"I told ya," said Sal, his voice distorted from the smoke in his lungs. He licked his finger and dabbed the edge of the glowing ember at the end of the joint he was holding.

"They never said shit about the union," I said, blowing out my own hit. Two weeks had passed with no luck.

"That's because you didn't even get that far."

He had a point. My prospects were looking dim and things were getting pretty crazy. We had been out every night and not just to Spoonful. We started hitting some of the trendier places around us, hipster lounges with sleek retro themes and pricey drinks.

"Nothing like a six-dollar martini," said Sal.

It was a different way to live, that's for sure. When he wasn't working the night shift, Dante came along with Sherry and sometimes Jasmine too, but Lila wasn't into it.

"I see enough clubs on the job," she said.

Besides, with all the Icons over at Spoonful, Lila was anxious to do some more. She just couldn't decide on a subject.

"How about John Lennon now?" I asked one day.

"I'm not ready for the Beatles."

"How about Kurt Cobain?"

"Too early for him."

We kicked around some other names but nobody clicked. Then I left and didn't see Lila for a little while. I missed hanging out but I was happy to leave her alone, painting.

"She's working hard," said Dante.

"Good for her," said Sal.

Too bad none of her work ethic rubbed off on any of us. Dante still spent his mornings at the bar while Sal and I went through endless T-bags. On top of all that, we started doing blow like it was 1989. We even picked up some of the ready rock that Aaron had his hoppers slinging on the corner.

"Good thing we're not shooting dope," Sal said with more than a trace of sarcasm as he fired up the pipe.

I didn't care what Sal thought. It was a good thing. Blow is blow and smack is smack. They're two completely different animals. Whether you snort it, smoke it or slam it, blow just doesn't take you away like smack. I know people get hooked, but for the life of me, I could never see why. You're up all night, running your mouth, jaw twitching, nose burning. You might want to fuck but you can't. All you can do is keep going. Before you know it, the birds are chirping and the garbage trucks are rolling. You're out hundreds of dollars and for what? We were doing it just to do something. We were bored. We didn't have to get up. Sal sometimes drove at night but I didn't have a job, just an increasingly futile search for one.

Not working was starting to really bum me out, and all that partying was expensive. The blow was adding up, especially since we weren't selling any of it.

"You should just get it going with Frat Row again," said Sal.

"Fuck them," I said. Mark had called less than a week after Lila bailed me out. I tried to brush him off lightly at first but he just kept on calling.

"C'mon, dude," he pleaded. "I'm really sorry about what happened. You'll never have to see those guys again."

Goddamn right I didn't have to see the CBOT crew. I was relieved when Paul called and told me those shady scumbags refused to cooperate with the police and no charges were being filed, but I still didn't want to run into those assholes and give them a chance to get any payback for Halloween. And I didn't want to see Mark and his idiot frat buddies either. Let them watch barnyard porn and have a big circle jerk. Fuck 'em.

That's what I told myself, but I was hurting without the business. I had already been to the bank three times, once to pay Lila back and twice more, pulling out a total of seven grand. I still had almost fifteen plus my bonds and the watch left in the box, but at this rate we would be kicking in doors before Christmas.

"You should come down and see Raj," said Sal. Raj was the surly Pakistani owner of Wicker Cabs, a small fleet of Checker Taxis where Sal did his driving. He was a real tightass with most people but for some reason he always put up with Sal's junkie bullshit.

"I couldn't take all that city driving. I'm in the car enough heading out to T's," I said.

"Well," Sal took another hit and handed me the joint, "I'm not sure what you're gonna do, but it's looking more and more like Starbucks isn't such a bad idea."

"Fuck you," I grumbled.

"I think you'll look good in a green apron."

"Oh yeah?" I narrowed my eyes at him, searching for a comeback, when suddenly I had an idea.

•

A few days later, Sal and I were at Spoonful, each with a catered plate of turkey, stuffing and other sides. Thanksgiving was the only day of the year you could get anything other than chili and we were taking full advantage of it. Sal's parents stayed down in Boca Raton and my mom was with Fran and Theo. We could've been at Fran's but neither of us wanted to go over there. It was no big deal. It wasn't the first time I was on my own for Thanksgiving and I figured it wouldn't be the last. Dante and Lila went to his mom's house and Sherry was with her brother's family in Naperville.

"You guys need another round?" asked Dana as she walked by with some plates for the table behind us.

"No thanks," said Sal. He turned to me and lowered his voice in an effort to mask his disgust. "Home Depot? Is that a joke?"

"I think I'll look good in an orange apron."

"No fucking way. You'll have to piss for that job."

"Dante's gonna help me out with that."

"Great start for your new career," said Sal. "Smuggling piss. What are you gonna do? Tape a test tube to your balls?"

"I'll figure something out."

"I can't believe you would sign on to work for such a corporate monstrosity. Fucking places are taking over."

"What the hell do you have against Home Depot?" The novelty of Sal's objection was starting to wear thin. "Have you ever even been inside one?"

"No way." Sal was emphatic. "I only know that North Avenue store and I refuse to go in there on principle."

I was going to work at that very store he mentioned, just west of the Chicago River on a grim strip formerly populated by hookers, dopefiends and other degenerates operating with virtual impunity. We used to roll down there every so often to burn the suburban pooh-butts coming in to score some ready rock or smack. When construction on the store started, the Chicago Police Department took a miraculous interest in the area and chased all the action away.

"Fuck," Sal went on, thinking. "I guess it's not so bad. I can always drop in there for a five-finger discount."

"Not while I'm working."

"Oh, no? That's exactly when I'm gonna do it."

I was about to let him know there was no way that was going to happen when I stopped myself. It was pointless arguing about it with Sal. Telling him I wouldn't help wouldn't stop him from trying to convince me to do it. Far from it.

"I'm just glad to get something going," I said finally, anxious to change the subject. "I don't want to hear it from my mom when we go over there for Theo's birthday on Saturday."

"What are you gonna be doing anyway?"

"I'll be a sales associate in the plumbing section."

"I'm sure your mom will be very proud of her son the..." Sal chuckled. "Plumbing section sales associate."

"Laugh it up, cabbie." I raised my eyebrows at him. "At least I'm not a junkie or a drug dealer anymore."

"Don't remind me," Sal said wistfully.

CHAPTER FIFTEEN

"Brings back memories, huh?" said Sal.

"Yeah," I mumbled, looking around.

Living in Chicago, we were less than ten miles from Elmwood Park but the place seemed liked worlds away, especially with all the old-time mom-and-pop stores and restaurants still hanging on after all these years. We were smoking a joint, taking it all in without much comment. There was always something sad about coming home, like the people we used to be and all the people we used to know were already dead. We took a few turns and stopped in front of the house where I grew up, a modest brick bungalow on a quiet street in the northwest corner of town. Dante was probably already there since he still lived with his mom only two houses over on the block behind us.

"Looks like Fran's already here." Sal gestured to the black Mercedes parked in front of my mom's garage. "Whatever happens, try not to get sucked into the bullshit like last time, okay?"

"I'll try." I puffed on the joint and handed it over. I started to pull into the driveway but changed my mind.

"Best to be ready for a quick getaway," said Sal.

"Tell me about it." I parked next to the curb in front of the house and sat back, remembering my previous visit.

•

It had been almost five months since my mom invited us all over at the last minute for a Fourth of July cookout. Rare as it was for me to make the trek out to EP, Fran and her son Theo were the guests of honor that day, as always. Fran was a real straight arrow, complete with a high-powered finance job, a Lincoln Park condo and all the other trappings of worldly success.

"If she wasn't divorced, she'd be perfect," Sal once joked.

Perfect or not, Fran and my mom were always bickering. Unlike the battles about my drug use or lack of gainful employment, their conflicts tended to be more abstract. They fought about shit like Fran's condescending attitude or my mom's constant criticism. They also clashed because Fran had spurned the Catholic Church, a cardinal sin that could not be overlooked.

"That poor boy hasn't even been baptized," my mom told Fran more than once.

My mom bought lottery tickets and clipped coupons and watched the local news. When my dad died, she got a job as a cashier at Dominick's. It wasn't a bad job, as far as jobs go. She worked hard and built up some pretty good benefits over the years, though she always seemed to be struggling financially. She was still pretty fit for a woman her age despite not taking the greatest care of herself. She drank and smoked and, as far back as I can remember, maintained a ready supply of Valium and other Mother's Little Helpers.

My mom thought Fran was a silly woman, knocking herself out to make it in a man's world. She was unimpressed by Fran's success in business, choosing instead to focus on her failed marriage and poor Theo who she thought was being "raised by the nanny." You would think the generous financial support from Fran's ex-husband, a downtown lawyer with a second wife and two more kids, should count for something but my mom didn't care.

"Money is no substitute for a father," she always said.

This made Fran absolutely furious. She was busting her ass, raising Theo by herself the best she could and getting nothing but grief for it. They were both fucking crazy as far as I was concerned. Even so, I was the closest thing to a mediating force between them, if for no other reason than either one could turn her sights on me.

So Dante, Sal and I rounded out the party along with this retired mope named Len who my mom met on some riverboat casino in Elgin. He manned the grill and did a pretty good job. He made sausages and pork chops, all the while getting increasingly sloshed on some rotgut cabernet in a box that he brought with him.

"He's had a long week," said my mom.

"Retirement is tough," Sal said dryly, careful as always to be out of earshot from my mom with whom he maintained a nauseating Eddie Haskell-like rapport.

We all did our part to get through this relatively benign, if ill-advised, occasion. Sal gave himself a booster in the middle of the party, just enough to maintain his trademark charm. Dante was gracious enough to help Len finish his box. I even held my own, chatting with Fran and playing catch with Theo before we ate. But it all went terribly wrong when Theo sat down next to me as I was having my after-dinner smoke.

"Do you mind?" said Fran.

"Do I mind what?" I asked, oblivious.

"The cigarette," said Sal.

"I'm almost done," I said. "And we're outside, for God's sake!"

"Michael," said Fran, trying her best to stay calm. "Please don't smoke around Theo."

"It's okay, Mom," said Theo. A quiet kid with bright blue eyes and a mop of dark brown hair, he always struck me as a good sport.

"That's not for you to say," Fran said to him in a sharp tone.

"Take it easy," I said to Fran and patted Theo on the back.

"A little smoke never killed anyone," said my mom.

"I never said it did," said Fran. She turned to me. "And don't tell me to 'take it easy'!"

"Why the hell not?" I said. "You're the one getting loud here for no good reason."

"Stop it, Michael," said my mom.

"No good reason?" Fran became hysterical. "I asked nicely and you just ignored me. Now put out the goddamn cigarette!"

"Fuck you!" I completely lost it myself. Her shrill tone set me off. "You did not ask 'nicely' and even if you did, you're acting like a crazy fucking bitch right now!"

"Oh!" exclaimed Sal.

"Goddamn it, Michael!" shouted my mom.

Even Len who was slumped over in a lawn chair, spent from all that grilling, perked up.

"That's it!" Fran announced, getting up from the table. She yanked

Theo off the bench and stormed into the house. Moments later, we heard the roar of her Mercedes as she sped off.

"Nice." Sal raised his eyebrows at me.

"Fuck you too," I said.

"Does this mean we're leaving?" asked Dante.

•

"That was fucked up," I said, recalling the scene.

"You better hit this again," said Sal as he handed me the joint.

We powered it down and each lit up a cigarette, taking a minute to wallow in the smoke before climbing out of the car.

"Fuck, I'm stoned," said Sal.

"Me too."

Weed was the key to making it through a trip to my mom's house, especially when Fran was there. We wandered up to the glass storm door at the entrance to the house. I reached for the handle when Theo appeared on the other side. He pushed it open with a smile.

"Hey, Uncle Mike," he said.

"Happy birthday, kiddo," I said. "You remember Sal?"

"Of course," said Theo.

"How's it feel to be six?" asked Sal.

"Seven," Theo corrected him.

"Damn," said Sal. "You're getting old."

Theo gazed at the small package in my hand. I got him a PlayStation video game, Delta Force. I didn't know much about games but the kid at the store said it was one of the best shooters out there. Sal pointed out that it's always fun to shoot stuff and I agreed, plunking down thirty dollars on the spot.

"Here." I handed the present to Theo. "Give this to your mom. You can open it when she says it's okay."

Though he certainly didn't have to, Sal had picked out his own sure thing for Theo, some gift certificates from McDonald's.

"These are for you too, buddy." Sal handed Theo an envelope and mussed his hair. "Have a Quarter Pounder on me."

"Thanks, Mr. Sal," said Theo. He turned and rushed down the hall to the kitchen as my mom came out.

"Michael," she smiled. "Salvatore, come on in."

We each gave my mom a peck on the cheek. I could hear Dante's voice behind her coming from the family room.

"Look what the cat dragged in," he spoke up heartily as we went in there. He was pacing on the carpet in front of the couch, beer in hand, talking football with my mom's boyfriend.

"You remember Len," said my mom.

"From the Fourth of July," I said.

"Those were some mean sausages," said Sal.

Len stood up and we all shook hands while Dante went on with his story. Sal and I doubled back to the kitchen when Fran walked in from the hallway that led back to the bedrooms.

"Hey, guys," she said with a polite nod.

"Frances," said Sal, addressing Fran by her full name, a habit I found vaguely annoying.

"Hello, Sal," said Fran. She had always been attractive, with classic Italian beauty to spare, but lately she was starting to look tired and a little thin. "Michael," she said to me stiffly. "Thank you both so much for coming."

"I wouldn't miss it."

"You guys want a beer?" said my mom. "Some wine?"

"I'll take a beer," I said.

"And I'll have whatever you're having," said Sal.

"Len brought some Merlot," said my mom.

"In a box?"

"You stop that," my mom said.

"I'm just joking around," said Sal. "You know me."

A real joker. My mom pinched Sal's cheek and I caught Fran staring at them with disapproval. Ever since we were kids, it seemed to bother Fran to no end how much my mom liked Sal.

"How have you been?" I asked her.

"Fine," she said. "Busy. How about you?"

"Same," I nodded.

"Michael just got a new job," said Sal.

"Really?" said my mom.

"What was your old job?" asked Fran. The question sounded harmless but I knew her little digs too well to let it pass.

"What difference does it make?" I snapped.

"I thought you were the maintenance man at your apartment building," my mom said to me.

"He is," said Sal. "Michael can fix anything."

"Is that so?" said Fran. "How would you like to come over and take a look at my dishwasher?"

"Are you still doing that?" asked my mom.

"When I can," I said, ignoring Fran. "It's tough with my new schedule. My hours change a lot."

"And what are you doing now?" asked my mom.

"Michael works for Home Depot," Sal said with mock enthusiasm. "He's a plumbing sales associate."

The conversation didn't get much better from there. By the time we sat down at the dining room table, each with a plate of my mom's lasagna, I was starting to feel strangely morbid. The framed photos on the walls around us didn't help. My mom still had strategically grouped school pictures of Fran and me at various stages of our development. Fran went from being a pretty little girl with big brown eyes and pigtails to a gawky adolescent with braces and bad eighties hair. I started out as a sunny kid with big front teeth and a bowl haircut only to become a surly teenager with a blank stare and some fuzz on my upper lip. There was a shot from my parents wedding, back when my mom had bouffant hair and my dad had pork chop sideburns. Most of the pictures were of Fran and me around the house or on one of our family trips to the Wisconsin Dells or Warren Dunes. One especially haunting photo showed the two of us with our dog, Magic, a black lab-setter mix who loved to run. She got hit by a car when I was fourteen years old. That was the last time I cried.

"So what do you think about Clinton?" asked Len. He was so clueless. Bringing up politics at our house in the middle of a meal was like torching the place.

"I think he's a stud," said Sal, fanning the flames.

I personally didn't care much for the man. I had heard Maurice and Clifford go back and forth about him many times. I tended to side with Maurice. Clinton was a little too slick to warrant my loyalty or respect but I absolutely hated the blowhards that were out to get him. Fran disagreed, of course.

"It figures you'd say that."

"And why, pray tell, is that?" said Sal.

"You two, stop," said my mom. She shot a look at Len who shrank impotently from the brewing conflict.

"He's a liar and a pig," said Fran.

"Are you saying I'm a liar and a pig?" said Sal.

"I'm saying that he represents a deteriorating moral attitude that I know you and," she paused to look at me before going on, "other people at this table wholly embrace."

"And who exactly are you talking about, Fran?" I goaded her.

"Never mind," she said. "Can we talk about something else?"

"How about them Bears?" said Dante.

"Fuck the Bears," I said.

"Oh!" exclaimed Sal.

"Michael!" said my mom.

"Sorry, Mom," I said. "I'm just kidding, Theo."

Theo took a bite of his lasagna.

"Watch your mouth," said Fran.

"What can I say? I guess it's that 'deteriorating moral attitude'?" I pressed Fran. "Who determines that anyway? The right-wing gasbags you love so much?"

"Knock it off," said my mom.

"Tell me, Fran."

"Enough!" my mom shouted. She stood up and pounded the table. The dishes rattled and we all jumped. "What the hell is the matter with you two? This is supposed to be a nice party for Theo!"

The whole room fell silent. Theo put his fork down with unconscious resignation and I felt bad. My mom had a temper which flared every so often but seeing her like that in front of everyone else unnerved me. She stood there for a moment, glaring at all of us before speaking up again as she stormed away from the table.

"I need someone to help me in the kitchen," she said.

That's when I noticed the slight limp in her gait.

•

"What's wrong with Mom?" I asked Fran.

We were in the family room an hour later speaking in hushed tones. Sal was in the kitchen helping my mom with the dishes. Dante had gone home to get a couple of hours sleep before work. Len had dozed off in front of the TV where Theo was locked in fierce urban warfare with a shadowy force of enemy soldiers bent on destroying some nameless American city. The fact that he was allowed to play at all was a miracle, given Fran's qualms with the violent content of the game. She had almost insisted I take it back when Theo managed to talk her out of that nonsense.

"I'm only shooting bad guys," he said.

"What a relief." Fran's voice rang with sarcasm.

"The kid at the store said it would be okay," I said.

Fran was already uptight about the PlayStation console my mom had gotten Theo for Christmas the year before.

"He's too young," said Fran. "I don't want him spending all his time playing video games when he should be learning to read."

"Isn't that what school is for?" my mom argued.

They went back and forth before agreeing to leave the unit at my mom's house. So after cake and a few more presents, Theo got down to the dirty business of blowing away the bad guys. By then, the positive vibe around the party had been restored and nobody brought up politics or anything else that might set off more fireworks. The relative calm allowed me to focus on my mom's condition. Her meltdown over my unpleasant but unremarkable exchange with Fran was one thing. Seeing her limp around like an old woman was something else.

"Is her back acting up again?" I asked Fran.

"It never stopped," she said.

"What about her pain meds?"

"She can't get them anymore."

"What do you mean she can't get them anymore?" I was appalled. "What about her other meds?"

"Her doctor is cutting her off." Fran looked me in the eye. "I was hoping maybe you could help her."

I felt a surge of indignation. "I guess it pays to know someone with a deteriorating moral attitude."

"For God's sake, Michael."

"I'm sorry," I said finally. I was being petty and I knew it. "Truth is... prescription drugs are beyond my area of expertise. What about all your high-flying financial contacts? Surely one of the partners knows some Dr. Feelgood."

"I wouldn't know," said Fran.

Of course she wouldn't. Fran was an insufferable tight ass and I'm sure everyone around her knew it.

"Fuck." I started thinking. "I don't believe this shit. What happened to her doctor? What's his name?"

"Martinelli."

"Yeah, that's it," I remembered. "Isn't she still seeing him?"

"He retired," said Fran. "His son took over the practice. Robert, maybe you remember him from high school?"

I racked my brain to no avail. "Doesn't ring a bell."

"He was two years behind me," said Fran.

That made him a senior when I was a freshman.

"That's right!" It finally came to me. "He played football with Dante. He was a little guy, a free safety."

"Now he's a doctor," said Fran.

"So why doesn't she go to him?"

"She does but he won't give her the medication."

"Did you try talking to him?" I asked. "You know, appeal to him, one success story to another?"

"It doesn't work that way."

"The fuck it doesn't," I said as Sal came in.

"Doesn't what?" he asked.

"Nothing," I said. "You ready to roll?"

CHAPTER SIXTEEN

"She's your mother, Michael," said Sal.

"Really?" I said. "Wow, she's my mother? Thanks, Sal. I sure am glad you cleared that up." We were in my car driving back from EP, passing yet another joint back and forth.

"I'm just saying."

"Don't get me wrong. I feel bad, even pissed. But what the fuck can I do about it?"

"It's not like you're asking to fuck his wife," said Sal.

"What the hell does that mean?"

"I mean the guy's a doctor. Your mother is in pain. He should help her. That's his fucking job. You just want him to do his job."

"First of all," I set him straight, "my mom is always in *some* kind of pain, if you know what I mean and I know you do."

"Fuckin' A right I do," said Sal. "All the more reason."

"Second of all," I continued, "he *is* doing his job, just not the way we'd like. He's giving her some other shit, some...fuck, I don't know what it's called, some lame-ass drug."

"No doubt engineered to not let anyone feel a moment of undeserved pleasure," said Sal. "Fucking fascist doctors. We should just go over there and..."

"And what?" I cut him off. "Rough him up? He's a young guy, our age. He used to be a football player."

"He was a safety," Sal scoffed. "Gimme a break. We're not talking about Dante here. We could definitely work him over."

"What is with you? She's *my* mother, like you said. Why do you want to kick this guy's ass so bad? What the hell did he ever do to you? And how would it help my mom anyway? Seriously, think about it. So we kick the guy's ass. Actually, I kick his ass and you get a few shots in after I drop him."

"Fuck you."

"Whatever." We both knew that's how it would probably go down. "So we pound the guy into the ground and then what? Tell him 'Frances Lira gets her pain meds or else'? This isn't fucking *Goodfellas*. The police will be knocking on my mom's door in nothing flat."

"I haven't figured that part out yet," said Sal as he reached for the joint. He took a hit and spoke up again, wisps of smoke coming out of his mouth with each word. "I guess I'm just bored. And this kind of bullshit really pisses me off. I like your mom. She's always been sweet to me, even when my own mother wouldn't let me in the house. I hate to see her in pain, especially when there's something that could be done about it, you know?"

"*If* there's something that could be done," I said. Sal was making some sense but I still wasn't convinced.

"Maybe we just talk to the guy," he went on, "threaten him, tell him, 'I know where you live,' that kinda thing."

"He could still call the police."

"And tell them what? All we did was talk to the guy."

"So what's gonna make him go along?"

"Fear, man," said Sal. "A couple bust-out motherfuckers like you and me? Who knows what we'll do?"

He had a point.

•

"I'm sure Candice knows somebody," said Lila. She was puffing on a post-coital cigarette in her bed later that night, with me sprawled out next to her on the mattress.

"Yeah?" I said. "Why do you say that?"

"Because she's got a major stash of pills."

"No kidding."

"One of the drawers in her desk, you know, in the office, is full of prescription bottles. If you're a little wound up or dragging before a party, she'll hook you up."

"Does that include blow?"

"Sometimes, but mainly pills."

"Still, it's not a bad perk," I said. "I wish I could go to my boss when I need a little boost."

"Please," Lila said. "You think it's hard dealing with John Q. Public in a warehouse full of building supplies? Try doing it naked on all fours in the..."

"I get the idea." I cut her off and steered the conversation back to my mom before she gave me any more details. "Thanks for the tip though, really. I'll keep it in mind. Thing is, my mom probably wouldn't go for it. Too much like scoring."

"Isn't that what she's doing?" asked Lila. "She knows what she wants, she goes to the doctor to get it, right?"

"She doesn't see it that way."

"Okay."

Lila had a trace of the contempt in her voice and I could tell she was ready to move on. Nothing drove her nuts more than people unwilling or unable to own up to their desires. If we weren't talking about my mom, she might not have bit her tongue.

"So what's going on with you?" I asked. "Your paintings are obviously coming along." I motioned to a couple new works looking down on us, Keith Moon and John Bonham. "You got kind of a dead drummer thing going right now, huh?

"I want to get high again," Lila said abruptly. She tamped her cigarette out and rolled over on her side to face me.

"Excuse me?"

"I don't mean to screw up your thing. I'm really proud of you cleaning up and getting a job. It's been good for me too, though I have to say...I miss it. I miss that feeling, Michael. I would love to share it with you but only if it's right, which it's not, which I get, but...I'm also willing to feel it on my own."

"Jesus, Lila." I knew this day would come. "What about your painting? Everything is going so good for you."

"What does that have to do with anything?"

"I'm just saying that it's kind of risky to start shooting dope when you got it all wired tight like you do."

"That's not the issue and you know it," Lila said. "I handled it before.

I can handle it again. As far as my paintings go…I'm an artist, it's what I do, whether my work hangs someplace where someone can buy it or not. I paint because I feel, sometimes more than I can stand. I have to get it out. Right now I'm in an incredibly productive phase and it does feel great but it hurts at the same time. It's hard to explain. What else can I say? I want some relief and I know it's out there. If you can't help me, I understand."

She finished with a detached stare that told me she was prepared to do whatever she had to if I said no.

"I can help," I said.

"You sure?" she asked, searching my face. "I'm sorry to put you on the spot like this."

"Don't worry about it, Lila." I sat up and reached for my jeans. "Just gimme a few days. And whatever you do, promise me you won't try to score from anyone else."

"I promise," she smiled. "You'll be my only."

•

A couple of days passed and I was driving to work, thinking about my life and the people in it. Lila wanted to get high and who could blame her? Certainly not me, though I couldn't help but worry about where that might go. As it was, I felt like we had already dodged a bullet. The week after Sal returned from the hospital, Lila and I both went for a blood test that showed no Hep C or HIV.

"I told you we were okay," said Lila.

"You were right," I said. "But better safe than sorry."

I had another concern regarding Dante. I figured once I started scoring for Lila, he'd probably catch on that she was getting high. I didn't want him to know but I understood how sometimes these things can't be helped. Even if you're really clean and careful, shooting dope is difficult to hide. Lila wasn't going to let that stop her. If I didn't score for her, she would find another way. Between the art scene types she was meeting through her exposure at Spoonful and the displaced homeboys popping up around her neighborhood, Lila could easily make her own connections.

Then there was my mom, with Fran and her pathetic moralizing tossed in for good measure. People like me are bringing down the country but maybe, just maybe, I could still score some pills for our ailing mother. And now Sal was on the case, having already done some crude recon on my mom's new doctor.

"I spent the day driving around EP. I know where he lives. I know where he works," he said. "I've seen him, too. He's still short but he got pudgy. I'm telling you, Michael, we can take him!"

Great. Charges for the fracas at Triple Chi just got dropped and now Sal was ready to go off on some citizen, my mom's doctor no less. Not that I didn't feel my own rage at this uptight asshole, jamming up my mom, a faithful old patient who just needed a little something for her pain. Still, she was a grown woman who could fend for herself. Fran didn't need to drag me into this bullshit. I cursed myself for bringing it up to Sal. What a fucking mess.

•

When I got to work, I grabbed my apron and my timecard, punched in and headed out to the floor. As soon as I reached my section, I noticed some copper fittings that needed to be sorted. It was the perfect task, mindless but productive. I dug in, trying to look so busy nobody would approach me. I was about halfway through the pile when a soft voice broke my concentration.

"Could you help me?"

I looked up, and lo and behold! It was our girl with the luxury digs, Chloe Sevigny, only older and stacked. I couldn't believe it. At first, I told myself that it couldn't be.

What were the chances?

My heart started racing. I felt like a teenager bumping into the girl I had a crush on. What was it with this woman? Was it her face? Was it her place? Was it the intimate glimpse of a different kind of life I had found in her darkened condo? I quickly studied her. Dressed in a gray suit with black pumps, she could not have looked more out of place among the grungy construction workers and frantic do-it-yourselfers rummaging through the boxes and bins around us. I almost forgot she had asked me for help.

"Of course," I said finally.

"I'm looking for a new toilet seat."

We were standing between two rows of orange steel shelves stacked high and full of everything you needed to build a bathroom from scratch. A large display of toilet seats hung overhead. You could spend as little as $9.99 on the el cheapo seat made from synthetic composite, round and white with plastic hinges. Or you could spend as much as $39.99 on an elongated model made of solid oak with real brass hardware. As luck would have it, I had broad expertise in this particular area thanks to the crack Home Depot training program.

"Okay," I nodded, motioning to the display above us.

"How do I know which one will fit?"

"What shape is your toilet?"

"I'm not sure. I know it's bright white."

"Is it round or oblong?" I asked.

A few more questions and I couldn't help but wonder what happened. Toilet seats last a really long time and her place was brand new. She also probably had a warranty for stuff like that. I almost said so before catching myself.

"I spilled some nail polish on mine," she said, as if she read my mind. "I didn't notice until it was dry."

"You couldn't chip it off?"

"Not all of it. I tried some nail polish remover too but that just made it worse."

"How about your boyfriend?" I asked, knowing full well she couldn't expect much from a douchebag like that. "Shouldn't he be taking care of this for you?"

"No help there," she said with a trace of discomfort. "It's oblong, by the way."

I hesitated, momentarily forgetting myself.

"The shape of the toilet," she added.

"Oh, yeah," I stumbled. "Hold on." I turned and quickly searched the display. "This one right here will work."

I pulled a flat box off the shelf and handed it to her.

"Thank you so much," she said with a sweet smile.

"You need someone to put that in for you?" I asked. Up until the words came out of my mouth, I didn't know if I would go for it.

"No, but thank you again..." she said, her eyes dropping down to scan my name tag. "Michael."

"You're welcome," I muttered as she walked away.

"Tough break, homey," said Hector from electrical as he walked past. I glanced around, suddenly self-conscious.

What the fuck was I thinking?

I spent the rest of the shift wandering the aisles, trying not to meet anyone's gaze. As I punched out, my boss, a pasty corporate drone named Scott, pulled me aside.

"You are aware of our installation services," he said or asked. He had a funny way of talking where you never knew which.

"Yeah," I said, once again recalling my fine training.

"Okay," he said. "I'm just trying to make sure. Because, as you should know, there is no independent solicitation of business allowed here in the store or anywhere on the premises."

I cursed that fucking bigmouth Hector as I felt a surge of anger and humiliation. Getting shot down in flames by a girl for being a working stiff with an apron and a name tag was bad enough. Getting reprimanded for it by this little pissant was the last straw.

"Fuck you, Scott," I said.

"Pardon me?" he asked, his face flushed.

"You heard me, motherfucker." I balled up my apron and tossed it on the floor in front of him.

•

When I got home from that last awful shift, I wasted no time getting on the phone with Mark. He was thrilled to hear from me.

"Just in time for the holidays," he said.

Indeed, I thought. "What's it gonna be?"

He told me what he wanted and I told him to get the money. I also told him to keep me away from the CBOT Crew.

"No problem, dude," he said.

I hopped in my car and headed out west where I took a seat at the dining room table and got right down to it.

"I'll take two ounces of blow and six bags," I said.

"Damn!" said Aaron. "I guess you back in business."

"Smack too?" asked T. "That sure didn't take long."

"It's not for me," I said.

"I heard that one before," she said.

"Remember what I told you," Maurice spoke up from the living room where he was watching TV with Clifford and Beverly.

"I remember," I said. "I'm telling you, the smack is for someone else. How is it anyway?"

"Ha!" said T.

"Solid," said Aaron.

I was glad to hear it. "Solid" meant no complaints. You get off but not too hard. If he said it was "tight" or "for real", I'd be worried about Lila falling out.

"Does Sal know you out here?" asked Janet.

"Oh, I almost forgot." I reached into my pocket for a wad of bills. "Five of yours, too," I said to T before answering Janet. "And no, Sal doesn't know about the smack. I don't want him to know either. This has nothing to do with Sal."

"Where that punk at, anyway?" asked Mookie. He walked past the table into the kitchen for a glass of Tampico. "He still owes me two dollars on our last game."

"I'm sure he's good for it." I handed Aaron the money.

"Uh-huh," Mookie scowled and headed back to his room. Janet followed him, turning into her room.

"A couple hypes too," I called after her. T got up to fill her part of the order and I lit up a cigarette.

"You gonna have to come back tomorrow for the rest, but I can have it for you here." said Aaron.

"Right on." I took a long drag.

"So what about that job?" asked Aaron.

"It sucked," I said. "I quit."

Aaron perked up. "So this gonna be a regular thing?"

"We'll see," I said, wondering myself.

•

By the time I got back, I was crippled with temptation. I spent the next two hours talking myself into and out of slamming a couple bags and only made it over to Lila's after getting good and stoned. Smoking and shooting had never worked for me. Whenever I tried to mix the two, I would get freaked out by the needle. So I smoked some weed to distract me from the craving which would only get worse when I fixed

Lila. After a seemingly endless wait outside her door, I knocked again and she finally opened up.

"I had oil on my hands," Lila said. "I started painting an hour ago when you didn't show."

"Sorry about that."

Lila gave me the once-over as she stepped aside to let me in.

"Look at you," she said.

"What?"

She peered into my eyes.

"Hello...hello...hello." She made her voice echo and it tripped me out for a second. "Is there anybody in there?"

"Don't ask," I said.

"You should see your eyes."

"What can I tell you?" I shrugged. "I stopped using Visine when I moved out of my mom's house."

She reached out for my hand but I pulled away. I had a wicked case of cottonmouth and was afraid that she might want to kiss me.

"You got a beer?" I asked.

"Help yourself."

I grabbed a High Life from the icebox and twisted off the cap, taking several long gulps.

"Man, that's good." I wiped my mouth.

"I can tell," said Lila as she watched me.

"Just gimme a minute here, all right?"

"Take as long as you need."

I finished one beer and grabbed another. Lila went to put some music on, since whatever was playing when I walked in—P.J. Harvey, I think—had stopped, leaving us in jarring silence.

"How about Soundgarden?" she asked.

"Perfect." I opened my second beer, took a sip and walked over to sit down next to her on the bed.

"You sure you're okay with this?" Lila asked, searching my face.

"I'm fine," I said. "I'm just a little stoned, that's all." I made a clunky move towards her but she backed away.

"I was hoping you could, you know..." She looked me expectantly.

"Of course." I should have known.

"Afterward, for sure," she said.

"Don't worry about it," I said. "We don't have to."

"I want to," she said. "Just not right now."

First things first.

"No problem, Lila." I reached into my pocket for the small Crown Royal bag where I kept everything. "You still got that..."

"Right here," Lila produced the contorted spoon and candle stub we had used to cook in the past.

"Whatever you do, don't do more than one bag at a time."

"I won't," said Lila. "I won't even do it alone, as long as you don't mind helping me out."

"Not at all," I said. "I'd feel much better that way."

I didn't relish the prospect of watching Lila get high, but even solid dope could kill you before you know it. That's the thing with smack. It's a fine line between the time of your life and the end of your life. That's why it pays to have a partner. I had never overdosed myself but I knew many people who had. More often than not, the difference between life and death was having someone there to revive you or call somebody who could.

"Good, because I don't want you to worry," said Lila. She held out her arm and I tied her off and went to work. It was easier than I thought. My hands were shaking so badly I almost knocked over the cooker, but I barely noticed the smell and handling the needle was no big deal. I still loved to watch the bliss wash over Lila's face, but I didn't feel the irresistible urge to join her.

I'll be all right, I told myself.

I packed everything up and stashed it behind one of the books in the shelf unit near the bed before lying back on the mattress next to her. Lila's breathing was heavy and slow, her eyes half lidded. She smiled and pulled me close, whispering in my ear.

"Do you need a map?"

CHAPTER SEVENTEEN

"Where have you been?" asked Sal.

"Nowhere." I had no prepared explanation to give him. I got home around midnight and didn't expect to see him there.

"Aren't you working bright and early tomorrow?"

"I quit."

"No shit?" His eyes lit up.

I quickly ran through the story about our girl and my clumsy attempt to ask her out. Sal just had to razz me about it.

"You got no game, man."

"Game or no game, I didn't have a shot."

"Why?" he scoffed. "Because of your name tag?"

"I'm telling you," I said emphatically.

"I don't believe it." Sal shook his head. "You forget. I met our girl too. If we weren't so desperate to score that night, I would've gotten her number myself."

"Maybe, maybe not."

"There's no 'maybe' about it," said Sal. "Even with that meathead boyfriend, I could've had her."

Sal was probably right but I didn't want to admit it. I went on with the story, eager to get to the part where I told my boss to fuck off before storming out of there.

"Good for you," said Sal, giving me the props I expected. "Fuck that place. Bunch of corporate pod people." He paused. "So, ah...does this mean we're back in business?"

"I'm making a run tomorrow," I said.

"Fuckin' A," Sal smiled. "That's what I like to hear."

I glanced at my watch.

"Shouldn't you be driving?" I asked.

"I am," said Sal. "I'm just taking a little break. You didn't see the cab out front?"

"No." I was still pretty stoned when I came in, not to mention a little giddy from my time with Lila.

"I tailed the good doctor again tonight," said Sal.

"Jesus, Sal." I shook my head.

"Guess where he is, right now?"

"What the fuck is with you?" I couldn't believe we were still talking about this asshole.

"Just guess."

"I have no idea. A bar?"

"A titty bar," Sal said triumphantly. "On a Tuesday night."

"So what?"

"He's got a wife and two kids, little girls, real cuties. I saw them all in their driveway last week."

"Okay, now you're starting to creep me out." I went into the kitchen for a beer.

"Can you believe this guy?" Sal followed me. "He won't give your mom her meds, yet he's leering at strippers when he should be home with his family."

"It's an outrage." I twisted open a beer and took a big gulp. "Another fucking hypocrite strikes again. What a shocker."

"I got an idea," said Sal.

"I don't even want to know."

•

"Are we all good?" asked Mark.

Two days had passed and we were in my car, parked outside a McDonald's in East Rogers Park. After the Halloween party debacle, we couldn't do any more deals at the frat house, which was fine by me. He took an ounce and a half and I was counting the money.

"Yeah." I pocketed the roll of bills and adjusted the rearview mirror. Sitting in parking lots always made me nervous.

"How about with everything else? I heard Brad and those guys aren't pressing charges?"

"You heard right." I gave him a hard look. "Just keep those fucking shitheads away from me."

"Hey, dude." Mark raised his eyebrows. "I wouldn't even know them if it wasn't for you."

"I guess not," I said. "Are they still calling?"

"What do you think?" he asked, taking one last look at the package I just handed him.

"I think I'm glad they're not calling me."

"I'll probably need two more before Monday night," said Mark as he climbed out of the car.

"Gimme at least a day," I said, cranking the ignition.

•

"Done with retail?" asked Paul.

"At Home Depot," I said.

"Right, you're still charging me retail." Paul let out a short sharp burst of laughter and caught himself. "Seriously, I don't know how you could stand it," he said, handing me a drink.

I had just stepped into his office on the sixteenth floor of an office building on Upper Wacker Drive. Nestled in the back of a bright, noisy room packed with bustling stockbrokers, Paul had set himself up right, with a leather sofa, a fully stocked wet bar and a plasma TV. He closed the door behind me with a heavy thud. The jarring silence made it feel like we were the only people in the building.

"What did that run you?" I asked, gesturing to the TV.

"You don't want to know," said Paul.

"Probably not," I agreed.

He sat down on the couch with a drink and a plate on the glass table in front of him. I handed him his package and walked over to the wall of windows looking down on the river.

"How about that view?" he asked.

"I'll bet it looks great at night," I said. What a life.

"That it does." He snorted a pair of lines and took a sip of his drink. "I'll tell you one thing...it sure beats working for a living!" He laughed for a moment and reined himself in again.

"Seriously, with all the money being made in the market these days? You have to be a glutton for punishment to work for somebody else, especially for the peanuts they were paying you. And those corporations are as bad as the government. A bunch of peons busting their asses at the bottom of the ladder while the fat cats at the top sit around getting rich, carrying on like they matter or getting blown by the interns. That reminds me...I gotta get me some interns." He chuckled to himself. "That kind of talk used to drive Fran nuts."

"I'll bet." I could just imagine.

"I won't even ask how she is," said Paul.

"She hasn't changed," I said. "Just gotten older."

"Haven't we all?" Paul sat back with his drink.

"So, Michael." He gave me that look. The pitch was coming and I knew it. "When are we getting you into the market?"

Not this again.

"I'll bet you never followed up on that stock I told you about. That's a shame because you would've seen it double in value in less than three months. That's a four hundred percent annualized return." He leaned forward. "I'd venture to say that's even better than dealing blow. Not to mention, you don't have to worry about getting thrown in jail or shot."

"Or beat up by rogue traders," I said with a smirk.

"I heard you and your friends were the ones that did all the beating," said Paul.

"Who told you that?"

"My man at the Board of Trade."

"So you haven't seen Brad or them?"

"I just heard about it." He puffed on his cigarette. "I guess Brad was motherfucking you guys from here to kingdom come."

"I'm sure he was." I almost made some comment about his stay in the hospital but there was no point running my mouth to Paul. "Well... I'm glad you appreciate the trouble I go to."

"You bet I do," said Paul. "That's why I'm offering you something better, a way out."

"How would you score?"

"Please," Paul said. "I can always score. I just like to throw my money your way if I can."

"Speaking of scoring," I said, recalling my mom's predicament. "You wouldn't happen to know any friendly doctors, would you?"

"Why? What are you looking for?"

"I'm not sure. My mom takes something for her back."

Paul got up and went behind his desk where he reached deep into one of the cabinet drawers. He came back with a prescription bottle filled with yellow oblong pills.

"What's this?" I asked.

"Lortab. Tens. I can't imagine she's taking anything stronger. If they're too much she can break them in half."

"Are you sure?" I had no idea.

"Positive," said Paul. "That's hydrocodone, the de facto medicine for anyone with chronic pain."

"Where do you get them?"

"A client of mine." He pointed to the bottle. "Dr. Love."

"You're joking." I looked down. Sure enough, the name on the bottom of the label read: "Dr. Jamie Love."

"You don't need these?"

"I've got another bottle," he said.

"What for?"

"Try one," said Paul. "Better yet, try two. They're not heroin but they make you feel pretty damn good. It's an opiate."

"No thanks," I said, shoving the bottle in my pocket. I wasn't looking for another habit.

"It's up to you." Paul cut himself two more lines and got serious. "So what about the market?"

Not again. "What about it?"

"I got another tip for you."

•

Two hours later, I finally escaped from Paul's office, my head spinning from the hard sell he gave me. He tried to start things off with a crash course on buying and selling stocks.

"I saw *Wall Street*," I told him.

"Then you know that information is the key," said Paul. "If you know what will happen with the company, then you pretty much know what will happen with the stock."

He went on to tell me how he could find things out from his many contacts here and there.

"You got inside connections," I said.

"And that's all you need, my friend."

Even though Paul came at me with the cheesy force of a used car salesman, what he said made enough sense to sell me on the idea. There was a lot of buzz about the market. People were getting rich. Working stiffs were quitting their jobs to trade stocks during the day. College kids were starting Internet companies. Even WXRT, "Chicago's finest rock," had added a daily stock market report to their otherwise quasi-indie music lineup. There seemed to be no escaping the madness, not even for someone like me who was being left out. Paul convinced me. The time had come to get in the game. I agreed to come back the next day with a five thousand dollar cashier's check.

"You won't be regret this," he said.

•

By the time I got home, it was dark. Sal was gone but there was a message from him on the answering machine.

"Michael, it's about six o'clock and I'm over at the Dreamboat Lounge in Stone Park. You should see this place. Fucking skank central. The good doctor sure is lapping it up though. I got Sherry and Jasmine here ready to work him over. He doesn't stand a chance. Get out here as soon as you can."

"Fuck!" I picked up the phone and called information, hoping like hell I could get Sal on the line. I quickly dialed the number. It rang and rang. No answer. I dialed it again. Same thing. A pit formed in my stomach. I dialed the number again. It must have rung thirty times. A gruff male voice finally answered, all but shouting over the Journey blaring in the background.

"Yeah?"

"I'm looking for a guy named Sal," I said.

"Sorry, don't know him."

"Are you sure?" I pressed him.

"I know who I know."

"Because he just called me from there."

"Look, pal," said the bartender with brewing irritation, "I'm kinda busy here. And there's too many people for me to ask around."

"He's a skinny guy with long black hair, tattoos, friendly," I spoke fast, thinking he might hang up any minute. "He's with a couple hot chicks. A tall brunette..."

"Oh, you mean Phil," His tone softened up a bit. "That guy's a real card. Hold on a minute."

I heard him set the phone down.

"Hey, Phil! You got a call," he yelled.

Then I heard Sal's voice. "Who's this?"

"What's up, Phil?" I asked.

"Where are you?" said Sal. He lowered his voice. "And what are you doing calling me here? You're blowing my cover."

"Your cover?" I was incredulous.

"I'm trying to keep it on the down low," said Sal. "Are you coming out here or what?"

"No, I'm not coming out there!" I yelled. Then I backed off, trying to figure out a way to subvert his mad determination. "I want you to abort the mission."

"You think this is funny?" said Sal. "Your mom can't get her meds and this guy calls himself a doctor?"

"Have you lost your fucking mind?" I couldn't believe what I was hearing. "This is insane, Sal. Totally insane. You're obsessed and for the life of me, I can't figure out why."

"Why ask why, Michael?"

"Now you're just talking crazy."

"So what if I am?" Sal snorted. "You know what's crazy? A couple junkies like you and me not getting high. *That's* crazy!"

"Is that what this is about?"

"I don't know," he said. "Maybe. All I know is that your mother's doctor is an asshole."

"Fuck him," I said. "So he's an asshole. So what? We don't need him anyway. I scored some pills through Paul."

"Damn," said Sal. "That was smart."

"I'm glad you approve." I was relieved to hear him say so. "Now can you give it a rest?"

"I don't know, Michael," said Sal. "That's not really the point anymore. Me and the girls came out here to make a movie and by God, that's what we're gonna do. We're all set up too. I borrowed a camera from Tony and we got a room at the Motel Six..."

"I don't even want to know," I cut him off. "Just leave me out of it. My mom too. Don't even mention her."

"What's your problem, Michael?"

"No problem. I just don't want any trouble, that's all."

"Well...you know," said Sal. "Sometimes trouble can't be avoided."

"This is not one of those times," I said. "I mean it, Sal. This is your thing."

"I can live with that," he said.

I hung up, hoping like hell not to get a call that night from the Stone Park Police. I picked up the phone again and started dialing my mom's number before I stopped myself. I hated calling my mom. That sounds terrible, I know, but getting on the phone with her was like going to the dentist. I'm not talking about getting a root canal or anything like that, more like a checkup where you have to sit still under a bright light while your gums get poked. Much worse on the phone than in person, my mom seemed to view getting a call as a license to start nagging. She would ask me if I got a job or a girlfriend. I'd tell her I was working on it.

"A handsome guy like you?" she'd say. "Honestly, how hard can it be? Look at Dante."

If she only knew. Whatever I told her, she was unconvinced. Thankfully, she could easily be distracted with a question about Fran or one of her sisters. She never got tired of bad-mouthing any of them. I'd pretend to listen, occasionally zoning out so flagrantly she would notice my inattention and harangue me for it.

"Are you smoking dope again?" she'd ask.

Just thinking about that phone call was enough to wear me out. Still, I had her meds and I wanted to get them to her. Whether I called first or not, I'd have to take a ride out there. I looked at my watch. Seven o'clock on a Thursday night. She was probably just sitting down to "must-see TV." Wild horses couldn't drag her away from *Everybody Loves Raymond*.

•

A half an hour later, I walked up to the front door of my mom's house and rang the bell. After a short delay, Len answered with a woozy smile. I could smell the cheap wine on his breath.

"Michael, what brings you out here?"

"Is Mom around?" I asked.

"She's watching TV," he said.

"Who the hell is it?" I heard my mom shout.

"It's Michael," said Len as I brushed past him and walked back to the kitchen where she was mixing herself a drink.

"Hey, Mom," I said.

"What's going on?" She looked worried.

"Nothing," I sighed. "Jesus, can't I just drop in to see you without something going on?"

"You could but you never do."

"Well, I got something for you."

"For me?"

"Here," I reached into my pocket for the pills and handed them to her. "For your back. How is it anyway?"

"Fine, thanks." My mom gave me a strange look before unfolding her glasses to read the label on the bottle. "My goodness. These will certainly come in handy." She looked closer, reading the small print. "Paul Willis? Does Fran know about this?"

"Not exactly." I was a little put off by her reaction, a far cry from the profuse gratitude I expected. "She was the one who told me you couldn't get your meds."

"She what?"

"She said your new doctor—Martinelli's son—was giving you a hard time. So I got some for you."

"For God's sake, Michael," she scolded me. "Don't you think you should have asked me first?"

It never even occurred to me. Whether her back was acting up or not, I knew my mom liked her pills.

"I don't know why Fran had to go and bring you into all this. Dr. Martinelli—the son that is—was mistaken, that's all. I had a nice talk with his father and we got everything all worked out."

"You did?" I felt a surge of aggravation.

"Of course, I'm a grown woman. I can take care of myself." She leaned back against the counter. "Honestly, Michael, I don't know why your sister has to be such a…"

"Control freak?" I interrupted.

"Exactly!" My mom nodded emphatically. "That's just the kind of pushy attitude that's landed her by herself all these years."

"What can I tell you?" I was pretty pissed at Fran myself though I didn't want to get into it. "She was concerned."

"Concerned?" my mom balked. "She needs to be concerned about herself. I was hoping she might want to meet Dr. Martinelli. He's only a couple of years younger and he's never been married."

"Meet him? I thought he had two kids."

"That's his partner, the brother. He got divorced after his wife caught him with the receptionist."

She offered a brief account of the affair based on gossip she heard from other patients. I only caught bits and pieces of what she said since I had suddenly become distracted by the sinking realization that Sal was out there scheming to trap the wrong guy.

"I gotta go, Mom," I said as I headed for the door.

"Mind if I keep these?" she asked, holding up the pills.

CHAPTER EIGHTEEN

"I thought you weren't coming," said Sal.

"I didn't plan to," I said, shouting over the Def Leppard blaring from the speakers hanging on the wall across from us. A loud neon sign underneath read "Dreamboat Lounge." We were standing at the bar with a motley group of bikers and businessman, frat boys and bust-outs like us. There were a few women hanging around too. They looked pretty rough, like they couldn't make the cut to be on stage. I'm sure some were trolling for johns.

Not far from the bar, dancers in various states of undress took turns seductively twisting their bodies around several poles arranged across a stage pulsing with flashing lights. Every so often, one of them would step across for a tip, usually a crumpled one or five tucked into her g-string or her teeth if she was completely nude. Thanks to the weed I smoked on the way to my mom's, the amplified sleaziness of the place was enough to make my skin crawl.

"You almost missed us," said Sal.

"Where are the girls?"

"They got him eating out of the palm of their hands, especially Jasmine," Sal said with glee. "Looks like the good doctor has got himself a case of jungle fever. Who knew?"

He cracked a shit-eating grin and took a sip of his drink. Sal loved getting over on people. And though I always chalked up his dopefiend moves to...well, being a dopefiend, I now saw that his motives could run deeper. Maybe it really was a matter of principle. Like Lila, Sal hated hypocrites. I did too, but not enough to go to such lengths. And if I did, I'd make sure I got the right guy.

“Where the fuck are they?” I barked.

Sal practically jumped at my tone. “They’re right over there,” he said, gesturing over my shoulder.

I turned and peered across the room. Sherry and Jasmine were nestled in a booth with a pudgy, middle-aged guy between them. I could tell immediately this guy was not the high school safety I remembered. The girls were all over him. He must have been a complete idiot or a raging egomaniac, because the scene was so over the top you’d have to be one or the other to fall for such a crude charade.

“Subtle, aren’t they?” I shook my head.

“What the fuck is your problem?”

“My problem is you got the wrong guy.”

“You’re telling me that’s not Dr. Martinelli?”

“That’s not my mom’s doctor,” I said. “That’s his philandering older brother, who’s also named…”

“Dr. Martinelli,” Sal gulped.

“This guy’s divorced.”

“I saw him with his wife and kids,” said Sal.

“I don’t know what to tell you. You caught him on visiting day, maybe. He fucked the receptionist, got caught, got divorced. My mom knew all about it.”

“You’re kidding!”

“Scandalous, I know,” I said. “Anyway, I’m not sure what your big plan was…film the guy, blackmail him, whatever, he probably won’t give a flying fuck.”

“Jesus Christ.”

“I’m putting an end to this right now,” I said as I started to head over to the booth.

“Hold on,” said Sal. “Let me.”

I raised my hands. “Be my guest. Just do it.”

Sal slammed the rest of his drink, set his glass down and walked away as the bartender appeared.

“What’ll you have?”

“Nothing.”

“It’s a two drink minimum.”

“Here,” I said, handing him my drink tickets. “Keep ‘em.”

He took them without a word and I directed my attention back to Sal standing over the booth. Things weren't going so well. Sherry and Jasmine had just slid out from behind the table and the good doctor clearly wasn't happy about it. Just as he got up to face Sal, I decided to go over there to try and keep things cool.

"Who the hell is this guy?" he said as I approached them. I had him by at least six inches, but he was much thicker and had a big gut just like Sal said.

"We don't want any trouble," I said.

"Then mind your own fucking business!"

"Sherry, Jasmine," I said. "Let's go."

Sherry made a move in my direction and Jasmine followed, but Martinelli grabbed her by the hand.

"Where are you going, baby?" he asked with nauseating tenderness.

"Step off, man." Jasmine pulled away from him.

"What?" said Martinelli, his face contorting with an almost comical blend of rage and disbelief.

"You heard her," said Sal.

"Fuck you, punk!" squawked Martinelli as he shoved Sal.

"That's enough!" I tried to get between them but Martinelli pushed past me only to get cracked in the jaw by Sal. He hit the floor like a rag doll and Sal pumped his fist.

"I told you I could drop him!" he crowed triumphantly.

I couldn't believe my eyes but I didn't have time to dwell on it. A pair of stone-faced bouncers were on the way over.

"Let's go, *now*," I said.

•

We almost didn't make it out of the Dreamboat Lounge. With Dr. Martinelli being such a dedicated regular and all, the bouncers didn't want to just let us go quietly. Even Sal's rapport with the bartender was useless, and all his fast-talking seemed to make things worse. Just when it looked like we were screwed, Sherry turned on the waterworks, insisting that Sal was only defending her. It was a brilliant ploy.

"Don't come back," said the bigger of the two bouncers as he pushed us both out the door.

"You don't have to tell me twice," I said.

"Well," Sal said once we were safely in the parking lot, "that certainly was exciting."

"What you talking about?" asked Jasmine. "That was whack!"

"Oh, come on," said Sal. "You guys were great."

"Thanks," said Sherry as she wrapped her arms around him.

"We did have that fool," Jasmine smiled.

"I'm just glad we don't have to see him naked," said Sherry.

"But now we don't get paid," said Jasmine. "Isn't that right?"

"Sorry," said Sal. "The good doctor was our meal ticket."

"It's early," said Sherry. "What do guys want to do?"

"We still got a room at the Motel Six," Sal said hopefully.

"Let's go back to the city," said Jasmine, ignoring him.

"We can go by Lila's," said Sherry.

My ears perked up. I had planned to head home for a quiet night on the couch with a T-bag, a six-pack and a couple of videos. Seeing Lila sounded much better.

"What do you say, Michael?" asked Sal.

"I'll race you over there."

•

"That's quite a scheme you had going there, Sal."

Lila spoke with detached amusement, having just gotten the scoop on the scene at the Dreamboat Lounge. It had been recounted to her in excited bursts from Sal, Sherry and Jasmine. I was keeping quiet myself, pacing around and taking in Lila's paintings. She was finished with John Bonham and Keith Moon and had already started a pair of new pieces, Duane Allman and Ronnie Van Zant.

"My southern rock series," said Lila.

Judging by her happy, warm expression, I could tell she was glad we came by. I could also tell she was high. I told myself it was no big deal, but as I walked around I began to feel uneasy. She had broken her promise, not that I could blame her.

"Sit down, Michael," said Lila. "Relax."

"I am relaxed," I insisted.

"Here." Sal handed me a beer. I twisted off the top and took a swig before sinking into one of the beanbag chairs. Sal rolled a joint and Lila put on some Lynyrd Skynyrd.

"Can't go wrong with Skynyrd," said Sal.

"Free Bird!" Sherry exclaimed, holding up her lighter.

"Fuckin' A!" said Sal, raising his own lighter.

Jasmine watched them carrying on, amused.

As the music played, I started to loosen up too. We smoked and drank and laughed a lot discussing the scene with Martinelli. Later, I caught Lila alone by the icebox while Sal, Sherry and Jasmine were spread out by the stereo, drunk and oblivious.

"So how you feeling?" I asked.

"Good," she nodded.

"Yeah?" I looked at her hard.

"Why ask if you already know?"

"You promised you wouldn't fix by yourself."

"I tried to call you," Lila said. "You weren't around. What else was I supposed to do?"

"You could've waited."

"Waited? Come on, Michael. I don't need to hear that, not from you of all people."

"I just want you to be careful." I cast a wary glance over my shoulder as I took her hand, flipping it over to see the inside of her elbow. "Good job. Nice and clean."

"I'm glad you approve," Lila said, taking her hand back. "But I also need you to understand, like I always did."

•

The next morning, we were once again parked on the couch, passing a bowl back and forth.

"Hey, man…is it me, or did you notice something kinda funny about Lila last night?" asked Sal.

"Like what?"

"I don't know. Something seemed off with her."

"She was just in her painting zone," I said. "You know how it is with artists."

"Maybe," said Sal. He was about to say something else when some pounding at the door made us both jump.

"Jesus!" yelled Sal.

"Fucking Dante," I groaned.

"Open up, you pussies!" Dante shouted through the door. He kept pounding until Sal got up to open it.

"Who's up for some tacos?" said Dante as he breezed in.

"It's ten o'clock in the morning," I said.

"But it's noon somewhere in the world," said Sal. He fanned his hand in front of his nose, raising his eyebrows at the strong smell of alcohol emanating from Dante.

"Look who's talking, potheads," said Dante. "C'mon. I know you're hungry." He fanned his own hand through the haze of smoke hovering around us.

"Just sit down for a minute while I get ready." Sal went back to his seat and fired up the bowl again.

"You hungry?" Dante looked at me.

"I got some errands to run."

"So I hear you hooked up with Mark again."

"Yeah," I nodded. "We'll see how it goes. I'll probably have a little something for you next week."

"You don't have to do that," said Dante. "I told you that before, when I paid off my car."

"I want to," I said. "It's the least I can do."

"Forget it," he said. "Once is enough. I mean it."

Dante was stubborn and proud and I knew that, but my guilt about Lila had me looking for ways to somehow do him right. He needed the help and I could give it to him. I should've just kept my mouth shut and handed him the money when I had it. The argument would've been much easier if I was already holding a wad of bills.

"Michael?" Sal asked, holding out the bowl for me.

"I'm good," I said. "I gotta go."

"That's cool," Sal nodded before continuing like I hadn't said anything. "So, you think something's going on with Lila?"

"What do you mean?" Dante turned to him.

"She seemed different last night," said Sal.

I wanted to somehow change the subject but I didn't want to put my foot in my mouth. I just sat there, tense and paranoid.

"When did you see her?" asked Dante.

"Last night, around ten o'clock," said Sal.

"I stopped by there earlier on the way to work and she seemed fine to me. She was in a good mood, that's all. Actually, she was in a good mood when I got there," he grinned. "She was in a better mood when I left."

I'll bet she was, I thought, fighting back a surge of jealousy.

"Fuckin' A," said Sal. "That explains it."

"You guys ready?" Dante pushed himself to his feet.

"Fuck it." Sal stood up and struck a commanding pose. "I love the smell of chorizo in the morning."

They both looked at me.

"Not today," I said.

"Suit yourself." Dante tossed his keys to Sal. "You're driving."

•

"You won't be sorry," said Paul.

"I hope not."

I couldn't believe all the paperwork involved. I hadn't signed my name so many times since I took the Iowa Tests of Basic Skills back at John Mills Elementary School. Account documents and tax forms and power of attorney this and release of liability that, and over and over again the statement that "past performance is no guarantee of future results."

"We have to tell you that," said Paul.

"Jesus," I said as I signed another form. "Let me ask you something. With all this red tape, how do I get paid?"

"Simple," said Paul. "After you make a sale, you call the office and they'll cut you a check."

"And when do I do that?"

"I'll let you know. First, we gotta get you into a winner. Something poised to really move."

"You're the expert."

"I've got just the ticket." Paul smiled.

By the time we were done, it was after noon. Paul fixed me a drink and told me about the stock he had in mind, a hot IPO.

"That's an Initial Public Offering," he explained. "Shares are extremely limited and usually reserved for my biggest clients."

"The rich get richer."

"It takes money to make money. But I'm making an exception for you since we're just getting started."

"How big of you," I said. "So what do they do, the company selling these shares? Did they find a cure for cancer?"

"Not quite," Paul laughed. "Much as I like you, Michael, the company that finds a cure for cancer will be just for me, if I can even get a piece. Fuck my clients."

"Nice." I wasn't surprised. "So what about this company?"

"They're an Internet stock. Petshop dot com."

I gave him a blank stare.

"They're gonna sell pet stuff over the Internet. You know, dog food and leashes and other accessories." He could tell I seemed dubious. "It sounds a little hokey, I know, but people love their pets. The stock is gonna skyrocket. Trust me."

What the hell did I know anyway?

"Like I said," I finished my drink and set it on his desk as I stood up, "you're the expert."

"It's gonna be a slam dunk." Paul slapped me on the back. "You'll see. Just keep your eye on the business page. It's gonna hit the market on Monday."

•

"Frances Lira Novosel," I said to the receptionist.

"Do you have an appointment?" she asked.

"No."

"And you are?"

"Michael Lira," I said. "Her brother."

"Please take a seat." She pointed to a cozy little waiting area that looked like a study carved out of some mansion on the North Shore. I picked up a *Wall Street Journal* and sat down on one of the leather armchairs. Just as I was about to dig into the shrill editorial on the Clinton scandal, Fran appeared.

"Jesus, are they really gonna impeach him?" I asked.

"They certainly should," she said with typical indignation. "But you didn't come down here to discuss politics, did you?"

"Of course not." I set the paper down. "I just happened to be in the neighborhood, so I thought I'd drop by for a little chat."

"Follow me," said Fran. She turned and led me down a warmly lit corridor to her own plush office with its view of Lake Michigan.

"Nice," I said, taking a look around. A group of framed photos of Theo sat on a wooden credenza opposite her desk. I picked up the one in the center, his school photo for that year. Fran must have forgotten to log the occasion in her daily planner because his hair was longer than usual.

"That's a great picture," I said.

"What's up, Michael?"

"I'll tell you what's up." I got right to the point. "I'd like to know why the fuck you wound me up about Mom and her meds."

"What are you talking about?" asked Fran. "You saw her at the party. I just told you what she told me."

"I knew you would say that."

"Then why are you busting my chops?"

"Forget it." I suddenly realized I was wasting my time.

"What are you doing down here anyway?" she asked. "Since when are you just 'in the neighborhood'?"

"I had some business with your ex," I said.

"Paul?" Fran's face twisted with a noticeable mix of curiosity and revulsion. "Like what?" Then she raised her hands. "Never mind. Don't tell me. I don't want to know."

"It's nothing like that," I said. "Not today anyway."

"I didn't even realize you two were still in touch. What's he doing these days? Is he married?"

"Not even close. He's the same as ever, still trading, making money hand over fist."

"I can just imagine," she said. "He's also probably breaking every law in the book."

"What difference does it make?" I asked. "With all the crooked shit going on? Tell me some of the partners around here don't bend the rules whenever it suits them."

"Think what you want, Michael. I'm just saying…" Fran looked me right in the eye. "Don't give him any money."

CHAPTER NINETEEN

"I can't believe you gave Paul five grand," Sal marveled for a moment before firing up the joint he was holding.

We were in my car a couple of nights later, driving over to Spoonful. Sal had been playing house with Sherry since Friday so we were just catching up. I had told him about the deal with Paul as well as Fran's ominous warning.

"I didn't *give* him five grand," I said as he handed the joint over. "He's just managing my investments."

"Fuckin' A," said Sal. "You sound like a real big shot. But I still don't see why you couldn't just give your money to Fran. Seems a lot less risky to me."

"You're joking, right? How about the fact that she's a royal pain in the balls? Besides, Fran works at a hedge fund."

"I don't even know what that means."

"It means they only deal with rich people."

"Like a high-stakes card game."

"Something like that," I said. "Only they always win."

"Of course they do." Sal got it. "The rich get richer. Well, fuck Fran. What does she know anyway?"

We turned the corner and went to the end of the block where we could usually find a spot. No luck. As we doubled back, Sal noticed the line of people gathered outside the door.

"Jesus," he said. "What the fuck is going on?"

I stopped and stared at the crowd for a moment. I didn't recognize a soul. Then I remembered.

"It's that time of year again."

Though there were some blues acts in the regular rotation, Spoonful had evolved into more of an all-purpose rock club than a straight Chicago blues bar, but once a year Danny worked his mojo and personally booked a week of top-shelf blues acts as a tribute to the venue's roots. The event was called the "Holiday Blues." Starting the first Sunday in December, the place would be invaded by yuppies and old-timers and everyone else but the usual suspects for seven days straight. Sometimes, big-name musicians passing through town on tour would come by to check it out. Steven Tyler and Joe Perry joined some old blues men for a couple of songs the year before. The year before that, Robert Plant dropped in, although he didn't play.

"Fuck," said Sal. "I forgot all about this."

"Me too," I said, knowing we had enough pull to get in if we really wanted. Dante, Lila and Sherry were supposed to meet us there, but that plan was hatched before we knew the place would be packed. I hated crowds. "Do you see them?"

"No." Sal scanned the line. "They must have gone in without us. What time is it?"

I glanced at my watch. "Ten o'clock."

"Fuck this," said Sal. "Let's head down to Tuman's. We can give them a call from there."

Tuman's Alcohol Abuse Center was the dive bar all dive bars would aspire to be, if they had any aspirations at all. For us, it was the place to go when we wanted cheap drinks and a change of scenery. We went over there for a couple of beers and made a half-assed attempt to reach someone at Spoonful. Sal was able to get Dana on the phone but there was so much noise in the background, he had to literally scream into the receiver. He thought he heard her tell him to hold on a minute. When she set the phone down, someone hung it up.

"Fuck it," said Sal. "We tried."

I was bummed out I wouldn't be seeing Lila but I decided to make the best of it.

"Two Crowns," I told the bartender. "Make 'em doubles."

"We're drinking whiskey tonight?" asked Sal.

"Might as well."

Sal and I started washing down double shots of Crown Royal with pints of Bass. Three hours later, we ran into our long-lost buddy Kenny. A wild guy with a macho edge, he was an auto mechanic by day and barfly by night. Kenny also had a wicked habit of freebasing cocaine into the wee hours. We had heard all kinds of crazy stories about why he hadn't been around.

"I thought you were in jail," said Sal.

"Fuck no," said Kenny. "I went to rehab. Court ordered."

"Good thing you're back out here abusing alcohol." I gestured to the drink in his hand.

"Stoli rocks?" asked Sal.

"Nothing but," said Kenny. "You guys wouldn't happen to be holdin' any blow, would you?"

"Funny," Sal grinned. "I was about to ask you the same thing."

And just like that, we were off on a three day coke bender. The party started with a couple chicks Kenny knew but they soon fled the scene. Before long, we were holed up at Kenny's ex-wife's place, a rundown frame house in the southwest corner of Ukrainian Village. She had just been sent to Dwight Prison for doctor shopping and multiple counts of prescription forgery. Kenny figured he only had another month or two before the bank evicted him.

"What are you doing back here anyway?" asked Sal. "I thought you guys split up a while ago."

"We did," said Kenny. "But I had nowhere else to go after rehab. Besides, she was already gone when I got here."

And that worked out great for us. After each score, Sal and I would snort some powder while Kenny cooked the rest into freebase. We would smoke it up and start over again, all the while slugging vodka, jamming music and talking shit about everything from cult movies to muscle cars to who had the best tits in porn.

"Cristy Canyon," Sal insisted. "Hands down."

"Jenna Jameson's my pick," said Kenny.

"Her tits aren't even real!"

"What do I care?"

"Who do you like, Michael?" asked Sal.

I liked Cristy Canyon too but I refused to get involved. By that point, I was sick of the relentless cocaine chatter and wasn't about to contribute my two cents just because I had it. I was also sick of doing blow, not that I could stop myself. Kenny had a house connection less than a block away. It was just too easy to keep running over there. I never went with him but Sal did. I asked him what the people were like.

"Imagine a Puerto Rican version of Aaron and T and them," he said. "Only a lot less patient."

Evidently, all the money they had made from our binge was not enough to compensate for dealing with Kenny coming back to score every few hours always vowing, "This is the last time!"

By early Wednesday, we were finally done. I went down last, around four in the morning. Six hours later, my eyes snapped open to the sound of the front door opening and closing not far from where I sacked out on the floor. Then I smelled the coffee. I turned over and saw Kenny seated in the armchair with a piping hot mug of brew in one hand and a folded *Chicago Tribune* in the other. He looked so calm, so…domestic, it was hard for me to reconcile this guy with the one I had just witnessed smoking rock for days on end.

"I got a whole pot in the kitchen." Kenny lifted his mug.

"You gotta be fucking kidding." I rubbed my eyes and sat up. "You actually *made* coffee?"

"Beats paying a dollar a cup at Dunkin' Donuts," he shrugged.

Of course it does, I thought. Who has a dollar for a cup of coffee when you need every penny for blow?

"And what's with the newspaper?"

"My ex forgot to cancel the subscription."

I glanced around, surveying the scene. Sal was still out on the sofa. The table in front of him was covered with empty beer cans and bottles and ashtrays stuffed with cigarette butts and spent glass pipes. The floor around me was strewn with empty CD cases, most with the artwork lying nearby or missing, having been torn out for the lyrics or some freaky image that we just had to see up close. A couple of pizza boxes were piled in the corner.

"Jesus," I muttered.

"You're telling me," said Kenny. "I'm thinking of checking myself back into rehab."

"Check me in while you're at it," I said. "Any weed left?"

"I think there are a few buds over there," Kenny gestured to a small wood tray on the table. I packed a bowl and roasted up before getting myself a cup of coffee.

"Holy shit!" said Kenny as I came out to join him. He was leaning forward, glued to the inside of the Tempo Section.

"What?" His excitement was starting to freak me out.

"You'll never believe who was at Spoonful the other day."

"Elvis," said Sal as he came to life.

"Close," said Kenny.

"I should hope so," he said. "The way you're carrying on. What time is it anyway?"

"Ten o'clock," I said.

"Fucking Keith Richards!" said Kenny. A huge Stones fan, he was beside himself with so much emotion I could almost picture him as a little kid on Christmas morning.

"No way!" Sal sat up.

"I'm telling you..." Kenny began to scan the article, reading choice passages aloud. "Late Sunday night, blues fans got a real treat when British rocker Keith Richards paid a visit to the "Holiday Bluesfest" at Spoonful..."

"It's Holiday Blues," Sal cut him off. "Not Blues*fest*."

"Figures. Newspapers always get shit wrong," said Kenny. He continued reading. "Richards took the stage with Chicago favorite Melvin Taylor and the Slack Band. The pair rocked and rolled through a medley of classics including 'Not Fade Away' and 'Voodoo Chile.' Afterward, Richards chatted with fans before leaving with an original painting he purchased from local artist Lila Davenport."

"What?" I grabbed the paper from him.

"Isn't that Dante's girlfriend?" asked Kenny.

"Fuckin' A!" said Sal. "What else does it say?"

I quickly skimmed the page. "That's it about Lila."

"I wonder if it was Brian Jones," said Sal.

"What about him?" asked Kenny.

"Nothing," said Sal, yawning. "Got any cream?"

•

"That must be from the other night," said Sal.

After unsuccessfully trying to reach Sherry or Lila, we were back outside our apartment, looking at a note that was folded up and stuck in the door jamb. It read: "Where are you guys?!"

"Is that Sherry's handwriting?" I asked.

"Maybe. I'm not sure what her writing looks like."

"Well, we tried to call." I unlocked the door and pushed it open. We went inside and Sal hit the button on the answering machine. The tape started to rewind.

"Fuck," he said, noting how long it was taking. "It's like we just stepped out of a time machine."

I nodded and waited while the tape started to play the messages from Sunday night. Sure enough, Sherry had called several times.

"Where the fuck are you?" she said on her final message. Sherry had to be really pissed off to swear like that.

Dante joined the effort with a drunken tirade about our "fucking junkie asses." Lila left the last message of the night.

"You guys will *not* believe what just happened!" she said.

The next message came from my mom early the following day.

"What's this I hear about you giving money to Paul Wills?"

"That didn't take long," said Sal.

I shook my head, still listening. We got a few more messages from Sherry and Lila. Neither sounded angry anymore.

"Just let us know you're okay," said Lila.

Frat Row had called twice.

"We're hurtin' up here, dude!" said Mark. "Call me."

Then I heard Paul's voice.

"You shady motherfucker!" his voice boomed. "I hope you're watching the stock 'cause it's a hell of a ride so far!"

"You gotta like the sound of that," said Sal.

"Fuck!" I had totally forgotten about the IPO.

I bolted out the door and around the building to where the mail slots were located. One of the guys upstairs left for work before the newspapers arrived so I grabbed his Tribune, ran back to our place and collapsed on the couch out of breath. Sal sat down next to me and tore out the business section.

"What's the symbol?" he asked.

"Hold on." I reached for my wallet. I flipped it open and pulled out a slip of paper with the symbol and the share price I had paid: $13.50. "It's on the NASDAQ."

Sal took the slip and scanned the page. "Holy shit!"

"What?" I couldn't tell if the news was good or bad.

"It closed at twenty-two even yesterday," said Sal.

He set the paper down and I snatched it up.

"So what's it worth now?" I wondered out loud.

"Depends on what happens today. Maybe you should call your broker." Sal snorted. "I can't believe I just said that."

"Me neither." I laughed, giddy at the prospect of my big payoff. I quickly got Paul on the phone. He told me the deal and said he had another hot tip if I was interested. He also said that he needed me to come by, meaning he wanted me to bring over some blow.

"Will do," I told him as I hung up.

"So?" Sal looked at me expectantly.

"It's at twenty-five and leveling off," I said. "Paul's gonna watch it for the first hour tomorrow and dump it if there isn't any significant movement. Not bad, huh?"

"Fuckin' A!" said Sal. "Where do I sign up?"

"Get some money together."

"I just might," he said. "But before I become a business tycoon, I'm gonna try Sherry again."

I sat down, still shocked from my good fortune.

"Wow," said Sal after he hung up. "It certainly is a banner day for those of us who have their shit together."

"What are you talking about?"

"That painting Lila sold to Keith Richards?"

"It was Brian Jones, wasn't it?"

"Yeah. And she got ten grand for it!"

"Fuck!" And I thought I was doing well.

"On top of that," he went on, "Jim, Jimi and Janis sold just yesterday. Twenty-five grand for all three!"

"No fucking way!" I was incredulous. "To who? Mick?"

"No," said Sal. "Just some rich guy. You know, probably some art scenester padding his collection."

"That figures."

"Anyway," he said, "I guess Lila already got calls from a couple galleries and an agent. She quit Anything Goes. Sherry's bummed about that but at least Dante will be happy."

"No shit?" Dante wasn't the only one. "Good for her."

"Definitely. Good for her," said Sal, though he sounded a little off. "So what's up for today?"

"I'm gonna give Mark a quick call back. After that, you want to grab a sandwich at Leo's?"

•

Sal wasn't hungry. He said he had some driving to do but I could tell by his grim expression something was eating him. We were both crashing hard after doing all that blow with Kenny but I knew it was more than that. Kicking dope had proved to be a good move for me. Sal wasn't seeing the same kind of payoff. I would've bet money he was on his way to see Janet and get high.

Sal's gonna do what Sal's gonna do, I told myself.

Besides, I had a busy day ahead of me. Having blown all the money I made from the last deal on our binge with Kenny, I had to dip into my savings just to cover the blow for Paul and Frat Row. I ran out to EP for some cash, my mind racing the whole way. Things were really looking up for me. By the time I got to the bank, I had decided to stake another ten grand on Paul's latest hot tip.

Fuck it. I still had three in the box.

I made a stop on the West Side, catching Aaron on the way out the door to his girlfriend's place. With the weather getting colder, the narcs were laying off the block and that made the deals a lot easier. We didn't have to go out to the projects. I could come back and pick up what I needed right there.

"No problem," he said. "Holler at me tomorrow."

Aaron took off and I went inside for some T-bags.

"Sal been out here today?" I asked T.

"Nope," she said with a puzzled look. "Why you asking me? I thought y'all stayed in the same place."

Before I could reply, Maurice walked in from the bathroom.

"I know why he asking," he said with a warm, relaxed smile. I could tell by the way he stopped to stretch and scratch his back the lucky bastard had just gotten high. "Don't worry, Michael. Sal still holding up, as far as *we* know."

•

It was dark when I pulled up in front of our place. Sal was gone, either driving or hooking up with Sherry or some other chick. I wasn't worried about him anymore, just as I was no longer basking in my good fortune with the market. I was raw from the session with Kenny and anxious about how deep I was getting in with Paul. On top of that, the news about Lila and her paintings started doing a number on my head. What if she became some famous artist? Would she have to move to New York or LA? Everything would change.

I got so worked up thinking about shit I almost headed back to the West Side. Having just seen Maurice flush with narcotic bliss, I knew they had what I needed to chase away these feelings. Shaking off the urge, I decided to drop by Lila's instead. I figured there was a good chance she was there, painting.

Walking up to her place, I could hear Patti Smith playing loudly inside. I rapped on the door and waited. Her car was parked on the street in front so I knew she must be home. I knocked on the door again, louder this time.

"Hello!" I shouted, somewhat self-conscious. I had met a handful of Lila's neighbors and I didn't want to disturb them. I'm sure they got their fill with Dante. I began to feel uneasy, my mind racing again. Maybe she was sleeping or taking a bath. Maybe she nodded off. And then, thinking of her newfound success, I was hit with the twisted possibility she might be dead of an overdose.

It would be all my fault.

I got close to the door and was about to yell her name when something shiny on the threshold caught my eye. Crouching down for a closer look, my heart leapt into my throat.

A round red splotch.

CHAPTER TWENTY

A normal person might have sprung into action thinking foul play was involved. I sprang into action thinking heroin was involved. If there was one thing I didn't miss about getting high, it was the blood. I'm not talking about the tiny red cloud in the cylinder, the one telling every dopefiend, "Help isn't on the way; it's here!" I'm talking about the drops and the streaks and the stains on your hands and your clothes and the floor or couch where you're fixing. Because no matter how careful or experienced or weathered you might be, sticking yourself with a needle day in and day out involves blood. If it's not yours, then it's somebody else's. Some people bleed more than others but everyone bleeds a little. After a while you get used to seeing it. I know I did.

Even so, when I glimpsed that crimson drop outside Lila's place, I completely freaked out. If Lila stuck herself badly, she could be inside nodding off while her life bled clean out of her. Without a second to lose, I stood up and kicked in the door, just like I did the night Sal and I broke into our girl's luxury condo.

"What the fuck, Michael?" shouted Lila. She was standing in front of a six-by-four foot canvas wedged into a large easel. She had a paintbrush in one hand and a cigarette in the other. A trail of red splotches led from the door straight to her.

I pointed to the floor. "I got spooked. Why didn't you answer?"

"Because I was working!" She glanced down for a second. "That's paint. What the hell did you think it was? Blood?"

"Never mind." I felt like an idiot.

"You thought someone broke in and stabbed me?" Lila laid the brush down and walked over to inspect the damage. "Jesus, Michael.

You scared the shit out of me."

"What's with the paint on the floor?" I asked.

"Forget that," she snapped. "What about my door?"

"I can fix the door."

"I should hope so." She took a closer look at it. "Goddamn it, Michael! I can't even close it now."

"I'm sorry. I'll run out to Home Depot right now."

"That was so fucked up." Lila wasn't even listening.

"I'm going." I turned to leave and felt her hand on my arm.

"Wait," she softened up. "I don't mean to be so..."

"It was a fucked up thing to do, I know," I said. "I thought something might have happened to you."

"Like what?"

"Forget it," I just wanted to move on. "Congratulations, by the way. I heard you quit Anything Goes." As the words came out, I realized how bad that sounded.

"Really?" She looked at me hotly. "Did you also hear that..."

"I'm sorry, Lila," I cut her off. "I didn't mean it that way."

"I hope not," she said, calming down. "Because a lot of great things have been happening."

"I read about Brian Jones. And you sold Jim, Jimi and Janis too? I'll miss those guys."

"Me too. But at least I got a show out of the deal," she said with a curious lack of enthusiasm.

"A show?"

"On New Year's Eve. Will you go?"

"Of course," I assured her. "We all will."

"I have to do four more pieces by then. That's why I quit. It's going to take everything I've got just to finish on time."

"You can do it."

"I hope you're right." Lila gave me a kiss on the cheek. "So what happened to you guys the other night?"

"You don't want to know."

"No?" She raised her eyebrows.

"We ran into Kenny. One thing led to another."

"I can just imagine."

"The real question is...how was it meeting Keith?"

"It was cool. He was really friendly. Funny too. He loved my paintings."

"I'll say. Ten grand?"

"He made the offer. I told him to pay what he felt was right. "

"That was a good way to play it."

"I thought so," she agreed. "Fuck, I would've given it to him just for all the exposure, not to mention...he's Keith. I've been thinking about painting *him*."

"Did you get a chance to hang out? You know, party?"

"Hell yeah, we got high in his limo. I wanted to blow him but he couldn't get it up." She was clearly fucking with me.

"That's not what I meant," I said, though something like that had definitely crossed my mind.

"We had a drink. It was hard to talk with everyone around. The place was a total zoo."

"I'm sure," I said. "How was Dante?"

"Fine. He wasn't that drunk yet."

"That's cool," I nodded. It was nice catching up but I wanted more than anything to get close to her. I wanted to touch her, to feel her, to know that we were still okay, but I didn't make a move. The vaguely distant look in her eyes warned me not to even try. I had never made Lila turn me down and I wasn't about to start.

"So...ah," Lila looked at me expectantly. "The door?"

"Of course."

I turned to survey the shards of wood around the broken lock. It would take some fixing but I could do it.

"No problem. I just gotta run out for a couple things."

I double-checked the make of the lock and started out the door when Lila grabbed my arm again.

"Michael?"

•

Lila wanted me to score for her. Lightning had struck and she needed a little something now more than ever. I understood all too well. Whether you're celebrating the good times or lamenting the bad, dope always helps. So after picking up my tools and running over to my former employer for a new lock and a length of jamb stock, I headed back out west. Janet had just finished up with a new package and I was able to get in and out. When I got back to Lila's, she took the bags and went into the bathroom by herself while I got to work. She came out fifteen minutes later, a new woman.

"You want something to drink?" she asked.

"You got a beer?"

Lila brought me a longneck and left me to it. "I'm taking a break, if you need me," she said.

A couple hours later, the job was done. I closed the door and walked back inside, hopeful. I had been kicking around this "handyman gets lucky" scenario ever since Lila got so angry about the door in the first place. She was back in the corner, laid out on the bed, eyes closed, her breathing heavy and slow. Sleeping or nodding—I couldn't tell which—she looked so peaceful and relaxed.

Tonight's not the night, I told myself.

What a bummer. I pulled the blanket up over her shoulders and kissed the top of her head. Her hair smelled like shampoo laced with turpentine. On the way out, I stopped to check out her latest work. The canvas was streaked with bright reds and yellows and oranges swirled together in a fiery vortex. A magazine clipping sat next to her brushes and palette on a small workbench nearby. I picked it up and there was Richard Nixon boarding a plane, arms spread wide, hands flashing "V" for victory.

"Nixon goes to hell," Lila murmured from the bed.

"Excuse me?" I jerked, startled.

"That'll be the name of the piece," she said in a barely audible voice. She cocked her head in my direction and reached under her shirt to scratch her chest. "He's my first dead president."

"Who's gonna be your second?"

"I don't know." Lila's voice trailed off. "Kennedy maybe."

"Cool." Going to heaven? I didn't ask. I was just glad that she wasn't out cold. Maybe tonight was the night after all.

"Thanks for hooking me up," Lila said with a yawn. "And for fixing the door too."

"That was my fault."

"You were just trying to save me." She smiled and closed her eyes and I could hear her breathing again.

No luck for the handyman after all.

I walked back over to the bed and kissed her on the forehead, feeling the warmth of her body. She'd be fine by herself. I took the extra key and locked the door on my way out.

•

"The Next Big Thing?" Sal scoffed.

He was looking at an invitation to the group show Lila was doing on New Year's Eve. She was one of several promising local artists being featured at the grand opening of some gallery on a newly gentrified stretch of Damen Avenue in north Bucktown. I hadn't seen Sal in a few days and he was in a foul mood.

"Lila didn't come up with that name," I said.

"I should hope not."

"What's your problem?"

"No problem," Sal bristled. "I'm just saying, The Next Big Thing? Sounds kind of…I don't know, corporate. Sounds like the slogan for a new line of distressed jeans or gym shoes. You know, something for all the fuckheads taking over."

"They are the ones buying stuff."

"Don't remind me." muttered Sal.

"Are you all right? You seem a little twisted."

"I'm fine," he said. "I'm just worn out. What with Christmas right around the corner and all these assholes out and about, scurrying to and fro, buying all this useless shit for their ungrateful families."

"Well, Scrooge," I said, "Do you think you can set aside your pain and suffering long enough to support Lila?"

"I'm shocked and positively crushed that you would even have to ask," Sal said, reverting back to his usual manner.

"I'll take that as a 'yes.'"

"What else are we gonna do on New Year's Eve? Fucking amateur night? Wouldn't miss it!"

"Good, because I'll need help with Dante."

Sal examined the invitation.

"Uh-oh," he said. "Open bar."

•

"Open up, you pussies!" Dante yelled through the door.

I first heard the pounding in my dream. Sal and me and my old girlfriend Tina and some other people I didn't know were outside this abandoned roadhouse—sort of like Spoonful in a ghost town. They were slamming dope and I was trying to kick in the door. Like those dreams where you punch someone in the face but your fist moves in slow motion or you're running and you don't get anywhere, my efforts were useless and incredibly frustrating. The door wouldn't budge but I could still hear one loud thud after another. When Dante started yelling, I finally woke up on the couch, bone tired.

After hooking up with Frat Row the day before, Sal and I pulled another all-nighter with Kenny. As soon as the sun came up, we covered the windows with blankets and towels and kept going until well past noon when we ran out of blow. Then we came home and crashed. Barely three hours had passed and I felt like shit. I could have easily slept the day away.

"What the fuck?" I grumbled and opened the door to let Dante in as a draft of freezing cold air swept over me.

"What the fuck yourself?" he said. "I've been out there for almost ten minutes. I thought you guys were dead."

Sal stumbled out of the bedroom. "Goddamn it, Dante!"

"Don't you start!" Dante growled at him and went into the kitchen for a beer. "Let's get something to eat."

"I'm not hungry," said Sal. "And I'm broke."

"I'm buying," said Dante.

"Thanks anyway," said Sal as he headed back into the bedroom. "Some other time."

"You're not getting a rain check," Dante called after him. He turned to me with an expectant look.

"Isn't it a little early?" I gestured to the beer in his hand.

"I don't have to be at work for another seven hours. Are you coming with me or what?"

"Let me brush my teeth."

•

"Two High Lifes and two bowls." I started to slip Dana a twenty when I felt one of Dante's meat hooks around my arm.

"I said I'm buying." He let go to reach for his wallet. "Make it one bowl," he called over his shoulder to Dana. "And a shot of Jack."

"Oh yeah?" She looked at the clock and looked back at Dante. "You're never gonna make it."

"Don't worry about me," said Dante. "I'm going to work."

"Whatever you say." Dana shook her head.

"I say bring me the fuckin' shot."

Dana turned and filled the order without a word. I didn't know what was up with Dante. He was a fuck-up and a bust-out and a bad drunk, but doing shots before work was still unusual.

"What's going on?" I asked him.

"Lila's cheating on me."

"What? No way?" I swallowed hard. "How do you know?"

"I can just..." Dante clammed up, glaring at Dana who had just come back with our order.

"Fuckin' dyke," he said as she walked away. "You just know she'd love to get her hands on Lila."

"I think you need to calm down."

"I am calm," said Dante. "I'm just saying. You know she wants to get with Lila. Who doesn't? I don't even care. I mean, I care, but what the fuck can I do about it? Lila's hot. I know she could have whoever she wants. I've always known that. It's not like I thought we'd get married. I'm just sad. I see things changing for her. She's gonna make it. She's gonna do all right. And you," he turned to me. "With your stocks and shit..."

"That's nothing," I interrupted him. "I don't even have a job."

"Fuck that," said Dante. "You know what job stands for?"

I had no idea but I knew he was going to tell me.

"Just over broke," he said emphatically.

"I never heard that one."

"Believe me, I know..." Dante gulped down some beer. "Because that's exactly where I'm at. Why bust your ass working for some needle-dick when you can just sit back and get paid?"

I remembered my asshole boss from Home Depot.

"I read the papers. I know what's going on. Everyone's making money in the market. Why shouldn't you?"

"Look at it this way," I said half-heartedly. "At least you don't have to worry about losing your ass."

"Whatever. It's something. Something better. You got an angle. You got a chance. I *had* a chance back in the day and I blew it. Even Sal... sure, he's just a cabbie, but you never know with him. One of these days he's gonna be driving some big shot around and he'll end up on a billboard in his underwear."

"What the fuck are you talking about?" I knew where Dante was coming from but I didn't want to admit it.

Dante downed his shot with a grimace and waved the empty glass in Dana's direction.

"Gimme your keys," she said.

"Fuck you."

"That's it. Get him outta here." Dana said to me.

"I'm driving, Dana," I lied. "I promise."

"I don't care. He goes."

"Dana, please," said Dante, looking contrite. "I'm sorry."

Dana looked him over with a combination of pity and disapproval before taking his glass.

"No more bullshit," she said.

"I promise," he said. "No more bullshit."

She walked away and I turned to him.

"Everything will be all right."

"Right," he nodded and sipped his beer.

Dana came back with the second of many rounds and even though he got shit-faced, Dante behaved relatively well. We went back and forth about Lila and football and life. Dante knew things were a mess for him, and he knew I did too, but he still let me tell him all the happy horseshit you tell somebody whose life is going down the drain. Maybe I was wasting my breath but it felt better that way. Three hours, a couple bowls of chili and I don't know how many drinks later and we had both finally had enough.

"Should I call you guys a cab?" asked Dana.

"Yeah," said Dante. "Sal can drive us home!"

We all had a good laugh at that one.

"I'll be okay," I told Dana. "It's only a few blocks."

I drove us back to my place in Dante's car. He was almost out by the time we got there. Sal was gone so I had to drag him inside all by myself. With a few hours to go before work, I left him on the bed to sleep it off as much as he could.

"Wake me up," he slurred.

Hearing his voice, I knew there was no way that he would get up and drive himself to work.

"Can't you just call in?"

"Too late for that. Just wake me up."

"Fine," I said, closing the door behind me.

"Hey, Michael," he called out. "Thanks a lot."

CHAPTER TWENTY-ONE

"Do you realize there are only five more shopping days until Christmas?" asked Sal. He had just donned a red Santa hat on his way out for a double shift in the cab.

"I didn't realize you cared."

"I don't," he said, "but I get the countdown from every other asshole I pick up."

"Well, what do you expect with that hat?"

"Better tips?" Sal walked out the door.

I don't know how he did it. We had been up all night with Kenny again after spending a chunk of the day drinking with Dante in what was starting to become a routine. Whether he was giving up or just bored, Dante had become a real pain in the ass. The fact that Lila was always painting or getting high definitely didn't help matters.

"It's like she's not even there," Dante said one day.

"It's all about the show," I told him.

And it pretty much was, though I still managed to get lucky every now and then when I scored for her. I couldn't complain. Things with Frat Row had slowed some, but I was flying high with the stocks. After dumping Petshop.com for a tidy profit, Paul had parlayed my earnings along with the additional ten grand I gave him into almost forty grand in holdings. I didn't how he did it and I didn't particularly care. All I knew was that I owned several stocks in companies and industries that I barely understood.

"What do they make?" I asked.

"Money," Paul said with his obnoxious cackle.

I wasn't the only one rolling either. Santa Claus came early to T's house. Mookie had gotten a full ride to Michigan State and T got some help securing a mortgage through the recruiter.

"We moving to Oak Park," she said proudly.

I couldn't believe it. Sal was unfazed.

"All the big schools make deals like that," he said. "You can't have your star running back going home to some shithole where he might get smoked while he's out with the homeys."

I was a little envious myself. Mookie was a blessing and T certainly deserved some credit for doing what she could to keep him on the straight and narrow, but they could not have done it without all my running around.

"Buy your own place," said Sal.

Even though I got over on him with Lila, Sal could practically read my mind at times.

"How hard could it be?" he went on. "Throw some money down. It's not like you got bad credit."

"I got no credit," I said.

"So what? You're a handyman. You're old-school. You get paid in cash," said Sal. "Talk to Stella. She must know some shady Polack who could set you up. How else do you think all these guys right off the boat get started?"

"I never thought of that."

The wheels started turning in my head. I knew I needed to make a move, a real one. All my deals had served me well and Paul had done me right with the stocks, but I needed something more solid. I needed something to actually do. I could buy an old place and fix it up. I could live there or sell it. If I moved quickly, I could spend the rest of the winter rehabbing and flip it in the spring for a quick profit. There were places all around our neighborhood, small frame houses and rundown brick two-flats. The Mexicans and other immigrants were selling, looking to cash in and move on before whitey completely took over. If that wasn't enough to push them out, the increased property taxes would soon do the trick. The more I considered the idea, the more it seemed like the perfect move for me.

Two days before Christmas, I stumbled across exactly what I was looking for, a frame two-flat on a block that was just good enough to show some promise but still shady enough for me to get a deal. A homemade sign jutting up from the small patch of grass in front read "For Sale by Owner." A phone number was written underneath.

I called the number and spoke to an affable man with a faint Irish brogue. I asked him how much and he told me three hundred thousand. Based on what I'd seen on the For Sale signs all around the area, that was a great price.

"And we don't have to pay any agents," he said.

I liked the sound of that. He said he would meet me out front the next day. His name was Tom Daly. He was a wiry old guy with a bright white mane who loved to talk. He was retired with a full pension from People's Gas where he had worked for thirty-seven years. During that time he amassed a small fortune in rental properties on the North Side in areas like Lakeview and Roscoe Village.

"You know how I did it?" he asked.

I could tell that was a rhetorical question.

"One place at a time!" He laughed heartily.

"So what's the matter with this place?"

"Absolutely nothing," he said. "This is a great place in a great neighborhood. You'll see in five years. You won't even recognize it around here."

"So why sell?"

"Too much opportunity," he said with a wave of his hand. "If I don't get out now, I never will. The wife wants to go to Florida. Imagine that! Florida! What am I gonna do down there?"

"Relax?"

"Bah!" he scoffed. "I'll relax when I'm dead. That's what I told her. She didn't much like it either."

He walked me through each of the two units, both empty since October. He had planned to rehab them himself until his wife put her foot down. The place was perfect, clean with solid mechanicals, wood floors and wood trim. I could rent them out "as is" or clean them up and sell them as condos.

"I already got the new zoning approved," said Tom.

It seemed like a great deal and I was ready to jump, except for the issue of financing. I told Tom I might have trouble getting a mortgage and he offered to carry the note for nine percent if I put fifty thousand down. The rate seemed a little high, but I knew I wouldn't get a loan anywhere else. Not anywhere legitimate.

"I couldn't get a mortgage when I was your age either," he said.

"Fair enough." I extended my hand. We shook and agreed to hash out the details after the holidays. I walked away, stunned by my good fortune. Could it really be so easy?

•

After the deal with Tom, I had some running around to do. In addition to my Christmas Eve trip to the new Target on Elston where I could get gifts for everyone on my list in one fell swoop, I had to get some money together. I called Paul and told him the bad news.

"I need to cash out," I said.

"What? Already?"

I filled him in about the building and he razzed me for my "bourgeois aspirations" before telling me to give him a week to make the sales and get the paperwork together. Assuming no big gains before all that, I still had to get another ten together. I had three in the box and almost two under the mattress but I needed at least five to live on. That still left me ten short.

"Borrow it from Fran," said Sal.

I thought he was kidding at first but the more I thought about it, the less ridiculous the idea seemed. Why not? It's not like I wanted the money to go to the racetrack or play the stock market. I wanted to buy a building, become responsible. I hadn't gotten high in almost two months, not counting the weed or the blow of course. I hated like hell to ask her but I didn't have much choice. My mom didn't have the money. Lila would've loaned it to me but that definitely wouldn't feel right. Even though she was a huge pain in the balls, Fran seemed like my best bet.

I would know soon enough.

After a harried afternoon shopping the next day, Sal and I got stoned and headed out to EP for Christmas Eve at my mom's house. She had gone all out with a pork roast as well as spaghetti with meat sauce. After dinner, Sal helped me orchestrate a charade to fool Theo into thinking that Santa Claus had landed outside.

"I can't believe he forgot his hat," said Theo. He had fished it out of the snow after we all ran outside in response to some bells Sal jingled while Theo and I were wrestling.

"He must have a spare in the sled," said Sal.

We went back inside where my mom had set out gifts from Santa.

"Mom, look!" Theo shouted. "He was really here!"

"That was fast," I said.

"No wonder he lost his hat," said Sal.

The rest of the evening went well. I was on my best behavior and Sal was too. We opened presents and sat around for a while, not saying much while Theo played with his new toys. I had a few extra glasses of wine, fortifying myself to ask Fran for the money. I finally pulled her aside in the kitchen. Much to my surprise, she was totally cool.

"Congratulations," she said. "I'm glad to help."

Ten thousand dollars wasn't a lot of money for Fran but she still could have easily given me a hard time. She did make me promise to close my account with Paul, but that was in the works anyway. I went home feeling good and looking forward to Christmas Day when Sal and I would head up to the Music Box Theatre. With that anxious bit of business out of the way, I was in the mood for some holiday movie magic. And that's exactly what we got at the annual matinee double feature of *A Christmas Carol* and *It's a Wonderful Life*.

"Best thing about Christmas," said Sal. "Movies."

CHAPTER TWENTY-TWO

"Any messages?" I called out from the doorway.

"I was in the shower. Can you close the fucking door before I freeze my balls off?" Sal stepped out of the bathroom with a towel wrapped around his waist. "Sherry?"

"Nope, no calls."

She spoke up from the couch without taking her eyes off her magazine. I glanced at the machine anyway. No blinking light.

"You want a beer?" asked Sal.

"Fuck no. I'm still working here."

I checked my watch. One o'clock in the afternoon. I had just come back from my third trip to the West Side in as many days. It was New Year's Eve and everybody wanted blow. Everybody except Paul, apparently. I hadn't heard from him in over a week, not since I told him I needed to cash out. I knew he might drag his feet when it came to issuing me a check, but I thought for sure he'd call me with an order for the big night. By that time I figured he should have my money, and I could pick it up when I dropped off his blow.

"Take a break," said Sal. "It's New Year's Eve, for Christ's sake. Have Frat Row drive down here."

"They are," I said. "I'm meeting them at the Map Room later."

"I could take care of Candice for you," said Sherry.

"Thanks anyway," I said. "You guys just chill."

I needed to stay busy. Back in the bedroom, I divided up the latest package. An ounce for Frat Row, a half for Kenny, a quarter for Candice and pair of eightballs for Paul, even though I hadn't heard from him. I left a half on the plate and walked out.

"For Kenny," I said, handing his order to Sal. "He should be coming by anytime."

"Excellent." Sal took the bag with a little too much enthusiasm.

"Don't even think about pinching any," I told him. "Like Kenny wouldn't notice? Besides, I left us a nice pile back there."

"Fuckin' A!"

"Just go easy, would you? It's still early."

"I'll keep an eye on him," said Sherry.

"Me?" Sal laughed. "Who's gonna keep an eye on you?"

"Great." I shook my head.

"Lighten up, Francis," said Sal. "And get your shit straight. It's gonna be party time when you get back."

"I thought it was amateur night," I said.

"If you can't beat 'em, join 'em."

•

First stop was the Anything Goes office. I walked in to find Candice pacing back and forth on the phone, trying to coordinate the entertainment for some last-minute parties.

"Suddenly, everybody wants girls on New Year's Eve," she said as she took off her headset.

"I'll bet you miss Lila," I said, thinking how glad I was that Lila wasn't one of the girls being lined up for the evening.

"I'm happy for her." Candice reached into her desk for six hundred dollars in twenties and handed them over to me. "I just hope she can handle it."

"Handle what?" I asked as I counted the cash.

"Well, success can sometimes be harder to deal with than failure. Lila's under a lot of pressure."

The phone rang and she grabbed her headset and got back to work. I almost waited around, but a big part of me didn't want to hear any more Candice had to say. She could probably tell Lila was getting high. It was her business to notice things like that. So what? Lila was painting and getting paid. Maybe the sudden recognition was a little weird, but Lila was smart and tough and she had her shit together. I wasn't especially concerned about Lila's coping skills. Still, Candice's remark did get me thinking. I hadn't seen Lila since earlier that week when she called me in the midst of a painting frenzy. She needed something to chill her out, and I was happy to help. So I scored some dope and brought it over to her place.

•

Lila had finished the Nixon piece along with another one featuring Kennedy waving from the Dallas motorcade.

"Just think," she said, gazing into the picture. "He had only minutes to live."

It was a morbid thought that fit the melancholy blend of blues and grays swirling around the image like the radar view of a thunderstorm being tracked on TV. She was also half finished with another piece of Bobby that had a flatter color scheme.

"He's not a president," she said. "But he's still an icon."

The Kennedys didn't strike me as especially original, though I made sure not to tell her that. We had sex and talked for a while and it felt all right, but I knew she needed some space.

"After Bobby's done, I have to come up with one more by the end of the week." Lila sounded matter-of-fact about her deadline. She was really cranking out the paintings, but she didn't seem to be stressing too much about it. I'm sure the dope helped.

"How about Martin Luther King?"

"Someday," she said. "I'd like to do him and Malcolm X, you know… sort of a yin and yang of the race thing. But for right now, I'd really like to get back to music."

"Still not ready for the John Lennon?"

"I can't deal with anyone else who got shot."

And then it came to me. "How about Elvis?"

She closed her eyes for a moment, deep in thought. She snapped them open and smiled.

"Perfect!"

She began brainstorming out loud. Skinny young Hollywood Elvis or fat old Vegas Elvis? Light, vibrant tones or dark textures?

"Like the oil and canvas version of one of those gaudy velvet pieces?" she said. "I could even mix the image and color scheme. Young Elvis with a dark future or old Elvis with a bright past."

"Either way, you can't go wrong with the King."

•

That was the last time we talked. I had been running around so much since then I never got a chance to see how Elvis turned out. So with over an hour before I had to meet Frat Row, I decided to drop in and check on Lila. I went over there, knocked and waited. No answer. I tried a couple times to no avail. That's when I remembered her extra key on my chain. I couldn't help but let myself in.

"Lila?" I called out.

Still no answer.

I walked in and took a look around. For a split second I thought I was in someone else's place. There was an Oriental rug next to her bed and a purple velvet loveseat in the corner, neither of which I'd seen before, but that wasn't what made it feel so unfamiliar. It was her missing paintings that transformed the space into something alien. Their absence was powerful. They were all gone, leaving patches of barren brick and block where they had once hung or leaned. I felt a burst of panic, as if Lila had disappeared with her artwork.

Then I remembered the show. It didn't start for hours, but she was probably already there, deciding where her pieces should hang or doing some finishing touches in place. I took a deep breath, trying to relax. Standing there in Lila's empty apartment was filling me with a muted sense of dread. I tried to pretend like it was nothing, like it was all in my head, but the more I told myself that, the more I felt the need to get the fuck out of there.

•

Besides, it was time to head over to the Map Room. A stock North Side tavern with a wide selection of imported beer, I had met Mark and Steve here before when I didn't feel like running all the way up to Evanston. I quickly scanned the place before spotting them huddled around a table in the back with a couple of buddies. Mark got up and approached me.

"I know you told me you don't want to meet anyone else," he said apologetically. "These guys are just visiting from out of town."

"Whatever." I just wanted to get done and get out of there.

"Michael, dude," Steve called out from the table. "C'mon over here and have a drink."

I was about to turn him down when the waitress came by and he ordered me a shot and a beer.

"High Life and Crown, right?" Steve asked, pulling a chair over for me at the crowded table.

They were already half-lit. Mark made some clumsy introductions.

"You're just in time, dude," said one of the guys.

"We could all use a little boost," said the other.

"On that note." I made eye contact with Mark, tilting my head in the direction of the restrooms.

"We'll be right back," he said.

We made the swap in the men's room and returned to the table where our drinks were waiting.

"I gotta get going," I said.

"We won't keep you," said Steve. "But we gotta have a toast."

"Happy New Year," said Mark, raising his shot glass.

"Happy New Year," we all chimed in.

If you can't beat 'em, join 'em, just like Sal said. I swallowed my shot, savoring the mild sweetness and that warm, fuzzy feeling of the whiskey flowing down my throat.

"This guy's hardcore," said one of the guys.

"You don't fuck around, do you?" said the other.

"Man, that's good," I said, ignoring these two clowns who had no business being there in the first place. I almost said so, but I stopped myself. Why not be cool? I took a swig from my beer and lit up a cigarette, figuring it wouldn't hurt to hang out for a few more minutes. Might as well if they were buying.

"So," I looked at Mark, "you hooking up your buddies from the Board of Trade tonight?"

"No, dude." Mark shook his head. "Those guys are laying low. You know…after the big bust."

"What are you talking about? Those guys got busted? How?" I couldn't care less about the CBOT fuckheads, but they could give me up to the police if they got pressed. This was terrible news.

"No, no, no," said Steve. "They didn't get 'busted' busted. Not for blow, that is."

"They got nailed by the SEC," said Mark. "They were part of some big stock manipulation scam."

"Pump and dump," said Steve. "You didn't hear about that?"

"Obviously not," I said, thinking hard. So if it wasn't a drug bust, then what was it? And why did I care? My mind started racing through the possibilities and I remembered Paul saying he sometimes traded through those guys. Jesus, did that include my stocks? I tried to stay calm and listen.

"It was all over the local news," said Mark. "Brad and Jack had to do the perp walk. They were smiling at the cameras."

"Anyone else?" I asked.

"Hell yeah," said Steve. "A bunch of guys higher up. Nobody at any of the name-brand shops though. That's according to my dad."

I wasn't sure what the fuck he meant by that.

"He works at Merrill Lynch, right?" asked one of the guys.

"He's a VP in the Internet group," Steve said with the pride of any douchebag bragging about his country club.

I could practically feel the color draining out of my face as my mind started connecting all the dots.

"Are you okay?" asked Mark.

"What else do you know about all that?" I asked.

Somehow, despite my rising panic I managed to sound like I still believed there was a chance this had nothing to do with me.

"With Brad and those guys?" He turned to Steve.

"Brad really didn't want to talk about it," said Steve. He paused and then came out with exactly what I didn't want to hear, but knew, deep down, had to be true. "He did mention something about that other guy. You know him. What's his name? The guy who hooked us up?"

"Paul Wills," I whispered for lack of breath.

•

"Motherfucking fuck!" I screamed and yanked on the steering wheel before turning my attention to the dashboard. I punched it several times, stopping only when my knuckles started to bleed. I wiped them on my jeans and took a deep breath. "Fuck."

I was heading east on Armitage after a futile attempt to reach Paul at his condo from the pay phone in the back of the bar. Then I called Fran and left the whole sorry tale on her answering machine. She had told me not to give Paul any money and I didn't want to hear it, but I needed to tell somebody who could understand how this happened. After reaching the recording limit, I remembered that Fran had jetted off to Acapulco days ago. Theo always spent the break between Christmas and New Year's with his father, and Fran would go down to Mexico for some much needed R and R.

Good for you, Fran.

I wasn't really into sun and sand myself, but at that moment I would've loved a vacation south of the border. Instead, I was freezing my ass off, racing around Chicago trying to track down Paul Willis. As I pulled up to Lake Point Tower, it occurred to me maybe Paul left town too. I could just see him kicking back on a chaise lounge, poolside, with a margarita in one hand, a cigarette in the other and a sly expression on his face. I ran inside and the doorman told me Mr. Willis wasn't in. I had no way of knowing if that was true or not, but I couldn't get past the lobby anyway.

So I headed over to his office. It was a long shot, but I didn't know where else to look. The building was almost completely dead. If not for a pair of dedicated stiffs breezing out the door late for the holiday weekend, I would not have gotten inside. I ran to the elevator and took it up to the twelfth floor where I got off and headed south down the corridor to Diamond Investments.

Definitely not one of the name-brand shops.

The door was ajar but the lights were off. Rows of desks, formerly occupied by Paul's gang of young brokers, looked like they had been abandoned in the middle of a busy day. Papers were strewn across the floor. File cabinet drawers hung open, mostly empty. The computers had wires hanging out of them and appeared to be missing parts. The only light came from the overcast sky outside and the cracks in the privacy blinds hanging over the window looking into Paul's office. I moved in that direction and accidentally knocked over a desk lamp. The bulb shattered with a pop.

"Who's there?" I heard Paul call out.

"It's me, Michael," I said, catching my breath. My stomach was in knots, like I was about to get into a fight.

"Come on in," he said.

Paul sat parked in his executive chair with ESPN flashing muted highlights across the plasma screen on the wall. He was sipping from a lead-crystal highball glass and smoking a cigarette, his jaw twitching, his eyes glazed. A plate of cocaine sat on the desk in front of him next to a stainless steel semi-automatic pistol.

"Jesus, Paul!" I recoiled at the sight of the gun.

"I'm not taking any chances."

"Expecting some clients, huh?" For the first time, it hit me that I wasn't the only sucker he got. I shook my head and gestured to the pile of blow. "You look like Tony Montana."

"Let me tell you," Paul looked up at me. "The cocaine cowboys don't have much on a pack of disgruntled investors."

"Really? Jesus, who are your investors?"

"Doesn't matter," said Paul. There was something strange about his voice, like he was talking to a mirror. "Because you never know what people will do when their money disappears. Then again, maybe the gun should be for me."

"Yeah, well..." I really didn't want to hear it. Paul blowing his brains out was not the worst thing I could imagine at the moment. "How about closing my account first?"

"I wish I could, Michael. I really wish I could." He shook his head and gulped down the rest of his drink. "But the Feds have everything frozen. I can't even pay my mortgage."

"Now I can't even get a mortgage."

"You'll be all right," Paul said with a wary glance at me. "That wasn't your whole nut, was it?"

"Take a guess!" My voice boomed and Paul jumped.

"I was hoping not." His voice trailed off.

"You motherfucker." I took a deep breath.

"I'm really sorry," he said.

"What the fuck, Paul!"

"I don't know what else to tell you."

"You could start by telling me how the fuck this happened."

"What do you mean how did this happen?" He looked genuinely surprised at my demand for an explanation. "You saw your returns. How the fuck do you think it happened?"

"I have no idea!" I shouted. "I thought the whole point was to invest money, get a good return and get paid."

"That is the point," said Paul. "But how do you get that good return? Do you know something that nobody else does? And if not, do you have some way to move the market?"

"I don't know what the fuck you're talking about."

"Never mind. Let's just say I cut a few corners, but nothing out of the ordinary." Paul was getting indignant now. "It wasn't supposed to go down like this. I was just playing the game like everyone else except I got singled out. If I were part of some big Wall Street firm, with friends in high places, this would've never happened."

"Is that so?" I couldn't believe my ears. "Then why the fuck didn't you send me to one of those big Wall Street firms? I was perfectly fine just putting my money in the bank! Fuck!"

I punched the wall next to the TV and my fist went clean through, much to my surprise. I could pack a punch, but I had never put my fist through a finished wall. Once the shock wore off, I collapsed in the chair across from Paul, rubbing my aching hand.

"You okay?" he asked.

"I should've listened to Fran."

"You should've," he agreed. "Hell, I should've listened to her years ago when she told me to clean up my act."

Could've, would've, should've. Paul snorted a few lines and got going about his own sorry travails. How he blew it with Fran. How his parents never gave a shit. How the finance clique always sneered at his degree from Roosevelt University. I just sat there, stunned.

"You want a line?" he asked.

"Fuck no," I shuddered.

My mind was racing enough as it was. I couldn't stop thinking about all that running around. The trips out west. The trips up north. The cutting, the packing, the bullshit. All that work. All those chances I took. All those times I could've been busted. Or ripped off. Or beat up. Or shot. All that for nothing. And now my big move with the two-flat was dead on arrival. I knew my luck was gone too.

There was only one thing to do.

CHAPTER TWENTY-THREE

"Where the fuck have you been?" asked Sal.

He was standing in the dining room, his arms folded. I pushed past him toward the bedrooms. "Where's Sherry?"

"She went home to get into her party dress. Dante's gonna pick her up later. They're coming here and we're all going out for drinks before Lila's show. Does that work for you?"

"I don't give a fuck what we do later." I pulled out a dozen hypes and a fistful of dime bags and tossed them on the coffee table. "Right now, I'm getting high."

Sal leaned back against the wall, slack-jawed and speechless.

That's when I put it to him. "Want to join me?"

"Fuckin' A! I thought you'd never ask!"

I knew Sal was down. Health issues or not, he had been chomping at the bit to shoot some dope. Driving was wearing on him and booze and blow just weren't cutting it. The only thing holding him back was me. He wasn't going to break before I did.

"What about the Hep C?" I asked, feeling compelled to say something even though I knew it wouldn't make a difference.

"What about it?" Sal scoffed. "I could still get killed in a car accident or die of cancer. Why not live it up while I have the chance? Besides, life is too long as it is."

He had a point, though I wasn't thinking that far ahead myself. All I knew was that I had tried to get on the right track, I got screwed, and I couldn't take it anymore. Unlike a lot of people who are fucked up and miserable and don't know what to do, I knew exactly what to do. Help was on the way.

•

An hour later, I lifted my chin off my chest and focused my gaze on the TV flickering across the dark room. Two men in trench coats were speaking in short bursts of French above the flashing subtitles. It was one of Sal's art house crime flicks. He loved the grim-faced characters and the bleached-out look of Paris circa 1970. He must have put it on for some background imagery because the sound was muted and a familiar, haunting melody filled the room.

"Come

Doused in mud

Soaked in bleach

As I want you to be..."

I rubbed my eyes and looked around. Sal was lying on his back on the floor, blowing smoke rings at the ceiling.

"How long was I out?" I asked.

"Not long."

"No shit."

"How you feeling?"

"You know damn well." I sat back, wondering if I had ever felt so good in my entire life.

"I can't believe how long we went."

"It was only two months."

"It felt like years." Sal stubbed out his cigarette and sat up. "I'm never going back now. Life is too short."

"I thought you said, 'Life is too long.'"

"It depends what's going on." Sal pushed himself to his feet and came over to sit next to me on the couch. "Hey, man, I never got a chance to tell you...Fran called."

"From Mexico?" I pictured her relaxing on the beach, soaking up some rays and sipping a Mojito. Good for her.

"Is that where she is?"

"Did you talk to her?" I reached for a cigarette.

"I did." Sal shook his head. "She told me everything."

I had no idea what he was talking about and it showed.

"About Paul and the SEC," Sal went on.

Thanks to the narcotic serenity that had washed over my entire being,

I had completely forgotten about my incredible misfortune. And at the moment, it really didn't seem all that important.

"Can you believe that shit?" I mused out loud.

"I'm really sorry, man."

"It's not your fault."

"It's still a bummer."

"Fuck it," I shrugged.

Sal turned up the music just in time for the chilling wall of sound that ended the song. When it was over, we each slammed another bag spiked with a little blow and sat there, swooning over the rush for a few more tunes before Sal got up and stretched.

"We better get moving," he said. "Dante and Sherry will be here any minute. It's New Year's Eve."

"Amateur night." I had completely forgotten.

"Whatever," said Sal, his face glowing from the speedball. "You could drop me in the middle of a dance club in Schaumburg and I'd have the time of my life right now."

He got to putting everything away while I wandered into the bathroom to linger under a hot shower. Between the smack and the blow and the soothing water flowing over my back, I felt the irresistible urge to sit down on the floor of the tub.

Bliss and heaven, indeed.

I sat there feeling the rush, periodically nodding out until the water got a little cooler. Just as I was thinking about turning it off and getting out, Dante's booming voice roused me.

"Let's go, motherfucker!" He poked his head into the shower with the wild-eyed look he always got after a few drinks. "What the fuck are you doing in there?"

"Chillin'."

He looked me in the eyes and shook his head. "You didn't."

"Don't start." I really needed him to cut me some slack.

"Fine. Fuck, I got nothing to say but get your ass in gear. Sorry about the stock shit, by the way," Dante paused before going on. "But I don't want to hear any crying about that, not tonight. It's party time!" He pointed at me and disappeared though my gaze remained fixed on the spot where he'd been standing.

Dante, what a prince!

•

"You guys going to Lila's show tonight?" asked Dana.

"Of course," said Dante as he waved his glass in her direction.

She took it without her usual attitude toward Dante when he was drunk and forgot his manners. Not even Dana was immune to the giddy vibe of New Year's and Lila's success. "Anyone else?"

"We're good, Dana," said Sal. "Thanks."

"You been nursing that beer for a half an hour," Dante spoke with a faint slur. "What are you waiting for?"

"Not a damn thing," said Sal. "I was well on my way before we even walked in here whereas you, my little droogie, are a work in progress." He shot me a quick look, making sure I was also keeping an eye on Dante. I nodded back, letting him know I was on it. We were all having a good time and we wanted to keep it that way.

"I never realized just how much Lila's paintings added to this room," Sherry spoke up, gesturing to the walls around us where some of Lila's work had recently hung.

"That they did," said Dana as she put Dante's drink in front of him. "I missed them as soon as they came down."

"Well, we're gonna head over to see some brand new pieces of hers right after this drink," said Sal. "Why don't you join us?"

"I don't think so." She shook her head.

"C'mon Dana," I spoke up, feeling all warm and friendly from the smack. "You can cut out for an hour or two."

Spoonful wasn't the kind of place to go all out on New Year's Eve. Other than a pair of no-name rock bands taking the stage later that night and the obligatory countdown, nothing much was planned. Dana had plenty of help behind the bar just in case it got busy, but she would still never leave her post.

"Go on, you guys," she said. "Tell Lila 'fuck yeah!'"

•

Sal hailed a taxi and the four of us piled into the back and headed over to the David Lloyd Art Gallery. Located in a faded rectangular brick building that had probably once been a machine shop or a truck garage, the gallery could not be missed. With a pair of spotlights shooting bright beams into the night sky as far as you could see, the scene reminded me of a nightclub opening or a movie premiere. Our cab pulled up to the curb where an actual red carpet led to the entrance. We all spilled out and headed up there. A buff bald black guy in a sharp suit stood guard holding a clipboard.

"We're friends of Lila Davenport," Sal told him.

"And she is?" he asked as if he was in the Secret Service.

"One of the artists," I jumped in. "She put us on the list."

The guy flipped through his clipboard before nodding his head.

"So we got Dante, Michael, Sherry and Sal," he said.

"In the flesh," said Sal. "Do we need a stamp or anything?"

"No, sir. Enjoy your evening." He directed us through a set of double doors that led into a vestibule where we were greeted by a striking woman in formfitting black from neck to toe.

"Welcome," she said with an affected pause. "To the next big thing." She handed us each a flyer that showed the layout of the gallery and the names and locations of the works of the different artists featured that night. "Be prepared to be inspired!"

"Is she for real?" Sal whispered in my ear.

"Where's the bar?" asked Dante.

No sooner did he ask than a guy in a poorly fitting tuxedo passed by with a tray of mini egg rolls.

"That way," he told us, pointing to the right.

Dante grabbed a snack and we followed the waiter's directions. We ended up in a space filled with larger than life, photo-like oil paintings of young people in party scenes. They were smoking and drinking and dancing. The subjects were mainly attractive women. Some were visibly drunk, others just clowning around. The pictures were cropped like zoomed-in fragments of memory. A woman laughing from the mouth down. A close-up of a couple hugging, the back of the man's head obscuring the woman's face. The intimate nature of the images made me recall the days when most of my time with friends wasn't all about scheming, scoring and slamming dope.

"These are cool," said Sal.

"Aren't they?" said an older woman from a small group that came in after us. "I love this artist."

I looked at the flyer to see who she was talking about.

"Shane," I said. "No last name."

"Like Prince," said Sal.

"I've seen this chick around," said Sherry.

"Shane's a chick?" asked Sal. "Where did you see her?"

"She dated a girl that dances with us."

"A girl?" Sal asked with interest.

"Sorry." Sherry knew Sal well. "She's gay, not bi."

Even high, Sal knew when to change the subject.

"Where's Lila?" he asked, looking around.

"And where's the bar?" asked Dante.

He was going to keep asking until he found it, so I figured I might as well find it for him. The place was like a labyrinth, with each room turning into the next. I walked ahead in the direction the waiter had pointed us and wandered by a wall of paintings that resembled incredibly detailed graffiti on canvas.

"I don't know about these," said Sal.

They were interesting, but they didn't really grab me either. The opposite wall featured a series of textured oil depictions of poppies growing in strange places. The middle of the Ryan Expressway. The pitcher's mound at Wrigley Field. They all showed a bewildered onlooker or two, gazing at the rows of red.

"These are just weird," said Sherry.

"I don't know," I said. "I like poppies."

"I do too," said Sal. "My favorite flower."

More people were coming through, and the place was getting louder and a little crowded.

"The bar?" Dante said impatiently.

"Of course." I pulled my eyes away from the paintings and moved on. We found the bar in the next room where a line was quickly forming. Dante and Sherry waited to get drinks while Sal and I scanned the area for Lila, who was nowhere to be seen.

"Her paintings are in the room after the next," said Sal, consulting his own flyer.

"We'll get there," I said. "What's the rush?"

Maybe it was just the smack, but the show totally grabbed me. I had always appreciated Lila's work, though I figured much of that had to do with appreciating Lila. Now I was seeing that maybe it didn't. We hadn't even found Lila's work, yet I was already into other pieces from people I didn't even know.

Dante and Sherry returned with our drinks and we moved on, pausing to glance at the works in the next room. They were modern, with simple shapes and bright colors on white canvas. They didn't seem to require much skill.

"I could paint better than this," said Sal.

I agreed. "They look like Theo did them."

"Hey, guys," a familiar voice called from behind us.

Sal and I turned to see Lila approaching from the next room. Unlike most of the people breezing through the gallery, she was casually dressed, in faded low-rise jeans with a long-sleeve blouse, her hair pulled back in a loose ponytail.

"Hey, honey." Dante walked over to kiss her on the cheek.

Lila wrapped her arms around his waist. "Thanks for coming."

"Wouldn't miss it for a million bucks," Dante smiled and took a gulp of his drink. He was already well on his way.

"How's the show going so far?" asked Sal.

"Okay," said Lila. "I guess. People seem to like my work."

"Where are your paintings anyway?" asked Sherry.

"This way." Lila tilted her head toward the next room.

Everyone moved in that direction, with me bringing up the rear. Lila hung back, waiting for a chance for us to talk privately.

"How are you?" she asked. "I heard."

"I don't want to talk about it."

Lila peered into my eyes and sighed. "Oh, Michael."

"What?" I shot back, hoping to discourage her from continuing.

"You were doing so well." She shook her head and I wondered what she meant by that. Was she talking about me making money and getting my shit together or me giving up dope? The more I turned it over in my mind, the more I realized I was in no mood to get into either.

"Fuck it. I'm not the first person to get burned by a shady stockbroker. I won't be the last. What I want to know is…how are you doing? Really." I gestured around me. "With all this?"

"I'm fine, Michael," she said. "Why wouldn't I be?"

"Just asking," I said. "This is a big deal."

"The next big thing," she said dryly. "I know. And I'm fine. Really. Not saying I couldn't be better though."

She moved in closer to me and grabbed my arm.

"Are you holding?" she whispered.

"How did you know?" I asked, not that it mattered. She must have figured out that losing everything and getting high went hand-in-hand, which they did. She knew I had just what she wanted, what she needed. She also knew I was going to give it to her.

"Meet me in the bathroom," she said.

"Men's or women's?" I asked.

"It's unisex."

"Perfect. Which way?"

"Right past my paintings." She pulled me along.

"I'll go in first," I told her. "Knock after a minute or two and I'll be all ready for you."

We went into the next room where everyone else was milling around, taking in Lila's work. We tried to slip by unnoticed when Sherry's reaction to the King stopped us in our tracks.

"Wow!" she exclaimed. "Check out Elvis!"

Wow indeed. The only canvas on the wall, the King was awesome to behold. Measuring five feet wide by eight feet tall, it truly was a larger than life piece—the largest she had ever done. It was also completely original in that it wasn't based on any famous photo or otherwise easily recognized image. Elvis looked young, like he did in Hollywood, but he had his Vegas jumpsuit hanging off his lanky frame. He was standing on the side of a dusty highway leading away from a glittery skyline in the distant background. He had an old hard shell suitcase at his feet and his thumb out.

"Leaving Las Vegas," said Sal.

"That's right," Lila nodded.

"It's incredible," said Sherry.

"You really did him right," I said, marveling at the piece.

"Thanks," Lila nodded again before giving me a covert stare. I had completely forgotten about the plan.

"I have to go to the bathroom," I said in a clumsy proclamation.

"I'll alert the media," Sal announced. "Breaking news."

Dante broke out laughing. "That's a good one." He threw his arm over Sal's shoulder, swaying a little. "I'm gonna hit the bar again. What can I getcha?"

"I'll take a bottle of the most pretentious import they have," said Sal. "When in Rome."

"Coming right up."

Dante headed one way and I went the other, and nobody suspected a thing. The unisex bathroom was the perfect place to fix. Usually, when you fix in a bathroom, you have to sit on the toilet seat with your works on your lap. If you're lucky and they have a residential-style toilet with a tank, you can use that as your work surface. The bathroom in the gallery was even better. It had a lock on the door and a marble counter around the sink with a crushed velvet wing chair right next to it. I quickly cooked up a bag and waited for Lila's knock. Almost a minute passed and I got antsy, so I sat down in the chair and gave myself a booster. It wasn't enough for a really heavy nod, but when I did finally hear the knock, I blew it off at first, forgetting why I was in there in the first place.

"Hello?" I heard Lila's voice.

It took a second before I got up to let her in. She immediately noticed the spent syringe.

"Michael!"

"Just give me a minute," I said as I went to work. "Please," I motioned to the chair. "Have a seat."

Lila sat down, rolled up her sleeve and tied off before offering me her arm. I rubbed the soft flesh inside her elbow until I located the sweet spot. Once I found it, I stuck the needle in and paused. She took a deep breath and a thin stream of blood seeped into the syringe. After gazing at the red cloud for a moment, I depressed the plunger and set my eyes on her face. I always loved to watch Lila as the rush washed over her. She was so fucking beautiful, dropping into a heavy nod right before I pulled out the needle. I even had a little Band-Aid all ready, though Lila wasn't much of a bleeder. She raised her head and gave me a warm smile.

"So you don't stain your blouse," I said, putting it on her.

She rubbed her nose. "You are so sweet."

"Are you gonna be all right?" I asked, packing up my works.

"Are you kidding?" She stood up and stretched before wrapping her arms around my waist. "Now, I'm ready."

"Just try to lay low for a little bit," I said. "You don't want to nod off while talking to some collector."

"Don't worry about me, Michael. Let's just figure out how to get out of here without being noticed. I know heroin is somewhat acceptable for artists, but I'd rather the world didn't know I was shooting up in the bathroom at my first show."

"Anyone see you come in?"

"I don't think so."

"I'll go first." I reached for the doorknob and Lila stopped me. "Wait a minute or two," I said, though she wasn't listening. I turned and she kissed me on the lips.

"Thank you," she said.

"You're welcome. Be careful."

I had just slipped out the door when Sal spotted me.

"It's a little early for another fix, isn't it?" he asked with a wink. "Not that I wasn't thinking the exact same thing."

Before I could think of a way to stall him, the bathroom door opened and Lila emerged, rolling down her sleeve. She buttoned her cuff and paused for another rush, obvious to any junkie.

Sal looked at me. "What the fuck?"

CHAPTER TWENTY-FOUR

"Oh, Sal," Lila said, stroking his arm. "It's okay, really."

She wandered over to a cluster of artists and hipsters who had just come in, leaving me to deal with the fallout from Sal.

He turned to me. "I can't fucking believe this."

"What?" I asked as if I had no idea what he meant.

Sal wasn't having it. "You know goddamn well what, so don't even start. Lila's getting high. And you just fixed her, in the bathroom. Jesus, Michael, you might as well be fucking her."

"Please," I scoffed, though Sal's reaction made sense. He was completely floored, probably as much by me not telling him as anything else. We didn't have very many secrets between us. But this one was out now, and all I could do was try to limit the damage.

"She likes to get off every now and then, and I help her out. What's the big deal?"

"Does Dante know?" he asked with a quick glance around.

"I don't think so."

"Well, don't tell him."

"Gee, thanks for the tip."

I was just grateful he didn't seem to have a clue I actually was fucking Lila. That was the real secret, and the only one I needed to keep to myself, the only one I couldn't expect Sal to understand.

"Now let me get one of those bags." He lightened up and snapped his fingers. "All this drama has me feeling a touch peaked."

"Knock yourself out." I reached into the fifth pocket on my jeans and handed him one of the tiny foil packs.

"I'll do my best," said Sal.

He made a beeline for the bathroom and I felt a surge of relief that the conversation was over and everything seemed to be cool. I turned my gaze back to Lila. She was now talking intently to a slight woman with a pale complexion, deep red lips and a shaggy glam rock haircut. Even with a cardigan over a T-shirt, jeans and scuffed Doc Martens, she managed to look sophisticated, like an artist you'd see profiled in a magazine. She wasn't my type, but there was still something about her that demanded my attention. She and Lila stood out from the group as if they were under a spotlight.

"That's Shane." Sal appeared next to me.

"Jesus!" I started. "That was fast."

"I don't want to miss anything." Sal smiled and dropped into a momentary nod. He came back to life, his eyes half-lidded.

"How do you know her?" I asked.

"I met her in line when I was getting a drink," he said.

"Met who?" said Dante. All of sudden he was right there, swaying a little with a mixed drink in one hand and a tall glass of beer in the other. "Here," he thrust the beer toward Sal, who took it, gazing suspiciously at the opaque amber brew.

"What's this?"

"It's from Germany," said Dante. "The bartender said it's made with wheat. That's why it's all cloudy."

"Cool." Sal took a big swig and wiped his mouth on his cuff. "The doctor did say I need more fiber."

"So who were you guys talking about?" Dante nudged me. "Got your eye on one of these artsy chicks?"

Sal tilted his head in Shane's direction.

"Oh, her." Dante scowled and sipped his drink.

"What's her story?" I asked him.

"Who knows?" said Dante. "Lila digs her."

"Excuse me?" I wasn't sure I heard him right. Dante had never been so casual about Lila's female dalliances.

"What can I say?" he shrugged with resignation. "She's obviously got something I don't."

"Yeah," Sal snorted. "A pussy."

"It's more than that," said Dante. He swallowed the rest of his drink, blinked a couple times, and lurched forward. At any moment, he would probably black out, walking and talking and interacting with absolutely no recollection of any of it the next morning.

"Easy there, big fella," said Sal, patting him on the back.

Dante stiffened up and got his bearings before continuing. "Look at them." He waved his glass. "Don't they make a great couple? They're both artists. They're both hot."

"I have to admit," Sal said, giving Shane the eye. "There's something quite appealing about her."

"Don't even think about it," said Dante. "She's all girl. Never been with a guy in her life."

"I heard." Sal rubbed his chin, thinking hard. "I might just have to put her to the test."

"Put who to the test?" Sherry walked up to us with a fresh drink in one hand, a cigarette in the other and a trace of blow on one of her nostrils.

"I wonder where you've been," Sal said as he wiped off the telltale white smudge and gave her a kiss.

"C'mon," said Sherry. She gulped her drink and took his hand. "You gotta see this painting."

"It's been stimulating," Sal said to Dante and me. "But you know how it is. Culture calls."

I watched them go and turned back toward Lila and Shane. They were now standing close together, engrossed in a private conversation. Shane reached up to push back a few strands of Lila's hair that had fallen loose from her ponytail.

"That flamer is the owner of the gallery." Dante gestured to a man walking over to Lila. He had cropped gray hair and wore glasses with thick frames. A taller man with a dark brown mane and deep-set eyes stood next to him. Lila greeted them both warmly.

"Which one?" I asked, vaguely curious.

"The older guy," said Dante. "With the glasses. That's his partner," he went on, letting the wrist of his free hand fall limp. "If you know what I mean."

I nodded and continued to watch with Dante. Now Lila and Shane and the gallery owner and his partner were all chatting each other up like they were the only people in the room. They looked like two couples. I felt a pit growing in my stomach.

"It hurts a little, doesn't it?" asked Dante.

"What did you say?" I asked, my mind reeling as his words sunk in. It was like Dante knew about Lila and me. And he was even empathizing with me, watching Lila get close with this Shane chick. It seemed so impossible I couldn't believe I had heard right.

"C'mon, Michael," said Dante with a deep sigh. "I may be dumb, but I'm not stupid."

"What are you talking about?" The surreal feeling was getting more intense by the moment. I did my best to look genuinely baffled, but Dante just ignored me.

"I know what's going on," he said. "I know Lila is getting high with you. And you're probably fucking her. You don't have to say."

The words hit me like a two-by-four.

"Look, Dante." I wanted to deny it, to say something, anything, but he shook his head.

"Don't bother," he went on. "I'm not mad. How could I be? Look at her. I'd want to fuck her too. As it is, I haven't given it to her in months. She deserves better. She probably deserves better than you, but at least it's a step in the right direction."

Dante paused and I just stood there, dumbstruck.

"You can't believe you're hearing this, right?" A twisted smile formed on his lips. "Think how unbelievable this must be for me. My best friend is shooting my girlfriend full of poison and then fucking her and I'm not gonna do a thing about it. What do you think Baldino would have to say about that?"

Baldino was Dante's co-captain of the Elmwood Park Tigers and another crazy fucker. He played center and gave as good as he got to the linemen trying to get past him. He ended up with a scholarship to a small college somewhere in Ohio.

"He wouldn't fucking believe it," Dante continued wistfully. "He'd say 'Cascianni! Stomp that fucker like you got a pair!' He used to yell that to me from the sidelines."

"I remember."

"That kid was tough," said Dante. "His dad was a Marine, you know, fucking rode his ass twenty-four-seven. I used to think he got a raw deal, but I know better now."

I almost spoke up, but Dante went on as if talking to himself.

"You know all I ever wanted to do was play football? That's it. I never even thought of doing anything else. Even when I got my knee kicked in and they told me 'no way,' I thought 'somehow, someway.' Pretty fucking sad, huh?"

"I'm sorry, Dante," I said. I meant it too. Dante's injury broke everyone's heart.

"Whatever. There's no point being sorry. What happened, happened. But I just can't let it go. I got nothing else. It's like I'm not even here. I'm walking. I'm talking. But I'm somewhere else, like I don't exist. You know I haven't been to work in a week? They didn't even notice I was gone. I went to get my check, expecting an earful from my asshole boss and he didn't say a word. He just handed me the envelope and went on talking on the phone."

"What did you do?"

"Nothing, man," Dante scoffed. "I put it in the bank."

"That's not what I meant."

"Then what did you mean?"

"Nothing. Never mind." I shook my head.

"You mean when I didn't go to work?"

"Yeah. I was just wondering."

"I bet you were," said Dante. He squinted, concentrating. "I went to the bar across the street. I meant to go to work, but when I got there and saw all the people hanging out, I said 'fuck it.' They looked a lot more fun than the usual morning crew. So I closed the place three nights in a row and slept in my car. Then one night I went by Lila's and saw you coming out. You were strolling and stretching, like I've seen you and Sal do. That's when I knew."

Dante always did have more on the ball than I gave him credit for. I cursed myself for being so careless, so casual. Then again, what could I have done differently? Would it have made a difference if I went out the back door? Sooner or later, these things always come out. A stray word or a look here or there and before you know it, everybody knows everything.

"I don't know what to say, Dante."

He nodded as if he understood and looked at the floor. I noticed some people walking by with noisemakers.

"Just do me a favor." Dante sounded strangely sober. "Watch out for Lila. Don't let her throw her life away on dope. After tonight, I don't want to see you guys for a long time."

"What do you mean by that?" My throat was so dry I could barely get the words out. I tried to repeat myself but my voice got drowned out by a big group coming through wearing hats and clutching tall glasses of champagne.

"Where's your bubbly?" a giddy young woman asked us.

I glared at her and she moved on.

"I'll get a couple glasses," said Dante.

He made a move for the bar but stopped just as Sal and Sherry appeared with a bottle of Cristal and a half dozen plastic champagne flutes. Sal handed us each one and started pouring. Lila came over to stand near Dante and eyed the bottle.

"I think that's supposed to be for the artists," said Lila. "From David's private stash."

"And what do we get?" said Sal. "Cold Duck? I think not."

He topped off everyone's drink and gulped down the rest straight from the bottle.

"That's charming," Sherry poked him.

Sal shrugged and handed the empty bottle to one of the waiters, who had traded in the finger foods for champagne flutes. Moments later, the smooth jazz that had been piped in throughout the space all night disappeared and the din of the crowd seemed to go up a notch. After the traditional countdown, the opening chords of "Auld Lang Syne" began to play. I felt Sal's spindly arm around my shoulders. He started singing at the top of his lungs along with half the room.

Should old acquaintance be forgot,
And never brought to mind?
Should old acquaintance be forgot,
And auld lang syne?

Everyone was swaying and singing whatever words they knew. All the while, I kept one eye on Dante, who was silently brooding throughout the celebration. Lila took him by the arm and his expression didn't change. I watched her rock him back and forth until the smooth jazz was back. He was drunk, completely tanked. There was a good chance he wouldn't remember a word of our conversation. If he brought it up again, I could play dumb and deny everything.

But I would still know that he knew.

"You ready to roll?" I asked Lila.

"So, where are we going?" Shane rounded the corner and approached us, holding a fresh drink. I guess she was part of the gang now. Great. The night just kept getting better and better.

"My place, I guess." said Lila. "We need to wrap up here." She turned to me and lowered her voice. "Can you bring some blow?"

"It wouldn't be New Year's Eve without it," I said, thinking of the two eightballs I had scored for that motherfucker Paul. Someone might as well enjoy them.

"So, Shane and I will meet you there as soon as we can get away," said Lila. The two of them went to the right, Shane leading Lila by the hand. Lila flashed me a sweet smile as she disappeared from view, but I felt an inexplicable burst of dread. Maybe it was Dante. Maybe Shane. I didn't know exactly what, but something felt very wrong. Thankfully, it was almost time for another fix.

•

The bitter cold seemed to be attacking us outside Spoonful where Dante's car was parked. We had gotten a cab from the gallery easily enough, but we were having a hell of a time getting Dante's keys. He was just standing there, still as a statue, apparently oblivious to the temperature in his drunken stupor.

"We need your keys." Sal pretended to turn the ignition as if Dante didn't speak English.

"It's fucking freezing out here, Dante. Don't you want to get in your car, where it's warm?" I asked him.

He just looked right through me.

"Fuck," said Sal. "Lights out."

"Your keys, Dante," said Sherry gently.

She always had a soft spot for the big lug, no matter what shape he was in. He gazed at her for a moment and started pawing himself while she reached into his coat pocket.

"Here they are," she said. "No big thing. Let's go."

Sherry handed me the keys and I unlocked the car so we could all pile inside. I quickly started the engine and turned on the heat. While the car warmed up, I got out to brush off the ice and snow and we were once again on our way. We stopped by our apartment to pick up the blow. I only took one eightball to Lila's and stashed the other one since I knew we would end up doing whatever I brought, and I wasn't up to hearing the manic coke chatter all night. I just needed to get myself right and be cool. From our place, we made another quick stop at a liquor store where I picked up a bottle of Stoli and a case of High Life. Just as we pulled up to Lila's, Sal whipped out the second bottle of Cristal he had stolen that night and waved it over his head as we climbed out of the car.

"Happy New Year!" he cheered.

CHAPTER TWENTY-FIVE

Lila must have been looking out for us because she opened the door just as I was about to knock. Sal flashed the blue bottle.

"How do you like me now?" he asked her.

"You're incorrigible." Lila sounded more impressed than pissed as she reached for Dante, helping me bring him inside. We walked him over to the bed where he immediately passed out. Lila pulled off his shoes, covered him with a blanket and planted a kiss on his forehead.

"Can I get some glasses?" asked Sal.

"Coming right up," Shane called out from the kitchen.

She appeared with some plastic cups and I couldn't help but notice how comfortable she seemed in Lila's place. She was friendly enough too, though not quite as outgoing as she had been at the gallery. Sal took the cups and popped open the Cristal, filling one for each of us while Lila put on some music.

"How about The Doors?" she asked.

"Old school." Sal approved.

He and I dragged a couple beanbag chairs over to the new loveseat and rounded up a couple extra blankets to roll up as cushions. I tossed Sal the blow and he laid out some rails.

"Who's up?"

"I'll take a bump," said Sherry as she hopped to her feet.

"So I hear you're into movies," Shane said to Sal. Lila must have told her that. I wondered what she said about me.

"I am," said Sal. "If they're good."

"Same here," said Shane. "I especially like the classics and foreign films. I can't deal with most Hollywood shit. Last week, I caught a

Sunday matinee at the Music Box, *Angels With Dirty Faces*."

"Oh yeah," said Sal. "You can never go wrong with Cagney.

Shane turned to Lila. "He'd be a good one for the Icons."

"I've been thinking about Hollywood," said Lila. "Cagney would be a good choice. Or maybe Clint. But I'd like to pick an actress. I've been meaning to focus on women for a while now."

"Well, you're off to a good start," said Sal.

He spoke just loud enough for only me to hear him, not that Lila and Shane were listening. They were already brainstorming possible female subjects while I dug out my works.

"Do you guys *have* to do that again?" asked Sherry.

"You know we do," said Sal. "Why even ask?"

"Don't hold back on my account," said Shane. "I don't mind at all. I've tried heroin before."

"Oh yeah?" Sal said with a laugh. "Something tells me you didn't try hard enough. Wanna give it another shot?"

"No thanks. I actually just snorted it. But you guys do your thing," said Shane. "I'm cool."

Gee, thanks for the permission. Aside from the whole thing with Lila, Shane's presence was getting on my nerves. She wouldn't take her eyes off Sal or me while we fixed. She just sat there staring, like it was some sort of performance art.

"Would you mind if I took your picture sometime?"

"Why would you wanna do that?" I asked.

"All my paintings start with a photo."

"It depends," said Sal. "No needles."

I looked at him, surprised. "When did you get so discreet?"

"I'm just fucking around." He smiled and rubbed his nose. "I don't care if you snap me slamming dope. Why should I? I'm a junkie, in case you hadn't noticed."

"I wouldn't paint anything you didn't want me to," said Shane.

"Either way, you're the artist," Sal said with a heavy nod.

Maybe she was the artist but there was no fucking way I wanted to end up in one of her paintings. God, she was annoying. Then I felt my own merciful rush. Once the dope hit me, I didn't care about Shane anymore. I was warm and comfortable. I turned to Lila.

"You up?" I asked casually.

Lila froze.

"It's okay, Lila," said Sal. "I know. Remember?"

With the excitement of the show and everything else, she had forgotten how Sal busted us earlier at the gallery. But even after his reassurance, she still seemed conflicted.

"What's the problem?" I asked.

Lila glanced over at the bed where Dante was sprawled and Sal did too. He didn't want to do his cousin wrong, but there's no getting around the secrets and lies that are always part of the deal when you have a habit like shooting dope.

"What he doesn't know won't hurt him," he said finally.

The same went for Sal and Lila, I thought as I recalled my disturbing exchange with Dante earlier that night.

"So," I put it to Lila once more. "You up?"

She gazed at the works Sal and I had laid out before turning and nodding to me. I quickly went to work, cooking up and loading a syringe. She dug out her leather belt and sat down next to Shane, tying off just as Sherry came back from the bathroom.

"I knew you were getting high," she said to Lila with a twitch of her jaw, quickly adding without a trace of irony, "not that there's anything wrong with that."

"Not that there's anything wrong with that," Sal repeated, mostly to himself. "You know, I don't miss Seinfeld one bit."

"Really? I loved that show," said Sherry.

I approached Lila and got in position to fix her. She flipped her arm over and I slapped the inside of her elbow twice until I found the vein. I laid the syringe on the soft flesh of her forearm and pricked the skin, staring silently at the wisps of blood that danced in the cylinder. Someone stroked my arm.

"Can I do it?" Shane spoke in little more than a whisper. I hesitated, feeling Lila's body clench with anticipation.

Despite the warm glow from my recent fix, Shane's request really put me off. Fixing Lila was like fucking her. Having done both, I could honestly say I didn't know which brought her more pleasure. She was louder when she got fucked, but she melted when she got fixed. I knew there was no way Shane could know this. She was probably just curious. Having never shot up herself, this was as close as she had ever been. I'm sure she also wanted to add it to her list of alternative experiences, all ready to break out when she needed some street cred or a little color as an artist. Fixing Lila was practically sacred to me and I sure as hell didn't want to share the experience with Shane, but I had to be cool.

"Go slow." I told her.

"Not too slow," Lila murmured and bit her lip.

"Here comes." Shane looked into Lila's eyes and steadily depressed the plunger. Lila sat back against the beanbag chair and let out a faint moan as the rush swept over her. I scooped up the needle and leaned back to watch. Lila took a few deep breaths and suddenly sat up just enough to grab Shane from behind the head as the two of them started kissing. In spite of the jealous thoughts I had only moments before, there was no getting around how hot it was to watch them kiss, their tongues flicking in and out of each other's mouths.

"Fuckin' A!" Sal said. "I think I gotta jerk off."

"That's nice," said Sherry.

"You want to help me out with this big thing?" Sal turned to her, pointing at his groin. Talk about wrecking the mood.

Shane pulled away and shook her head.

"What can I do with these guys?" Lila asked her.

"I wouldn't know," Shane sat back, smiling with satisfaction.

With the impromptu girl-on-girl show over, we chilled out and partied some more. We drank and smoked some weed that Shane had on her, every now and then jamming out to the music. It didn't take long before Sal and Sherry started powering through the blow and running their mouths like crazy.

Still on a Doors kick, Lila put on *American Prayer* and zoned out, bobbing her head and reciting the words along with Jim and the music. I wasn't sure if Shane was into the Doors, but she was definitely into Lila and never took her eyes off of her. Between the smack, blow, booze and weed, I was wiped out. I moved away from the group and crashed hard in the first spot I found.

Hours later, I woke up with a jolt. It took me a second to realize I was still at Lila's place, lying on the rug about ten feet from her bed, my leather coat balled up as a pillow. Someone had thrown a blanket over me. Though I could hear him snoring, I couldn't make out where Sal went down. Sherry either. They must have set up some kind of camp over by the kitchen. I lifted my head up and glanced around, rubbing the sleep from my eyes.

And then I remembered everything.

How I had lost it all just the night before.

How I unleashed my habit, one more time.

How Dante knew about Lila and me.

It all came back to me with a hot surge of anxiety that shot through my entire body. Time for another fix. I reached inside one of my coat pockets and grabbed what I needed. Just as I was about to sit up, the sound of heavy breathing stopped me cold. I turned toward Lila's bed, my eyes now fully adjusted to the darkness. Between the pale moonlight seeping in through the windows and the red LED numbers on her clock radio, I could see everything clearly over there.

Lila and Shane had both shed all their clothes and were lying on the rug next to the bed with a blanket barely covering them. Lila was on her back with Shane on top of her, grinding away. Lila let out a moan and Shane covered her mouth and kissed her, all the while their bodies undulating together. I could hear Lila's breathing getting faster and faster until it stopped with a faint whimper. Then Shane let herself go as Lila grabbed her from behind and took control. The two of them came together. They did it again and again. It was raw yet tender and much hotter than any all girl porn I'd ever seen. I felt like an intruder watching like I was, but I couldn't take my eyes off this transcendent scene. That's when the beauty of what I saw before me collapsed under the weight of my new reality. I could now add Shane to my list of disturbing developments. Happy Fucking New Year.

Much as I needed a fix, I didn't want to interrupt them. I didn't want Lila to know that I saw her. Not that it mattered. She wouldn't care. She'd tell me it was no big deal and we were still okay. Just like her and Dante. I didn't want to hear it. I lay back and closed my eyes, resolving to wait it out.

"I'll get us some water," Shane said in a low voice.

I turned my head to see her roll off Lila and dig through the clothes piled around them. Her cardigan hanging just low enough to cover her, she got up to go the kitchen. That was the break I was waiting for. When I saw the light from the icebox, I let out a loud yawn and sat up, rubbing my eyes and looking around.

"Hey you," whispered Lila. "What are you doing up?"

"I could ask you the same thing," I said. "What time is it?"

"Four-thirty," said Lila as she furtively wriggled into a T-shirt and panties. I pretended not to notice.

"Hey, Michael," said Shane as she gently handed Lila a glass and sat down next to her, reaching for the blanket to cover up.

"Hey," I mumbled back and quickly went to work, cooking up a fix before turning to Lila. "Can I borrow your belt?"

She didn't say a word. I could feel her eyes on the needle.

"Lila." Shane nudged her.

"Of course." Lila snapped out of it. She plucked the belt out of the pile on the floor and handed it over. I wrapped the worn leather around my arm, found the sweet spot and just like that...

All my troubles were gone.

I wasn't in the habit of waking up in the middle of the night to fix, but things were never such a mess. The smack hit me like Dante did that quarterback in the '88 semis. I fell straight back, with the needle still hanging from my arm as the rush swept me away. A priceless moment of rapture faded to black before blurred images and frantic voices drew me back into semi-consciousness.

"Michael? Michael?" Lila sounded hysterical. She was nearby, though I couldn't make her out. "What's the matter with him?"

"I'm calling 911," said Shane.

"Fuck that!" said Sal. The voice of reason. I could feel his hands on my face. "He'll be okay. Gimme some ice in a bag!"

Moments later, a chilling sensation on my groin yanked me a little further back into consciousness.

"Keep that on his balls," said Sal.

A few minutes passed and my vision became clearer. Once I got control of my limbs, I pushed Sal away from me.

"I'm all right, I'm all right."

Sal backed off and I removed the bag of ice Lila had been diligently holding in place.

"Thanks a lot," I said.

"Thanks a lot?" Lila sat back and stared at me with rage. "What the fuck!" Her eyes welled up with tears.

"You almost died," she said, her voice fading.

"I'm sorry," I told Lila. "This is why you have to be careful." I looked around at everyone. "Just say no, right?"

Nobody thought that was funny.

"How about not slamming dope in the middle of the night by yourself?" said Sal. "You're lucky I woke up and not him."

He gestured to Dante who was still out cold on the bed.

"He'd have your ass halfway to the emergency room by now. Probably would've wrecked a couple cars in the process. And then you'd be in a world of misery, assuming you were still alive."

Sal was right. I was lucky he was there. If Shane had called the paramedics and they arrived in time, I would've gotten a shot of Narcan. That's the antidote that works by literally ripping the active ingredients in the heroin—the opiates—from the receptors in your brain. Those receptors happen to be in the same region that controls important stuff like breathing. Assuming you haven't gone into complete respiratory failure, you end up with one hell of a headache and no buzz. If you have gone into respiratory failure, then your heart will soon follow and you might get the adrenaline shot a la *Pulp Fiction*. If that doesn't work, you better have Mario Andretti behind the wheel of the ambulance or you're not going to make it. The ice on the balls trick was your best bet. Sal learned it from Maurice, who would never even consider calling for help.

"We fend for ourselves up in here," he once said. "Ain't nobody in the hood waitin' on 911."

Of course not. Who wants to deal with paramedics and the police when you don't have to? The ice down there shocks your system, kind of like jump-starting a car. We didn't believe him until we actually tried it on Kenny's brother a couple years back after he just got home from a three-year stint at Stateville Prison. Just like me, he slammed a bag and instantly fell out. I grabbed the phone to call for help, but Kenny stopped me. A trip to the hospital would've meant a parole violation and a trip back to the joint. So we did like Maurice had told us, and booyah! The guy made it. He went back to jail anyway, but at least it wasn't because of some chickenshit overdose.

"Fuck," I muttered. My brush with death had really worn me out. I needed to sleep, and I needed a break from myself and everyone else, if only for a bit. "Thanks, Sal, you guys."

Nobody said a word, and the lights went off.

•

I didn't come to until almost noon the next day. Lila and Shane were on the couch and Sherry sat behind me at the table in the kitchen, eating a bowl of Froot Loops. She had slept clean through my near death experience. Sal and Dante were both nowhere to be seen. The sky through the windows was white with falling snow.

I got up to get a look outside. "Holy shit."

"It's really coming down," said Shane.

A thick white blanket of fresh snow covered the entire street. The wind was howling away, blowing up drifts that looked four feet deep in some places. The only cars I saw were parked against the curb and they were getting buried.

"How long is this supposed to go on?" I wondered out loud.

"They predicted around twenty inches," said Lila. "And the coldest temperatures yet this winter."

She walked up close to me. "How are you feeling?"

"I'm fine," I said with a slight shiver. I didn't really need it, but the weather and the general vibe made me want my next fix. I felt cold and lonely, and all the fucked up events of the day before were flooding my mind once again.

"Promise me you'll take it easy today, okay?" Lila said, staring me directly in the eyes.

"Of course." I would just have to fix in the bathroom. "Where's everyone else?" I asked, gesturing to the empty bed.

"They were gone when we woke up," said Lila.

I took another look outside and recognized Dante's car, covered with snow right where we left it.

"Sal went to get some coffee," Sherry said absently.

"I've got coffee." Lila frowned.

"No cream," said Sherry. "You know how he is. That was like...I don't know, almost an hour ago."

"Did Dante go with him?" I asked.

"Not sure," she said. "I was still half asleep."

I took a couple more drags, tamped out my cigarette and headed into the bathroom. I was a little wary at first, being that I almost dropped dead only hours before. But once I got the needle in place, I figured what were the chances it would happen again?

The next thing I knew, someone was pounding on the door.

"Did you fall in or what?" Sal was back.

I lifted my chin off my chest and gathered up my works. When I opened the door, Sal gave me the once-over.

"We all straight?" he asked.

"I'm fine," I said. "Not sure what happened last night."

"You fell out."

"It was pretty fucking scary," said Lila.

"I remember," I was feeling sheepish. "I'm sorry.

"Anyway." Sal motioned toward the kitchen, ready to change the subject. "I got coffee and donuts."

"Where's Dante?"

"I don't know," he said. "We were just wondering the same thing. His car is still out there."

"He probably went to get some breakfast," said Lila.

"Probably," I said, pausing for the rush.

CHAPTER TWENTY-SIX

"I don't know about you," said Sal. "But I'm starting to get the feeling something is up."

A couple of hours had passed, and we were all lying around Lila's place, smoking weed and jamming some Monster Magnet. We had already polished off all the donuts and even the breakfast sandwiches Sal picked up for Dante. The whole time, I did my best to carry on despite a gnawing sense of dread that was growing stronger by the minute. I kept replaying my conversation with Dante the night before. It freaked me out how he knew everything but he didn't seem to care. And one thing he said kept coming back to me.

"I don't want to see you guys for a long time."

What the hell did he mean by that? And what, if anything, did it have to do with his disappearance? I couldn't help but tie the two together, and I couldn't tell Sal about it either. I felt remorseful and rattled and shaken to the core.

Still, Dante occasionally wandered off, usually late at night after enough alcohol to kill most people. Sometimes we'd find him passed out in someone's lawn or slumped on a stoop. Other times he'd stumble into a neighborhood tavern. We'd drag him out after getting an earful from some harried bartender. But these scenes always took place before we got home or back to wherever we were crashing, and we were able to track him down. That's why this particular episode was so unsettling, especially to Sal and me. Hungry or not, Dante wasn't one to get up and at 'em, not in the middle of a blizzard and not when we still had a half a case of beer left.

"Well, what should we do?" asked Lila. "We need to find him."

She knew Dante as well as anybody and she was also concerned by this unprecedented disappearance. Shane rubbed her back but Lila didn't relax. She sat up straight, her jaw tight.

"He must have gone down to the place on the corner," she said after a while. "He's been there before."

"That shithole tavern where that guy got shot?" asked Sal.

"That was months ago," said Lila. "Besides, they have booze and a TV and he was really looking forward to the Rose Bowl."

"We all were. We watch it every year. I can't believe he would just leave without us." He shot a pointed look at Lila and Shane. "Then again, maybe he woke up and felt like a third wheel."

"What are you saying?" Lila confronted him even as she put a little distance between her and Shane on the loveseat.

Sal shook his head but kept quiet.

"I'm really sorry about all this," Sherry spoke up. "But I have to get home. I need a shower and some clothes."

"I'll take you," said Sal. He got up and went over to the window. "Looks like it finally stopped snowing. We'll take Dante's car. I've still got his keys. Michael, can you help me dig it out and then check that bar, see if he's there?"

"No problem." I was glad there was something I could do. "Sherry, you might as well wait in here. It's gonna take a while to get the car out with all this snow."

•

"Fuck, it's cold!" Sal's voice pierced the eerie silence in sharp foggy bursts. The whole block was so dead it felt like we were the last people on earth.

"I heard that," a voice called back. We both whipped our heads around to see another brave soul out there, some old-timer shuffling by on the cross street.

"Happy trails, man," Sal muttered as we stepped into what looked like a foot of snow covering the sidewalk in front of Lila's building. "Times like this, I wish I would've joined my parents in Boca."

"Fuck that," I said. "Between all the old people and the crackers down there, you'd go nuts."

"Maybe," he said, musing. "Then again, Fort Lauderdale, Miami...

shallow, scantily clad women. What more do you want?"

I ignored Sal, too distracted by the weather to join him on his little fantasy detour. Digging out Dante's car was going to be a total bitch. I was just glad I had my stash and didn't need to get out to the West Side anytime soon. I took a moment to survey the arctic landscape around us. This was the first real storm of the year and it was a motherfucker. The snow was thick and heavy, and it was still accumulating in drifts everywhere you looked, thanks to the icy wind howling past us. Dante's car was directly across the street. Neither one of us had a shovel, but we did have a couple plastic trashcan lids that we'd swiped from the dank storage area in the basement.

"I wonder how Shane is getting home. That's *if* she's going home." Sal sounded disapproving, no doubt on Dante's behalf.

"It's not all that," I told him and myself. Given the difficulty of the task at hand, I couldn't help but let go of the drama with Lila. "Fuck it. Let's do this."

I turned and began trudging across the street. Sal followed at first before breaking into a sprint, high-stepping right past me and over the partial drift building on the driver side of the vehicle. He kept going until he reached the passenger side where something stopped him dead in his tracks.

"My God!" Sal stepped back, dropping the trashcan lid.

"What?" I ran around the car. That's when I saw him.

Dante was flopped on his side across the front seat of the car with the passenger door hanging wide open. A layer of flaky snow had blown inside. Sal began frantically wiping it off Dante's face. It had the grayish pallor of a corpse.

"Help me!" he shouted.

I dashed around to the driver side and tore open the door, climbing inside on top of Dante. I brushed the snow off his stiff, lifeless body and put my ear to his chest.

"Well?" Sal stared at me, his eyes welling up with tears.

"I don't hear anything," I said.

"Fuck that!" Sal shoved me back to listen for himself.

He started pumping Dante's chest and breathing into his mouth. I watched and waited, hoping this wasn't really happening. After what seemed like an eternity, Sal collapsed on his belly, hugging Dante tightly, weeping. The big lug was dead.

"Goddamn it!" I screamed at the top of my lungs and dropped to my knees, pounding my fists into the street until the packed snow around me was red with spattered blood.

•

"Did you get the car started?" asked Sherry.

Sal and I were speechless, staring right through her. Sherry looked us over—Sal with tears streaming down his hollow cheeks and me with blood smeared on my knuckles and face—and covered her mouth. Lila rushed over when she saw us.

"What happened?" she pressed us. "Where is he?"

"He's gone," said Sal, his voice cracking.

"Gone? What does that mean?" Lila stared at him in horror.

"It means he's dead!" Sal started to get in her face before I pulled him away. "He's out there in his car, frozen stiff!"

Lila shrank back from him, buckled and fell to the floor, crying out with a furious agony unlike anything I had ever heard. I stepped between them, glaring at Sal.

"Knock it off!" I told him.

I turned to help Lila up, bracing her limp form against my chest as she shook and sobbed uncontrollably. Sal brushed past us without a word and went into the kitchen for a glass of water.

"Shouldn't we call an ambulance?" said Shane.

"What good would that do?" asked Sal. "He's already dead!"

"You can't just leave him out there!" choked Lila.

Sal wasn't listening anymore. The cooker was already going. I could smell the relief.

"We'll call them," I said. "Afterward."

•

"They said it'll probably be a while." Shane spoke quietly as she hung up the phone.

"I'll bet," Sal murmured in between nods.

He and I were slumped at the table in sad, silent oblivion. Lila was curled up on the bed, whimpering next to Sherry. Shane approached them and stroked Lila's back, murmuring something in her ear. She got up and put her coat on, sitting down with us for a moment to lace up her boots. As perfectly numb as I felt, there was no getting away from Shane's palpable disgust with Sal and me. From the moment I opened my eyes after that first rush, I could sense her disapproval even through my narcotic haze.

"I'm out of here, guys," she said. "I told Lila to call me if she needs anything. So sorry about your friend."

And then she was gone. Fuck her.

About fifteen minutes later, we heard the sirens and I looked outside and saw the ambulance along with a squad car. By the time the police knocked on the door, we were ready for them. I did most of the talking and fared pretty well, but they were still plenty suspicious. There were two of them, about our age, a chubby white guy and a woman, Puerto Rican from the looks of her. All the veteran cops, the ones who were too jaded or too lazy to bust anyone who wasn't black, Hispanic or waving a gun, no doubt had the day off. These two asked a lot of questions, all the while blatantly checking us out.

"And about the deceased," asked the male cop. "Was he drinking excessively last night?"

"It was New Year's Eve," I said.

"Any drugs?"

I gave him an emphatic "no" and the two of them eyeballed me for a second. I could almost hear the tiny wheels inside their heads grinding away. Two young women laid out crying, a pair of tattooed grease balls and a dead body? I'm surprised they didn't shake us down right then and there. We hadn't done anything illegal but that never stops them. If they think you're a junkie, they can do whatever the fuck they want to you. Sal and I knew the drill and we were ready, our stash and works all double-wrapped in plastic and taped to the inside of the lid of the water tank on the toilet. After the initial grilling, they asked me to walk them outside to see Dante.

"We need a positive identification," said the female cop.

"Right now?" I wasn't prepared to see Dante like that again and it must have showed.

"I can do it," said Sal as he grabbed his coat and pushed past me with grim resolve.

•

"Fuck," I said, pulling the key from the ignition.

The gray sky was already getting darker. After watching the ambulance pull away with Dante, I had gone back out to his car to join Sal. We didn't have any other way home and figured the car had to be moved anyway. It seemed like a good idea to try and fire it up like we originally planned. We hopped inside where the faint smell of Dante's Drakkar Noir still clung to the stale fabric that drooped from the interior of the roof. I held my nose and turned the key. The battery had just enough juice to give us a moment of false hope before it went completely dead. Click, click, click.

"Just like Dante," Sal said bitterly. "Fuck this." He shook his head and climbed out of the car.

"Where are you going?" I asked.

"I'm walking." He flipped up the collar of his black leather coat, jammed his hands in the pockets and got moving. I really didn't have any choice but to go with him. The snow had stopped falling hours ago, yet it seemed like everyone around us had holed up for the day. Other than a handful of stray plows doing the bare minimum to keep the streets passable, nobody had so much as picked up a shovel as far as I could see. All I needed was to get a call from some gloomy official telling me they found Sal's bony ass in a snowdrift.

"Wait up," I called after him.

It took us almost an hour to reach North Avenue, only halfway home. The conditions were much better up there. Most of the snow had been pushed off to the sides of the streets, leaving only a grungy sheen of slush for the SUVs and Volvos passing by us. Here and there we came across gaggles of post-college types, clad in parkas, yakking as they poured in and out of the trendier bars and restaurants.

We passed a couple more obnoxious assholes I would've gladly mugged on the spot if only we had an extra minute, but we didn't. Instead, Sal and I hiked and smoked and occasionally made surreal small talk until we reached our apartment. There we dug out my car, which mercifully started right up.

"We can give Dante's car a jump," said Sal. "I'll drive Sherry home. Then we'll head out to EP."

"If it's not too late," I said, hoping it would be. I knew what we had to do and I wasn't up for it, not yet anyway. Maybe after another fix and some sleep.

"It doesn't matter how late it gets," said Sal. "I gotta tell Aunt Rosie tonight. I'll never hear the end of it if she finds out from the coroner."

"You'll never hear the end of it anyway."

Dante's mother, Rosalie—Sal's Aunt Rosie—was Sal's mother's youngest sister. The two of them were so tight when we were growing up that whenever Sal or Dante got in trouble, which was quite often, they both heard about it from their mothers.

"Why don't you watch out for your cousin?" each mother would say. "Keep him on the straight and narrow."

Sometimes they blamed me. "Stay away from that Michael Lira," they would say. "He's going to lead you astray."

My mom said the same things, mostly about Sal. None of that lasted though. With time came the comfort of the familiar. We all had our shady sides and our mothers knew it.

"You should probably let your mom know," said Sal.

"I'll call her tomorrow," I said. Or not. She would find out soon enough, one way or another.

"Suit yourself."

We drove the rest of the way back to Lila's, each mired in our own thoughts. Sal was probably wondering how the fuck he would break the news to his aunt. I kept flashing back to the night before and what Dante said to me.

"I don't want to see you guys for a long time."

My throat felt tight as I ran it all through my mind. In the end, I just couldn't make sense of what happened. Dante was depressed, no doubt. Maybe he somehow knew, deep down, he wouldn't make it much longer. The way he drank and brawled, death was always a possibility. Maybe he was going to pick up and leave, like I had thought about doing. Lila, too. It wasn't that far out. Dante's life was a mess and he was in pain, but I still couldn't believe that he went out there and froze to death on purpose.

When we got to Dante's car, Sal and I went to work without a word, just like the guys in those old French heist movies he loved so much. In less than ten minutes, we had the old Iroc fired up and ready to go. I disconnected the cables and tossed them in my backseat while Sal sat inside the vehicle and warmed it up. After a few minutes, he got out and approached me.

"I'm ready when you are," he said. "Go get Sherry and I'll drop her off and meet you at Dante's house."

I nodded and tramped across the street to Lila's door.

•

"Do you think he knew how much I loved him?" asked Lila.

We had been sitting in silence at her kitchen table for a while before she finally said something.

"I know he did, Lila," I said, doing my best to comfort her. "And I know it meant a lot to him."

"I really, really loved him, right from the start," she went on as if I hadn't said anything. "It was easy. He loved me so much, and I could always make him happy. Maybe it wouldn't last but I know it helped. He deserved to be happy."

Lila put her head in her hands and let out a muffled sob. Then she sat up and looked straight into my eyes.

"Do you think he knew about us?"

Her question caught me completely off guard. She searched my face as I tried to avoid her gaze.

"No way." I knew the truth but she didn't have to. Things were fucked up enough. I didn't want her to feel any worse.

"I can't believe he's gone." Her voice cracked, and a fresh wave of tears streamed down her cheeks.

"Me neither," I said, taking her hand.

She moved over and I held her for a moment until she pulled away, rubbing her eyes and face.

"I just don't know if I can take it," she said. "I feel so fucking… rotten, so guilty."

"This wasn't your fault, Lila. It wasn't anybody's fault."

I was trying to convince myself as much as her. She pushed herself up and walked over to the windows. I followed her.

"Are you gonna be all right here alone?"

"I don't want anyone to know about us."

"Of course not."

"I'm not saying forever," she continued. "People move on and it's okay, but not right away."

"Don't worry." I was glad to hear her talk that way. With everything that happened, I wasn't sure where we stood, *if* we even stood. I didn't think I could get through it all without Lila. I wrapped my arms around her and looked over her shoulder down at the spot where Dante's car had been parked.

"What was he doing out there?" she asked.

"Who knows?" I knew then and there I would probably never stop asking myself that same question.

"Oh, God." Lila took a deep breath and turned around to face me. I grabbed her by the waist and pulled her close. She began to sob again, her face buried in the wrinkled front of my shirt, her body heaving in my arms. It felt like she could go on that way all night. I didn't want to leave her but Sal was waiting for me. So I picked her up and carried her over to the bed where I gently laid her down.

"Lila," I whispered.

"I know you have to go. But before you do," she wiped her nose and swallowed. "Will you fix me?"

CHAPTER TWENTY-SEVEN

"Where the fuck have you been?"

Sal was livid by the time I finally pulled up in front of Dante's house to get him. He slid into my passenger seat and slammed the door so hard, I'm surprised it didn't fall off. I turned up the heat inside the car and aimed the vents in his direction.

"I'm really sorry, man."

"You want me to freeze to death too?"

"Why didn't you wait in the house?"

"I *was* waiting in the house!" he bellowed. "I was in there for over two hours listening to my Aunt Rosie going on and on. When she wasn't wailing with grief, she was on the phone, calling people, waking them up to tell them. I told her that could wait but she wouldn't listen. She was beside herself. One minute she's pounding on the kitchen table and sobbing on my shoulder, the next minute she's handing me my mom on the phone..."

"How was that?" I interrupted, trying to concentrate. I was still high from fixing with Lila and hadn't really thought about how rough it must have been for Sal.

"How the fuck do you think it was?" he snapped. "She wanted to know how this happened. What the fuck was I supposed to tell her? I have no idea myself! The whole thing is so fucked up, I can't stand it. And you know how what it's like in there." He shuddered, rubbing tears from his eyes. "Pictures of Dante all over the place. Pictures of us as kids, all shaggy hair and smiles. I couldn't take it anymore. I practically ran out of the house."

"I'm sorry." I didn't know what else to say.

"Where the fuck were you, man?" said Sal.

He turned and caught me zoning out on my waning buzz, the last vestiges of the dope I shot with Lila before nodding off for almost an hour and a half. When I came to and saw the clock, I bolted down to my car and flew out to EP as fast as I could. The roads were icy as hell and I almost ended up in a ditch more than once, but I made it in pretty good time. Still, when I saw Sal shuffling toward me over the packed snow on Dante's street, it hit me how bad I had fucked up.

"I was taking care of Lila," I said, realizing how weak this excuse sounded the minute I put it out there.

"Goddamn you!" Sal pounded on the dashboard. "I'm out here getting raked over the coals by my aunt and my mom, the two of them hysterical, all but blaming me for Dante and you're doing what? Getting high with Lila, catching some z's..."

"It wasn't like that," I cut him off.

It was hard to sound convincing when that was exactly what happened. Sal stared at me for a moment and turned away, making a show of his disgust. Then, to my relief, he dropped it. He leaned back in his seat and let out a deep breath.

"Never mind. I don't want to hear it. You should've been here. You weren't. You got high. I can't blame you. If I didn't have to do all the talking...believe me, I would've fixed up before going in there myself. I just got one question..."

"Don't even ask," I cut him off. Before he could say another word, I whipped out a Ziploc bag with some works and the three bags we had left, not counting our emergency stash at home.

"Fuckin' A," said Sal, his anger fully abated.

At least I hadn't completely let him down.

"I figured you could use a little something."

"We gotta make a run," he said, examining the bag. I had been thinking the same thing.

"Tomorrow." I turned on to Harlem Avenue. Life goes on, I thought absently. My mind started wandering when a familiar smell brought me back. Sal already had the cooker going.

"What are you doing?" I asked. We never just broke out the smack like that, not while driving. If we absolutely couldn't wait to get anywhere private, we'd park on some dark side street or pull into a fast food parking lot.

"Just keep going," he said. "And be careful, would ya? It's pretty fucking slick out there."

"Ah...aren't you forgetting something?

"What's that?"

"We don't fix and drive, Sal."

"We're not fixing and driving," he said. "I'm fixing. You're driving. Now keep your eye on the road. I'd like to make it home in one piece if you don't mind."

"We could pull into the KFC." I pointed to the brightly lit building with the red and white roof on the right.

"Or Denny's?" I pointed to the left.

"Michael." Sal hissed my name with the loaded hype clenched between his teeth and I backed off. It was the least I could do after leaving him out there like that. What difference did it make anyway? Things had changed. I could feel it.

The monkey was taking over.

I had never thought of it like that, the monkey that is. On one hand, there was the sickness, like any disease, to be warded off at all costs. On the other, there was the incredible anticipation of the rush. It was similar to the giddy expectation many people feel when they're about to get laid or go sky-diving or eat a big, juicy steak, only much more intense. Now there was something else, something more pressing, more persistent, something that didn't have to make sense and wouldn't take no for an answer, like a monster...or a monkey. And now it was on my back, digging in. I realized I couldn't care less that we were fixing and driving. I just needed to get high.

"We'll just stop for a minute," I said.

No answer from Sal. He already had the needle in his arm and was depressing the plunger. I pulled off Harlem and parked on a dark block in River Forest. After Sal fixed, I did the same and we cruised home without saying a word.

•

"How on earth could this happen?" asked my mom.

We were in my room at the house. Aside from some of her old clothes piled on the twin bed, it was exactly the way I left it. The walls were covered with posters and tapestries, a shrine to classic rock. My first stereo, a cheap component system in a prefabricated rack, no longer worked but had yet to be thrown out. I was rummaging through the closet, trying to find my only suit—the one I wore to my high school graduation and my dad's funeral.

"I have no idea," I sighed.

My mom had followed me in, peppering me with questions about Dante and every detail about what happened on New Year's Eve. She was getting on my nerves and I felt perilously close to telling her to shut the fuck up. When she shuffled over to my desk and sat down with a grunt, I pounced on the opportunity to change the subject.

"Is your back bothering you again?"

"A little bit."

"Are you getting your pain meds?"

"Don't you worry about me, Michael," my mom said harshly. Word had gotten back to her about the doctor and some shady guy who decked him at the strip club. Right after it happened, she called me and brought up the incident, somehow knowing that I had *something* to do with it. That seemed like a long time ago.

"I gotta go." I yanked out the suit. It was wrinkled with a thin layer of dust across the shoulders and a red striped tie that already had a knot in it wrapped around the hanger.

"You better get that to the cleaners," said my mom. "I bet Marathon on Conti Parkway can do it for you by tomorrow."

"I'll get right on that," I said as I walked out.

My mom trailed me to the front door.

"You know the wake is tomorrow night at Sabbatini's?" she called after me. I stopped without turning to face her.

"Yeah, I know," I said over my shoulder.

Like I could forget.

•

On the way back from EP, I made a stop at the good old Midwest Bank and Trust. The same pretty girl walked me down to the safe deposit boxes and left me in the private room, telling me to take as long as I needed. Less than a minute later, she looked surprised to see me coming back up the steps.

"It doesn't take long to empty it out," I told her.

I had stuffed the cash, Rolex and the envelope labeled "United States Treasury" into my pockets, leaving everything else behind. I went home and dumped it all on the coffee table. Sal was nodding out on the couch. I fixed myself and we sat there, smoking cigarettes and occasionally exchanging a few words. Eventually, Sal turned his attention to the coffee table and took in what was in front of him. He picked up the envelope and looked inside.

"Oh!" Sal raised his eyebrows. "Wish my parents would've bought me some savings bonds."

"Me too," I said.

"How much are those worth?"

"Face value is two thousand."

"But that doesn't include interest. How much would that be?"

Neither one of us had any clue.

"It's probably a lot," I said finally.

"You should maybe give them to Fran," said Sal. "To hold, you know, for a rainy day."

Not a bad idea. I had cleared out the box without really thinking it through. I felt like my world was falling apart. I didn't want to have to run out to EP every time we needed to score and I knew that would be more and more often the way things were going. But I didn't want to squander everything I had either, not when I could just pawn the watch until we got something else going. And if that something fell through, at least I would still have the bonds. I knew they'd be harder to get out of Fran than any safe deposit box.

•

"You really still have Dad's watch?" asked Fran, her tone hushed.

She cast a wary glance in the direction of my mom, who was talking nearby with a small group of people from her church. I pulled back my cuff and raised my fist. The watch, heavy and loose, shifted on my wrist, the bracelet clicking softly.

"Do you always wear it?" She sounded astonished.

"Not always. I try to save it mainly for funerals and the shooting gallery." I was annoyed by her question. "What do you think? It's not like I hang with the gold Rolex crowd, you know."

"I don't know anything, Michael. I'm just glad you still have it. And I'm glad to hold on to these." She held up the envelope with the bonds before sliding it into the pocket of her suit coat. "I wish you would tell me why you're giving them to me."

"Just do it, would you?"

"I will," she said. "That's why I'm asking about the watch. I can take that too, if you want."

"Thanks, but no thanks." I really didn't want to talk about my plans regarding Dad's watch with Fran.

"I'm so sorry about everything, Michael." She took my arm for a moment. "Things with Paul, Dante..."

"There's no comparison!"

"I didn't say there was!" She lowered her voice. "I just mean I know you were doing so well, and then it all fell apart for you so suddenly. And now with what happened to Dante. I only hope you don't use all this as an excuse to throw your life away, Michael."

I nodded silently while she searched my face. She obviously wanted more of a response but I had nothing for her. It was Dante's wake and the last thing I needed to hear was some motivational speech from Fran. She finally marched off to grab my mom and the two of them left me there in the lobby of Sabbatini and Sons Funeral Home, the place to be when you're dead in EP.

Sherry and Sal were still in the room where Dante was laid out between a pair of large framed photos flanking his casket. One showed him as a smiling toddler, cradling a football that was almost as big as he was. The other had him in uniform our senior year, posing on one knee and leaning on his helmet with a crazed grin on his face.

After walking up to see him in his casket, Lila broke down and bolted for the ladies room. I went after her and that's when I ran into Fran. Having finished my business with her, I was standing around waiting for Lila when the funeral director, Vincent Sabbatini, approached me with a warm but impersonal welcome. The son of Giuseppe, the old man who started the business back in the late sixties, Vincent was a nice enough guy but nothing special.

His father, however, had been a bona fide character right out *The*

Godfather. Hardworking and genial with a vaguely sinister edge, he had a way of comforting you without going too far. He was the only person who said anything that helped when my dad died. I'll never forget when I walked into the funeral home and saw my dad's name in those white plastic letters that snap into the black placards they place outside the rooms. Giuseppe came up behind me. He put his hand on my shoulder and said with his thick Italian accent, "Sooner or later...we all gonna get our names up there." I don't know why but that made me feel a little better at the time.

"I think I'm okay now," said Lila, her voice breaking into my thoughts as she reappeared next to me. Recalling the day of my dad's funeral, I had completely forgotten about her.

"You sure?" I asked. She still looked a bit shaken.

"I'm fine." Lila hooked her elbow around mine and we went back into the crowded room to meet up with Sal and Sherry. We found them milling around in the back. Sal looked at me.

"I want to go up there and see him again."

"All right," I said. "Let's go."

The place was filling up and getting louder. I recognized some of the people coming in. They were classmates and teammates, parents and teachers and of course, Dante's extended family. I did my best to look through all of them, but I couldn't help making occasional eye contact. When I did, I would offer a polite nod, careful to keep moving lest I get cornered in some awkward conversation. I was in no mood to make polite small talk with anyone.

Dante's mom was sitting in the front, weeping into the arms of his grandmother, a little wisp of a woman with long gray hair and a hooknose. His father sat on the other side of the room with his second wife and two daughters, a teenager and a pretty young woman in her twenties. Dante's parents had divorced when he was little. There were problems when Dante was born and his mother couldn't have any more children. Many in the family thought this played a big role in the failure of the marriage. The divorce was bitter but never kept Dante and his dad from being close. A large man with square-jawed appeal, Dante's father was a force. He must have missed Sal and me before, but this time he made sure to call us over on our way up.

"Sal, Michael," he said, looking weary but carrying on with his usual strength. "How are you boys holding up?"

Before we could answer him, he continued.

"Will you two help carry him?"

"Of course," said Sal.

I nodded in agreement, grateful to be asked.

"I'll call you up after the eulogy tomorrow," he said.

His younger daughter reached over and gently took her father's hand and Sal and I figured that was our cue to go. We turned and approached the casket where a fat little old lady was on her knees saying a prayer. She pushed herself to her feet and waddled off and we walked up next to the mahogany slab. Dante was laid out in a dark suit. His silver tie had a pattern on it made up of tiny footballs. Between the odd set of his jaw and the heavy layer of color on his lips, the body in the casket looked more like a version of Dante made out of wax than our old friend.

"He looks dead," I said, trying to stave off the grief I felt creeping up on me.

"He is dead," said Sal, his voice cracking as he reached out to touch Dante's hand. "The big lug."

A line had formed behind us and we had to move on. I put my hand on Sal's back and he reluctantly pulled away. We made our way to the back of the room and joined Lila and Sherry.

"Let's get outta here," said Sal.

•

"Where the hell are we going?" asked Sherry with unmistakable distress as she peered out the window.

"We'll be okay," said Lila.

"Relax, Sherry," said Sal. "They're just black people."

"Fuck you, Sal," she said. "You guys want to kill yourselves, don't bring me along for the ride."

"It'll just be a minute, Sherry," I said.

I tried to give her a reassuring look through the rearview mirror but she just folded her arms and turned her head away. Fuck it. We were definitely breaking protocol, but running the girls back into the city just to drive back out to the West Side was a huge hassle. I pulled up in front of T's place and parked.

"You want some blow?" Sal asked Sherry.

"Are you kidding me?" She glared at him.

"Grab a couple twenties," Sal said to me. "Just in case."

I climbed out of the car and hopped over a mound of slush to the sidewalk when I heard a car door close behind me.

"Hold on," said Lila.

"What are you doing?"

"Coming with."

She didn't say so, but I knew Lila didn't want to wait in the car with Sherry and I couldn't blame her. We walked up to the door. I rang the bell and Janet buzzed us in.

•

"Sorry about your man," said T.

"He in a better place," said Beverly.

"That drink ain't to be messed with," said Clifford.

Lila and I were sitting in the dining room with everyone, waiting for Janet to hook us up. Maurice came out of the bathroom.

"I forgot to thank you the other day," I said to him.

"Why's that?" He asked with a curious look.

"I fell out on New Year's Eve," I said. "It was fucked up, man. I didn't even know what hit me."

"Damn, boy." Maurice shook his head. "I told you to go easy after all that time. What you do?"

"We put ice on his balls," Lila said matter-of-factly.

"You playin'!" Aaron laughed. "That shit don't work."

"The hell it don't!" Maurice huffed. "He sittin' right here."

"It did work," said Lila. "I held the bag of ice myself."

"Damn, girl." Aaron was impressed. "You a dopefiend?"

"I'm a stripper," she said as she lit a cigarette.

"She's an artist," I corrected her.

"No shit," said Aaron.

I noticed him checking out Lila. Even Mookie poked his head out of his room to get a look.

"It was scary as hell," she said.

"I'll say," Beverly called out. "Praise the Lord! Y'all could've been having two funerals tomorrow."

Just then, Janet came out with our package.

"Where Sal at?" she asked.

"He's in the car," said Lila.

Janet looked confused, but I got up from the table before she could ask any more questions.

"We gotta run," I said to the room.

Everyone called out their goodbyes as T walked Lila and me to the door, undid all the locks and let us out.

"Nice people," said Lila.

CHAPTER TWENTY-EIGHT

"You remember how to get there?" I asked Sal.

The first words spoken in hours, they hung there in the car unattended like some shitty job nobody wanted to do. Lila, Sal and I were driving over to pick up Sherry after spending the night at Lila's in a narcotic haze. We had pretty much shot dope from the minute we got back from the wake the night before until the minute we left that morning, all the while barely talking. Now we had to rejoin the world and say good-bye to Dante one last time. We had almost an hour before the service at Old Roman Catholic Church English Rite, where Dante, Sal and I all put in more than a little time growing up.

Sal lit a cigarette. "I'm sure I can find it."

•

Forty-five minutes later, he and I were standing in a dim nook off the lobby outside the chapel. We were stalling really, waiting until the very last minute to go in for Dante's service. Sherry and Lila had just headed for the ladies room when an elderly nun shuffled by us, almost passing without a word. Then she stopped and turned, extending her gnarled hand in my direction.

"Sister Gladys Cantori," she said with a polite nod.

I instantly recognized the name. A decent enough looking woman back in the day, she had aged beyond recognition, even for me, the guy who could never forget a face. I reached out to shake her hand.

"Michael Lira," I said, gesturing at Sal. "And this is..."

"Salvatore Bono," she cut me off. "I remember."

"Nice to see you," Sal muttered.

"It's been a long time," she said with mild reproach. "I'm sorry about

Dante. God's will is often hard to understand."

I had nothing to say to that. I didn't want to hear about God's will or otherwise prolong this uncomfortable exchange. As it was, I felt overwhelmed by nostalgia due in part to the distinct smell of the place—a vaguely musty blend of cheap cleaning products and wood varnish. I kept flashing back to the good old days when we were all, as Sal put it, "shaggy hair and smiles." If not for the smack, I might've broken down crying right there on the spot.

"In any event," Sister Gladys went on, "may you both learn from his mistakes." She nodded at us again and walked away.

We watched her go for a moment before Sal spoke up.

"Learn from his mistakes?" He looked indignant.

"What else is she supposed to say?" I shrugged.

"Who?" Lila asked, walking up to us with Sherry in tow.

"One of the nuns from when we were kids," Sal said absently.

"Jesus," I murmured, still thrown off by her appearance. "She looked so old I didn't even know who that was."

"Are you okay, Michael?" asked Lila.

"I'm fine." I looked at her.

Dressed in a dark suit with her hair in a tight bun, Lila might've been an executive, like Fran, if not for the fresh traces of mascara streaming from her eyes. Sherry was dressed in a similar outfit. Even Sal managed to scare up a sport coat and slacks. He borrowed them from his cousin Tony. Sherry just had to do a little improvised tailoring with safety pins to keep everything from sagging too much off his bony frame.

"You look great," said Tony as he walked by us with his wife and a few other stragglers.

"Thanks." Sal rolled his eyes, "If anyone else tells me I look great, I'm gonna go postal."

"But you do," said Sherry. "You clean up well."

"Like it fucking matters. We're at Dante's funeral!" Sal's voice cracked and he took a deep breath, shaking his head. "I'm sorry. Can we just get this over with?"

He started to head inside while I lagged behind, momentarily considering a quick fix in the restroom. Sal read my mind.

"Don't even think about it," he growled.

•

The church was packed. If Dante had been the kind of guy who gave a shit how many people came to his funeral, he would've been impressed by the turnout. Walking in and seeing everyone crowded into the pews, all for Dante, I felt my heart clench inside my chest.

"Wow." I heard Lila whisper.

"Everyone loves a football star," said Sal.

Choking with sorrow, his voice resonated over the back few rows and several people turned their heads. We found a spot on the aisle in the last pew. Settling into my seat, I took in the surroundings and was hit by a fresh wave of emotion. The vaguely tinted illumination from the elaborate stained glass, the rich dark wood everywhere you looked, the graphic sculpture of Christ on the cross looming over the altar...it all brought me back. I hadn't seen the inside of a church since my dad's funeral more than ten years before.

There was a sudden wail from the front row. I craned my neck and saw Dante's mom, standing with her hand over her mouth, gaping in our direction. The priest had just appeared next to us in the doorway with Dante's casket on a cart right behind him. He turned and sprinkled it with holy water, intoning something in Latin, and solemnly marched toward the lectern with Vincent Sabbatini trailing him.

The rest of the mass was in English. Dante's funeral was like every other Roman Catholic funeral I had ever been to. There was a prayer for eternal rest for the faithful departed and another prayer for absolution. Then there were scripted readings. It was all bullshit as far I was concerned. Dante was gone, plain and simple. Just like my dad. Time would pass and the world would turn and before any of us knew it, we would stop thinking about him every day. He might pop into our minds every so often, but life would go on like he never even existed. The same went for the rest of us. Our names would go up on some black placard and that would be the end, period.

After all that praying and reading and talk of sin, the priest announced Communion. Sherry was the only taker in our group, though I have to admit, I could have used a drop of wine myself. The priest reverted back to Latin for the final prayer, this time with some incense in addition to the holy water. Once he was done, he called Dante's father up there to say a few words. This was fairly unusual. Most Catholic funerals don't allow for traditional eulogies since you're supposed to be ordained before you can address the congregation from the lectern. But sometimes you can work something out if you're a big shot and a good Catholic—meaning you don't make a show of your sins in the community and you give lots of money to the Church. With the exception of his divorce, which was probably ruled as an annulment, Dante's father was exactly the kind of guy who could bend the rules. Gracious and grateful, he thanked the priest and delivered a short but stirring expression of love for Dante that brought almost everyone, myself included, to tears.

I felt bad for the man. Dante's father had always tried to do right by his son. The divorce made it tough. Though he moved to River Forest, a definite step up in the world, he was around EP regularly. He went to all Dante's football games from Pop Warner through senior year. They would always grab a bite to eat afterward and sometimes Sal and I tagged along. When we were kids, Dante's father even treated us to a couple of Bears games. After the flood of scholarship offers came in, he drove Dante around to scout out colleges, taking time off from his booming contracting business—at the peak of the building season. He had been a starting tight end at Wisconsin and really wanted his son to go there too.

When Dante chose Michigan State instead, his father didn't hold it against him. Even after the fight that ended it all, a senseless brawl with some shitheads from Melrose Park, Dante's father remained supportive. He never even turned on Sal or me like many parents would've done. Of course, we each took a pretty bad beating that night too. Sal ended up with a fractured cheek and bruised ribs. I lost two teeth and half the hearing in my right ear. When it was clear that Dante would never play football again, his father tried to help him find a new direction. He fixed him up with Donnatella and everything was set to go. Then Lila came along. Sitting there in the back of the church, running through the history, I couldn't help but wonder how it all might have turned out differently. For a moment, I forgot myself and where I was when Sal nudged me.

"Let's go," he said.

It was time. Dante's father had summoned us to the front of the chapel. There we joined Sal's oldest brother Carmine and his cousin Tony, along with Baldino and another former teammate, Steve Ferguson. With the exception of Tony, none of us had seen each other in years. Carmine moved to Miami right before we graduated and had lived there ever since. Baldino, I recently learned, had made his home in some far-flung town in Ohio. Likewise, Ferguson had settled in one of those faceless far-west suburbs that might as well have been in Ohio. Meeting over Dante's casket like that was depressing and surreal but at least we could focus on the task at hand. We each grabbed a polished mahogany handle and lugged the casket out to the hearse without a word exchanged between us. It was heavy and I noticed Sal struggling, though he tried to hide it.

•

The interment was at Saint Joseph Cemetery, just a short run up Thatcher Avenue from the church. Being part of the official funeral party, we got to ride in one of the limos behind the hearse and run a few red lights, a good distraction. I was really starting to miss the rush and looking for anything to take my mind off the grief festering inside me. I told myself it was almost over. It had been a cold, grey day, but the sun came out from behind the clouds just as we arrived at the cemetery. Between the tears and the glare off the accumulated snow cover, my eyes ached. We piled out of the car and carried Dante to his final resting place. He was going in the plot Dante's father had originally purchased with his mom.

The priest intoned some more Latin and sprinkled the casket with holy water again. He recited one last prayer in English and made the sign of the cross over the casket. Finally, the time had come to drop Dante into the ground. When the casket started going down, Dante's mom lost it. Her cries of sorrow set off a chain reaction that left Lila and Sherry sobbing as well. Sal hung tough, barely. I was out of tears myself and ready for a fix.

After each taking our turn with the shovel, Sal and I rejoined Lila and Sherry and tried to get out of there before anyone noticed we were gone. Lila had driven my car over to the cemetery and she had the keys out, ready to go. We almost made it but Sal's mother caught us before we could reach the car.

"You're coming to the house, right?" she said to Sal and me, without even glancing at Lila or Sherry. "You know your father sprung for quite a nice spread."

"Thanks, Ma, but we're really not hungry." Sal looked at the ground as he moved in to give his mother a quick peck on the cheek. He tried to pull away but she grabbed his arm.

"I wonder where you're off to," she said angrily. "What's more important than being with your family at a time like this?"

"We're just tired and really sad," I jumped in, trying to defuse her wrath. "I'm so sorry for your loss, Mrs. Bono."

"Thank you, Michael," she replied in a tight voice.

I turned and walked away, traipsing through the snow to avoid everyone else. That included my mom, who made a move in our direction at first, only to think better of it.

•

Sal had the cooker going before we even got out of the cemetery. By the time we reached the city limits, the three of us were all nodding so hard I had to pull over and let Sherry take the wheel. She drove to her apartment, parked in the tow zone out front and left us in the car without a word. I was coherent enough to drive by then but still feeling no pain.

"Thanks for driving, Sherry," I called after her as she slipped into her building without even looking my way.

Sal came to life. "What was that?" He sat up and glanced around. "Where are we? What happened to Sherry?"

"She went inside." I tilted my head toward her building. Between the funeral and all that dope we slammed in the car, Sherry obviously wanted to get the fuck away from us and I couldn't blame her.

"Oh." Sal lit up a cigarette. "I'll call her later."

I got behind the wheel and drove us to Lila's where we ran into Shane, the last person I wanted to see at the moment. She was leaning back against her old VW bug and smoking a cigarette while the engine puttered away. She came over when we pulled up.

"Hey," I said, rolling down my window.

"How was it?" she asked.

"Sad." I told her brusquely. How the fuck did she think it was? I nudged Lila. "C'mon, girl. You're home."

She stirred and stretched and noticed Shane at the window.

"Shane." Lila looked glad to see her. "What are you doing here?"

I could have asked Shane the same thing. I could have gotten worked up by her intrusive presence at such an emotional time. They hadn't even covered Dante's casket and here she was already sniffing around his girlfriend. I could have easily gone off on her, in my mind or out loud. But I couldn't find it in me to really care much. I knew Lila better than anyone. She might spend some time with Shane but she would be back before long. She hardly had a choice.

•

"What's going on with Mark and Steve?" asked Sal.

A few days had passed and we were at home in front of the TV. We had planned to put on a movie but ended up just slamming dope and zoning out to *The Jenny Jones Show*.

"Haven't heard, man." I rubbed my nose and focused on the rush for a moment. "I think they're still off."

"Off?"

"From school."

"Shouldn't they be partying even more?" Sal looked puzzled.

"Not if they're back at home with their parents," I explained.

"Doing what? Playing Monopoly? Doing chores?"

Sal shook his head and lit up a cigarette. He had a point. I hadn't heard from Mark since right before everything went to shit on New Year's Eve. I grabbed a smoke from Sal's pack and sunk back into the couch. It had snowed really hard after Dante's funeral. We got like twenty-seven inches dumped on us in less than two days. And though the city kept up for a while, things eventually ground to a halt. A simple trip to the corner store was a major commitment, fraught with peril. If you didn't come home with frostbite, you could slip on some ice and crack your head open. This just made it that much easier to stay inside and slam dope. We hadn't even watched any movies. Every time Sal put one in, we nodded off.

He and I had been holed up for days and we were getting on each other's nerves. The inside of the apartment felt like death, and it smelled that way too. A stale blend of cigarettes, charred metal and body odor seemed to permeate every square inch of the place. I had tried to call Lila a few times but her phone just rang and rang. I figured she unplugged it, losing herself in a haze of smack and paint. I didn't worry about her anymore. She knew what she was doing. Besides, Shane was probably keeping an eye on her, among other things. Sal left a few messages for Sherry but she didn't call him back. Our only contact with the outside world was a single message from my mom, bawling us out for not going by Dante's house after the funeral.

"I don't know what the hell has gotten into you." Her voice was bitter. "But I am really disappointed...in both of you!" Click.

I was always in the doghouse with her, but for Sal to get it like that was truly something special. So much for the Eddie Haskell routine. Fuck it. I had more pressing concerns than my mom and what she thought. Our stash was running low and the money I managed to salvage wouldn't last long at the rate we were going. I had to make some kind of move and fast. Sal thought Frat Row was our best bet.

"Just give Mark a call," he said.

"Fuck that."

Out of the question. I also wondered what was going on but I didn't want to pick up the phone and give him any ideas. Mark always called me. I had what he wanted, not the other way around. I named the price. He paid it. If I started soliciting him, that could change. I'd look desperate. He might even try to get over on me.

"You know we're down to the reserves," said Sal.

"I know, I know." I didn't want to hear it.

"And I'm flat broke."

That was nothing new. "You know, driving wouldn't kill you."

"Of course I know," Sal scoffed. "Hasn't been that long."

"It's been over a week."

"Really? A week?" He thought for a second. "Fuck, you're right. So what? How about bereavement?"

"What about it?" I had no idea. "I'm just saying."

"I'll give Raj a call tomorrow," he said. "In the meantime, somebody has to run out to the West Side."

"Somebody, huh?" I stubbed out my cigarette. "I take it you're not volunteering."

"Not today." Sal forced a weak smile. He laid his head back on the arm of the couch and I thought I noticed a faint yellow tint to the skin on his face. "I'll hold down the fort."

"No problem," I said, feeling an unexpected burst of concern. Sal was really not well. "You just chill. I'll be back soon."

•

I figured we weren't the only ones running dangerously low on dope, so I started my car and ran up to the corner to give Lila a quick call. There was no answer again but I was pretty sure she was there and her place was on my way. I parked out front with my hazards on and ran up to her door, knocking twice. After a moment, I heard someone inside shuffling toward me. A pair of deadbolts clicked and the door opened a crack. Lila appeared in ratty wrinkled clothes with her hair in a loose ponytail and specks of paint dotting her face.

"I tried to call," I said, noting her disoriented gaze. I had never seen Lila like this before.

"You did?" She looked high and smelled like turpentine. "I must've forgotten to plug the phone back in."

"I figured as much." I glanced around. "Where's Shane?"

"I don't know." She sounded like she didn't care either.

"I'm on my way to score," I said. "You need anything?"

"What's wrong, Michael?" Lila seemed puzzled by my tone. She stroked my arm and pulled me closer. "Are you in a hurry?"

"Not really," I said. "And don't ask me what's wrong. It feels like everything is wrong. Anyway, I'm double-parked."

"Why haven't I heard from you?"

"I told you. I tried to call. You weren't picking up."

"Oh." Lila paused with marked confusion while I walked over to the wall and plugged in the phone. It rang instantly and she threw up her hands. "That's why I unplugged it in the first place," she said as she went to pick up. "Hello?"

She listened for a minute before speaking up. "No problem. I can do it." She listened some more and finally said, "Thanks for saying so, Candice. Tell Jasmine I hope she feels better."

"Don't tell me you're working again." The words slipped out before I could stop them. "Fine." She set the phone down hard. "I won't tell you."

"But why?"

Lila folded her arms and looked away from me, tight-lipped.

"Forget it." I raised my hands.

"What's your problem?"

"Nothing. No problem. Like I said, I'm making a run."

"What's the rush, Michael? Jesus, we haven't talked in days."

"I'm sorry," I said quietly. "I'm just a little off."

"I understand. I am too." Lila came over and grabbed me by the waist. "I'm going to heat up some leftover Chinese after I hop in the shower," she said. "Do you want to join me?"

"For the Chinese or the shower?"

"Both," she smiled.

"Lemme move my car."

CHAPTER TWENTY-NINE

"And a box of Reds," I said to the man behind the counter.

He was a grizzled Korean guy with the telltale lump of a gun under his shirt. I set a forty-ounce bottle of High Life down on the counter next to the register and reached for my wallet. He handed me the cigarettes and dropped the beer into a thin paper bag, glancing at the front window. Fresh snow had just started falling.

"How about this fucking weather?" he said.

"That's winter in Chicago for ya." I gave him a ten, grabbed my stuff and practically glided out the door. "Keep the change."

What a difference a shower and some chicken fried rice make!

It was more than that. For the first time since Dante's death, I felt a glimmer of happiness, or at least the possibility of it. After getting cleaned up, Lila and I screwed around and hung out for a while. We smoked a joint and had a few beers. Lila showed me her latest work—a pair of busy oils. She had decided to go with jazz greats, Miles Davis and Charlie Parker so far.

"What about Billie Holiday?" I asked.

"Shane asked me the same thing."

"I'll bet. On that girl-power tip."

"She's not like that." Lila poked me.

"She's exactly like that." I poked her back.

Other than a stray jab or two about Shane, we spent the rest of the afternoon getting along just like we used to. We didn't shoot any dope but we fucked a lot, much to my relief. When I noticed the sky outside getting darker, I decided it was time to get going. I still needed to score that night and I wasn't sure how bad the massive snowfall would jam things up. Probably not much. The drug trade tends to work like the mail. Through rain, sleet or snow, people keep slinging. You just might have to wait.

I collected a couple hundred dollars from Lila, gave her a kiss and headed down to the corner store before jumping in my car. I had hoped to beat the traffic but got caught on the Ike in the rush of cars driving home from work, no doubt people cutting out early because of the weather. I still made it to Austin Boulevard at a decent clip. I was going so fast when I pulled off, I almost slid into the intersection at the bottom of the ramp.

"Fuck!" My heart slammed against my chest. I took a few deep breaths, grabbed the steering wheel with both hands and proceeded with caution when the light turned green. It took a few blocks to get used to the surface streets, much slicker and narrower than any by my place. I could practically hear Clifford grumbling about how the city doesn't care about black folks. I made it all the way to Erie Street without any problems, only to hit the brakes a little too hard before making the turn. My car skidded into the rear end of the beat-up Ford Tempo in front of me with a crunch.

"Motherfuck!" I pounded the steering wheel and pulled over while the other guy did likewise. We both climbed out of our cars and he came right over and got in my face. Short and husky, he had his thick afro tucked inside a white hairnet. He wore a generic blue uniform sporting a patch on the shirt with his name embroidered on it— Willard. Just a working stiff on his way home from a long day. Willard must've come from Ferrara Pan, the candy factory in nearby Forest Park. He smelled like a box of Lemonheads.

"What the fuck is your problem?" He was seriously pissed off.

"I'm sorry, man." I held up my hands, really meaning it.

"Sorry ain't gonna fix my car." Willard walked around his vehicle, inspecting the damage to the rear end. The mostly plastic bumper was completely cracked up. "Look at that shit!"

"I don't know what to tell you," I said.

"You can start by telling me the name of your insurance company." He looked me over and I knew we were in for problems.

"That's the thing, man," I started to say.

"Don't you 'man' me, motherfucker!" Willard growled. "If you don't have no insurance then we callin' the police right now."

"The police? C'mon, is that really necessary?" I was trying to reason with him. I sure as hell didn't want to get jammed up filling out some report only to get a ticket on top of all that. I didn't even know what the penalty was for driving without insurance. I reached into my pocket for the wad of twenties I was going to use to score. "I'm sure we can work something out."

One look at the cash I was holding and Willard pegged me.

"You raggedyass junkie motherfucker! I wondered what your white ass was doing out here."

"I'm picking up some rib tips," I offered half-heartedly.

"The fuck you are!" Willard wasn't having it. He gave me another once-over. "I've seen your ass around the way. You and that skinny motherfucker."

Now that I got a good look at the guy, his face was familiar to me too. I made sure not to say so.

"Here's four hundred," I said. "It can't be more than that." I tried to hand him the bills but he batted my hand away.

"Four hundred? You out your mind!" Willard scoffed. "That there's gonna cost you at least a thousand."

That's when I lost it.

"A thousand dollars? You gotta be fucking kidding me!" I stepped to the guy, looking down into his face. I had at least six inches on him and I wanted to make the most of it. "Your whole fucking piece of shit car isn't worth a thousand dollars!"

"Step the fuck off, motherfucker!" Willard shoved me.

I slipped but stayed on my feet. It was on now. I was just about to rush the guy when the quick burst from a police siren stopped me dead in my tracks. An amplified voice followed.

"Hold it right there!"

Willard and I both turned our heads toward the street where a pair of Chicago's finest was climbing out of their squad car. It was another salt-and-pepper combo, this time an older black guy and a fresh-faced Hispanic woman, both in crisp blues.

"What the heck is going on here?" asked the black cop.

A cop who doesn't swear. Not a good sign.

"Nothing, officer," I replied.

When Willard didn't say anything, I thought maybe I was going to catch a break. Usually when something goes down in the hood, everyone clams up around the police. You might be at a guy's throat one minute, but you quickly set aside your differences and work together to get over on the Man. Willard had threatened to call them earlier but I knew that was just his way of trying to squeeze some more money out of me. I would've done the same thing.

"It doesn't look like nothing," said the younger cop. "Looks to me like you rear-ended this guy." She flashed a wicked smile at Willard, goading him. "Like he drove right up your ass."

"Look at my car!" he whined. My hope for solidarity against the police evaporated on the spot.

"Well," the black cop spoke up, putting his hands together. "We should all know the proper procedure for this situation. You two need to exchange information," he started counting off. "Your name, your address, the name of your insurance company..."

"He don't have no insurance!" Willard blurted out.

"Way to go." I shook my head at Willard and he scowled, knowing he just fucked up. He should've taken the four hundred when I offered it. He'd have to sue me now. Good luck with that, Willard.

"Is that true, sir?" asked the black cop.

"I can't find my card," I said. "Thought I had it."

"How about your license and registration?" the other one asked.

As I dug into my pocket, I could feel her sizing me up. An hour later and she and her partner could've had a field day with me. Fuck them. Whatever trouble I was already in, I silently thanked God I wasn't holding yet. I reached for my wallet, pulled out my driver's license and handed it over to her.

"My registration is in the glove compartment."

"Have you been drinking?" She glanced at the card. "Mr. Lira?"

I almost laughed out loud. Granted, I had been partying with Lila a little while earlier but never thought twice about driving.

"I had a couple beers this afternoon," I said. "But I'm not sure what that has to do with anything."

"Drunk driving causes most accidents," she said.

"I'm not drunk," I said.

"Maybe not," said the older cop. "But you don't have to be inebriated to be officially driving under the influence."

"You gotta be kidding me." I couldn't hide my disgust.

"I never kid about the law!" he snapped.

As bad as things were going up to that point, I still thought I had a chance to walk away from this particular scrape with a couple of tickets. But once he mentioned "the law," I knew I was fucked.

•

"You gotta get me outta here," I said into the phone.

"Jesus Christ," said Sal from the other end of the line. "You can't throw a snowball in that neighborhood without hitting a dope spot and they gotta bust your balls for some two-bit fender bender?"

"Tell me about it."

"You should've just paid the guy for his bumper."

"I tried to pay him! But this fucking cocksucker wanted a thousand dollars."

"Oh!" Sal exclaimed. "What's he drive?"

"Fuck him. He won't get a dime out of me now."

It was cold comfort. The whole sorry mess was going to cost me a lot more than a grand before it was over.

"A fucking DUI," Sal marveled. "After all this time."

"Total bullshit. I was barely over the limit. And they didn't even give me the field tests!"

"They probably don't have to when you got an open forty in the car," said Sal. "You should have never blown."

"Thanks for the tip. You my lawyer now?"

"I just can't believe it. Even Dante never got a DUI."

"It's ironic, I know. Perhaps you could mull it over while you're driving out here."

No answer from Sal.

"Are you coming or what?"

Still no answer. He had obviously nodded out.

"Fuck!" I was about to bang the phone on the desk where I was told to make my call when I noticed the cop who directed me there watching.

I took a deep breath and tried again. "Sal?"

"Yeah, yeah," he said faintly.

"Stay with me," I said, my voice ringing with frustration.

"Sorry, man," said Sal. "Your timing is not the best. I waited for you all day. I finally had to dip into the reserves."

"Well, I'm glad *you're* all better now," I said, trying to mask my rising panic. Between the florescent lights glaring overhead in the dingy office where I was sitting and the sickness creeping into my limbs, I was starting to freak out.

"I'm feeling pretty fucking shitty myself." I spoke as calmly as I could. "Thing is I could use a little help, too, you know? A little help from my friends? Can you handle that?"

"Fuckin' A," said Sal. "I'm on it."

•

Four long hours later, I was sprawled in the backseat of Lila's car. It had been more than twelve hours since my last fix when she and Sal got me out of that godforsaken police station. My hands were shaking so badly, Sal had to work the hype. It was the least he could do after making me wait. I really let him have it too. He took it for a while before finally pushing back.

"You didn't want me to show up empty-handed, did you?"

He had a point but I didn't care. Everything was fucked. When it was all said and done, that sorry little mishap had cost me more than half the cash I had left. Bail alone was twenty-four hundred dollars. And getting back my impounded car would cost another twelve, two hundred for towing and storage and a thousand for unpaid parking tickets. I told them to keep the damn car. Fuck it.

"Twelve hundred buys a lot of trips on the el," I murmured and sat up after getting knocked on my back by the rush.

"What are you talking about?" asked Lila.

"Michael is merely trying to come to terms with the loss of his beloved Disgustang," said Sal.

"No way! I can pay to get the car out," she offered.

"Forget about it," I said with a clumsy wave of my hand.

"At least they didn't take the cash you were holding," said Sal. "The narcs pull that shit all the time."

"Speaking of narcs," said Lila. "Could one of you please climb up front with me so we don't look so, I don't know..."

"Shady?" Sal raised his eyebrows.

"Exactly." Lila nodded and let out a wry laugh. "Who's going to pick me up if *I* get thrown in jail?"

•

The sun came out in force the next day and the temperature had shot up at least twenty degrees. By the time I was up and heading over to the corner for some cigarettes and a bottle of OJ, all the snow had melted off the tops of the parked cars. Tiptoeing and hopping my way back, I was so focused on avoiding the deep, soupy puddles of slush I didn't notice the man approaching me from across the street. When I finally glimpsed him right up on me—lean and leathered with a shock of white hair—I recognized him immediately. Then I remembered his voice on the answering machine a few days prior. I had ignored it as if the call was for someone else.

"C'mon, Michael," said Tom Daly. "It hasn't been that long."

"No...of course not." I looked down, avoiding his scrutinizing gaze. "Not at all. I just didn't expect to run into you here."

"I tried calling you," he said. "I left messages."

"I know, I know," I said. "I've been meaning..."

Before I could get the words out, he cut me off. "Backing out of the deal, huh?" He looked disappointed.

"I don't have the money to put down," I said. "Not anymore."

I stood there in front of him, fighting the nod from my morning fix. The idea of buying a piece of property with a mortgage and insurance and property taxes and all that other worldly shit seemed ludicrous. I would have laughed but for his earnest expression.

"What happened?" he asked without a trace of judgment.

"It's a long story," I said, hoping to leave it at that.

"I've got a few minutes," he said. "C'mon, Michael. We had a deal. At least tell me what happened."

I started to tell him the tale, leaving out the most unflattering details about Paul and, of course, myself. As it turned out, Tom Daly didn't need to hear much before he went off.

"Hucksters and charlatans, the lot of 'em," he said of Paul and his ilk.

He didn't think much of the people they duped either. "Dreamers and fools! They all think they can sit on their asses and get rich...throwing their money at companies they don't know anything about. All these dotcoms? Tell me, what is a dotcom anyway? What the hell is it that they do?"

"I wouldn't know." I stated the obvious.

"You're better off jumping on a plane to Las Vegas," he went on. "At least you know your odds." He shook his head. "Michael, you seem like a smart kid. You should've known better. You work hard. You save your money. Why throw it away like that? You had the right idea. Buy a piece of property. Land. A building. Something real. Something that's gonna be worth something no matter what."

"Tell me about it."

"Well," he said. "Not much you can do about it now. Live and learn, I suppose." He looked at me with genuine regret in his eyes before he patted me on the back and started to walk away.

"Hey," I called out to him as the question occurred to me. "How did you find me anyway? My address isn't listed."

"I wasn't even looking," he said, turning toward me. "I came by here to talk to the owner of the building."

•

"Going condo?" Sal was beside himself. "I can't fucking believe this shit!"

"That's not for sure," I said. "If my buddy Tom Daly buys it, he might just raise the rent."

"Great," said Sal. "As if we don't already pay enough for this shithole." He stubbed out his cigarette. "Besides, I thought that guy wanted to retire."

"His wife wants him to."

"She'll get her way. They always do. How do you think my parents ended up in Boca? My dad hates it down there."

"Whatever," I said with resignation. "It's out of our hands. If it's not him, it'll be somebody else."

"I'll tell you one thing." Sal had broken out his works and was cooking up a fix. "We're not paying any more rent for this place if all they're gonna do is throw us out when it goes condo."

•

We spent the next few days slamming dope and licking our proverbial wounds. During that time, we learned our building really was going condo, thanks to another faceless North Side developer. Our building manager, a frumpy guy who always seemed to be doing four things at once, filled me in when he stopped by to see if I could fix a broken p-trap in the unit two floors above us. I almost told him to call a plumber but since I figured the poor slob would probably soon be out of a job, I didn't want to leave him high and dry. So I went upstairs and helped him out. When I got back, Sal was crashed out and Mark had left me a message.

"Long time no talk, dude," he said. "Gimme a call."

"It's about fucking time," I said to Sal as he came to.

"No shit." He rubbed his eyes and stretched his back. "Too bad you can't call him back."

"What?" I grabbed the receiver, put it to my ear and didn't hear a thing. It didn't exactly come as a huge surprise. After months of unpaid bills and notices, AT&T had finally cut us off.

"Perfect timing, huh?"

"I'll be right back," I said, heading for the door.

I ran down to the corner store to use the pay phone. Sure enough, Mark was back at school and everyone was ready to party.

"Can you hook us up?" he asked.

"What do you need?"

"Two, like before."

"No problem," I told him. "I'll call you."

I hung up and ran back to rifle through what was left of my cash, twelve hundred.

"Well?" Sal called to me from the living room.

"I'm four hundred short," I said. "Got any cash?"

"Yeah, right. You're gonna have to get the money up front."

What a pain in the balls. I walked back out to join Sal in the living room. He was on the couch tying off with the loaded syringe at the ready. While he lined up and fixed, I sat down next to him with my head in my hands. I was right back where I started. I was tired. I knew I needed money and I knew I could make it back, but I couldn't imagine all that running, especially without a car. I felt like I didn't have the energy or the luck to do it again. I lifted my head and reached for a cigarette just as Sal dropped back in.

"Well?" He pulled the needle from his arm and sat back, itching his chest. "What are you gonna do?"

CHAPTER THIRTY

"Gonna make a big old burn bag, huh?" said Aaron.

"For real?" said T. "That ain't like you, Michael."

"Fuck it," I shrugged. "I'm tired of these guys."

"Time to cut 'em loose," Sal backed me up.

"You do real good with those boys." T looked at me. "Don't see why you fittin' to shut it down again right now."

"Too much bullshit," I said with a wink in Sal's direction. "Unless of course you want to start fronting me."

"Shiiittt," said Aaron. "The way y'all be slamming?"

I was about to explain why our slamming wasn't a factor when I noticed stuffed moving boxes piled around the apartment. Most of the framed pictures that had cluttered various pieces of furniture were missing too. Others had been taken down from the nicotine stained walls, leaving bright patches like little windows to nowhere.

"Somebody going somewhere?" I asked.

"Me and Mook," said T. "We got us a place in Oak Park."

"They done with us West Side niggas," Aaron smiled.

"What about us?" said Sal, only half-joking.

"We done with you, too," T laughed.

Janet walked up behind Sal and wrapped her arms around his neck.

"It's okay, baby," she said. "I'll still take care of you."

"You will, huh?" He cracked a lecherous grin. "I assume you're referring to more than the T-bags, right?"

"Maybe," Janet teased him. "If you lucky."

"Well, I'm definitely lucky," said Sal as he spun her around and pulled her close, pushing his chest up against those massive breasts. The rest of us just ignored them. Sal and Janet's thing had never been right out there in the open like that, and I for one was happy to keep it that way. But Clifford spoke up from the living room where Beverly was parked next to him in front of a rowdier than usual episode of *The Montel Williams Show*.

"Since me and Bev movin' into Mook's room," Clifford called out over the noise from the TV, "You two gonna have to learn to keep it down when you goin' at it."

"Oh!" exclaimed Sal.

"You stop that." Beverly slapped Clifford on the arm.

"Don't worry." Aaron looked at me and I could tell he was getting back to business. I'm sure he wasn't happy about losing the sales to Frat Row but he knew it was out of his hands. "Janet got the weed now too. And if anything else come up, I'll be around."

"So when's all this jumping off?" I asked, feeling a little sad about T and Mookie just being gone like that.

"Place gonna be ready March the first," said T.

"Well, congratulations," said Sal.

"Thanks," said T. "Y'all come by and see us sometime."

"We'll do that," I said.

Steering the conversation back to my original question, I pulled out the package I had just paid for and looked at Aaron and T.

"So what do you think? How hard would it be to turn this into a couple ounces of rock?"

"Not hard," said T. "If you a magician."

"That's helpful." I shook my head and turned to Maurice.

"Somebody know how to do it," he said. "They got to. Where else do all the bad blow come from?"

"I don't know nothing about that," said Aaron. "Ain't my thing."

"Me neither," said Janet. "Everything we get is ready made and correct. We don't need nobody coming back on us."

"These guys aren't gonna do shit," I said. "I just need to get out the door before they figure out what's up."

"First you need to find someone that can cook," said Aaron.

•

"We weren't even sure you'd still be around," I said to Kenny as he stepped aside to let us in.

"How much longer you got this place?" asked Sal.

"Another week, give or take," said Kenny. "The landlord said he's gonna call the sheriff."

"Fuck the sheriff," said Sal.

"That's what I told him," said Kenny. "His deputy too."

He closed the door behind us and led the way over and around the mounds of trash that had accumulated since our last bender more than a month before. He looked awful—pale and gaunt with his hair pulled back in a loose, greasy ponytail. His lips were cracked and he had several burns on his hands. For all we knew, he had been going since we last saw him on New Year's Eve. The place sure looked and smelled like it. A stale combination of cigarette butts, spoiled beer and charred plastic permeated the air. We all took a seat on what was left of the ratty living room couch.

"Still fixing cars?" I asked.

"I'm off on comp," said Kenny. "Hurt my back lifting a trans."

"So what really happened?" asked Sal. I was thinking the same thing. We both knew Kenny's affinity for daredevil stunts.

"I fell while I was surfing the el," Kenny smirked and lit up a cigarette. "Shop's fighting me tooth and nail. I'll probably get cut off and canned any day now. So what's up?"

"We got a little proposition for you," I said.

Sal had come up with an idea that was simple but brilliant. Since Kenny knew how to cook the impurities out of cocaine, we figured he could just as easily cook them right back in.

"And then some," said Sal.

"What for?" Kenny looked aghast.

"Some people we're looking to burn," I said.

"No shit," said Kenny. "Who are they?"

"Nobody," said Sal. "Just some frat boys. They came by Spoonful one time, real candyasses."

"That's right," said Kenny. "I heard one of 'em puked on Lee."

"The night Dante tagged him," Sal said wistfully.

"I forgot about that," I said, feeling a pang of emotion. The big lug. I thought about him all the time and I was sure Sal did too, but neither one of us had spoken his name in days.

"Sorry I didn't make it to the funeral," said Kenny.

"You didn't miss much," said Sal.

"Dante was a good guy," said Kenny. "Crazy fucker."

A moment of silence passed. I didn't want to talk about Dante anymore so I tried to get things moving.

"So, Kenny," I put it to him. "Can you do it?"

"That depends."

I pulled out the ounce I bought earlier and told him he could keep a quarter if he could somehow cook the rest into something that looked and smelled like good rock.

"How much?" he asked.

"Two ounces," I said.

"Fuck!" said Kenny. "Can't you just break it up and mix in some bunk shake? Tell 'em it's from the bottom of a key."

"I already do that," I said. "But I still need a lot more rock to make this work."

"These guys are idiots," said Sal. "But they're not that stupid."

"You think you can do it?" I looked at Kenny.

"I'll do my best," he said, his gaze locked on the bag.

I cleared a spot on the coffee table, dumped out the blow and quickly broke off a quarter. All the while, I could practically feel Kenny's eyeballs on the pile in front of me.

"Looks good, doesn't it?" said Sal.

He just had to fuck with Kenny, as if Sal or I wouldn't be drooling over a big pile of smack. I grabbed the tattered copy of *Swank* lying nearby and tore a page from the lesbian spread, folded it twice and dumped the rest of the blow on there.

"Here you go," I said, handing it to Kenny.

"This could take a while," he said.

"Better get to it," I said. "We'll wait. And you can have your piece as soon as you're done."

Kenny disappeared into the kitchen while Sal and I fixed up. I ended up nodding off for a while. By the time Sal nudged me, Kenny had finished. Somehow he had cooked up something that looked, smelled and even tasted like the real thing. It came back in two chunks, one about twice as big as the other. They sat in the middle of a red plate with white powder spread over it like a gourmet dessert.

"What happens if they snort it?" asked Sal.

"Nothing," said Kenny. "They'll get a little numb, taste the baking soda and probably pick up the phone."

"Good thing we're disconnected," said Sal.

"It won't hurt anyone, right?" I asked.

"Fuck no," said Kenny. "Maybe their feelings."

"Fuckin' A," said Sal as he gawked at the plate.

"That's something, isn't it?" I was blown away myself as I handed Kenny his reward. "You truly are a magician."

"I try," he said as he headed right back into the kitchen.

"Knock yourself out," Sal called after him. "You deserve it."

•

I wanted to get the deal over with as soon as possible, but we needed a car and Sal couldn't get the cab until the next night. Once he did, we drove up to the Triple Chi house for the last time. Sal parked and waited for me outside.

"Keep the engine running," I told him.

Kenny had come through like a champ but I still felt nervous when Mark greeted me in the lobby and told me Steve was upstairs. The house was quiet, except for a gaggle of frat guys coming down the stairs as we were going up. The collective blast of cologne as they walked by almost knocked me on my ass. Up in the room, everything went as usual except for one tense moment, at least in my head.

"The stuff looks different," said Steve.

I felt flushed but kept my cool and didn't say a word. Mark opened the bag and took a whiff.

"Smells okay." He nodded and gave me the money.

It took everything in me not to bolt down the stairs and out the front door the moment Mark let me out of the room.

"I'll call you," he said.

You do that.

•

"Well, well, well," said Dana.

Sal and I had just walked up to the bar.

Having made a clean getaway from the Triple Chi house with an even two grand, I felt like celebrating with a few drinks.

"Let's do it," said Sal.

We dropped the money at home and the cab at the stand and caught a ride over there with one of the other drivers. Dana came over as soon as she saw us.

"Haven't seen you guys since New Year's," she said. "By the way, I was really sorry to hear..."

"No sweat, Dana." Sal cut her off. He didn't want to talk about Dante any more than I did.

"How are things around here?" I jumped in, glancing around. "Seems kind of slow for a Friday night."

"I think people are hibernating," said Dana. "Hey, how's Lila doing? Haven't seen her or Sherry either."

"Neither have we," Sal said abruptly. He hadn't heard a word from Sherry since the funeral and I knew it was bothering him. "But since we're not hibernating and it's colder than a witch's tit out there, I could use a little warming up. How about a couple Crowns?"

Dana raised her eyebrows. "Coming right up."

"And a couple High Lifes," I said with a nod as I peeled off a twenty and laid it on the bar.

Dana came back with our drinks and took the bill without a word.

"Here's to..." Sal hesitated with his glass in the air.

"Fucking Frat Row," I said.

"Fuckin' A," said Sal.

We downed those drinks and many more, and though it certainly wasn't our custom, each one went down with a different toast. They got more outrageous as the night went on and the place slowly filled up with more people. By the time Dana was making noise about cutting us off, we were drinking to Monica Lewinsky and the blue dress.

"That shit's better than Springer!" said Sal.

"Fuckin' A!" I said, mimicking him.

Sal tipped his glass only to have it suddenly knocked from his hand by some yuppie asshole that had pushed his way up to the bar. It hit the grimy wood floor and shattered into pieces.

"Watch where you're fucking going!" Sal got in the guy's face.

"You watch where *you're* going!" The guy puffed himself up and looked down his nose at Sal. "Fuckin' punkass bitch!"

"You!" Dana pointed at the guy. "Get the fuck outta here!"

"Fuck you, cunt!" The guy spit the words at her and everyone around us started backing away from the scene. I felt my heart pounding against my chest as the adrenaline surged through me. For one long moment, I considered braining him with the longneck in my hand but I set it on the bar instead.

"Get lost or I'm calling the cops!" Dana grabbed the phone but the guy ignored her, turning to Sal.

"Fuckin' pussy!" he barked at Sal as he shoved him back into me.

I grabbed Sal, pushing him aside as I stepped to the guy. Before I could even get my hands up, he caught me with a glancing blow that slid off my cheek but still stung.

"Motherfuck!" I shook it off and lunged at him, but the guy turned his back and ran for the door with the crowd that had gathered quickly parting to let him through.

"What the fuck!" said Sal.

"Let him go, Michael!" said Dana.

"Fuck that!"

Dana reached over to grab my arm but I pulled away from her and charged out the front door with Sal behind me.

"There he is!" Sal pointed across the street. The guy stood still for a moment before darting into the alley halfway down the block.

Right then and there, I should've known it was setup.

"We got him!" I said as I broke into a run.

I was in such a hurry, I didn't even slow down when Sal slipped in the puddle behind me. In seconds, I turned the corner and was immediately blind-sided by a crushing blow to the face. I heard something crack and felt the blood begin to gush from my nose, running down into my mouth and across my chin. I raised my hand to wipe it away and immediately caught another blow to the stomach. Buckling over, I fell to the ground, choking on the blood in my throat as I heard a familiar voice I couldn't place at first.

"How's that feel?" he said. "Looks painful."

Then it hit me. Brad from the CBOT Crew. I rolled over and saw him and his limey sidekick Jack standing over me with Mark, Steve and the douchebag from the bar all but cowering in the background.

"What a bloody cunt," said Jack.

He pulled me up by the front of my jacket and slugged me in the jaw. Even though I saw stars for a moment, he didn't have much.

"Fuck you," I groaned, getting my breath back.

I rolled back over on my hands and knees and tried to push myself to my feet when I saw Brad approach me out of the corner of my eye. He reared back one hiking boot and I braced myself, covering my face just as Sal finally made his appearance.

"You motherfuckers!" he shouted.

"Piss off!" Jack sneered. "Little wanker!"

I heard a brief scuffle before seeing Sal drop to the cold, damp pavement not far from me.

"Fucking pussies," said Brad. "Not much without your big fucking ape here to protect you, huh?" He gave Sal a sharp kick in the gut and turned his attention back to me, calling over his shoulder to Mark and Steve. "You guys gonna stand around and pull your dicks all night? I'm not the one that got ripped off."

Mark just stood there, his eyes wide with fear. Steve and the other guy appeared to be thinking it over.

"Cunts and wankers, the lot of you," said Jack with disgust.

He went over and grabbed Sal, like he did me before, but just as he was about to slug him, Sal flicked out his switchblade with a shimmering flash and plunged it into Jack's thigh.

"Jesus fucking Christ!" he cried, desperately clutching at his leg while Sal yanked out the blade and stuck him again, this time in the mass of flesh above his elbow.

"How's that feel?" Sal mocked him.

"You fucking cunt!" Jack wailed.

He collapsed to the ground where two small pools of blood began to spread out and glisten in the moonlight. Sal pulled out the knife, rolled over and sprung to his feet just before Brad could get to him. I couldn't believe my eyes. I felt like I had suddenly been dropped into a toned-down version of some cheesy grindhouse flick, like so many Sal and I had watched on video. By that time, Mark, Steve and their buddy had fled the scene. Brad was another story. While Jack writhed around in pain, he slowly circled closer to Sal.

"Fucking grease ball," he spit. "I'll snap your arm like a twig before you stick me."

I got up to help Sal and Brad shot a look in my direction.

"I'll take both of you fucking cocksuckers myself," he said with a ring of doubt in his voice.

"I don't think so, Brad," I said calmly as I paused to stomp on Jack's injured leg. He let out a blood-curdling scream.

"Knock that shit off!" said Brad.

It wasn't clear if he was yelling at me or Jack. Either way, all the crying was extremely unsettling.

"You gotta get this guy to a hospital," I said to Brad.

"Maybe you want to join him," Sal said with a wicked smile.

For a split second, he looked pretty menacing, though Brad didn't seem to notice. He lunged at Sal and caught him by the wrist, twisting his arm until the knife hit the pavement. Sal scrambled to pick it up but Brad kicked it away and landed a blow to the back of his head. Sal's knees buckled and he dropped. Brad was about to kick Sal in the face when I took him down hard with an open field tackle.

Dante would've been proud.

He had me by several inches and at least forty pounds, but the impact stunned him for a moment and I had my way. I crawled on top of his chest and delivered a flurry of punches to his face. Other than a split lip, they didn't seem to do much more than shock him back to life. He covered up with one hand and caught me upside the head with the other. The force rocked me back and he was able to push me off. He tried to get on top of me but I wriggled away. When he pulled me back, I wrapped him up before he could start beating on me. Now it was a wrestling match. If I hadn't been so fucked up, I could've taken him. Having been tossed around for years by Dante, who was much bigger and stronger, I knew how to scrap. But between the smack and the booze and the cheap shot I took rounding the corner into the alley, I wasn't in the best shape that night.

"Kick his fucking arse!" yelled Jack from his bloody spot.

I was just glad not to hear any more whimpering. I could've used a cheer from Sal myself but when all I got was a faint moan, I knew I was on my own. I struggled with Brad for what felt like forever before he managed to get me in a headlock. He squeezed tight, choking me while I tried in vain to break loose from his grip. My strength was gone. It took everything I had just to claw at the forearm crushing my windpipe. As I felt my consciousness slipping away, it occurred to me that this could really be it. I was fucked.

Then I saw the bright white light.

CHAPTER THIRTY-ONE

And I heard the deafening roar. A horrible screech followed along with the acrid smell of burning rubber.

"What the fuck?" Brad loosened his grip and shoved me to the ground, where I inched over out of the light and caught my breath. Kenny had just pulled into the alley in his 1970 Chevelle SS.

The cavalry was here and we hadn't even called!

I stole a look at Sal crawling over to retrieve his knife as I pushed myself up on one knee. Kenny pulled up closer to Brad and rolled down his window, calling out to us.

"You guys all right?" he asked.

"Mind your own fucking business!" said Brad.

"Fine," Kenny said casually. For a split second, it seemed like he might back out of the alley and drive away. Then he pushed open his door and stepped out of the car with a sawed off pump shotgun dangling from one hand. Before Brad could say or do anything, Kenny racked the gun with a loud cluck-click. He stuck the barrel in Brad's face. "Except this is my fucking business, asshole!"

•

"That was fucking awesome!" Sal crowed.

"Unbelievable," I spoke up from the backseat of Kenny's car as we sped away from the alley where we left Brad and Jack.

"It was nothing," Kenny said over his shoulder.

"Nothing, he says." Sal shook his head.

"Hey, you actually stabbed that guy!" said Kenny.

"What the fuck was I supposed to do?" said Sal. "I should've stuck him again. Brad too, that fucking scumbag."

"I can't believe you showed up when you did," I said. "Why the hell were you up in that alley anyway?"

"I was driving by Spoonful when you guys ran across the street," said Kenny. "You didn't hear me yell?"

"Fuck no," said Sal. "And what about this?" He motioned to the shotgun propped against the seat between them.

"I was thinking of pawning it," said Kenny.

"Don't do that," said Sal. "It could come in handy again."

"I thought those guys weren't gonna do shit," said Kenny.

"Those weren't the guys," I said.

"They weren't?" Kenny looked puzzled.

Sal jumped in with a quick explanation. Burning Frat Row had left the CBOT Crew with nowhere to score for a little while and Mark had obviously wasted no time in telling them it was our fault. Between that and the beating they got from Dante on Halloween, those guys must have jumped at the chance for some payback.

"Fucking pussies," said Sal.

I wasn't sure, but I figured he was talking about Frat Row since two thirds of the CBOT Crew had just kicked our asses.

"You think they'll be back?" asked Kenny.

"I doubt it," I said. "We should still lay low for a while."

"Or maybe we should go after them," said Sal, still amped from the fight. "You know, strike first."

I could understand where he was coming from, but we had enough to worry about without going to war with the CBOT Crew.

"Where the fuck did you get this thing anyway, Kenny?" Sal motioned to the gun again.

"My father-in-law gave it to me when we moved to the city," Kenny said. "Sort of a housewarming present."

"Nice." Sal nodded and picked up the gun, running his hand over the smooth black barrel. "How do you pump it?"

"Keep it down." Kenny pushed the barrel down below the dash. "There's a little button you push while you rack it."

"Jesus, be careful," I warned them. I was still pretty freaked about nearly getting the life choked out of me. The last thing I wanted was to accidentally get my head blown off.

"Don't worry," Kenny said. "It's not loaded."

"You gotta be fucking kidding!" said Sal.

"Of course not," said Kenny. "You think I'm driving around with a loaded gun? That would be just plain stupid."

His indignation was funny as hell under the circumstances. I would have laughed if my throat hadn't been so swollen and sore.

"What's the Chevelle doing out anyway?" I asked. Kenny always garaged his vehicle during the winter, like most classic car owners in and around Chicago.

"When my comp ran out and I got canned, I had to clear out of the shop," he said. "The house too. Sheriffs came this morning."

"That sucks," said Sal.

"Tell me about it," said Kenny. "I thought I had a few more days. I barely had time to gather up my shit. Plus I thought they were gonna bust me. I was done cooking up what you gave me, but the smell..."

"They don't give a fuck," said Sal. "They just want the house."

I sat back and realized I was on top of a pile of matted clothes, some still on hangers. Two plastic milk cartons were wedged behind the driver's seat, both stuffed with a hodge-podge of random household items. I could see CDs, magazines, a clock radio and some plates and mugs. His coffee maker was shoved under the passenger seat next to a tackle box. His tools must have been in the trunk.

What a drag.

Kenny was homeless and he just saved our asses. That meant we now had a new roommate, at least until we got sent packing from our own place. It also meant another habit to feed. We had just made a nice score thanks to Frat Row, but it wouldn't tide Sal and me over for long. With Kenny and his habit around twenty-four-seven, I knew things could get desperate pretty quick. After Kenny accepted our offer of hospitality, I asked him straight out about his financial situation. He didn't have any cash to speak of, but he did have a steady stream of unemployment checks coming his way for a while.

"Get canned and get paid," said Sal. "You gotta like that."

•

After mercilessly ribbing me for my two black eyes, Maurice had hooked us up with a currency exchange where Kenny could get an advance on his checks. We spent a week or two doing speedballs—it was hard to keep track. The apartment became a prison with regular furloughs to the West Side. Between Kenny's cooking, the accumulating trash and our collective lack of personal hygiene, the place smelled more like death than ever. As bad as we were right after Dante's funeral, this was much worse because of the blow. I used to enjoy a bell ringer once in a while but now it was a constant thing. I couldn't resist spiking my shots, yet every time I felt that telltale chill, I regretted it. My chest would pound, my throat would grow tight and an overwhelming sense of dread would pour over me. The monkey was digging in deeper every day. Sometimes, I thought I heard someone standing outside the door or lurking under the window.

"It's all in your head," Sal would say.

"That doesn't make it any less real."

I also kept thinking about Dante. I tried not to but the blow kept winding me up, getting my thoughts racing places out of my control. Every time the rush faded and the blast took over, I'd see him in my mind. Sometimes, I remembered him on the field, tearing through one feeble block after another to make one of his many big plays. I saw him celebrating afterward, dropping to one knee and spreading his arms wide as he threw his head back and roared like some super-powered gridiron beast. He seemed so alive. Other times, I saw him on New Year's Eve, big and beat, hanging his head as he told me that he was basically giving up. I honestly couldn't say which was more painful to recall, but they both hurt.

Each day was more miserable than the last. I tried to think back to the last time I had felt anything beyond hopelessness and regret. Then I remembered. Leftover Chinese and a hot shower with Lila. I pictured her and me, tangled up in the sheets with several takeout containers next to the bed. She seemed like a lifeline I might be able to grab onto, the only thing that might bring some relief. That afternoon when Sal nodded off and Kenny crashed out at the same time, I headed out the door.

•

"Michael."

Lila had a paintbrush in her hand and an expression that told me I shouldn't have come. My heart sank.

"Not a good time?" I asked.

"Who is it, babe?" I heard Shane's voice.

"Babe?" I raised my eyebrows at Lila.

"It's Michael," Lila called over her shoulder, looking me over with a blend of disapproval and concern. She was just about to comment when I offered up my own observation.

"You don't look much better than me."

And she didn't. Lila was as thin as I'd ever seen her, with oily hair and the washed-out complexion you get from an overworked liver.

"Nice," she said, shaking her head. "So glad you dropped by."

"I'm sorry." I pulled her close and basked in a moment of comfort when I felt her arms around my waist. "Can we talk?"

"Sure," said Lila. She pulled away and headed back in. "You want something to drink?"

I grabbed her hand and lowered my voice. "I mean, alone."

I had just uttered the words when Shane appeared from around the corner of the kitchen, slipping her coat on.

"Hey, Michael." She nodded at me and turned to Lila. "I'm taking off. Want to meet for a drink later? After work?"

"Maybe," Lila murmured. "I'll call you."

"I'll wait to hear," said Shane.

You do that.

Shane walked out the door without another word, leaving an awkward silence in her wake. Finally, it was just Lila and me. I reached for her again but she had drifted over to her latest piece. John Coltrane. At least she was still painting.

"So you're working tonight?" I asked.

"Yeah."

Lila picked up her palette and was practically ignoring me now, gently dabbing paint on the canvas.

"Somebody get sick again?" I asked. "How's Sherry? Nobody's seen her around."

"She's okay," said Lila. "She got pretty shook up after Dante. She needed some time alone to figure things out. I haven't seen her myself but we're getting together tonight—at Excalibur of all places." She gave a slight shudder. "Whatever. We're doing one last party as a sort of favor for Candice. Then I'm done. Sherry too."

"One last party, huh?"

"That's right."

"I see." I just hoped she meant it this time. "I understand you're on the cusp of fame and fortune. But what's Sherry gonna do if she's not working for Candice?"

"She's moving in with her mother." Lila sounded a little sad.

"Her mother? Doesn't she live in Canada?"

"Toronto," said Lila. "As the child of a resident, her college tuition is totally covered by the government. Sherry's going back to school to get a degree. Nursing maybe, or social work. You forget that she's only twenty-two."

"A young-un," I nodded. "Good for her."

Hearing about Sherry cheered me up a little. At least someone was doing okay. I started wandering around, distracting myself with some of the new work that had sprung up.

"This is different for you." I wasn't sure what else to say.

I was standing in front of a four-by-six-foot oil of a party scene. A slim girl in low slung jeans and a lime-green tank top that left her flat, tattooed midriff proudly exposed was shimmying up to another hottie on a dance floor. The second girl was only partially visible in the foreground and still needed some color. I recognized the style immediately.

"That's Shane's," she said.

"What's it doing here?" I asked with a little too much tension in my voice. So much for playing it cool.

"She ran out of space at her apartment," Lila said. "She lives in a tiny little studio."

"Maybe her paintings shouldn't be so big."

Lila's eyes flashed, but I stopped her before she went off.

"I'm sorry, Lila," I said, meaning it. "Listen, I'm not here to bust your chops about your job or Shane."

"Good," Lila snapped. "Because you have absolutely no right. Not to mention, I haven't seen or heard from you in weeks!"

"I know, I know." I dropped my head and closed my eyes.

I had to gather my thoughts and courage. If I were the type who prayed, now would've been the time to do it. I knew I wanted out. I wanted a new life but I didn't know where to go or how to get there. All I knew was that I didn't want to go by myself. I loved Lila and I thought maybe she loved me too. I hoped that would be enough.

"What is it?" Lila put down her brush and palette and came over, gently taking my hands. I lifted my chin and took a deep breath.

"Will you go away with me?" I asked.

"What?" Confusion dimmed her expression. I could feel my hopes slipping away but I went on. It was now or never.

"I need to get the fuck out of here," I said. "I need to get away from Chicago and all the bullshit. For good."

"What about Sal?"

"I'll miss him but I'll get over it."

"You don't mean that," said Lila. "I know it's been hard. It's been hard for me too. It'll get better. You just need to get out of that apartment, scale back on the drugs. You need to clear your head and come up with a real plan."

"I need more than that, Lila." I fixed on her gaze, hoping to still somehow get through to her if my words failed. "I need you."

"You can have me," she said in a soothing tone. "Any time you want. You should know that."

"Not when Shane's here." I said, grabbing at the only tangible obstacle I could come up with.

"Oh, Michael," said Lila. "Is that what this about? Like I said, any time you want. And if it makes you feel any better, Shane said you could even join us sometime. If you want, that is."

I was probably the only straight guy in America who couldn't be tempted with that particular scenario.

"You told her about me? About us?"

"She guessed, but don't worry. She's cool with it."

"She's cool with it?"

I couldn't believe she had thought this through and discussed it with Shane. I also couldn't believe she figured some hot threesome could substitute for what I was proposing. Lila's attitude was heart-breaking, but I wasn't going to let her change the subject.

"What about California?" I asked. "A few months ago you were talking about going back. Now would be the perfect time." I went over to the window and blurted out. "Look at this shitty weather!" Hearing my voice, I almost cringed. I sounded crazy.

"Michael, please." Lila looked at me with more sadness and pity than love in her eyes. "Things have changed."

"I'll say," I agreed. "Look at us. Look at you."

I grabbed her arm and rolled up her sleeve to reveal the tracks. "You're a junkie, Lila. How long can you go on like this?"

"You've gone on for years," she said, yanking her arm back.

"You're not me," I said. "I'm just saying that..."

"I know what you're saying." Lila interrupted me. "You've had enough and I don't blame you, but that's on you. I'm okay."

"You don't seem that okay to me."

"I didn't ask for your fucking opinion!" Her sudden burst in volume made me jump. "Jesus, get over it, Michael. You can't save me. I can't save you."

"Fine."

We both stood there silent for a moment. Lila walked over to the kitchen table to retrieve a newspaper.

"I take it you haven't seen this." She handed over a wrinkled copy of the free Chicago weekly *Newcity*.

I took the paper and immediately recognized Lila's toothy grin. She was standing behind a three foot by five foot canvas with her head peaking over the top of a headless, life-size sketch of her nude form in heels and a sexy pose. The title of the accompanying article read: "Showgirl Shows Well!" I quickly scanned the text. It was a brief profile of Lila with some flattering commentary on the pieces she showed at "The Next Big Thing." I was as happy for her as I could be, though I didn't need to see the plug for Anything Goes.

"Well?" said Lila. I looked up and she was standing behind the gimmicky canvas shown in the photograph, smiling.

"Good for you," I said with resignation. I knew it was a lost cause now. I just wanted to go home and fix.

"It is, right? I've already gotten calls from a bunch of agents and Neil—you know, he owns the gallery—he said all but one of the pieces sold."

"Yeah? Which one?"

"Believe it or not, the King."

"It's only a matter of time," I said. "Congratulations."

I went over to where she was standing and picked up the canvas, setting it aside so I could give her a hug.

"It'll be all right, Michael," said Lila. "You'll see."

I knew she was wrong about that but all I said was goodbye.

•

"Where the fuck have you been?" said Sal.

"Out," I said, closing the door behind me.

I had only been gone for a couple hours but our place struck me as even more disgusting than it was when I left, like all the junkies on the West Side had traipsed through there while I was gone. Sal and Kenny were huddled over the coffee table, each looking uniquely desperate. Having noted with grim acceptance our dwindling reserves of cash and smack, I knew this day would come.

"I know a place we can hit," said Sal.

"Oh yeah?" I looked at him. "How can that be? You haven't driven in..." I hesitated, trying to remember.

"This is different," said Sal. "Some yuppie douchebag that lives in one of those lame new condos across the street went on vacation."

"We saw the cab pick him up an hour ago," said Kenny.

"You should've seen this guy," said Sal. "All the luggage? Imagine Madonna going on tour."

"Let me get this straight." I looked Sal in the eye. "You want to rip off some guy who lives *right across the street*?"

"We're not gonna pawn anything around here," said Kenny.

"Of course not," I shot back. "There's nowhere around here to pawn anything anymore anyway!"

"What are you getting so worked up about?" asked Sal.

"It's a stupid idea," I said. "We're liable to have the cops knocking on our door just to ask if we saw anything."

"So we tell 'em we didn't see shit."

"We can't let it come to that," I said, gesturing around us. "Look at this fucking place. You think they're just gonna ask a few questions and be on their way?"

"Well, what do you suggest we do?" Sal folded his arms. "Because we gotta do something. And we gotta do it now."

Sal was right. With less than five hundred dollars and only a few bags left, we would be retching within a week. The time to act was short. Once you got the monkey on your back, you gotta feed it, constantly. Finding the ways and means to score is a twenty-four-seven gig. You might get lucky and hit it big now and then but you're always looking ahead. Plotting. Planning. No matter how much you get or how close the scrape, you always gotta keep at it. Day in and day out.

"Whatever we do," I said. "We have to be smart."

"Too bad we don't know anyone holding a bunch of cash," said Kenny, "Or drugs."

He got up and grabbed his gun, pacing the room as he pumped the barrel. Cluck-click.

"Jesus," I said, realizing just how crazy things could get.

"What about your buddies on the West Side?" said Kenny.

"Are you outta your fucking mind?" Sal was appalled. "That's the best connection we got."

"So we cover our faces," said Kenny.

"That's not gonna stop a bullet," said Sal. "You think Aaron hangs around there for the conversation? And what about Mookie? A big fucker like that. Young, dumb and fulla cum."

"I thought he moved out," said Kenny.

"Fuck no," said Sal. "Not for another month."

"It's out of the question," I growled.

I couldn't believe Sal was seriously considering the risks of Kenny's plan. Even if we could get away with it, robbing Aaron and T was a fucked up idea. They were our friends. We couldn't do them like that. No fucking way.

"At least I had an idea," Kenny said. He dropped the gun on a pile of dirty laundry and slumped back down on the couch.

Sal went on, getting worked up now. "Not to mention, Janet would make me in a minute. And Beverly would probably keel over with a heart attack. I can just see it."

While Sal clutched his chest and tried to imitate Beverly in cardiac arrest, my mind wandered back to Lila. Something about the gun got me thinking. Then it hit me.

•

"The ski mask way," whispered Kenny.

He pulled the fluorescent orange wool blend down over his face. Sal and I did the same as some heavy techno beat throbbed in the distant background. We had picked up the masks earlier that day at Zoot's Workwear on Cicero Avenue just south of Irving Park.

"Stay warm," said the old guy that rang us up.

We'll get right on that, I thought. Now we were in a completely different world. Excalibur was a nightclub located in the heart of River North, only a few blocks from the Rock 'N Roll McDonalds and a dozen other popular tourist traps. It was housed in a striking red granite building that looked like a small castle. I think it used to be some city building but it had been Excalibur as long as anyone could remember. The place was big and loud with several levels, some with private rooms for everything from corporate functions to bachelor parties. We had booked the penthouse for Dante so I knew exactly where to go. It was a large private area with the comfortable feeling of somebody's finished basement. Since you could pretty much do whatever you wanted up there, it was the perfect venue for Anything Goes.

The penthouse had its own separate entrance, a stairway leading directly out to an alley behind the club. Sometimes there was a bouncer inside the door at the bottom of the stairs checking a list, but we caught a break that night. The coast was clear all the way up to the top. We were on a landing just outside the entrance. I glanced at my watch and wondered if we were about to make a huge mistake.

"No turning back now," Sal muttered grimly.

CHAPTER THIRTY-TWO

"Holy fucking shit!" said Kenny. He hit the gas and we peeled out. "That was fucking killer!"

"Slow down," I said. It was hard to get any words out.

"Okay, okay. Good point." He tapped the brakes and glanced at Sal in the backseat. "How much did we get?"

Sal was rifling through a handful of bills with a faintly sick look on his face.

"Twenty-three hundred," he said finally.

"Fuck!" said Kenny. "Not bad, huh?"

Neither of us had anything to say. What was the point? Kenny wouldn't understand. The robbery went off perfectly but for one minor hitch. We were a little late. More than a little late. We planned to get there just before the girls got started, before they earned any of the cash we were stealing. But by the time we burst through the door, they were already naked and halfway through the show.

"So you used to bang that chick, huh?" Kenny asked Sal.

"Her name's Sherry," said Sal.

"She's fucking hot," said Kenny. "Lila, too. Man…at least Dante had himself a fine piece of ass."

I would've punched Kenny in the face if I hadn't been so racked with guilt. When I saw Lila and Sherry doing their thing, I freaked out and screamed at them to put some fucking clothes on. Hearing Kenny go on about how hot they were made me sick to my stomach. It's a good thing he seemed to pick up on that. He shut his mouth and we were all quiet for a few minutes, until the inevitable wave of paranoid second-guessing started. Kenny, having hit the pipe pretty good before we went in there, got things rolling.

"You think they knew it was you guys?"

"I'm sure," said Sal. "Sherry looked me right in the eye, just for a second though." He sounded miserable.

"Do you think they'll tell anybody?" asked Kenny.

"No fucking way," said Sal.

They continued to go back and forth while I retreated into my own thoughts. I was certain Lila and Sherry would never say shit to the police if they had made us, but I still thought there was a ghost of a chance Sal was wrong and they hadn't. I'd made sure not to make eye contact with either one and, aside from my initial outburst, Kenny did all the shouting. The whole scene was completely surreal. Kenny waving his shotgun around. Lila and Sherry, standing there in the middle of a room full of yuppie assholes, naked at first, then in their silk shorty robes. Despite her quick look at Sal, Sherry appeared completely terrified, shaking and staring down at the floor whenever my eyes passed across her. Lila was defiant, telling me to fuck off when I yelled at them. After that, she crossed her arms and stared at Kenny and his gun the whole time. The guys were no problem at all. Some of them were so shitfaced, they didn't seem to grasp what was going on at first. At least one of them thought it was a gag.

"Enough is enough, Spud," he said to one of the others.

"This ain't no fucking joke, douchebag!" Kenny stuck his gun in the guy's face. "Now gimme your watch and your wallet!"

They got the message and the mood quickly grew tense as Sal and I made the rounds, each with a tall kitchen garbage bag. Still, nobody said shit. All we got was a moment of hesitation from Lupe, the squat Mexican woman who came with the girls to lug the gear and collect the cash. Lupe also made change so the guys would have small bills for tips. She was one of several relatively non-threatening chaperones who worked for Candice. I always thought it was fucked up that she didn't hire more physically threatening types for the job, given all the drunken slimeballs the girls had to deal with.

"That would be a big turnoff," Sal once said.

He had a point. Whatever the reason, I was glad not to face some big bruiser that night. It was a great score, enough to feed the monkey for at least a couple of weeks. I just needed to find out if somehow things were still cool with Lila.

•

"She doesn't want to see you, Michael," said Shane.

"Excuse me?" I raised my eyebrows.

She was speaking to me through a narrow gap between Lila's door and the jamb I recently installed. I had called repeatedly but the phone just rang and rang. I finally decided to go over there. After knocking several times, I tried to let myself in. My key still worked. I thought that was a good sign until the door came to an abrupt stop from the chain latch. Shane's face appeared.

"Please don't make this any harder than it has to be," she said. "You really have to go."

The threesome was definitely off the table.

"What the fuck is going on?" I gave her the most puzzled look I could muster. Depending on what Lila actually knew or just thought she knew, I figured I might have a chance at outright denial. That meant giving her the impression that I didn't know shit. Everything I was about to hear was news to me.

"Michael, please..."

"Don't gimme that 'Michael, please.' shit." I cut her off.

"What do you want me to say?"

"Talk to me, Shane! What the fuck is going on? I can't get Lila on the phone. Now I come over here and you're telling me to take a hike as if I'm supposed to know why..."

"You mean to tell me you don't?" She glared at me. She knew. That meant Lila knew. "You didn't hear what happened? You haven't been out? You haven't talked to anyone?"

Her face contorted with hostility.

"Of course not. You guys were just doing what you guys do, holing up for days, sticking yourselves twenty-four-seven, too fucked up to know or hear anything. How silly of me to think otherwise."

"If you're accusing me of being a junkie," I said, still hoping against hope to come out of this without admitting anything. "I plead guilty as charged. No big surprise there."

"Just stop!" I heard Lila yell. She approached us from inside, her heavy footsteps resonating out the door. Standing in back of Shane, Lila stared at me with silent, burning contempt.

"I'll take it from here," she said. "Let me talk to him alone."

I knew this conversation was going to be rough.

Shane closed the door for a moment to undo the latch and opened it again, brushing past me hard as she left.

"I'll be over at Leo's if you need me," she said.

Lila turned her back while I watched Shane go, bracing myself for what I just confirmed would be a bitter confrontation. I walked inside, closing the door behind me.

"How could you?" Lila asked. She was pacing in front of the windows, smoking a cigarette. "How could you do it?"

"What are you talking about? Do what?"

"Fuck you, you fucking liar!" she fumed. "Don't you dare!"

I was prepared to stick to my story no matter what but my resolve crumbled under the weight of Lila's anger. I had never seen her in such a state. She was literally trembling with rage. She looked a little sick too, with dark circles under her eyes, a runny nose and a layer of sweat covering her skin.

"Did you even stop to think about it, Michael? Did you even stop to think about what it would be like for Sherry and me? How did you think it would feel to be standing there naked, in a room full of guys, getting robbed at gunpoint? Did you even stop to think about me? Or am I just another mark like your little frat buddies? Am I just another sucker for you to beat?"

"Of course not," I sputtered, rattled by the force of her wrath.

"Are you sure about that?" she asked. "You don't sound sure. You don't look sure. You look like someone who feels pretty bad about something. Then again, maybe that's just an act. I don't know. I don't know anything anymore. I thought I knew you!"

"You do know me."

Lila continued as though I hadn't spoken.

"How could you fuck me over like that? And Sherry? My God, she's just a kid. I told you! She's going back home. She's going back to school. She's getting a life. Now she's got one more trauma to get over. Not like she didn't have enough already with the dope and all our other bullshit... and Dante." Lila's voice faded into a whisper and her eyes welled up with tears. I took a step toward her but she held up her hand. "Don't touch me! Don't you ever touch me again!"

She wiped her cheeks and took a deep breath.

"This is not all your fault. I take full responsibility for my part here. Sherry was my friend. I should've looked out for her. I should've..." Her voice trailed off for a moment before she lit into me again. "She hasn't slept in days. Not since she was robbed by masked gunmen! How could you, Michael? How could you be so..." She searched for the right word. "Brutal. That's what it was. It was brutal. You're a brute, Michael. A fucking lowlife brute!" After building to a scream, she calmed herself down and looked me dead in the eyes.

"To think that I loved you."

•

"So what did you say to her?" asked Sal.

A couple of days had gone by. Kenny was finally passed out after the wicked run he started right after the robbery. Sal and I were sitting on the couch after our morning fix as a few rays of sun peeked in through the twisted aluminum blinds. I had just told him about my confrontation with Lila, leaving out select details, like the last words she uttered to me.

"To think that I loved you."

Aside from the brief reprieve I got with each rush, they had been tormenting me ever since I walked out of her place. Not that it really mattered anymore. But if she had said she loved me before, things might've been different. As it was, I told myself she would come back around, she would give me another chance. I told myself a lot of things but my hopes were fading with each passing day.

"Michael." Sal nudged me.

"Yeah?"

"So what did you say?"

"Nothing," I said. "What could I say? She's done with us, at least for now."

We sat in silence until Sal spoke up again.

"Why didn't you tell me about Sherry?"

His question caught me off guard. Haunted by my thoughts about Lila, I had forgotten all about Sherry.

"She's going back to Toronto and you didn't tell me."

"I didn't want to bum you out," I said. "What for? Would that have changed anything?"

"No," said Sal with resignation. "Probably not."

•

Another week or so passed and I woke up to some frenzied activity around me. Sal and Kenny were digging through the clothes and the trash piled throughout the apartment.

"Where the fuck did they go?" asked Sal.

"What?" I asked. "What are you looking for?"

"The watches," said Kenny. "From the bachelor party."

"Fuck," I mumbled, sitting up.

It was crunch time again. Feeling the desperation around me, I decided to check on my dad's watch. I had wrapped it in plastic and stashed it in the dank utility room across the small inner courtyard of our building. Nobody knew where I put it but I wanted to be sure. It was still there, hidden on the header over the door behind a piece of broken drywall. The watch was safe where it was so I returned to our place through the back door when Kenny saw me.

"Where were you?" he asked.

"Nowhere."

"We found 'em." Sal held up the pair of white plastic bags. "Time to go see Stella."

•

"I was certain I had seen the last of you boys," Stella said as we walked into the store. "Did I not say so, Nico?"

She turned to Nicolas, parked behind the other end of the counter looking as surly as ever. He barely glanced up from the newspaper opened in front of him. I was surprised that moron could even read.

"What can I say?" said Sal. "We missed you."

"Of course, of course." She looked us over, sizing us up like she always did when we hadn't been around for a while. There was clearly nothing social about this visit. Much as we were all trying to keep things friendly, everyone knew what everyone else was about. We were there to get every penny we could out of Stella and she was there to pay us as little as possible.

"That guy come back for his guitar?" Sal asked, trying to lighten things up.

Stella continued to watch us, paying particularly close attention to Kenny. Sal noticed and introduced him.

"By the way," he said. "This is our associate, Kenny."

"How do you do?" Stella nodded politely and gestured to Nicolas. "My nephew, Nico."

Hearing his name again, Nicolas pulled his nose out of the paper just long enough to cast his suspicious gaze at us.

"Not a big talker, huh?" said Kenny.

"So what can I do for you today?" Stella directed the question at Sal and me. "I know you boys are not here to shop."

"You do, huh? You must have ESP." Sal grinned, still trying to work the natural charm that always seemed to fail with Stella.

"What do you have for me?" she asked.

Sal reached into his coat pocket for the brown paper bag where we had consolidated the loot before coming over. He dumped the watches on the counter and began to spread them out. Watching Stella watching him, I couldn't help but notice the expression on her face. Unlike any I had observed before, her look conveyed a blend of revulsion and pity, as if we were condemned. It was subtle and fleeting but unmistakable, and it sent a chill down my back. Stella slipped on her bifocals and we were back to business as usual.

"I had no idea you boys owned so many watches," she said.

"What can I say?" Sal shrugged. "We got a deal on them."

"Sure you did," Nicolas laughed to himself, still reading his newspaper. "You see them, you take them. What a deal."

"Ever think about a career in comedy?" Sal said to him. "You got a real gift there, buddy."

"I am not your buddy!" Nicolas pushed himself to his feet.

"Easy, Nico." Stella raised her hand.

Nicolas sat back down, glaring at the three of us.

"Don't you fucking eyeball me," Kenny snarled at him.

"Watch your mouth, you!" He leaned over the counter.

"Fuck you!" said Kenny.

"That's it!" Nicolas stood up again, this time so fast his stool fell over with a crash. That's when Stella lost her temper.

"Enough, I say!" She shouted at all of us.

After one last furious look, Nicolas got back to his newspaper, sulking in angry silence. I grabbed Kenny by the arm and looked him in the eye, hoping that he could take a hint and chill the fuck out. When he kept quiet, I turned back to Stella.

"We've collected them over the years," I said, referring to the watches. I really didn't have the energy to put much into this tedious charade. "Some were gifts."

She picked up a watch and carefully examined it. Made of stainless steel with a fitted metal bracelet and three sub dials, it looked like one of the nicest in the bunch.

"'Congratulations, Bruce! Class of '91'," said Stella. She was reading from an inscription on the back.

"I got that from my cousin," said Sal.

"Of course you did." Stella set it down. "I am sorry, but I am not interested in any of these." She waved her hand over the rest.

"What?" Sal couldn't believe his ears.

"Why?" Neither could I.

"You know why," said Stella as she glanced up at the security camera mounted over the door behind us.

"C'mon, Stella," said Sal. "You can turn that thing off."

"But I do not wish to."

"Fuck this!" Sal totally lost his cool. He started scooping up the watches and tossing them back into the paper bag, some clanking loudly against the wood counter.

"I am sorry, boys," she said.

"Sorry ain't gonna help," said Sal.

"Let's get the fuck outta here," said Kenny.

"What did I tell you!" Nicolas pointed at him.

"Piss off, Nicolas!" said Sal.

"You sure about this, Stella?" I asked. "You're not interested at all? Not even one goddamn watch?"

•

"So you got a gold Rolex, huh?" said Kenny. We were back in the Chevelle, heading down Ashland Avenue.

"It was my dad's," I said from the backseat.

"Is it in the apartment?"

"Are your tools in the apartment?"

"What the fuck do my tools have to do with anything?" Kenny's face reflected genuine confusion.

Fuck him. I wasn't gonna be the one to spell it out. I also wasn't gonna be the one to finance our next bender with my dad's watch, not while Kenny was sitting on at least five grand in tools, not to mention his car.

"Well?" Kenny asked, waiting for some response from me.

Sal jumped in. "I think what Michael means to say is that his dad's Rolex isn't the only thing of value we have."

"I get it." Kenny nodded at him. "So he's got the watch and I got my tools. What do you got?"

I had been thinking the same thing but I never would have put it to him like that.

"I got your backs," Sal huffed. "Both of 'em."

"Listen," said Kenny. "If Michael is ready to part with the watch, that's cool, but I'm not pawning my tools. That's my livelihood, man."

"*Was* your livelihood," Sal muttered.

"Whatever," said Kenny. "I'm not gonna part with them."

"Let some other people part with *their* valuables," said Sal.

"Exactly," Kenny heartily concurred. "Anyone but us."

They moved on while I zoned out on our dwindling options. With less than a hundred dollars between us and only a handful of bags, I knew we would reach the end of the line before long. Where that would take us was anyone's guess. Jail and the morgue were always on the table. Rehab was out of the question. Running through one grim possibility after another, I was stricken with regret.

If only I hadn't picked up the needle again.

If only I hadn't blown it with Lila.

If only Dante hadn't died.

If only.

I folded my arms tight against my body and hunched over.

"You all right back there?" asked Sal.

"I'm fine," I said, sitting up and trying to steel myself against the wave of hopelessness rushing over me.

"Don't worry, man," said Sal. "We'll hit some bottom feeders, dump these watches. I bet we clear at least five hundred."

•

"How y'all doin'?" asked Aaron.

"Not bad," said Sal. "Not bad at all."

We had just spent the last four hours running from one sleazy pawnshop to another, fighting tooth and nail for every dollar we could get out of the rogue's gallery of miserly owners. Now it was time to shoot our load, almost six hundred, and Sal was pretty fucking happy about it. I was too until I got a strange vibe off Aaron.

"What's goin' on?" I asked him.

"Not much," Aaron frowned and I knew right then and there we were fucked. "Police got the package."

CHAPTER THIRTY-THREE

"I can still hook you up," Aaron nodded at Kenny. "Take me five minutes to go round the way."

"Excellent!" Kenny rubbed his hands together.

"Fuck him!" Sal lost it again, worse than he did with Stella.

"Jesus," said Kenny. "What the fuck did I ever do to you?"

"Who cares?" said Sal. "We need some fucking dope!"

"Yo, chill the fuck out!" Aaron snapped at him. "Ain't shit anyone can do right now."

"What happened?" I asked, trying to stay calm.

"Narcos got our boy, took down a whole bunch of spots too."

"It's the middle of winter for God's sake!" said Sal. "What the fuck are they doing?"

"Police doin' they job," Clifford declared from the living room.

"You just gotta be cool," Aaron said to us, ignoring Clifford. "It ain't gonna be more than a few days."

"A few days?" Sal's eyes bugged out. We didn't have enough dope to make it through. "When did all this jump off?"

"Night before last," said Aaron. "It was all over the news. I can't believe y'all didn't see it."

"We don't watch the fucking news," said Sal.

"Ever heard of the newspaper?" asked Clifford.

"We've been busy," said Sal. "Where's Janet at?"

"And Maurice?" I added, suddenly noting their absence. With T and Mookie also gone, I had never seen the place so empty.

"They went down south," said Aaron. "Ain't lookin' good."

"There's no smack on the entire South Side of Chicago?" I asked.

"Sure there is. On the West Side too. It just ain't nothin' you want to mess with," said Aaron. "They slingin' some junk alright. They spikin' the bags with shit from the hospital."

"It's called Fentanyl," said Beverly from her place on the couch.

"How do you know that?" asked Sal.

"I saw it on the news just this morning," she said.

"Of course you did." Sal shook his head.

"Motherfuckers fallin' out all over the city," said Aaron.

"Is it any good?" I asked.

That was always the question. Junkies hear about a spate of overdoses and all they want to know is whether the problem was the smack or the poor souls who couldn't handle it. Some will even flock to a spot, looking to find out for themselves.

"From what I hear, it ain't that good," said Aaron. "And that's just if it don't kill you."

"Fuck, I don't believe this," said Sal.

I was speechless. As bad as I thought things were earlier, they had officially gotten worse. I thought about the monkey and how we were going to feed it. Disaster has a way of breaking everything down and making you see what's important. It's kind of like finding out that you have cancer. All of a sudden, you realize that you can live without your hair or even a lung or part of your face. You'll do whatever you have to do just to stay alive. You'll go without. You'll live without. Fuck getting high. Sal and I weren't ready to face the sickness. Not even close.

"What the fuck are we supposed to do?" asked Sal. "What are Janet and Maurice gonna do?"

"They looking," said Aaron. "But if it ain't there, it ain't there. Besides, Maurice got a stash of dollies somewhere."

"Yeah?" Sal perked up some. "Enough to share?"

Dollies were tablets of methadone, a synthetic narcotic that stopped the pain of withdrawal. You could chew them up or dissolve them in water. Most junkies got them doled out one dose at a time from a special clinic, and that was only after a long consultation, usually with some underpaid former hard case trying to walk the straight and narrow. The places were awful, dirty and sad with dopefiends lined up like hobos at a soup kitchen. Sal and I went that route during the last big bust a year or so earlier.

"If Maurice don't have enough to go around, I got a guy that can hook you up," said Aaron.

"That's cool," I said, trying to relax. At least we wouldn't get sick. That was something. I reached for the Sun-Times sitting on the top of the pile at the end of the table. Sure enough, the headline on the front page blared "Painkiller/Heroin Combo Causes Rash of Fatal ODs!" As Aaron headed out the door to score for Kenny, I tried to read the article but I couldn't concentrate. I sat back while Kenny and Sal wandered into the living room to join Clifford and Beverly for an unremarkable episode of *The People's Court*.

"I kind of miss Judge Wapner," said Kenny.

"Not me," said Beverly. "That man was mean."

Aaron soon came back with some ready rock for Kenny who was now smoking too much to cook for himself anymore. The minute Aaron walked in, Kenny wanted to head back to our place, but Sal and I couldn't leave yet. We were stuck, waiting for Janet and Maurice to return.

"You mind if I..." Kenny raised his eyebrows at Aaron.

"On the left." He pointed back to a bedroom.

"I think I'm gonna join you," said Sal. "Michael?"

"I'll pass," I said. I was edgy enough.

When Janet and Maurice got back half an hour later, Sal rushed out of the bedroom to get the word. The inevitable bad news hit us like a death in the family.

"It's tough out there," said Maurice.

"Sorry, baby." Janet stroked Sal's head.

"I can hook y'all up with some dollies though," said Maurice. "Ten dollars each."

"We'll take as many as you can spare," said Sal.

Maurice went into the kitchen and returned with some orange tablets in a baggie. I took them and did a quick count.

"How do we take these?" I asked as I paid him.

"Figure a quarter tablet for each bag you slam regular," said Maurice. "Only take enough to get right. No more. You don't want to get hooked on this shit."

"We'll be careful," I said.

And I meant it. From what we had heard, methadone was way harder to kick than heroin. Supposedly, the process lasted a couple of weeks as opposed to a few days and was incredibly painful.

"Like getting your skin pulled off with pliers," Maurice once told us. He had kicked Methadone twice.

"We'll be careful," I said.

"Thanks a lot, Maurice," said Sal.

"Just stay away from that smack they spikin' out there."

Sal and I nodded solemnly before Janet pulled him close.

"You be careful, baby," she said, hugging him tight.

Watching the two of them, I had a terrible thought.

"Oh fuck! We gotta go!"

•

"I'm sure she's okay," said Sal.

"Just drive, Kenny," I said. "As fast as you can."

"But whatever you do, don't get pulled over," added Sal.

"Thanks for the tip," said Kenny. "I wish you guys would've clued me in before I hit the pipe that last time."

"You could let me drive," I said, already knowing his response. I had heard it many times before.

"No way, man," said Kenny. "No one drives the Chevelle but me."

"Then fucking drive," I snapped. "I'm sorry if my concern about Lila is killing your buzz."

"Jesus, Michael," Sal chided me. "Give him a break."

"I'm just saying," Kenny said. "Bad timing."

I didn't give a shit. It's never a good time to overdose. All I knew was that every minute counted. Lila had no TV and she didn't read the newspaper. I was sure she had no idea about the bad dope.

We went the rest of the way without another word between us and Kenny rose to the occasion. He juked and jagged down the side streets to get around traffic and made it to Lila's neighborhood in record time. I started to feel a little better. Then we turned the corner and I saw the flashing lights from the ambulance and the rollers parked in front of her building.

My God.

"Fuck!" said Sal.

Kenny slammed on the brakes.

"This is as far as I go, man," he said.

"Open the fucking door!" I shoved the front seat.

Sal pulled the latch and I pushed the seat forward, pinning him against the dashboard as I slipped out of the car and ran inside. I bounded up the stairs and raced down the hall to Lila's door where I almost collided with a pair of uniforms coming out. Younger guys, no older than Sal or me, they both had buzz cuts and expressionless faces. One of them spoke into his radio.

"Just another overdose," he said.

"Slow down, guy," the other one said to me.

"What's happening in there?" I said. "Is she gonna make it?"

"We're not paramedics," said the cop.

"What the fuck does that mean?" I tried to push past him but the other cop holstered his radio and grabbed me.

"Look, guy," he said. "You better just dial it down a couple notches before we have a fucking problem here."

"Everything is under control," said the first cop. "Stay back."

"We just want to know if she's all right." Sal spoke up from behind me. I turned to see him approaching us, panting heavily, completely worn out from the trip up the stairs. The cop loosened his grip on me and I pulled away from him.

"The medics are taking care of her," said the first cop.

"Just let them do their job," said the other cop.

"Thanks, officer," said Sal.

That wasn't good enough for me. I made another move toward Lila's door. The first cop drew his club and blocked my path.

"I'm not gonna tell you again," he warned.

"Of course, officer," said Sal as he tugged on my arm. "He's just upset, you know. Lila's a good friend."

"Yeah?" said the other cop. "Then why don't you get her into rehab? Check yourself in while you're at it."

"Fuck you," I said, plenty loud enough for him to hear.

"What the fuck did you say?" The cop puffed himself up and made a move in my direction, but I didn't give a fuck. I was out of my mind, ready to knock his ass out.

"Nothing." Sal jumped in. "He didn't say anything. We're backing off. We're waiting. No trouble here. No trouble at all."

The cop eyeballed me hard as his partner pulled him away. The two of them disappeared back into Lila's place.

"Fucking pigs," I said.

"Jesus fucking Christ," Sal glared at me. "Would you just chill the fuck out? You're gonna get us both locked up!"

I took a deep breath, folded my arms tight and leaned back against the wall. Moments later, the cops came back out with the paramedics behind them. One pushed Lila on a gurney while the other pumped air into her lungs. She looked like she was already gone, her complexion deathly pale with a vaguely bluish tint. Shane trailed behind all of them with tears streaming down her cheeks. She didn't even look at us.

•

"So where did they take her?" asked Kenny.

"Martha Washington," said Sal.

We were all back home after watching Lila's ambulance take off, sirens wailing. Sal and Kenny were sitting on the couch while I nervously paced in front of them.

"That place is a shithole," said Kenny.

"How do you know?" I asked.

"That's where they took me when I had my seizure."

"That's where they take all the ODs around here," said Sal.

"When were you there?" I asked Kenny.

"Right before I went to rehab."

"I thought that was court ordered," said Sal.

"It was," said Kenny. "Cops went through my pockets when I went down, hit me up for possession."

"Fucking cops," I spit out. "I fucking hate 'em!"

"Well, that's where they got her," said Sal, giving me a sideways glance. "We'll go by there first thing tomorrow."

"We should be over there right now!"

"Why?" asked Sal. "There's nothing we can do. We'll just be standing around. And there might be police sniffing around, trying to figure out where she got the smack."

"I really doubt that."

"You never know," said Kenny.

"Whatever." I didn't have the energy to argue about it anymore. We had planned to finish off our meager stash and I couldn't think of a better time to do it. I felt like jumping out of my skin, screaming with guilt and rage and self-loathing. Lila was laid up in some rundown city hospital barely clinging to her life, and it was all my fault. If she died, I didn't care how long I stayed around after her. With Dante already gone and Sal on his way, life just wasn't what it used to be, not that it was ever that great.

"So how do you want to do this?" asked Sal.

He was referring the paltry four dime bags we had left plus an extra one Sal had miraculously spotted in the matted carpet underneath our coffee table. Normally, we would just split the fifth bag, but given our respective habits, an extra half bag for each of us was a waste compared with a full bonus for the lucky one.

"You take it," I said.

"Fuckin' A!" said Sal.

Much as the extra smack would help, I felt like I deserved to suffer. If Shane hadn't called 911, Lila would've ended up like so many other junkies, just another corpse laid out in the county morgue. Picturing her like that gave me a chill and I recalled one of the last things Dante said to me on New Year's Eve.

Watch out for Lila.

If I truly believed Dante was up there watching me, I would've cracked up right there on the spot.

"Can you hook me up?" Sal's voice broke into my thoughts.

I looked up and saw him holding a loaded syringe. Between his Hep C and all our running, Sal was in terrible shape, the worst I had ever seen him. As thin as he had always been, he was starting to look downright emaciated, always dragging, complaining about this or that pain, even when he was high. All of his most prominent veins had collapsed, making it harder and harder to fix.

"What do you want me to do?" I asked, taking the syringe.

Sal pulled his hair back off the right side of his neck.

"Any questions?" He flashed a weary smile.

"That's fucked up," said Kenny.

"Shouldn't you be hitting the pipe?" Sal asked him.

Kenny gave Sal the finger then hit the pipe while I went to work on Sal, firing all three bags into his jugular vein. It was an intense way to fix we called tree-topping. According to junkie lore, it's supposed to be easier on your liver, since the smack has such a direct path to your brain. Whether or not that's true, the rush is much quicker and stronger. You just need a partner you can trust or a mirror and a steady hand. After setting the needle down, I waited for Sal to pull out of the nod.

"Well?" I gazed into his eyes, searching for some response.

"Holy shit," he said finally. "I think I just saw God."

"Not yet," said Kenny.

•

Once Sal got his bearings, I had him fix me the same way and I sat around with my chin on my chest for the rest of the night before crashing out. When I woke up the next morning, the sickness was already waiting for me. My legs were sore and I felt queasy. I headed straight for the kitchen where we left our stash of dollies. I took one of the tablets out and split it, dropping half into a glass of warm water and stirring the mixture with my finger. I gulped down the orange tinted drink like a shot of Southern Comfort or anything else with a taste you want to avoid. The artificial sweetness reminded me of the cold medicine I took as a kid. As soon as it hit my gut, I felt the methadone kick in. Along with an immediate end to the aches and nausea came a slight dulling of the senses, just enough to feel vaguely impaired but not in a good way. There was no rush. There was no real relief, just a temporary reprieve from total misery. I took a minute to adjust to the feeling and returned to the living room where Sal was pestering Kenny to drive us to the hospital.

"It's either that or I'm calling a cab," he said to Kenny.

"Don't be stupid," said Kenny. "That's a waste of money."

"I don't give a fuck."

"Wow," I said. "I didn't think you cared that much."

"Well, I'm certainly not going crazy like some people," he said pointedly. "But I know Dante would want us to check on her."

I wasn't sure how much Sal had figured out about Lila and me, but I could tell my reaction to her overdose had gotten him thinking. I didn't care. I was just glad he wanted to go the hospital. For all we knew, Lila was dead. Most ODs are fatal in the first few minutes but some people make it to the ER only to die later on.

"So let's go," I said.

Kenny was in no shape to drive. He had been up all night smoking rock and slugging vodka and he was finally ready to pass out. It took a few minutes, but Sal talked him into letting us take the Chevelle. He gave us the keys with a lot of huffing about what would happen if we brought it back with so much as a smudge on the tire.

"Would you feel better if I chugged some Stoli and hit the pipe first?" asked Sal. "I heard that's what the owner likes to do."

Kenny flipped us off and we were out of there.

"By the way," said Sal. "I'm driving."

"Be my guest."

CHAPTER THIRTY-FOUR

"We're here to see Lila Davenport," Sal said to the older black lady behind the desk.

"I think she's gone," she said.

I felt my heart explode in my chest.

The lady started tapping on the keyboard in front of her.

"Uh-huh," she nodded. "Her people came for her this morning, moved her to Rush."

"So she's going to be okay?" I almost choked on the words, I was so anxious to get them out. Lila was alive.

"I'm no doctor," said the lady.

I fell back into a nearby chair, breathing hard.

"Of course not, ma'am," said Sal. "Thanks for your help."

•

"So her people came for her, huh?" Sal was back behind the wheel of the Chevelle. He cranked the engine and hit the gas a couple of times, blasting us out with the crisp, throaty roar of the 454 big block under the hood. "Isn't her dad some rich guy?"

"I know he's a lawyer in Beverly Hills," I said, trying to remember what else Lila had told me about him.

"That's what I thought." Sal dropped the car into gear and started driving. "It figures. The guy probably showed up, took one look around and said, 'fuck this.'"

That's exactly what happened, according to Shane. She was puffing on a cigarette near the entrance to Rush Presbyterian Hospital when we got there. Looking forlorn from a distance, she stood up straight when she saw us approaching. In the wake of Lila's overdose and all that followed, it seemed Shane let go of her animosity towards us, at least temporarily. She described how Lila got moved that morning and briefed us on her condition.

"They have her on a ventilator. She's stable right now..." Shane's voice cracked. "But she's not going make it if she doesn't start breathing on her own."

"Fuck," said Sal.

"My God," I whispered.

"That's all I know. Her dad's here and he's the only one allowed to talk with the doctors. He won't tell me anything else and he won't let me see her. The guy's a real prick. He doesn't seem to get that his daughter would be dead right now if I hadn't called for help. All he did was grill me like I was on the stand. He asked if I was her 'lover' like it was a dirty word. He didn't believe me when I told him I never touched heroin, that I was trying to get Lila to stop. Aside from the nature of our relationship, all he wanted to know was where she got her drugs. He asked me over and over. Then he turned his back on me like I wasn't even there. Fucking asshole."

"Where did she get the dope?" I had to ask.

"I have no idea," Shane said bitterly. "That was her thing, her own private thing. One time, I asked if she always has to shoot up when I'm over. I never saw another needle after that. But I also saw a lot less of her."

Much as I never liked Shane, I felt a bond with her at that moment. I knew exactly how it felt to have Lila push me away. Without thinking, I pulled her toward me for a long tight hug, swallowing her slight frame in my arms as she sobbed into my wrinkled shirt.

•

"What the fuck was that?" asked Sal.

"What the fuck was what?"

We were back in Kenny's car after leaving the hospital without even bothering to go in. Sal started the car, gunning the engine as he peeled away from the curb.

"You know what," he said. "With Shane. I didn't realize you two were such bosom buddies."

"We're not," I said. "She's just sad and scared...like us."

"You mean like you."

"What are you trying to say?"

"Nothing," said Sal. "Forget it."

"How am I supposed to be?"

Sal looked like he wanted to say something but he kept quiet.

"Lila's our good friend. Not to mention, she was Dante's girl. You said so yourself this morning. We need to look out for her."

"Then you probably shouldn't have turned her on."

"That's helpful. Just what I want to hear right now. Jesus, Sal!"

"I'm sorry," he said. "You're right. What's done is done. She wanted to get high. She would have found a way. You think we should try to get a hold of Sherry?"

"I'm sure Shane will try to call her if she's even still around." I said. "I wouldn't bother. Besides, there's nothing anybody can do. They can't see her. They can't help her. They can't do shit."

"They could pray for her," Sal snorted.

"Like I said."

•

We went back home and sat around, trying to focus on a movie. *Pulp Fiction* seemed like a good choice for taking our minds off Lila and the whole fucked up situation. It didn't work. I was completely twisted and felt like I would kill for some real smack. By the time the credits rolled, Kenny was up and itching to score some rock.

"I'll even treat," he said.

"Fuck it," said Sal.

I agreed. Any distraction was welcome. Unfortunately, Kenny was completely broke so his generous offer required a trip to Stella's.

•

"I'm not gonna miss my Snap-Ons," he said. "I always thought they were overpriced *and* overrated."

"Damn," said Sal.

I knew what he was thinking because I was thinking it too. Kenny was giving up. He walked Stella and Nicolas out to the car to show them all his tools. Some were in plastic or metal cases and the rest were neatly arranged in a pair of shiny steel boxes, each with multiple drawers that locked shut.

"So what'll you give me for the lot?" asked Kenny.

"You are offering them to me?"

"I just wanna know what they're worth."

"I will give you two thousand."

"Two thousand?" Kenny was incensed. "You gotta be kidding. The boxes alone cost more than that."

"That is all they are worth to me," Stella shrugged. "Nobody comes to my store to spend so much."

"I guess not," said Kenny. "Nobody but cheap lowlifes." He continued under his breath. "Just like you."

"What did you say?" Nicolas barked.

"Nothing," Sal jumped in. "Nothing at all. Kenny just happens to be really attached to his tools."

"Then he should not show them to me."

"Maybe not," Sal agreed. "Let's just forget about it. We got another transaction to get through."

Everyone cooled down and went back into the store, where Stella counted out three hundred dollars in twenties. Kenny took the cash, and Stella got his complete collection of chrome-finished Snap-On wrenches, ratchets and sockets in English and metric sizes.

"I still got my Matcos," Kenny told himself out loud.

Not for long. One trip turned into many more over the next three days. By the time we all finally went down amid the accumulated debris in our place, Kenny was left with nothing but a Craftsman variety set in a plastic case. Your average weekend warrior fixing his house had more tools. I had tried to stop the madness more than once. I felt like I was going insane from lack of sleep, but Kenny wasn't having it and neither was Sal. In the end, I had little choice but to join them on their crusade of self-destruction.

It wasn't like I had anything better to do.

Every time I hit a peak, I would soon crash and start thinking about Lila. Unable to even remotely face the possibility that she wouldn't make it, I distracted myself remembering the past. I was way too fucked up to actually have sex but that didn't stop me from going there in my mind. I usually started with our frenzied early encounters, in bathrooms, in my car, in the storage room at Spoonful. I went back to many other times we were together hanging out, like when we saw *Out of Sight* and went to Margie's Candies or the nights we spent fixing and fucking at her place. I would try to stay there with her but I always ended up back in the robbery at Excalibur and the terrible scene at her place afterwards.

To think that I loved you.

The words would ring through my head over and over until I took another hit and told myself I could make it right. I could get her back. I *would* get her back. I would get her back and we would get our shit together. We would leave Chicago and start a whole new life somewhere else, far away from everything we had been and done. All I had to do was get to the hospital and get past her father.

Just do it, I told myself.

But every time I made my move, the toxic gravitational pull inside the apartment proved overwhelming. It didn't help that I was losing my mind. Between the so-called relief I got from all the crack we were smoking and the increasingly terrifying prospects of facing the world outside, I couldn't bring myself to walk through that door. Lila was out there barely miles away but she might as well have been on another planet. Much as I hated what it was doing to me, there was no walking away from that pipe once I got going.

•

Eventually, I went down. I'm not sure how long it was but hours after I hit the floor, I slowly sat up to rub my eyes as they made the painful adjustment to the light from the overcast sky outside. Sal and Kenny were still out cold. After my dose of methadone, I went into the bathroom and doused my face and hair in the sink, careful not to dwell on my reflection in the mirror. I knew I looked terrible. I was just glad to be alive with enough hours between me and the pipe that I had no desire to hit it again anytime soon. Still, I felt shaky and anxious. For all I knew, Lila was dead, though I didn't really think that was a possibility. Someone would've been in touch. Granted, our phone had been cut off weeks before. I tried to remember if Shane knew where we lived. I wasn't sure.

I went back and forth in my head, becoming increasingly agitated as I scrounged around for a little something to take the edge off. I finally found the last of the last T-bag we had left. I packed a bowl, took a few hits and instantly regretted it, my mind and heart racing with fears of the worst. I had to get over to the hospital before I got bogged down any more. After a frantic search, I finally located Kenny's keys in the couch between a pair of beer-soaked cushions. I bolted out the door and sped straight to Rush, only to find that Lila had already been released.

"Thank God!" I exclaimed.

The woman behind the desk nodded politely, though not without a long, strange look. I hustled back out to the car and took it a little slower on the way to Lila's place. When I got to her block, I scanned the street for her car but didn't see it. Unsure what to make of that, I parked and went up. When I got to her door, it was wide open. I went inside and felt a chill wash over me. Everything was gone. The furniture, the artwork, everything. I heard voices and saw a pair of women, both blonde in faded jeans and T-shirts. One was sweeping the floor while the other wiped down the counter with a sponge.

"Excuse me," I said to the one closest to me. "Where is Lila?"

She started to say something in Polish and I knew I was wasting my time. On the way back to the car, I remembered the lady at Martha Washington days before.

Her people came for her.

Of course they did. Her dad didn't fly halfway across the country to just sit around in a hospital waiting room, hoping his daughter would be okay. He was there to take her home.

Lila was gone.

•

"I'll give you one fucking guess," said Dana.

Her nostrils flared as she lit up a cigarette. I knew I was in for some major attitude but I didn't care.

"She went back to California with her dad?"

"So what the fuck else do you want to know?"

"How do I get a hold of her?"

"Fuck if I know." Dana shook her head. "You think I'd tell you if I did? After what you pulled on her and Sherry? I can't believe you have the fucking balls to even come in here."

"I don't know what you're talking about," I said automatically.

"Sure you don't." Dana stubbed out her cigarette as some yuppie douchebag approached the bar. "You'll have to excuse me," she said. "I've got a paying customer here."

Dana went to work while I stood there letting it all sink in. I caught a whiff of the chili and realized that I was famished, but I knew I sure as hell wasn't getting a bowl on the house. When the guy next to me pulled out his wallet to pay for his Coronas, I thought about mugging him right there on the spot. That's when I knew it was time to go. I wasn't ready to head back home, so I parked the Chevelle next to a Dunkin' Donuts and finished the pack of cigarettes I had lifted off Dana on my way out of Spoonful. Alone at last, I might have said a prayer or shed a tear over everything that had already gone down or was yet to jump off, but I was numb from despair, not to mention all the drugs and the biting hunger in my belly. Instead, I sat there and blankly puffed on those Newports, one after the other, cursing the nasty menthol taste with every drag.

•

"Where the fuck have you been?" yelled Kenny.

I closed the door behind me and tossed him his keys.

"Don't worry. The car's fine."

"How is she?" Sal asked.

"She's gone," I said.

"What?" Sal's eyes went wide.

"She died?" Kenny asked.

"No, no. She moved."

"What the fuck are you talking about?" said Kenny.

"She made it, thank God." Sal put it all together. "She got out of the hospital and her dad took her back to California."

"That's right."

"Fuckin' A," said Sal. "I'm glad to hear it. That's the best thing that could've happened to her. Lila was never cut out for all this." He waved his hand around our filthy apartment.

"Were any of us?" I asked.

"You know what I'm talking about," said Sal. "Lila went to college. She has her degree and her talent, not to mention her family. She's probably locked up in some beachfront rehab center right now, swapping war stories with Robert Downey Jr."

"Who the fuck is that?" asked Kenny.

"This is good news, Michael," said Sal. "Really. Great news. Speaking of which," he added. "Janet came by. The smack is back."

•

Not quite. The smack was back, but the deals were different, and not to our favor. Aaron wasn't moving any more packages. He still had the ready rock for his hoppers to sling and Kenny was happy about that. But if we wanted smack, we had to take a ride with Maurice over to the projects and it would cost us twice as much.

"They twenties now," Maurice told us.

Of course they were. Maurice was just another junkie, angling for his own bags. It still hurt. We never even found out what went down with Aaron and the packages. Not that it mattered. Somebody got busted. Somebody got capped. Hell, maybe somebody quit.

Shit happens, just like it does in the real world. It's no different than going out to dinner, only to find that your favorite restaurant has turned into a sports bar. All of a sudden, you realize you're going to have to learn to live without that special dish you always ordered there. You might wonder why, but you're hungry and you have to eat. So you just move on, one way or another. After getting bent over by Maurice on our first go-around, Sal and I tried some other spots, but they ultimately weren't worth the trouble. We'd freeze our asses off in a long line. The smack would be lousy and the service even worse. Some of them were run by sawed-off punks who treated everyone like shit. Try scoring from some twelve year old calling you "bitch." It gets old fast.

These spots were downright dangerous. On more than one occasion, I found myself scanning the desperate faces around me, wondering who I could roll without much of a fight. I'm sure other people were thinking the same thing. And if the other junkies didn't get you, the hoppers or the thugs backing them would. We saw one guy get beat down for being a dollar short. They knocked him out cold with a sucker punch and pissed on his face while he was laid out in the snow. Then some junkies picked his pockets.

"Now that's some shameful shit," said Sal.

Rolling up in Kenny's car didn't help much either. We got hard stares from the boys in the hood at every intersection. It was only a matter of time before somebody tried to jack us for it.

"This is fucked up," said Kenny.

He was right. We were reckless but we weren't crazy. It's one thing to run yourself into the ground with drugs. It's quite another to get your head blown off by some gun-toting thug who wants your car and can't wait two seconds for you to hand it over. So we sucked it up and cast our lot with Maurice, which meant we had to work twice as hard. After kicking in a few doors and getting hosed by Stella one too many times, we decided to try a new, more direct path to cash. A small branch bank had opened up a few blocks from our place. Though the building sat on a lot bounded by a fairly busy intersection, the drive-thru ATM was far back from the street, just off the adjacent alley. Even better, the two nearest buildings across the alley were both gut rehabs, so there was never anyone around at night.

We worked out a system to rob people using the ATM after dark. Kenny hung around the exit, watching for cops or anybody else that might come along and jam us up on that end. I took a position near the entrance, leaving Sal to deal with the people. Between his looks and his nature, we figured he was the least likely to end up in some fucked up confrontation that would get us all busted. So while Kenny and I watched each end of the drive-thru, Sal squatted nearby in the alley with Kenny's shotgun. When someone in a nice car pulled in alone, I would whistle. Once the mark got to the ATM, Sal would creep up behind the vehicle and wait for the driver to lower his window and reach for the machine. As soon as they did, Sal would skulk around, pop up and pretend to rack a shell. Almost everyone recognized that sound. Cluck-click. If not, they quickly got the idea when Sal laid the end of the barrel on their car door.

"Do what I tell you and you'll be fine," Sal would say.

They always complied. He would instruct them to withdraw the maximum daily limit from their account, four hundred dollars as it turned out. He would take the money and ask hand for some photo ID. After a quick inspection, he would say something like:

"Thanks a lot, so-and-so. You've been a big help. Please don't say a word about this to anyone. If you do, I might have to come by your house, since I know where you live."

It was a creepy little spiel, especially coming from Sal who still had traces of his freakish allure. Nobody ever said shit. All they did was nod and take back their ID, no doubt thankful that they hadn't gotten their head blown off. If someone tried to pull in while Sal was doing his thing, I would stumble in front of the car, forcing them to stop and stalling them one way or another. I'd ask for directions or money or just babble like a crazy man. This routine worked well a handful of times, but eventually the police got wind of our scheme. One of the people we ripped off or someone at the bank reviewing the security tapes must have clued them in, because they had a pretty good sketch of Sal. We saw a flyer plastered on the wall outside our corner store. A big bold caption underneath Sal's mug read: "Have you seen this man?"

"Fuck," said Sal, tearing it down.

"I'll say." I glanced around, paranoid we were being watched. "They probably got the place staked out right now."

Sal stared at his likeness.

"We need another gig," he said.

"Obviously." I took the flyer and crumpled it up. "But until then, I might have something to tide us over."

CHAPTER THIRTY-FIVE

"Michael." Fran stood wedged between her front door and the jamb, looking me over with a mixture of horror, pity and frustration. "What are you doing here?"

"It's nice to see you too, Fran," I said.

"It's just a little late," she said. "I'm trying to put Theo to bed. It's a school night, you know."

"A few minutes late to bed aren't going to blow his chances at the Ivy League." I pushed past her into the oppressively elegant foyer of her Lincoln Park row house. Between the antique vases on display and marble tile floor, I always felt like I was going to break something whenever I walked through there. "This won't take long."

"Who the hell is that?" my mom called out from the kitchen.

"It's Michael," Fran said over her shoulder.

"Michael?" My mom repeated my name with surprise.

"Mom?" I was surprised too. "What are you doing over here?"

"I had my carpets cleaned today. Those fumes are like poison." She came into the foyer to join us. "Why are you here?"

"I'm just passing through."

"What's your hurry?" She looked at me with concern.

"Didn't you hear?" I asked dryly. "It's Theo's bedtime."

"Cut the bullshit, Michael," said Fran.

"Is that necessary?" my mom asked her.

"We all know why you have to go." Fran glared at me.

"Then you should know what I need."

"I'm sorry, Michael," said Fran. "You can't have them."

"What do you mean I can't have them?" I knew she would resist at first but I thought I could bully her into handing them over anyway. "They belong to me, Fran."

"I don't care," she said.

"What are you two going on about?" asked my mom.

I wanted to keep her in the dark about everything going to shit, but my unfortunate timing made that impossible.

"Just hand them over, Fran," I said.

"No, Michael." She folded her arms. "You told me to hold on to your bonds and not to give them to you no matter what."

"Your savings bonds?" my mom said to me. "My God, I can't believe you still have them."

"You'll thank me for this later," said Fran.

"Goddamn right," my mom agreed.

"Fuck later!" I roared. "I need 'em *right now*!"

My voice echoed in the space around us. Fran and my mom were speechless and I was too. We heard footsteps and Theo appeared, timidly shuffling into the room.

"Hey, Uncle Mike," he said.

"Hey, kiddo," I said with a knot my chest.

A tense silence filled the room until I spoke up again.

"I know what I told you before, Fran," I said as gently as I could. "I appreciate you taking it to heart and all..."

"Don't listen to him, Fran," said my mom, choking up. "Look at him. He's killing himself and he doesn't even..."

"Shut the fuck up, Mom!"

That's all Fran needed to hear. She grabbed Theo, pulling him close as if he might somehow get hurt from all the bad language.

"Get out, Michael."

Realizing that I had crossed the line, I tried to tone it down, but it was too little too late.

"I'm sorry, Fran," I said. "I just want my..."

"Get the fuck out!" she screamed. "Now!"

"Gimme my fucking bonds!" I growled.

"Fuck you!" said Fran. "I'm calling the police."

"I'm getting the phone," cried my mom as she burst into tears.

•

"So what happened?" asked Sal.

"What the fuck do you think?"

I had just hopped back into the car where he and Kenny were waiting. We were parked on the street in front of Fran's house.

"Did you get the bonds?" asked Kenny.

"Fuck no! I'm lucky I didn't get arrested."

"She would've never called the police." Sal shook his head. "Even if she did, what the fuck are they gonna say? They belong to you. They got your name on them."

"That doesn't mean shit," I said. "Look at me. Whose side do you think the cops are gonna take?"

"I'm just saying..."

"I know what you're saying and I'm telling you that's wrong. If the police show up, I'm fucked, even if they are my bonds. Now could you please get going before we have to find out for real?"

I knew going to Fran's might be a long shot. What I didn't know was that my mom would be there and it would get so ugly. I could have easily gotten bogged down replaying the whole miserable scene in my head, word for word, had I not been so preoccupied with the urgent business of scoring. That was the thing, from then on, twenty-four-seven. There was nothing else. We stole. We robbed. We fucked people over. We did whatever we had to, and then we went to the projects with Maurice. We hated the place but the smack was always there.

One day, we saw an old friend.

"Jesus, is that who I think it is?" asked Sal.

He pointed out the window at one of the tenements. I followed his direction and sure enough, sitting in a doorway with some stray crack whore was my former stockbroker, Paul Wills.

"You should beat his ass," said Kenny.

I thought about it for a moment but I didn't see the point. He looked worse off than any of us. Kicking his ass wouldn't help me score and that's all that mattered anymore.

Day in and day out.

Soon another flyer went up in our neighborhood, this one with a sketch of me. We had mugged a couple coming home from the bars late one night in Wicker Park. He resisted and I beat him down. She got a good look at me and told the police. We noticed more rollers up and down the streets. All of a sudden, things were way too hot.

"This isn't working, Michael," said Sal.

"Tell me about it."

We both looked at Kenny.

"I don't give a fuck what happens," he insisted. "I'm not gonna smoke my car."

That pretty much left me. All Sal had were his TV and videos, and they were the only thing keeping us from going completely insane, thanks to the electricity I pirated from the utility room.

"Go ahead and call Stella," I finally said to him. "Tell her I'm bringing in the watch. Make sure she has the cash on hand."

Sal nodded and got up to trek down to the phone on the corner.

•

"So how much is she gonna give you?" asked Kenny from the driver seat. We were on our way over to Uptown Pawn.

"Twenty-five hundred," said Sal.

"What a rip-off," said Kenny.

"What the fuck do you know about it?" I said, feeling low enough without his attitude.

"She *was* only gonna pay two grand," said Sal.

"Fucking tightwad," Kenny muttered.

He had been a real head case for the last few days. When he wasn't sulking like some teenage outcast, he was maniacally running his mouth. I knew it was all that rock, finally taking its toll. The rest of the trip passed with barely a word between us. Kenny parked right in front of the store and we went inside. As usual, Nicolas was behind the counter, giving us the evil eye.

"Where's Stella?" Sal asked him. He wasn't in the mood for any of Nicolas's shit and neither was I.

As if on cue, Stella appeared in the doorway leading out from the storage area behind the counter.

"Hello, boys," she said.

I put the watch on the counter and reached into my pocket for the paperwork that went with it.

"It's all there," I said.

Stella slipped on her bifocals to get a closer look before gently picking up the watch. She had seen it before but only as collateral for a loan I was going to repay. This time she looked at it like an investment. I imagined that she had some cousin or brother-in-law lined up to buy it, some guy like her, a Polish hustler living the American dream. He might have a small construction company or cleaning service overflowing with business. Those guys were everywhere. They were tough and they worked hard. Some were flashy. A guy like that would happily pay twice what Stella was giving me.

"It is gorgeous," she said.

"So you'll take it," I said, hoping to move things along.

I wanted to get paid and get going. We were all out of smack and we still had to pick up Maurice, run out to the projects and get home before the sickness came calling again. Not to mention, Nicolas's withering scrutiny was starting to get on my nerves. Kenny was too, poking around in his tools on display behind us. When I could no longer stand the loud clanging steel, I turned to tell Kenny to knock it off, but he was walking toward the door.

"I'll be right back," he said.

"You brought some more tools?" asked Stella.

"Something like that," Kenny smiled cryptically.

Sal and I turned back to Stella. I was just about to ask for the cash when the bell attached to the front door jingled.

"I'm back," Kenny announced.

I wouldn't have even given him a second look had I not seen Nicolas's jaw drop. I heard Stella gasp.

"What the fuck are you doing, Kenny?" asked Sal.

I turned and saw Kenny approaching with his shotgun pointed right at us. He pumped the barrel. Cluck-click.

"You guys better move," he said to Sal and me.

"What is this?" Stella hissed with disbelief.

"What's it look like?" said Kenny. "I want my tools back."

"Go ahead and take them." She sighed and shook her head, directing a quick, sad look at Sal and me.

"We didn't know anything about this, Stella," said Sal.

"Fuck you, Sal," said Kenny. "Don't be such a pussy."

"Watch your mouth!" Nicolas bellowed.

His voice boomed in the cramped space and we all jumped. That's when Kenny lost it.

"You watch *your* mouth! Stupid fucking Polack!" He marched up to the counter and stuck the barrel in Nicolas's face. "I'll blow that big fat fucking empty head of yours clean off, you keep it up!"

I flinched at Kenny's tirade. I was sure any moment Nicolas would lunge over the counter, wrap the gun around Kenny's head and stomp him into the ground. I was wrong. Nicolas didn't budge. In fact, he barely blinked. It was like he had slipped into some sort of trance that made him oblivious to his surroundings. He just stood there with his belly pressed against the counter and his hands at his sides. He was completely still, his dead-eyed stare aimed right through Kenny.

"Knock it off, Kenny," said Sal. "This isn't what we do."

"Take your watch." Kenny pushed me and looked at Stella. "We'll take the money, too. All of it. Everything you got."

"C'mon, Kenny," I said.

"Jesus fucking Christ, Michael! You too? That's your dad's watch she's holding! Your dad! It's all you got left of him and you're gonna let this fucking bitch..."

Kenny never got to finish, or if he did, it got lost in the blast from the pistol Nicolas had drawn. The bullet passed so close to my head, I felt a whisper in my ear. It struck Kenny in the cheek just below his left eye. His face opened up like a cherry pie that had been torn into by some fat kid trying to win a prize at the county fair. A hot red mist of blood spattered across Sal and me and the counter in front of us. Stella recoiled in horror.

"Nico, stop!" she screamed.

"The gun's not even loaded!" yelled Sal.

Kenny buckled and fell in a crumpled bloody heap on the floor.

"Fuck!" Sal dropped to his knees to kneel over him.

Kenny must have been dead already. If not, God help him. Turning my eyes away, I heard Stella gasp again and I knew Nicolas wasn't finished. He aimed the gun at Sal, but just before he could squeeze the trigger, I swatted the barrel aside. Another blast echoed through the store. I heard a whimper and saw Stella slump over on the counter, blood pouring from a gaping wound in her neck.

"My God, Nicolas, stop!" shouted Sal.

Seeing what he had done, Nicolas cried out and for a split second, I thought for sure he was through. I rushed over to check on Stella, stepping in the pool of blood on the floor in front of the counter. That's when I got a whiff of smoke streaming from the barrel of the gun now pointed inches from my head. I turned towards Nicolas and my heart leapt when I saw his face. He looked like he was possessed. But before he could squeeze off another round, Sal reached across the counter and grabbed his arm. The gun went off again, this time taking out one of the front windows. There was a loud crash and broken glass littered the store. I recognized my chance and jumped over the counter to charge at Nicolas, wrapping my arms around his thick torso. A pungent stew of vodka, body odor and stale cigarettes filled my nostrils. Nicolas was a slob with a big old gut on him, but his body felt hard as an oak tree.

I remembered Dante.

I would've sold my soul right then and there to be wrestling him, the big lug, instead of that homicidal maniac Nicolas. No deal. We crashed to the floor with Sal tumbling over the counter on top of us, clinging like a tick to Nicolas's outstretched arm.

"Get the fucking gun!" I screamed at Sal.

I barely got the words out before Nicolas caught me with a painful blow to the side of my head. Then he hit me again with a backhand and I felt the sweat from his hairy forearm on my cheek. My right ear started to ring.

"I'm doing the best I can!"

The gun went off again.

"Oh!" Sal yelped.

"Sal?"

I turned and saw him roll away from Nicolas. He sat up against an old console TV clutching his stomach. Blood was seeping through his shirt between his fingers, running down onto his jeans.

"I'm hit," he said faintly.

With his arm free to wield the gun as he pleased, Nicolas pointed it at me and squeezed the trigger. Another bullet just missed, coming so close I felt a quick faint breeze on my neck. I didn't think he would miss again, so I dug deep and went for the gun. Just as I got both hands around his wrist, Nicolas punched me in the gut with his free hand. The blow knocked the wind clean out of me. I dropped to the floor, fighting for a breath. Nicolas grunted and pushed himself to his feet. I rolled away from him and turned over just in time to get another look straight down the smoking barrel.

So this was finally the end. Fuck it.

I was ready to go when the gun suddenly jerked upward before going off again. A bullet struck the ceiling and plaster dust rained down on both of us as Nicolas dropped the gun, desperately grasping at the back of his neck with both hands. He spun around and I saw Sal's switchblade buried to the hilt in the narrow band of flesh between Nicolas's back and his head. He struggled violently, jerking back and forth like some horror movie villain that suddenly got outdone by the cowering victim. Just as he managed to get both hands around the handle of the knife, he keeled over, completely limp. Sal stood behind him, dead on his feet and ghostly pale with blood soaking his entire midsection all the way down past his crotch.

"Fuck." He collapsed on the floor.

"Sal!" I rushed over to where he had fallen and knelt down next to him. His eyes were half-lidded and his lips colorless.

"Remember what Mr. White said." He spoke in little more than a slow whisper. "The gut is one of the most painful places to get shot, but it takes a long time to die from your wound."

"I hope Mr. White knew what the fuck he was talking about," I said. "We gotta get you outta here."

Sal blinked slowly. "What about Stella?"

I swallowed hard and approached the counter, tiptoeing over all the blood on the floor. Stella's wrist was dangling over the front edge. I reached out to check for a pulse but as soon as I felt her cold, damp flesh, I knew.

"Oh God." I snatched my hand back and turned to Sal. "I'm not touching Nicolas."

"You don't have to," said Sal. "His eyes are still open."

"Jesus." I cringed and stole a look. "And Kenny?"

"You have to ask?"

That was it. We couldn't get out of that place fast enough. Moving Sal would be a chore but I could do it. I went back over to where he was sitting and reached under his knees with one arm and his back with the other, hoping to carry him like a bride over the threshold. As soon as I tried to move him, he howled in pain.

"Fuck me!" he yelled and I relented.

"It hurts, huh?"

"Whatever gave you that idea?"

"C'mon," I urged. "We can do this!"

I got in position and started to lift him again, as carefully as I could. This time he really let loose.

"Fuuuccckkkkkkkk! Fuck! Fuck! Fuck! No, Michael, I can't!" he panted. "No fucking way."

"Well, what the fuck?" I asked. "What are we gonna do?"

"You go," said Sal, his voice low and grim. "Take Kenny's car and get the fuck outta here while you can."

"And where am I supposed to go?"

"Go to California. Find Lila."

"What?" I couldn't believe it.

"You heard me."

"I don't know what you..."

"Don't bother, Michael," Sal cut me off. "I know."

"How?"

"Forget it," he said. "None of that matters now. Just do me one solid before you go."

"What about all this? How can I just leave you here?"

I waved my hand at the scene around us, taking it in. What a bloodbath. I almost threw up. Aside from wakes and funerals, I had only seen one dead body before. Some guy overdosed in a shooting gallery not far from T's place. They dragged his body outside and left it by a dumpster. That freaked me out at the time, but it was nothing compared to the horror show before my eyes.

"Snap out of it, Michael." Sal's voice broke into my thoughts. "Stay focused, okay? Nicolas went nuts. It's not our fault." He caught his breath and labored to point one bloody finger at the camera above us. "The whole thing is on tape."

"That doesn't mean shit."

"It'll have to do." Sal winced in pain. "Fuck the police. They're gonna get me no matter what. You can't help with them, but there is one thing you can do..."

"What's that?"

"Fix me," said Sal.

"What? How?"

"I'm holding."

"You're what?"

"I got two bags in my fifth pocket here," said Sal.

He began fidgeting with his jeans before I brushed his hand aside. I gingerly reached into his pocket and found a small tin box, the kind made for holding electrical fuses. I smeared the blood off and slid it open. Sure enough, there were two foil packs tucked inside, each marked with a black heart.

"What the fuck, Sal? I thought we were out." I took a closer look, noting that I hadn't seen any bags marked that way in months. "How long have you had this shit?"

"Since the summer," he recalled. "I skimmed them back when we were swimming in smack, you know, for an emergency."

"I'd say this qualifies." I shuddered and felt the faint cramp in my stomach. The sickness was coming.

Sal noticed. "Michael, man, I'm in serious pain here. You can't even imagine. I need the all the help I can get."

I fingered the bags. "You know the ambulance is gonna be stocked full. They'll give you exactly what you need."

"Michael, please!"

"Fine." I reached inside Sal's coat, pulled out his works and got busy. Whether I could talk him out of a bag or not, the police were on their way and I had to get going.

"Exactly what I need, my ass," Sal went on bitterly. "One look at me and I'll be lucky to get a fistful of Tylenol."

"Well, don't worry." I loaded up the syringe and flicked out the air bubbles. "Help is on the way."

Sal's eyes lit up at the sight of the needle. "Fuckin' A..."

"Where do you want it?" I asked.

Between his collapsed veins and the blood seeping from his wound, I was sure he would opt for the jugular, but I wanted to string things out and give him another chance to do right by me.

"I'm glad you asked." He sat back with a grimace. "How about a bull's-eye? For old time's sake."

"Comin' right up."

I clenched the hype in my teeth and grabbed Sal's left arm, the one with the bull's-eye tattoo inside his elbow. I hiked up the sleeve as gently as I could, tied him off and massaged the flesh in search of a vein. It seemed hopeless at first, his limb all skin and bone with nowhere to stick the needle. Finally, I managed to dig one out, right under the round red patch of ink in the center. I lined up the needle and Sal took a deep breath.

"You sure I can't get a little..." I couldn't help but ask.

"Goddamn it, Michael!" He exhaled and sat up. "Please!"

"I'm sorry, Sal, really." I meant it too. Fuck the monkey. Fuck the sickness. I was acting like an asshole. Sal was probably dying. I stroked his back and he relaxed again.

"Let's try this one more time. Here comes."

I fired up the shot and turned away, unable to watch. When I turned back, Sal's head was dropped over with his eyes shut. For a moment, I thought he was gone too. I pulled the needle out and felt for a pulse. It was weak but steady. Then I heard his breathing, slow and heavy. I felt a surge of relief and Sal spoke up, just as the sound of sirens in the distance began to float in from the street.

"Go," he said. "And don't forget the watch."

EPILOGUE

When I pulled off Route 80 just past the Iowa state line, I had no idea know where I was until I saw the green sign: Princeton, Pop. 946. I certainly hadn't planned on stopping in any crackerass towns on my way to California, but the engine was overheating and I knew I wouldn't make it much farther. Goddamn hotrod.

It was a bad break but I welcomed the distraction. I was losing my mind, replaying every gory detail of the scene at Stella's ever since I hit the road hours before. Up until then, I had been racing from one stop to another on the way out of town. After gathering a few things at my place, I stopped at Ashland Pawn where I said good-bye to my dad's watch for the last time. The surly Arab behind the counter beat me down to eighteen hundred.

Whatever.

The next stop was T's place where I picked up Maurice for a quick run out to score some dope for the trip. I figured a couple dozen bags would last me a week or so, enough time to get to Los Angeles where I would find other spots. After we scored and went back to T's, I ran inside to check for news about what went down at Stella's. Beverly informed me there was a report on the killings but nothing about Sal. Aaron and Maurice told me to take care and I was out of there.

I jumped in the Chevelle not knowing if Sal was alive or dead. If he was alive, I only hoped I'd see him again. I already missed the crazy bastard. A big part of me wanted to stay and make sure things got straightened out with the police, not that I could do much. If he made it, Sal would manage just fine. If he didn't, then I'd get pinched for nothing. The only thing to do was keep going.

Fuck it.